KEEPER OF THE WAY

Keeper of the Way

Published by Odyssey Books in 2018

www.odysseybooks.com.au

A Cataloguing-in-Publication entry is available from the National Library of Australia

ISBN: 978-1-925652-19-2 (pbk)

ISBN: 978-1-925652-17-8 (ebook)

Cover design by Simon Critchell

Typesetting by Odyssey Publishing

KEEPER OF THE WAY

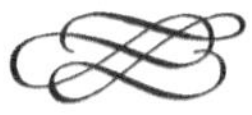

PATRICIA LESLIE

ODYSSEY
BOOKS

CHAPTER 1

Isle of Skye, 16th century

Ethne M'Kynnon had taken a long time to die; many generations had passed through her healing hands. No other had lived so long.

'May the Graces welcome thee,' Katrin mumbled. 'May they hold you close and coset thee ...'

The chill in the ground reached through Katrin's stockings and skirts, and skin to her bones. Before her, a low mound of freshly turned earth leeched its unprotected moisture into the air. By morning it would be rock hard.

Warm breath plumed from Katrin's mouth and became frosty mist. A hand-spun and quilted blanket stretched around her shoulders, each patch a loving reminder of mothers and grandmothers, of busy fingers gnarled and ache-ridden too young; their perfect stitching a counterbalance to the imperfection of everything else in their lives. Katrin kept vigil over the old woman's grave. Ethne's mind was clear, until the final fluttering of sunken chest.

Ethne was the last of the three sisters. The youngest, Caoimhe, had fallen in love with an Irishman and sailed away to his homeland, never to be seen again. It was said that Lilas, the elder sister, raped and left for dead, had stolen her tormentor's dagger. She used it to slash his throat as he slept and then had thrown herself from Dún Ringill.

Two sisters taken by the sea. One left to long life and solitary guardianship.

... Bury that which I hold sacred beneath me. Place my oldest possession at my head ...

Katrin reached out to the headstone she'd placed in position as the sun set. It was the hearthstone by which Ethne often knelt as she cooked and brewed, where she set cauldrons of soup to keep warm, where countless children warmed their toes on frosty evenings as they listened to the old woman's stories. One side of the stone was carved in ancient symbols: a quaich, a dagger, and circles within circles. Around the edge of the stone was a border of angled strokes. Facing the grave was an arched symbol: more of the angled lines and a tightly woven weave above the semblance of a skull.

The stone was as cold as the ground that held the remains of the old woman in its embrace. Katrin pulled a pouch from the pocket of her skirt. Inside were the leaf-thin seeds of a wych elm tree.

... Plant wych elm to shade me ...

Katrin dug a hollow behind the carved headstone and dropped the seeds inside. She covered them with earth, the pouch, and dried heather. Little enough protection from the heavy frosts to come, but what else could she do?

... Share my story with your daughters. There will come a time when one of them will take my place ...

It was said that Ethne and her sisters were the descendants of Scáthach; that they could trace their blood to the Fortress of Shadows across the waters of Loch Slapin and Loch Eishort. Dún Ringall and Dún Scáith had stood guard over the shared waters for centuries past. Scáthach had long since joined the mist of history and now it was Ethne's turn.

Katrin was glad she was not expected to take the healer's place of guardianship. Sacred relics and villagers would not be her responsibility. She felt movement within her swollen belly, the first kicks of the child she carried, and wept at what she had lost this day and what she would lose in days to come. She would share Ethne's stories nevertheless and let fate decide the rest.

'Once upon a time, my daughter,' Katrin rubbed her belly, 'a crone as old as the world walked these fields and cared for these people, your family. Her magic kept us safe. She was one of three sisters borne of a people who no longer walk this earth …'

Katrin looked up to the black sky and glittering stars. A light drizzle had started. Tiny raindrops mixed with tears and numbed her face. Her clothes, damp now, started to freeze and Katrin trembled. She rubbed her arms for warmth and silently promised those who had gone before, and those yet to come, that she would remain vigilant.

Winter would not last forever.

CHAPTER 2

Isle of Skye, 1850

*L*ord Algernon Benedict's experience of riding horseback did not include day after day of rain, wind, and winding muddy trails. And it showed. His forehead was stuck in a permanent scowl of pain and frustration. His back bowed under the weight of the constant precipitation; his riding coat long since soaked through slapped heavily against the horse's rump with every gust of wind. Each jarring step shuddered through his body. Rest breaks had become torture. He'd taken to spending them atop his horse to avoid the shooting pain of stiffened hips and knees.

A break in the clouds and momentary cessation of heavy rain was promising, but it had only retreated to a drizzle, the wind a breeze, and the sun had remained hidden. As the morning became afternoon, the weather deteriorated once more.

'We'll have to find shelter, m'Lord.' Ross MacNab had managed to remain relatively invisible for the first several years of his employ with Lord Benedict. Since his promotion to head groom, after the previous had passed on, avoiding notice was no longer possible. Even so, he showed only bare deference, and since they'd left the estate Benedict often felt as if the man found him somehow amusing. The closer they came to the Isle of Skye, the land of his mother's family, the less subservient and more confident the groom became.

On the ferry from the mainland to Kyleakin, MacNab had shared words in Scots with the ferryman, who'd laughed and looked away as if to avoid offending. And then the man had the audacity to give advice on negotiating for horses and accommodation, intimating that he should do the talking and his Lord should keep quiet!

'Do not take me for a fool, Mr MacNab. My family also have their roots in this island. I am neither ignorant of customs or tradition.'

MacNab's eyes narrowed and he spoke rapidly in his native tongue to the ferryman, who nodded and replied, before turning back to Lord Benedict. 'But you don't speak Scots or the local dialect, m'Lord, and some islanders will not be speaking English and some'll be disinclined to be respectful to an unknown Englisher travelling on the quiet, so to speak.'

Benedict had turned away, dismissing the men and hiding the blush he had felt creeping across his face.

Damn, the man. He'd started to hate his groom's no-nonsense practicality right there at that miserable wharf. Yet it was the same practicality that had seen them fed, accommodated, and discreetly provided for throughout the journey. In Kyleakin, MacNab had arranged horses; in Broadford, accommodation and men.

And as the small band of men and horses topped yet another hill, dipped into yet another valley, Benedict recalled now the coarse living quarters of the ferryman's cousin, dark and rank, yet dry, and the bowl of broth they'd been offered was warming, if rather bland. After days of wet and cold, even those simple lodgings would be more than welcome.

Benedict kept a wary eye on his head groom. There was no denying that the man was a boon. His practical nature extended to travel and intricate negotiations. He knew he'd have not got far with any other, or indeed on his own. Yet even after these long months of travel together, MacNab remained something of a mystery. He often had long conversations with folk. Translations into English were, however, brief.

The crofter in Kyleakin had scratched his head often and cast many long dangerous looks at the lord. After their meal, horses had arrived, saddled and provisioned. MacNab dropped a small purse of coins into the man's waiting hand, collected the reins and walked the laden beasts to Benedict who waited, out of the rain, back straight, jaw tense.

'You've bought yourself three sturdy animals and enough provisions to get us to Broadford and beyond. We're hunting your missing sister who was tricked into marriage and is in grave danger from one of the northern lairds.'

'I don't have a sister,' Benedict had replied, releasing clenched fists to take the reins being offered. 'And I would prefer it if you discussed these stories with me before sharing them with others.'

MacNab had feigned interest in the saddle. 'You do now,' he'd said. 'That little story got us a fair price too, and some information.' His lips thinned in what may have been a cold smile as he adjusted the cinch. 'Seems there's rumours of troubles on the western side of the isle.'

'Will these rumours hinder or aid us?'

MacNab had given the saddle one last tug, handed Benedict a set of reins, and walked around his own horse to make ready to mount. 'We'll know soon enough.' He pulled himself upward and heaved a leg over the saddle. 'We'd better be off before the crofter starts talking. He's off to the tavern for an ale with your purse.'

'Does the man not know the meaning of discretion?'

'I'm sure he does. It's his sense of time that worries me. I'd say we have a quarter hour of discretion depending on how fast he drinks.'

MacNab turned his horse's head to the trail that led away from the croft and to the Broadford road. Benedict mounted his horse, fidgeted in his saddle, and followed, frowning at his groom's back.

MacNab had embroidered the tale of a sister still further in Broadford, adding witchcraft and thievery. Two burly brothers and a taciturn man who smelled of sheep, were willing to guide them to the other side of the island. MacNab had spoken to others as well, but when questioned the groom had muttered that he was simply asking about weather and trail conditions, local news, and the like.

Benedict had listened to each utterance, but even when the men spoke in English, the accent was so thick it may as well have been in Gael.

The men they were now travelling with weren't much better. MacDonald, MacDonald, and MacGregor, they'd been introduced as. Of the MacDonalds, one was Allan and the other Alleg, and so alike in appearance and voice that he couldn't tell which was which. As they answered to either name with a friendly grin it didn't seem to matter. MacGregor apparently had no other nomenclature. His grin was more of a grimace, and the anticipatory gleam in the man's eyes left Benedict with a sour taste in his mouth.

Lord Benedict was roused from his thoughts when his horse came to a sudden stop, nose to rump of the horse in front.

In front of them, gorse-covered hills rolled down to the rocky shores of a loch. The men dismounted, climbed a mossy rock and pointed in various directions, arguing and casting doubtful glances at the leaden sky.

Benedict could see the jumbled remains of a fort in the distance. His pulse quickened. MacNab climbed down from his perch and came to report.

'We're not far off, but we've come the back way and this storm'll reach us first. MacGregor says there're caves we can wait it out in.'

Benedict wanted to dismount, remove his boots and stockings, and feel the cold earth on his skin. So close to his destination. He was on the precipice of change. His lightness of chest heightened his senses as his heartbeat raced. MacNab put a hand on his while pointing out toward the water and the ocean beyond.

'M'Lord, we need to seek shelter in a cave. We've been lucky with the weather so far, just rain, but there's wind coming in and the temperature's dropping. The trail'll be a torrent within minutes.'

Benedict ignored the man, soaking in the elation he felt a moment longer, quivering with the effort to control himself. He opened his eyes and saw the water running like rivulets around islands of tufted grass. Each step the men made as they returned to their horses sunk them ankle-deep in black mud.

Benedict met MacNab's gaze, surprised at the concern showing in his usually stoic face. He nodded, and the groom let out a held breath, patted Benedict's leg and turned to his own mount. He called out instructions to the others and MacGregor took the lead, weaving his way from the main trail along an alternative that vanished between stands of dripping gorse and dipped steeply down to the shore.

The rain hit within minutes and slowed them to a crawl. They couldn't afford to have a horse come up lame in this wretched weather. Benedict was trembling with cold and the strain of the descent by the time the ground flattened out and became hard enough for the sucking sound of hooves sinking into bog to turn into the clack of striking rock.

The loch had disappeared in the deluge and even MacNab's hunched back was a mere ghost of the man a few feet away. Water cascaded from the hills behind and rushed over the cliff edge beside them. Benedict was too numb to do anything but follow. MacNab kept turning in his saddle, his face shadowed beneath his wide-brimmed hat. Benedict had the sensation that time had slowed; that the world was this narrow cliff, the bloody rain, and MacNab—who was either completely trustworthy or not. Benedict attempted to loosen his aching back by rolling his shoulders, trying to sit straighter in the saddle to no avail. He was frozen in this tiny world, crooked and bent like an old man.

MacNab pulling at his arms startled him into wakefulness. A flickering of light in the corner of his eye was a fire being started. The thunder in his ears was rough oaths and curses as the men removed coats and saddles, and dragged stumbling horses as close to the cave wall as they could.

Benedict let his feet drop to the ground as MacNab pulled him free and then held him up while his legs wobbled. One arm held tight around the man's shoulders and the other around his chest, and he was led to the fire, eased to the ground.

'Keep your coat on while I see to your horse,' MacNab said.

Benedict thought he'd nodded, but wasn't sure, and huddled inside the coat as much as he could, appreciating the warmth of the fire on his face while he watched the men work. He tried to remember something about MacNab, something not quite right, but cold had made its insidious way through to the centre of his being. His thoughts were sluggish. The groom muttered something about being frozen through and Benedict thought he was probably right. He was sure he had feet inside his boots and hands inside his gloves, but he couldn't feel them.

MacNab was in front of him then, still muttering, pulling off his boots and rubbing his stockinged feet. His toes tingled.

'Old lady'll have my guts if you die from cold under this blasted rock.'

Benedict wondered who he was talking about, but as the tingling seared into stinging pain, he forgot MacNab and started worrying about his toes.

And then feeling came back to his fingers and ears and face, and for a time pain was his constant.

Benedict lay on the ground, his coat spread beneath him, warmth from the fire laying a shroud of comfort the entire length of his body. He stared at a stumpy wall of rocks, gaps filled with grass and mud that protected the fire and those seated around it from the elements outside. An iron pot sat in the middle of the fire, its contents bubbling.

'MacNab,' he said, or thought he did, as the man ladled something hot into a mug before him. One of the MacDonalds stoked the fire and the flames burst upward, filling the cave with heat until the wind cut through and chased it away. Had he spoken aloud or was the man ignoring him?

'MacNab!' he said again, forcing sound through his raw throat and past cracked lips.

The man glanced at him and shuffled over, mug in hand. He pressed his other hand against Benedict's forehead, they were warm from the fire, and then leant in to hook his free arm under him and help him into a sitting position.

'You passed out. No fever.' MacNab pushed the mug into Benedict's hand. 'Drink this tea. Stew'll be ready soon.'

Benedict brought the mug to his mouth. The tea was strong and sweet. He narrowed his gaze through the steam and tried to remember what it was about MacNab that had set him on edge.

'Drink up afore it gets cold.'

The man's rough pragmatism hid whatever it was like a cloak. He appeared fully focused on ensuring his lord's wellbeing.

Benedict sipped the tea. He would just have to take him at face value and trust him.

Two days cramped into a shallow cave with four men and seven horses was nearly the undoing of Lord Benedict. The brothers took it in turn to pace from the back of the cave to the front, peer out at the dismal sky, swear vociferously, return to their place by the dwindling fire, and drop as if boneless to the dirt floor. MacGregor made odd little noises, but otherwise remained motionless, arising only to take care of business in a sheltered nook outside the cave or attend the fire.

MacNab let the brothers spearhead haphazard exchanges that ranged from gossip, witchcraft, and faeries to Lord Benedict's poor sister. Judging by their sneers and disturbing chuckles, it was just as well that Benedict's sister was a figment of MacNab's imagination.

Benedict kept his jaw set and his back straight, refusing to be drawn in to the crude innuendo of the brothers.

He discovered that their close quarters enabled him to understand more of the Scottish brogue. Enforced observation allowed him to connect words to their stance, hand movements, and facial expressions. These men were far more emotional and expressive than he gave them credit for.

Even MacNab became more readable. Plainly writ on the man's face was a mix of complex emotions that came and went like the tide. He kept his face tight when talking to Benedict, controlled with an edge of irritation when the MacDonalds were in full flight, and concerned when he happened to look across at MacGregor, angry when the latter cleared his throat.

Benedict hadn't shared the finer details of their journey with his head groom. Only that he had business to attend to with a distant relation, which he preferred few people as possible knew about. With endless days to fill, or so it felt, Benedict allowed thoughts of his family business to encroach on the cold and wet.

His great-grandfather had travelled to Skye hunting a legend and finding only death, or so the family was told. He'd reached the shores of Loch Slapin, where Benedict now hid in a cave from the weather, and was never seen nor heard from again. Only a third of his entourage had returned: a ragtag group of half-starved, half-insane servants with tales of witches, ghosts, and faery mounds. The man's wife had sent one of their factors up to the island to investigate, and after that, one of her sons, and after that a witch finder. None had returned.

Algernon Benedict was the first of the family to approach the mysterious island since that time, and he'd been sure to keep his reasons for travelling to himself. He didn't trust anyone, not even MacNab.

Especially not MacNab.

On the eve of the second day, much to MacNab's consternation, Benedict asked the MacDonald brothers what they knew of witches and if they'd ever met one. By the time they'd consumed the last of their provisions, he'd managed to convince the pair they would make fine witch-hunters. MacNab tried to intervene and talk sense, but the brothers had fanciful imaginations, and an inflated opinion of their own bravery and prowess.

MacGregor grunted and rolled over to sleep.

The morning of the third day came clear and still, and with the distant sounds of a village coming awake, the group packed their gear in readiness to move on.

The rain held off for an entire day, but heavy clouds were coming in with the night, and Benedict suspected they were in for another dousing. He'd spent the day riding alongside Allen and Alleg, feeding their desire for action, prodding their ambitions, and nurturing a misplaced sense of justice.

MacNab whispered to MacGregor, who mumbled something beyond Benedict's hearing. He understood the gist of it though: trouble, injury, and fools.

Benedict smiled and kept his pace. It had taken most of the day to reach the village, the trail still treacherous, but their arrival was imminent. One more bend. One more gorse bush. One more straggle of sheep.

An abandoned croft, its black stone walls looming in the twilight, marked the edge of the village. Beyond the derelict fences and weed-riven garden lay a collection of cottages that had themselves seen better days.

'The witches won't live in the village,' Benedict said to Allen MacDonald. 'They'll live in the shadows of the ruined fort, guarding their ill-gotten treasures. My sister will be imprisoned by cold stone and evil guardians.'

The fire of battle reflected in Allen's eyes. He straightened in his saddle, nudged his brother along and the two took the lead, chests puffed with arrogance, pride, and determination to rid the world of evil.

'What are you doing?' MacNab asked. 'Allen and Alleg are dangerous when riled.' He made to hold Benedict back and thought better of it, not sure apparently, but proving to Benedict that he could no longer be trusted.

～

With the suddenness and timing of a message from God, the rain returned. It bashed the ground, drummed on roofs, and cut through the thin vestiges of warmth Benedict's damp coat had given him. The noise was atrocious. Thunder boomed across the loch, echoed in the hills, and rumbled on itself as it traversed the valley. Lightning struck out from behind the mountaintop of Blà Bheinn, casting a net of power and anger across the black sky.

The MacDonalds rode the thunder through the village, struck down a farmer, sent his wife into a ditch, and descended into a frenzy of wanton destruction.

Villagers came out in force, armed with pitchforks and axes to protect their families. Fishermen holding aloft wicked-looking gaffes and poles came up from the waterfront.

MacNab spoke to MacGregor in Scots, hot urgent words, and the older man peeled away from the group and headed into the maze of fields and bog behind the village. Yet the groom remained beside Benedict, holding tight on the reins of his nervous horse, wrapping the cracked leather around his fingers, alternating a steely glare from the MacDonalds to the cottages, and putting himself and his steed between villagers and his master. Benedict ignored him. What he wanted was at Dún Ringall. He urged the MacDonalds onward, cutting through the angry villagers like a spear, into the dark of the night and the pelting rain, to the promontory that held the remains of a once mighty stronghold, and a once powerful family.

Dún Ringall had guarded its secrets in solid silence for millennia. Now it was a ruin, but there were still secrets to protect. The last croft-house before the ruin stood like an ageing sentry. An old woman appeared in the doorway. Another pulled at her arm and dragged her from the oncoming men.

Benedict urged his horse forward. Legend passed down through his family spoke of this house and the witch within. The woman who'd cast a spell upon his ancestor and sent him wandering aimlessly through the Cuillins toward Cailleadch's Mountain, where he'd passed into mist and never been seen again.

'Witch,' he said. He vibrated with energy and dug his heels into the horse's flank. It jumped forward. 'Witch!' he yelled, voice hoarse, forgetting for a time that this woman could not be the same who'd cursed his long dead forebear.

All around them the sounds of battle, men yelling, women screeching. The brothers were somewhere in the din. Benedict didn't know where or if they even still lived. He didn't care.

The women ran.

And then a shadow passed between Benedict and his prey. MacNab realised at the last what his master intended to do; sacred duties and connections replaced inner conflict. As Benedict tensed, ready to give chase to the women, MacNab drew his horse between them and jumped from the saddle, tackling Benedict to the ground.

The fight was messy, each man hampered with sodden clothes and slippery ground, each desperate to succeed. Benedict was startled by the attack, but not surprised. He'd seen the confusion and anger on his groom's face grow throughout the afternoon.

First blood went to MacNab: a gash on Benedict's cheek he barely felt.

'Traitor!' he growled, and thrust out with the short dagger he kept sheathed on his belt.

MacNab grabbed his wrist and forced the blade away. He brought his fist up. Benedict turned his head, crouched, and let the devastating punch slide off his head. He darted in quickly and cleanly, catching MacNab off-balance, pulled his dagger free, and plunged it between the man's ribs.

Last blood went to Lord Benedict.

Benedict fuelled the desire for revenge with the lust for the hidden treasures his ancestors had long desired. His distant grandfather hadn't been the first of the Benedict line to lose their life on this desolate stretch of coast. He too had followed old stories of an ancestor who had disappeared on this very spot. Murdered and cast into the sea. Benedict men had left life behind in this place for centuries—not anymore.

Benedict forced his way into the croft, tearing a heavy curtain from the doorway and kicking over a stool. The hearth fire guttered out. Wind swirled around the room, causing an arc of brilliant golden candlelight to flash and then die in its wake. Curtains in windows flapped. Another door, large enough only for a small child or an adult on their hands and knees, stood open in the far corner. Benedict, struck with cold clarity, understood; the women at the front door had diverted attention from someone sneaking out the back.

MacNab's was a delaying tactic. It had cost him his life, but it had worked.

Benedict threw down shelves and tables; canisters of flour and acrid smelling powders coated the floor. He ripped at curtains and quilted bedding. The kitchen fire flared as shreds of straw landed within its hearth.

He howled at the ceiling and the wind receded for that moment as if in retreat. He strode out into the night. Figures were hiding in the bushes. Others were striding down from the village. Time was escaping him. He rounded the croft, searching for the trail down to the beach and stopped, frozen as a figure drifted along the broken ramparts of the fort.

'You're a fool. Like your fathers before you.' The voice was soft. It trickled like a tumbling brook in his head. 'You don't even know what you're looking for.'

The figure stretched upward into the night, absorbed some of the crackling energy, and sent a cobweb of light to the ground. 'You must seek knowledge, not violence. Only then will you know what you've lost.'

Benedict's mouth was dry, his tongue glued in place behind grimacing teeth. He couldn't move, couldn't speak, barely perceived what was happening.

'Go away, fool. Do not return until you find wisdom, until you've learned what is at stake.' A round carved stone appeared in Benedict's hand. 'Take this. One day you'll have need of gifts. Let this be the first.'

The figure shifted from male to female, armoured to begowned to naked, long armed and legged to short and stumpy, beautiful and ethereal to bedraggled and so ugly Benedict shook in his boots with fear.

Then it floated over the loch and sank into the water, a sheen of light haze beneath the surface before fading into inky black.

Full use of arms and legs, mouth, and brain came back in a rush and he turned to see angry villagers, led by MacGregor hefting a claymore over his head as he roared toward him.

Benedict pocketed the gift and ran.

MacNab's corpse lay where he left it.

Run.

Paddocks pock-marked with rocks, divots from sheep, cows, tree roots, tussocks of grass, all drenched in the downpour, and each sitting in stinking, marshy bog-mud. Stars obscured by cloud, the moon a ghostly presence above.

Run.

She was soaked through within minutes. Water trickled down her thighs, indistinguishable from the dirty water that splashed up her skirt with each clomping step.

The clash of arms rang in her ears, drove her onward. Sheriff's men or witch-hunters? She only knew that she must flee and hope that her brothers could protect her mam and granny from whatever ill was about to fall upon their heads.

Run, Mam had told her. *Follow the shoreline to Old Artair's wharf. A silver coin for passage across the loch. A cousin will meet you at the old fort, help you on your way. Run.*

The ruins of Dún Ringall, almost invisible in this miserable blackness, loomed overhead and she struck her hand out to drag her fingers along the slick rock. Not far now. She crossed the headland, saw the post marking the path down to the wharf and rushed onward. Halfway she misstepped and slid the rest of the way on her backside, mud and pebbles lodged in her clothing, but she made it to the bottom with nothing more than bruises. Her possession clutched to her breasts, safe for now. Ahead, a protected rush light showed where Old Artair waited in his boat.

'Artair!'

'Just yerself then, lassie?' he asked, taking her hand and helping her aboard.

'Aye. Mam says to give you this, n' would you please take me across to the old fort?'

Artair winked, folded her fingers over the coin, and pushed her down to sit in the bow. 'It'll be a miserable trip in this weather. You keep this. You'll be needing it more than I soon enough. I heard there was trouble and knew someone would be along. Hunker down and hold on. Likely to be some unsettled water between here and Dún Scáith. Mark my words, lassie. Unsettled, indeed.'

Halfway across the loch she twisted in her seat for a last look at home. A fire had been lit. Dún Ringall looked like a stubby black finger at the centre of a conflagration. For a scant moment, she caught her breath and tears formed as she feared for home and family, but no, it would be the signal fire. A warning beacon for the opposite shore. She turned to Dún Scáith hoping for an answering flame, a sign, anything.

The night remained unyielding. Only Artair's strength and knowledge of these waters would see her to safety. From Dún Scáith, no flicker of hope appeared.

Sydney, 1879

The grounds of the Botanical Gardens, in the corner between the governor's stables and Macquarie Street, was cleared for construction in January. A short nine months later, the pleasant aspect of nature with a view to the harbour beyond had become a brash edifice of archways, towers, cavernous halls, and a grand dome. The noise and business of the place could be endured; the electric lights used so that work could continue all night long, less so. The residents of Macquarie Street had complained long and bitterly at the destruction of their peace and quiet, and of course, their views. The Garden Arms and Travellers Rest Hotel, the last of its type along this stretch of road, had welcomed the new business. Residents had complained about that as well.

And now it was September. The Garden Palace was all but complete and the international exhibition due to open the next morning.

Rosalie observed the construction and consequent arrival of crates full of exhibit items with avid interest. Many of the curators and supervisors were guests at the hotel. She and her husband,

James, kept them entertained and well fed, making many useful business and personal contacts in the process.

Being the proprietor of the closest hotel to the Palace had many advantages and, on behalf of his wife, James Ponsonby did take advantage.

Which is why Rosalie was given access to the exhibition a week before its opening and several times thereafter as well. Rosalie had made her own friends and was able to enter the building from a side door long after most of the curators had gone home or to the Garden Arms for the night.

The morning was a few short hours away. After this night, the vaulted spaces of the ceilings would echo with the voices of the thousands of visitors sure to pass beneath throughout the day. Voices and smells would impregnate the wood, form a sheen over the exhibits that could not be cleaned away. The dust sprites in the air would carry the memory of people from one day to the next. This night, the air held only the fading recall of workers unpacking exhibits, placing, cleaning, labelling. The faint sense of the museum director and colleagues making their final inspection, harrumphs of approval, last orders, and pats on the back for a job well done hung around the various glass cases, marble statues, and examples of industry and culture.

Rosalie cared only for the giant statue she now stood in front of. Since its installation, the stout bronze figure atop its rock of granite had fascinated her. At times it appeared to be the embodiment of something else. She circled the statue, composed, hands clasped in front of her, eyes looking upward searching for a sign, anything really that could shore her confidence. On reaching the front-facing aspect, she paused. The metallic face was stern and unforgiving. She stood upon her pedestal, mistress of all she surveyed. A mere representation all that was needed to exert her influence across the seas to a landscape thousands of miles away.

Rosalie dipped her fingers into the purse that hung from her waist and pulled out a bob of dried heather and wattle held together with a strip of fabric cut from her grandmother's *arisaid*. She placed the gift on the bannister that surrounded the statue and fountain below it.

'*Caud Mile Failte.*'

Footsteps in the distance warned of the night watchman returning to the nave that ran from the north entrance to the south. His footsteps were unhurried, occasionally pausing. Time to leave. Rosalie stepped away and toward the southern entrance and the side door, which the guard left off the catch on the nights she visited.

A brush of sound and she half-turned, suddenly anxious; the statue shimmered and a ghostly figure of an old woman with long white hair appeared. She leant down and reached out for the flowers. Their eyes met as the apparition held the bob to her nose. Her face was tinged blue, her lips an earthy tone, eyes sparkling green and blue.

'So formal, Daughter?' She bowed, holding the flowers out in one hand, her staff in the other. 'I thank and bless thee, child.'

The old woman straightened and tapped her staff once upon the bannister. In the spot that Rosalie had left the spring of flowers sat an egg-shaped stone. Rosalie returned to the statue, trembling and excited. 'Thank you, Grandmother.' She took the gift and placed it in her purse. Its weight settled against her skirts with welcome warmth.

A cough warned that the night watchman was much closer now.

Rosalie bowed her head, whispered 'Thank you', and left. A last glimpse as she reached the exit door showed that the old woman who wore the night around her shoulders like a cloak was gone. The cold statue of Queen Victoria only remained; a silent sentinel over her garlanded domain.

CHAPTER 4

Sydney, 1882

Clement's fingers itched to adjust the starched collar that circled his neck like a manacle. He held them firmly in check, gripping the head of his maple and ivory cane, strangling the carved elephant hand-piece and grinding the opposing tip into the floor with all the strength of his frustration and irritation.

One day off the ship that had posited him and his father in this abysmal outpost and he missed the isolation of being at sea already; still had his sea legs. Every now and then he had to catch himself mid-lurch as if solid ground had transformed itself into the swell of the ocean, as if Poseidon loathed to lose even one soul from his watery clutch.

Business was business, and his often occurred in grimy bolt-holes. An open window let in the smell that lingered around dock areas. An aromatic tinge of sheep and tar, and a pleasant view of the quay. Boats thumped against each other and the jetties they were tied to as soft fat waves rolled from sea to shore. Even here the sea called him. He had the urge to strip himself of shirt and collar, and answer. His toes squirmed to the desirous sensation of sand and saltwater on his feet. Business came first. Pleasure later.

His father's factor in Sydney, a portly man, appeared from an inner sanctum, pumped up like an ageing cockerel, hiding his fluster and confusion as he rolled down his shirt sleeves and adjusted his cravat. Clement's skin felt raw and hot from the layers of clothing he was forced to endure in this warm, dry climate. The least the factor could do was be prepared.

'Did you not receive my note that I'd be calling at this time?' Clement's words came clipped and mean. He caught a glimpse of an old, poorly inked tattoo on the man's forearm just before the cuffs came down to hang loose around his wrists.

'My apologies, your Lordship. Time got away from me. We've had a dashed time building a case against a former man of some position. He diddled the books at the museum of all places ...' The man stopped fussing with his clothes, one step away from Clement, and held out a meaty paw of a hand. 'I'm George Boseman. You're Lord Benedict, I presume?'

'My father, Lord Benedict, is resting from the voyage this after-noon. I'm Clement Benedict, authorised to undertake all business on my father's behalf.' Clement touched his hand to Boseman's and was enveloped in two pincer-like clumps. He rode it out and, once free of the grip, pulled his kerchief from his pocket to wipe the man's sweat from his skin.

'You're aware of our requirements? Do you have a report?'

'Of course. Of course. I've had eyes out everywhere and have narrowed down a list of women who match your description. A more specific description would have produced more exact results. But you work with what you've got, what? Come into my office. We'll take some refreshment while I report.'

'We have no better description,' Clement replied.

Boseman's office was overstuffed and airless. His window remained closed, the glass clean so he could see out. Clement caught a glimpse of ships' masts bobbing away to the tune of the water below. He took the glass of pale liquor offered and sat down on the hard chair reserved for clients.

'Hearsay is all we've been able to glean,' he continued. 'We've had people searching in America and Canada as well with no luck. It seems most likely the woman came here.'

Boseman was nodding, his cheeks reddening. 'That may be. No woman with the surname MacKinnon and hailing from Strathaird arrived in Port Jackson during the period specified. So we widened the search to anyone at all from that area and found several. A steady stream, in fact. One must wonder if there are any Scots left in their homeland! A sorry business that is, but good for us here in the colonies …'

'I didn't come all this way to converse on the topic of clearances, or British politics. Get on with it, man!'

Boseman returned to his report. 'Right then. Many of the emigrants are untraceable. They often moved on from Port Jackson within days of landing, and in all directions. We've done what we can and narrowed the list down to three possibilities. One of those is someone I happen to know. A canny businesswoman. Rosalie Campbell travelled with her aunt and uncle in 1852, all of whom hail from Broadford on Skye.'

Clement noticed a gleam of perspiration on Boseman's forehead. It dripped a track through the gutters of skin to his beady eyes.

'How well do you know this woman?'

'Quite well. A canny businesswoman, as I said. She married James Ponsonby and the two took over the Garden Arms Hotel and Travellers Rest. Did quite well with the business. Mr Ponsonby passed away last year. I expect his widow will soon sell the hotel and retire to a quieter life.'

Clement's stomach lurched a little as Boseman described the first woman. Canny …

'In my experience, clever women are not necessarily apt for the quiet life.'

'She is clever indeed, cunning. Very good at predicting political and economic changes and, of course, knows all the right people. But still, a woman, with a family to look to. She'll come around.'

'You sound envious. Are your personal views colouring your report, sir?'

Boseman's face reddened as he rubbed the back of his neck. 'Her background fits your description, Mr Benedict, so any feelings on my part are coincidental. Her aunt fits the bill as well. She currently resides in the far north of the state on an isolated property. One other I've been able to trace: a Mrs Elsa Ricci, formerly Adam, born in Portree, Skye.'

'Where is this woman now?'

'She lives with her husband south of here near Botany Bay. They have a small holding near the Aboriginal settlement at La Parouse. I can arrange for a carriage and a guide if you'd like to make the trip.'

'And Mrs Ponsonby is in the city?'

Boseman nodded. 'The hotel is on Macquarie Street.'

'Very well. Portree is some distance north of Broadford and our evidence thus far leads to Sydney rather than any regional areas so I'll not concern myself with either Mrs Ricci or Mrs Ponsonby's aunt for now. Mrs Ponsonby herself, though, yes, she does fit the bill, as you say. The woman I'm looking for would have to be clever …'

Clement had the unusual sensation of his chest expanding, yet not enough breath to fill it. He left the shady businessman to his subversive dealings and returned to the narrow street with its bustle of sailors and traders, and relaxed; more buoyant now, with the scent of brine in his nostrils, than he'd felt since making land aboard the *Orontes*.

'Perhaps not such a dismal locale after all.' Plans were finally coming together, and all of a sudden the warmth and the noise and the smells were as welcome today as they'd been anywhere else on his travels.

CHAPTER 5

The Botanical Gardens were a forest of trees and shrubbery, drawn from England and forced into a lifetime of servitude on the other side of the world where winter was as summer in their homeland. Confusion must no doubt reign in this foreign land, at least for those who yearned after memories of the past. Local fauna interspersed with the exotic plantings of England and Europe and appeared dowdy in comparison. Or so Algernon Benedict thought. The new world was at a distinct disadvantage from the old. Stories could not be easily gleaned from plants, and animals that appeared so young and old. Fibrous bark peeled away from tall straight trunks of trees, leaving behind colour and pattern as confusing as the shape and smell of the leaves. Vibrancy of blossoms imprinted on his mind; the local fauna's saving grace. Everything else was complete rubbish. Algernon shrugged away heat and itch and beads of sweat forming on his skin and thought about his son.

The boy was sneaky. No doubt about it. Benedict counted on it. He was also observant and had an excellent grasp of cause and effect. He'd identified the potential of difficulty Mrs Ponsonby might equate to and had secured an ally in the battle to come.

George Boseman would make a useful tool in this isolated city even if he was somewhat of a country bumpkin compared to the businessmen in London.

Clement certainly had his uses; as such, Benedict was prepared to overlook the seedier side of his son's character—the fondness for illicit activities. He watched him now, still dressed in his black dress coat from his evening's entertainment the night before and helping himself to the expensive liquor at the side bar of the gentleman's club. He cut a fine if somewhat jaded figure with his waistcoat unbuttoned and his silk tie hanging loose around his neck. Benedict wasn't sure how Clement managed his subversive tastes and preferred not to know. The only thing that mattered was the collection of relics that would reinstate his family's position and quench a fair amount of the revenge they had long sought on those who had cursed them.

His fingers itched with the need to return to his room and check on his belongings. Benedict stood, ignored Clement's raised brow, and pushed past the waiter on his way over with a glass of sherry. He'd go for a short walk. Visit the gardens or the museum. Perhaps pay a visit to Mrs Ponsonby's tearooms.

The waiter, drinks tray left on the bar, rushed over with Mr Benedict's coat, hat, and walking stick; hovering behind the elder gentleman as he poised, indecisive it seemed, in the doorway.

'Father, what are you doing?' Clement ignored the waiter and nudged his father.

Benedict heard his son's voice as a distant, irritating buzzing and shook away the weight of the younger man on his arm. A walk might be the thing. He should see his enemy's natural habitat for himself; find out what sort of woman he was dealing with. If she were anything like his wife, she would be easy to conquer. Threats bundled up as promises had always worked with Margaret. Without him she would have nothing, and even though her family had owned the country home for generations it was his now, and so was she.

His mother, too, knew her place in the world and always acquiesced to her husband, and later her son. He tried to draw an image of his mother and failed. A shadowy silhouette in the background wearing a white cap over pale gossamer thin hair was all he could come up with.

A walk through the streets of this jumped up little city was just what he needed.

A group of gentlemen came in the front door of the club, showing each other in, commenting on the weather, chattering about plants and animals in plummy English accents; the youngest, a Scot by the sound, excited about the sighting of dolphins following his ship in through the headlands. The smell of dust and mud tainted with horseshit and a faint trace of native blossom wafted in through the front door. The men shook off their over-coats in the foyer, and the scent of the colonies was cut off by the closing of the heavy oak door.

'Father?'

Benedict ignored his son and turned to the gleaming staircase that led up to the guest rooms. With all these newcomers, another check on his belongings wouldn't go astray.

Entering the Union Club was like walking into any of the popular gentleman's clubs of London. Algernon Benedict felt at home amid the walnut-clad walls, overstuffed leather lounges, sumptuous light-ing, and discreet staff.

Clement stepped aside for the newcomers. Give him a music hall and a lively tavern any time. He watched his father disappear up the staircase, followed by the puppy-dog of a servant. Stifling a yawn, he considered respite in his room, but shrugged that thought aside as he made eye contact with the last of the Englishmen, who shared a secret look that suggested he'd rather be anywhere but in the stuffy old Union Club.

Clement's lips twitched in a grin. Sport was to be had with this new bunch of pretentious somebodies and, perhaps, confederates to be made. He followed them into the lounge.

'It's a little early, don't you think?' said the youngest member of the group. 'I've got an appointment at the museum shortly and a talk at the exhibition hall to attend …'

'Soda water for Mr Ridlay,' ordered one of the others. 'I'll have a nip of whisky. Something Scotch, if you please.'

The oldest gentleman in the group eyed Clement, seating himself in the wingback chair his father had vacated, and shuffled over. 'Interested in a little company, sir? I don't believe I've seen you around. New in town?'

The others followed and Clement recalled a photographic image he'd seen of a waddle of penguins. He pointed a finger at the waiter, enough to ensure a drink would arrive without any delay, and waved to the seats beside him. 'Be my guests.'

A gruff snort came from one of the gents and a drag of heavy chairs over thick rugs as the waddle gathered around.

'I'm new in town too,' said Mr Ridlay. 'Hopped off the boat yesterday, though it was in harbour for near a week. You? I mean, how long have you been in Sydney?'

Clement accepted his glass from the waiter, sniffed at the amber liquid it contained, and quaffed it down. 'A few days,' he admitted. 'My father and I are exploring the colonies instead of touring the continent.'

'Introductions are in order!' The older gentleman who interrupted the start of the conversation had a thick girth covered over by a tight vest and stained jacket. His wiry walrus moustache and bushy eyebrows wiggled with every word. 'My name is Walter St Leon. This young gent on your left with the Scotch brogue and the red face is Mr Alexander Ridlay. Over here are Messrs Stenton, Crosse, McIntyre, Benisso, and Hunt. You probably guess from Mr Benisso's olive complexion that he's from the continent. Nice, isn't it, Louis? Or Naples. I can never remember which. The rest of us are from various quarters of Britain except for Mr Hunt, who is native born.'

The native-born Mr Hunt was clean-shaven with brown hair, and a twinkle in his eyes as he leant forward to shake Clement's hand. Clement stood with the same action, and bowed to his new friends. 'Clement Benedict. My father, who you've just missed, is Lord Algernon Benedict.' Clement proceeded to shake the proffered hands.

Mr Walter St Leon's bushy eyebrows caused a ripple effect in his bald scalp as they rose and dipped, mightily impressed with the status of Clement's father. Most people were, which is why Clement made sure to always mention it.

'I don't believe I've heard of Lord Benedict. Where's his estate? North or south? Your accent certainly doesn't give you away. Mind you, I've not been back home for nigh on five years and was usually busy in the back of some museum or other, so it's not likely I would've heard much about anyone. Interested in the natural sciences at all, Mr Benedict?'

Clement was starting to wish he'd followed his father's lead and returned to his room for a rest after all. His eyeballs were burning: a sure sign of impending headache. St Leon's bombastic mode of speech was abrasive to say the least.

'We're all connected to the Royal Society, Mr Benedict. In Australia for scientific purposes … mostly.'

Clement enjoyed the sound of Mr Ridlay's voice, Scottish brogue with velvet undertones. Where most Scotsmen were clipped and raucous, Mr Ridlay's speech was gently soothing. Ten to one, he'd been to elocution lessons and learned well enough to be understood without losing the hints of his heritage.

'And adventure,' added Mr Hunt. 'I've been showing these gents up and down the coast for the past six months. Stenton, Crosse, and McIntyre are studying animals. Benisso draws pretty pictures of flowers, and St Leon is studying the natives. Ridlay, why are you here again?'

'Pretty flowers,' was the answer, and Clement enjoyed hearing the edge in the young Scot's voice. Not all gentle velvet then. 'I have a commission to identify as much of the flora as I can, collect samples, and render likenesses. I have a particular interest in Aboriginal agricultural methods.'

Clement dropped his hand on the Scot's arm and gave it a squeeze. 'The Garden Palace has an excellent exhibition of flora and fauna from around Australia, and a grand collection of paintings and sketches from artists and botanists. The Scott sisters, in particular, have quite an eye, and I do believe some of John and Elizabeth Gould's illustrations are available for perusing as well.'

'An admirable collection of weaponry from the Aboriginal tribes too. Some are my own contribution, given to me by a tribe I befriended out west.' St Leon didn't have the overall appearance of a man interested in, let alone on friendly communications with tribes in any direction. 'I'd consider it an honour to show you and Lord Benedict the collection and provide commentary ...'

Clement gave a slow nod. It might prove a distraction for this father. 'Are there any items of a religious nature? My father is quite interested in artefacts of a more spiritual purpose rather than warfare.'

'The local savages aren't much for religion, Mr Benedict. Their main focus is survival in the wild Australian bush. Killing and fighting, yes. Praying to gods? No. Culture is something they have yet to aspire to.'

Mr Ridlay objected, 'Perhaps we just don't know them well enough, Mr St Leon. I haven't heard of a single society yet where culture does not run deep. Warfare and survival are, on the surface, easy to observe. The details of spiritual belief are often hidden much deeper ...'

'Nonsense! I've talked to many an Aborigine. They can barely grasp the concept of language let alone higher beings.'

'Perhaps they just don't like you,' Mr Hunt mumbled as he waved the waiter over for another round of drinks.

'What was that, Hunt? Are you being impudent?'

The remaining gentlemen diverted the conversation to flora and fauna with recommendation to Clement on where the best locations were to observe kangaroos, koalas, and wombats. Cigars were passed around and the air in the warm room became cloying and thick with smoke.

Clement re-joined with desultory non-committal chitchat, finished his drink, and rose. His eyes throbbed with the need for sleep, and if he didn't escape soon he felt sure his skull would crack in two.

'So very nice to meet you all,' he said, excusing himself from the group. 'There's an excellent program of music at the Garden Palace in the evenings; perhaps I'll see you at one of the concerts or wandering around the exhibits. Good day.'

'Come to one of the Society lectures, Mr Benedict. I'll leave details with the concierge. I'm sure you and your father will find something of interest to be heard.'

'Most kind.' A rapier of pain slid into the top of Clement's head and cut through brain matter to the base of his skull. He shook Mr Ridlay's hand, refrained from any more nodding. 'Good day,' he repeated.

The door from the lounge was opened with a soft swish. 'May I bring anything to your room, sir?' the attentive doorman asked.

'Nothing,' Clement croaked out. 'I do not wish to be disturbed.'

St Leon's grumbling voice was cut off as the door closed. Not even a murmur of sound filtered through into the foyer. Clement headed for the grand staircase, hoping that his father was indeed resting. Pain inflamed his eyes and his temples throbbed. He made it to his room without meeting any fellow guests, or his father, along the way. The curtains were drawn and the dresser held a porcelain pitcher of water and a bowl. He sloshed water into it and splashed it over his face, lacking the energy for more vigorous cleaning. He pulled his necktie from his collar, unbuttoned his shirt and shrugged off his coat. He needed sleep and quiet and darkness. He poured a nip of brandy from the decanter beside his bed, sipped, appreciated the burn on his lips, and sunk onto his bed.

～

Carpeted floor muffled footsteps yet Algernon could still hear his son's footfall as he came up the stairs, along the hallway, slowed at the door, and then moved on to his own room. They shared a suite on the first floor: two comfortably fitted-out bedrooms with a modest sitting room between them. Algernon sat by the window of the sitting room, hands protectively over a highly polished thuja wood box. It had once been his grandfather's, purchased in some African market on his travels, and used as a receptacle for the most precious of items: family heirlooms passed down the line to Algernon and, eventually, to Clement.

He waited; his son moved around his room, the thud of shoes being kicked off, a clink of crystal, and the soft twang of bedsprings. It was nearing noon and Clement was only just getting to bed. The old man wasn't sure which perturbed him most: the fact that his son kept exceedingly late hours and regularly slept through the day, or that by tea he'd be awake and refreshed, ready to go again.

With no further sound or movement from his son's room, Algernon let his attention come back to the box in his lap. He ran his fingers over the cool wood and, with both hands, lifted the lid. Inside, nestled in black velvet, was an old shallow cup. The cup was banded in willow and sat, crooked, on a base of carved elmwood. Twin handles, cut into the same piece of elm as the base, were large enough to be held between thumb and forefinger. The bowl showed the smooth surface of the willow bands tapering inward. Liquid could not be held in the cup. Algernon had tried. It seeped through the willow. A circular edge around the centre of the base suggested that a piece was missing. It was this piece, among other items, that brought Algernon on the three-month journey from London to Sydney.

He'd come into possession of the cup some months before, looking for answers to missing pieces of the puzzle that was his family history. A history riddled with holes and stories of loss and betrayal. Algernon's grandmother had talked of hereditary power. He'd always thought she'd meant the kind of power that came with status and wealth and position.

Algernon's first visit to the Isle of Skye, some thirty years previous, was full of hardship and violence. He'd sought to learn more at every turn, to find wisdom, but it wasn't until the discovery of the simple willow and elm cup in a forgotten grave that he'd realised the power his grandmother talked of had nothing whatsoever to do with money and everything to do with the kind of power that can make money seem like a gaudy plaything. Who needed money when you could command governments and armies?

Clement had accompanied him on his second trip and insisted on a carriage ride across the island, and stopping to inspect every ruin and cracked gravestone they came by. But it was Algernon who had stood at the edge of Loch Slapin at Kilmarie and suggested they traverse the rocky shores, memory overlapping the peaceful scenes. A long time ago, he and his men had ridden through town hell-bent on overcoming any obstacle. Now, without even foul weather to contend with, he passed stone cottages and skirted struggling gardens and hungry sheep, and with far less obstruction than expected, found the grave at the end of a path flattened through the long grass. Sheltered by a towering elm tree, the headstone faced a castle so ruined it appeared to meld into the cliff. Grass grew where once tall walls had loomed; shrubs of berries filled the corners of rooms open to the sky and long since empty of human life or use.

'She's here,' he'd said. Algernon had known that at their feet lay a missing piece of his grandmother's tales. *Why did I not see this that stormy night?* A sharp sting of icy memory came to him then: a man's body prone and bleeding, eyes vacant, chest still of breath and a corporeal being who lived below the loch's stormy surface.

'We're not prepared,' Clement said, though he knelt in the dirt and wiped his hands over the crumbling gravestone. 'We'll have to come back when we're ready.' He dug a shallow pit at the base of the stone. 'There's something here.'

Algernon knelt at the stone, the grave between them. 'Careful.' He pushed Clement's hands away and probed the ground until a round outline appeared at his fingertips. He dug deeper until he could pull the object free, retrieved a kerchief from his pocket to clean hard-pressed mud away, and felt a frisson of energy as his skin brushed, for the first time, against the carved wood and willow cup.

Clement pushed sods of loose dirt into the hole the cup had left and patted down patches of grass to hide the evidence of what they were about to take. He asked no questions, merely got to his feet and helped Algernon do the same, gently encouraging him to leave. It was near dark by the time they reached their carriage and the restless horses. The carriage driver grumbled at the wait in the cold, and, as soon as the men were seated, cracked his whip and they returned to the halfway tavern they'd left early that morning. The next day saw them back at Broadford and preparing to board the ferry to the mainland, a storm whipping their backs all the way.

Some months later, Clement had vanished from their country estate. On his return, grey and haggard, he'd presented his father with a heavy lead-lined chest. Inside, shrouded bones, the gravestone, and a long curved-blade dagger. The smell of decay had filled the room. Algernon could still smell it on his hands even though he was in Sydney and the bones were on the other side of the world. Most of them, anyway.

Algernon flicked a corner of velvet back from the base of the box. Below it wrapped in tissue paper was a single bone. The stench of the grave wafted into Algernon's face and nausea filled his gut. Indigestion burned its way upward. His eyes watered. He dropped the fabric, replaced the cup and the lid. He sat back in his chair smiling, tears tracking his cheeks, and let the buzz of energy run through his entire being. The smell was truly awful but the sense of being on the abyss of wondrous things to come was exhilarating. He closed his eyes and imagined great warriors clashing weapons, and the thrill of victory. A whisper on the edge of consciousness called him. A woman's voice in a language he couldn't understand, angry and desirous, calculating and lustful. He lost himself in her singsong tones, yearning to comprehend.

A thud brought him from his reverie. He was kneeling on the floor, the box open before him, its contents spread out on the rug. The bone had somehow come free of its wrapping and pointed, accusingly it seemed, at the cup lying a few inches away on its side. The cup pulsed with light for a moment and he could almost see the missing disc in its centre, then it faded to nothing. Just an old cup on the floor, the bone just a bone, the smell of death a memory in a hot stuffy room.

Shuffling sounds came through the closed door and Algernon realised that Clement must be awake. He collected the artefacts, returned them to the box, and stood, realising as he looked out the window that noon had come and gone, and teatime was fast approaching.

CHAPTER 6

Florentine Ponsonby straightened her skirts and patted down her flyaway hair. She knew from experience it looked as good as it was going to get. With only scant moments left before she needed to see her mother in the kitchen downstairs, she collected her purse, her fingers brushing over the handwritten book of verse her sister had given her. Thoughts of her sister were a balm for the nerves that threatened to rip through her stomach if she gave way to them.

Butterflies, her mother would say. *A sign that you need to stand up and be brave. Only cowards and the ignorant did not feel the twisting twirling flight of butterflies within.*

Florentine smoothed the thick material of her vest before slipping it over her blouse, glad that there was no outer sign of the turmoil below, and twirled slowly to inspect her skirt. She didn't have the means to be the most fashionably dressed woman in the city, but she made the most of what she did have. One of her mother's many friends had brought the fabric of her vest, a rich green, from England along with pattern books and silk thread. Florentine's mother, Mrs Rosalie Ponsonby, knew the true value of a respectable outfit. Sydney society was particular and a woman had to look impeccable if she wanted entry to the right events. Her responsibility was to ensure that some of those 'right events' were held in the tearooms at the Garden Arms and Traveller's Rest Hotel. While today's meeting was to be held elsewhere, the Ponsonby women were always welcome.

Rosalie worked her entire life to be respectable and comfortable, and her children planned to honour their mother's efforts and continue the tradition. Not that there was anything wrong with being poor, but a person could achieve far more with their life if they didn't have to also concentrate on barely surviving in a world where poverty and starvation were far too easy to come by.

Florentine had too much to do for that. The butterflies settled as she thought ahead to the meeting of the Women's Literary and Geographical Society she was about to attend. The society was a relatively new organisation formed by Mrs Harris, the Lady Mayoress, as a means for women of a certain education and economic status to discuss books, news, and current affairs. Meeting places were shared from month to month. Tonight, Florentine was walking to the King Street home of Misses Mary and Elizabeth Young. The Misses Young were the only daughters of George and Henrietta Young, who owned a large successful sheep station in the country. With an older brother and his wife already managing the property, and younger siblings old enough to help their doting parents as needed, Miss Mary and Miss Elizabeth had decided that country life was far too stultifying to suit them. Their clever arguments with their father concentrated on the lack of suitors to be found so far away from the city, and with their mother, the desire to further educate themselves on the afflictions of the age. In other words, they needed to be where the action was and stuck on the wide brown lands of western New South Wales was slowly killing them.

Rosalie had sniffed when Florentine shared the program of discussion. 'Women's storytelling through quilting … A group of women sitting around sewing and talking … we've being doing that since the dawn of time.'

'There's a little more to it than that, Mother.' Florentine was certain that her mother did not understand the importance of the meetings.

'Just remember to think before you speak and pay attention to what you are sewing before you thread the needle.'

How her mother went on.

Florentine closed the door on her bedroom and walked along the hallway to the staircase that punctuated the hotel from ground floor to top. The Garden Arms was one of the few hotels on Macquarie Street. Its longevity and reputation was a result of careful planning by its owners and their ability to appease their neighbours. The uppermost level held the family bedrooms, with the youngest children relegated to the sloping eaves beneath the roof at the back.

The floor below had four airy rooms with large windows and lace curtains overlooking Macquarie Street, a guest living room at the top of the main stairs, and smaller box-like rooms that over-looked the hotel courtyard. By law, the hotel was required to have only four rooms available for traveller accommodation so the extra was more often used for storage. At street level was a taproom and tearoom, distinguished from each other by an ornate iron gate and a potted cabbage palm between each doorway.

Mrs Ponsonby had planned the layout well. Each day the bar was full of men and the tearooms full of women, all of them drinking, eating, and discussing the affairs of the world.

Florentine didn't know it, but the birth of the Women's Literary and Geographical Society had taken place in her mother's private tearoom during a high tea she'd hosted for the likes of Mary and Elizabeth Young and the Lady Mayoress, who mentioned the idea at her very next monthly reception to certain women of Sydney's governing body. It was agreed that a society to educate themselves and others would be organised: first meeting to be held at the Garden Arms Tearoom and subsequent to be held at member's homes, as voted on at the conclusion of each month. Rosalie was sitting by the fireplace in the kitchen, her feet resting on a worn footstool, a basket of yarn and knitting needles in her lap. Opposite her sat the family nurse and cook, Honora Keogh, leafing through a journal of recipes, home help tips, and sewing patterns. Aunty Nora knew the children as well as Rosalie herself, and looked up with a wicked twinkle in her eye.

'Time to be off at last, I take it? You look well dressed for your secret women's business.'

'Aunty, don't be mean,' Florentine replied, 'and there's nothing secret about it. We'll only be talking about current affairs and litera-ture. And hopefully not too much about sewing.'

Rosalie looked on, pensive, as the needles clicked together in her hands, pulling in brown yarn from the basket, and turning out neatly knitted rows on their way to becoming a vest for one of the children.

'Your brother will come with you tonight. Nora has packed him some food and a flask of warm tea. He'll wait and walk you home afterward.'

'Mother, no! I don't need a protector. I'm perfectly capable of walking on my own.'

'Nevertheless, he'll go.' She nodded her head toward the folded newspaper on the side table. Florentine picked it up and flipped it open. Strange happenings were reported in the Gardens across the road, right down to the wharves and over to Darling Harbour. The Young household was not too far from stories of brigands and thieves. 'It will be dusk by the time you return, getting dark. I would feel better if Drew was with you.'

'Some deterrent he would be. He's only fifteen!' Florentine slapped the paper down on the table and cut off Rosalie with a shake of her head. 'Don't worry. I'll look after him.' And she left the room. She wanted to stamp her feet in frustration, but contented herself with a firm closing of each of the doors she walked through instead. By the time she reached the courtyard and the gate to the alley beyond where her brother waited, her temper had calmed somewhat. Drew shrugged and started walking.

The boy knew his sister well enough to keep his mouth shut and his thoughts to himself until she indicated his conversation would be welcome. His solicitous silence added an extra balm to her nerves and disgruntlement. She gave him a sidelong glance, sighed, and relented.

'What will you do while I'm at the meeting? It will be awfully boring for you and there's nowhere to wait inside. You should go home and come back later.'

'Not a chance, Florrie. I'll find something to occupy my time.' He jiggled the basket he was carrying. 'I could just spend the whole time eating. You'd think we were going to the ends of the earth with all the food Aunty Nora packed.'

Tucked in with the picnic were some books, a sketchpad, and drawing materials. Spending an hour or so away from the family wouldn't be such a hard chore. As the only boy, Drew often found the constant noise and attention of his female relations trying.

'I shan't rush then,' Florentine answered.

The winter sun was warm on their backs as they walked along Macquarie Street, past the Gardens and the looming exhibition building on their left, dwarfing the trees and tall iron boundary fence. Shadows cast sharp lines across its pale surfaces and added a mysterious air to arches and domes.

'That place gives me the shivers.' Florentine had a view of it from her bedroom and had seen it at all times of day and night, and in all types of light and weather; nothing seemed to effect or damper its noble presence on the skyline. The building, with its turrets and spires and dark-eyed windows, was a constant reminder of an encroaching world every morning and an exclamation mark at the end of every day.

'It's just a building made of wood and nails and plaster. What's inside it is more important. I've been inside dozens of times and still haven't seen everything.'

'That's because you stop and inspect every item and read every label. I find most of the collection slightly abhorrent. All those stuffed animals staring at me with their glassy eyes as if it's my fault they're dead and on perpetual display.' Florentine pulled her coat tight to ward off imaginary chills. 'The statues are nearly as bad. I would much rather see everything in its natural habitat than … caged and boxed.'

'Statues in their natural habitat? Where would that be then? Some quarry in East India?'

Florentine flung her purse at her brother and hit him in the chest. 'What I mean is that I would rather go to the Parthenon to see a Greek statue where it's meant to be seen than one put on a pedestal in Sydney. It's all out of context.'

'And I would rather be exploring and observing the animals and plants myself as well, but we're on the other side of the world with no money of our own to sail away to far-flung destinations. Did you know there's a collection of weapons and masks from tribes in Guinea? And Aboriginal shields and canoes and spears too.'

'Yes, I did, but there's not much there to say what the women do while the men are off hunting and making war. It was a much better collection during the Great Exhibition. Remember that? We found something new every week.'

The Great Exhibition had ended two years previously, and the Ponsonby girls with their brother tagging along had visited each weekend to admire everything from the room full of French ceramics to the vast collection of minerals. Anastasia, a talented artist like her brother, had filled a dozen sketchbooks with reproductions of the display rooms and later created beautiful watercolour renditions, which she'd presented to their parents the Christmas before their father had passed away.

Brother and sister turned down Hunter Street, dodging passersby and avoiding shop wares that crowded the footpath. Drew pulled Florentine out of the path of screeching children chasing each other along the street. The fading smell of fresh baked goods wafted across to them from Mrs Shadler's bakery. Amy Shadler's bread was nearly as good (and sometimes better) than Honora's. Drew suspected that his old nurse quite often bought loaves from the bakery; something about the taste of the soft bread was different. Honora had regularly taken all the children along to visit Mrs

Shadler when they were small, and the smell of her bakery was often to be detected in the kitchen of the Garden Arms.

'Stop dawdling, Drew. I'll be late.'

They rushed past the bakery and the hotel on the corner of Phillip Street and down Elizabeth Street, crossing the road in front of the New South Wales Royal Society. A young man had just alighted from a carriage and was standing beside a battered leather portmanteau. Florentine almost tripped over it and looked up with a stab of annoyance.

'I'm awfully sorry, Miss. My fault entirely. I hope you haven't hurt yourself.' The gentleman's voice trailed away in embarrassment. Florentine bit back on her opinion of oversized luggage lying around the footpath as she realised that the source of irritation was already being moved away.

'Thankfully not,' was all she could come up with. The gentleman had a Scottish accent, and underneath his hat and broad coat she discerned a certain pleasing aspect. The knowledge that he must be a member of the Royal Society to be carting his luggage to their front door was also pleasing and she decided straight away to make his acquaintance.

'Flor, you'll be late.'

Florentine's scowl at her brother was interrupted by the young gent returning to the footpath.

'Please don't let me keep you any further,' he said. He tipped his hat and waved to the carriage driver. 'I have a rather important appointment myself. Perhaps we'll meet again under less violent circumstances?'

'I barely grazed your luggage, sir; I would hardly call that violent …' Florentine started to say before Drew tugged on her elbow and dragged her away. 'Another time would be lovely.'

They were past the vacant block of land before Florentine could afford another word, this time to her brother. 'I could have spared one moment to speak, Drew. I didn't even find out his name. Did you hear his accent? Just off the boat, I'm sure of it, and a scientist too …'

'If he is a scientist then you'll probably bump into him again at one of your talks or at the Palace. I'll keep an eye out for him myself if you like. Right now, you have to get to your meeting and I have to … well, I have plans as well, if you must know, and you are putting a right spanner in the works.'

'Plans, Drew? Are you meeting someone?'

They'd almost reached King Street and the sidewalk was overflowing with fashionable young men in tightly tailored sack suits. Older men in dark frock coats reminded Florentine of black wings flapping in the shadows waiting to hide evidence of evil doings. Such a man visited the family a day after her father's funeral to convince their mother that she was not capable of running the hotel without him. He was given short shrift by Mrs Ponsonby, who had managed the business for twenty years already by that point and didn't give two figs for the interloper's false concerns. A week later, the same man in his black crow suit attempted a petition to have her declared unfit to run the business.

His interference cost the Ponsonby family quite a bit in legal fees, licences, anxiety, and temper, but he didn't win. Rosalie Ponsonby was made of stern stuff and now her name was engraved on a brass plaque she'd had made especially and fixed above the front door of the hotel.

Florentine scanned the faces of the suited men and was relieved to see he was not there waiting to pounce as they rushed by. She suspected they made Drew nervous as well, because he bumped into every single frock coat they passed. A chorus of disgusted grunts were aimed at his hunched back like a grit-laden wind, but he ignored them all and crossed the road without a word or a glance in their direction.

'They'll think you're a hooligan,' Florentine stated as soon as she caught up to him.

'Don't care what they think.'

They walked on in silence until they reached the residence of the Misses Young: a two-storey terrace with a well-kept garden and imposing iron balustrade and gate that opened with a creak when Florentine gave it a push.

'What are you going to do while I'm inside, Drew?' A vague sense of unease spread through her and the soft flap of wings brushed between them. Drew was a sensible enough lad, but only to a point, and she had the sudden wish that he could come to the society meeting with her.

'Might go to the billiards room around the corner,' he answered with a shrug avoiding her gaze. 'Charley and Pete might be there.' Charley and Pete were brothers, either side of Drew in age, who regularly frequented such haunts. They were a known pair of larrikins and each had felt the sting of Rosalie Ponsonby's sharp words whenever they'd dared to enter the Garden Arms Hotel. Florentine was sure though that the ring leader of the trouble-making activities was none other than her quiet brother, who was full of ideas and plans, only some of which he shared with his sisters.

'Or I might go see if Mr Bell's got his new shipment of books in yet. He might need help putting them on the shelves.'

'Or reading them …' Florentine smiled. The lure of new books exceeded the lure of billiards and a room full of cigar smoke and stale beer.

Drew nodded. 'Of course.' He tapped his pocket and coins jingled. 'I've been saving in case the new Mark Twain came in.'

Florentine had the urge to visit the bookshop with her brother. Mr Bell's bookshelves were filled with the latest books and journals. He and Mrs Bell were considered experts on all things literary. Mrs Bell would likely be at the meeting and Florentine's nerves renewed. She hoped the other women wouldn't consider her an ignoramus and that they would talk about books she'd read, or at least heard of. The front door of the terrace opened behind them.

'Miss Ponsonby. Welcome. You're just in time for tea before we start.' Miss Mary Young stood in the doorway with a smile halfway between friendly and haughty. 'Do come in.'

Honora Keogh was friend, confidante, nurse, and cook at the Garden Arms Hotel since the days when William Ponsonby was the proprietor. She'd arrived in Port Jackson off the *Lady Peel*, one of nearly two hundred orphan girls from the workhouses of Ireland, barely speaking English, but strong and capable. Honora had been a week in Hyde Park Barracks with the other orphans when William Ponsonby had come looking to employ a domestic servant to assist his wife at their hotel. He'd picked her randomly, provided her with a room to herself to live in (her first such), and paid and treated her well. Mrs W Ponsonby was a frail English woman who had not come to terms with either the sea journey from her homeland or the tropical climate of Port Jackson. It fell to Honora to do most of the cleaning while the cook at the time, Mrs Lonergan, took care of the kitchen. Between them they kept the Macquarie Inn, as it was known back then, as comfortable and homey as they could. When Mrs Ponsonby failed to survive her lying in, puerperal fever taking her two days after giving birth to a stillborn son, William lost interest. Despite Mrs Lonergan and Honora's best efforts, the inn slipped toward becoming a squalid hovel.

James Ponsonby, younger brother to William, arrived just in time. Or rather, Honora acknowledged, Rosalie arrived just in time. The young couple had met aboard the *Sir George Seymour* and married within a day of landing in Port Jackson. The new Mrs Ponsonby was strong as a horse and nobody's fool. Within a week, the inn was cleaned from top to bottom, kitchen restocked, and new rules set in place. James was given the care of his grieving and ofttimes inebriated brother. The two were charged with keeping the peace in the main bar and providing entertainment. Rosalie had found, Honora still didn't know from where, an old piano. James was quite proficient, and William had a deep gravelly voice. They accompanied each other every night for a year before William was trampled beneath the hooves of an ill-tempered horse. He was buried beside his wife at the Devonshire Street Cemetery.

Mrs Lonergan left the Ponsonby employ not long after, keen to try her hand at the goldfields, and Honora was promoted to head cook. The Ponsonbys then embarked on a continuous plan of improvement for the hotel, starting with a new name: the Garden Arms Hotel and Traveller's Rest. Carpenters were employed to update the rooms. Self-taught Rosalie took on Honora's education, and improved her own, by poring over magazines and newspapers, especially those that provided the latest recipes, decoration ideas, and current affairs.

By the time her eldest daughter was married, with one bairn running around and another newborn, and her second eldest daughter had received her invitation to attend the Women's Literary and Geographical Society meeting, Rosalie had become something of a power force in Sydney's business and social life.

Honora recognised the same determined personality in Florentine.

'Headstrong that one,' she said. 'Just like her mother.'

'And her mother before her,' Rosalie added. 'All the more so for the education.'

'I'm still not convinced that all that reading and learning is good for her.' Honora tutted. 'I can't see her running around after a brood of wee ones and cleaning up after a husband.'

'Nor can I.' Rosalie slipped her feet into her shoes and put her hands on the armrests of her chair to force herself into standing position. 'Perhaps she's not meant to. Our Anastasia's managing well, but Miss Florentine is a different kettle of fish. It's time to move again. We'll have dinner orders starting soon." She nodded her head toward the young woman efficiently kneading dough at the kitchen table. "Your Bridie has a dab hand with the cakes and sweets, but she's not got the strength yet for hearty meals.'

Honora agreed. Young Bridie had the makings of an excellent cook and had created some wonderful accompaniments to the staple menu the Garden Arms provided their guests, but she liked to experiment and didn't have the patience for the cuts of meat and basic vegetables the guests preferred.

The women made their way to their positions within the hotel; Honora to the pantry to retrieve vegetables and meat from storage, and Rosalie to the front of house and their soon to be clamouring guests.

~

Rosalie missed the sound of her husband's piano playing on Sundays. He'd a fine ear for music and a light touch on the ivories. His voice wasn't a patch on his brother's fine baritone, but he had the talent to make up for it with the music and produce a sound that was pleasing to the ear.

She walked through the hotel at a sedate pace, preparing herself with each step to be Mrs Ponsonby, proprietor. Any crack in the calm demeanour she showed the customers would set tongues wagging and rumours flying. She was sure that George Boseman, ambitious and greedy lawyer that he was, had the ear of someone in the government—he was too well informed and overbearing to not have.

Luckily, the president of the United Licensed Victuallers Association was a long-time friend of her husband's and godfather to the Ponsonby children. And Rosalie had contacts in the Colonial Secretary's office as well. She was also well informed, extremely cautious and level-headed, and knew exactly what she was doing.

Still, Boseman was a worry. There was something about him she did not like even before he'd tried to muscle her out of business. A certain cross-eyed look and cocky swagger he had about him; the memory of his presence in her home had stirred old fears. She'd found that in the three months since his last visit, a sense of dread haunted her dreams—asleep and waking.

Rosalie could hear Honora laughing at some ridiculousness of Bridie's in the kitchen as she passed by. Women's voices chatting, someone singing in a high contralto (not well at all), and the clink of teacups carried down the hallway from the ladies lounge ahead. She'd pop her head in for a cup of tea with whoever was there before moving on to the main bar. Tea and a quick chat gave her the strength to be stern later with the men.

The door pushed open as she reached it and she held it so for the maid to come through with her trolley laden with empty teacups and soiled plates.

'Mary's just pouring fresh tea now, Mrs Ponsonby,' the maid said of the waitress inside. 'She's saved you some of Bridie's pretty little cakes too.'

'Thank you, Alice. Are our guests behaving themselves this afternoon?' The behaviour of the guests was a running joke within the close circle of the hotel. Guests who didn't behave, male or female, were politely asked to leave until they felt better, and were welcomed back in the days following as long unseen friends.

Alice paused and leant closer to Rosalie's ear to whisper, 'Mrs Whittle's tea is more whisky than tea. She's quite gay as you've probably heard. Someone told her she could sing.' Alice giggled and moved toward the kitchen. 'Of all the most dreadful noises ...' Kitchen sounds swelled as Alice opened the door and drowned out the last of her less than respectful opinion of Mrs Whittle's singing. Rosalie sighed. She'd need to have a word with Alice about keeping her opinions, if not to herself, then at least in the kitchen rather than the hallway. Again.

Mary had already started pouring Rosalie's tea and passed her a dainty porcelain cup as soon as she entered the tearoom. Rosalie was a stickler for perfectly brewed tea, and Mary knew exactly how she liked to take it.

'Thank you, Mary.'

Mary blushed, bobbed a curtsy, and returned to serving the guests.

Rosalie moved among the women, pausing to have a quick word here and there, answering greetings, and encouraging Mrs Whittle to take more of Mary's tea and another of Bridie's cakes. A signal across the room to Mary and a fresh cup was brought across straight away. Rosalie stayed with Mrs Whittle a while longer, so she couldn't top up the tea with liquor and then, finishing her own now cool tea, Rosalie said her farewells, placed her empty cup on the sideboard, and steeled herself for the more boisterous main bar.

She felt the cold fingers of dread as soon as she walked in. Her feet soaked them in through the floor and they inched their way up her solid legs. Her woollen stockings did nothing against the shock. Petticoats and skirts were no barrier from a cold that travelled the length of her body until it was all she could do to not shiver. The room was warm with the hot breath and bodies of the men who filled it, yet Rosalie was chilled to the bone. She set her face against the ill will that fluttered around her, clamped her lips down on a scream, and searched the room as discreetly as she could for the harbinger of the dread she felt.

Someone was here who shouldn't be, and Rosalie knew that her family's past and the secrets she kept had finally found her. Her mother's words, whispered in fright as she sent her only surviving daughter to the other side of the world thirty years previously, came back to her as if it were only yesterday; the smell of the cold stone cottage and the sea, the sound of the ocean crashing against the cliffs, trees swaying wildly in the storm strengthened wind. The touch of the sheepskin bag her mother had made to hold the things that were most precious to her—to them all.

'Go swiftly, daughter, and be safe. Stay forever on your guard and never let them have power over you.'

Rosalie hadn't understood who 'them' were or why she had to flee her home. Her mother's urgency was unmistakeable, and she had done as she was told. First to Dún Scáith and then Broadford to hide herself among fellow travellers, and then down to Falmouth, where she had boarded the *Sir George Seymour* as a distant relative's 'help', and finally to Port Jackson, where she had changed her name through marriage, and did her utmost to put herself and her family in a position of strength through fiscal and social means, and education.

Crossing the room, tucking her skirts away from half-drunk men and end-of-day discussions of high importance, her mother's soft burr sounded in her memory. She didn't know who it was she had to be on guard against, but deep down in her waters, to the very core of her being, she knew—they were here.

~

'And the mantelpiece was overflowing with china knick-knacks and the fire was fair bursting from the grate beneath. Doilies made from Irish lace covered the back of every chair and it was all I could do to keep my shoes on and not run my feet over the soft floor rugs. From Persia, Miss Mary said …'

'Sounds fussy,' Drew responded to cut through his sister's chatter. 'Did you talk about books at all or just gawk at the furnishing?'

'Don't be rude, dear brother. Of course, we talked about books, poetry, and politics. Miss Devereaux, who is engaged to Edwin Walker, one of Mr Salwey's clerks, was in a huff about a bill to amend the Right of Dower.'

'What's that?'

'It's about when a husband dies and the right of his widow to inherit some of his property, or at least the value of it in cash perhaps. Miss Devereaux says it's a continuation of restricting the legal rights of women and should be quashed.'

'Miss Deveraux's not even married yet.'

'But she will be and Mrs McLaughlin, who is very married, agrees. More so, her husband agrees as well and he's a member of the Legislative Assembly.'

'Luckily for Ma then that Da knew what he was about and signed nearly everything over to her before he passed and left the rest to us in his will.'

'Very lucky. That old Mr Boseman would have had the Garden Arms otherwise. Did Mr Bell have your book in?'

Drew's grin was wide as he pulled the cloth back from the picnic basket to show that several books had replaced the food. On top was a brand-new copy of Mark Twain's *A Tramp Abroad*. 'Not only that, he gave me two others for helping him unload the crate, and Mrs Bell another for helping with the cataloguing.'

'We won't see you for days with all of that to read.'

The pair continued chatting as they navigated their way down Elizabeth Street. It was past six o'clock and there were quite a few people out walking, enjoying the mild evening and a few more staggering their way home from the hotels. Neither noticed anything untoward as they approached the corner and turned toward Macquarie Street. They slowed their pace and looked about them. Dusk was fast becoming dark night and the flickering gaslights that lined the street did little to banish the shifting shadows of the trees. Window light seemed to stretch out from the buildings and vanish in between the fine cracks of the wood-block paved road. Wind whistled up from the harbour and bats flapped overhead.

'Where is everyone?' Not a soul could be seen, not even silhouettes in the windows and doorways they passed by. Without waiting for an answer, brother and sister clasped hands and ran the rest of the way home.

The air around them thickened with dread, swirled with threat of the unknown. The squeak of bats in the treetops sounded like distant screams, their leather wings flapped through the sky as they started on their nightly rounds.

Somewhere along the road, a wagon trundled. Its wheels clumped through a pothole. Footsteps splashing and the scrape of rough brooms over the road's surface followed behind. The acrid stink of disinfectant carried to Florentine and a knot of fear started to unwind. Wagons, brooms, and disinfectant were normal sounds and smells. The block boys were out cleaning the streets. The shadows retreated, and evening peace restored.

Pools of light leeched across the lane leading to the rear of the Garden Arms. Florentine heard a worry of voices through the open windows of the ladies lounge. One of the female voices sounded familiar, another carried the same Scots brogue of their mother; a deep male Irish voice wove a story in between, about dangerous roads and omens, colicky children, and played out mines.

'Anastasia's home!' Florentine and Drew scampered the rest of the way. Pushing the wooden gate open with a bang, rushing through the kitchen door, past Honora and Bridie still busy cooking and cleaning, down the corridor and, at last, into the ladies lounge. Pale faced, eyes glittering with a mix of emotions, they burst into the room.

'Ana! John!' The pair hugged their older sister tightly and then separated enough to draw their brother-in-law into the embrace.

'Your Aunt Flora has arrived as well.' Rosalie's strained voice cut through the room.

Florentine relaxed her grip on her sister and blinked away a hot tear. 'We've missed you so much, Ana.'

Anastasia pushed her away and held Florentine's shoulders until she was standing upright and steady. Drew wiped his face with the back of his hand and reduced his hug to a handshake as John pulled him away from his sisters.

'Come and meet your aunt,' Anastasia said, and the pair turned to the stranger in the room. 'Mrs Heffernan, this is Florentine and Drew.'

'Enough with the formalities. We're all family here. Flora is a perfectly suitable name to be met with. Come here, children.' The woman with the voice so like their mother's wore a man's brown travelling coat with buttons opened to reveal a soft cream blouse and tan linen skirt. Other than a few creases in the skirt, Flora Heffernan showed little sign of her journey, though she had travelled far and by roads much rougher than in Sydney. Her grey hair was pulled into a low bun at the nape of her neck, and her collars were loosened enough to show the tanned skin of someone who spent a lot of time outdoors.

Florentine curtsied and Drew bowed, and both were hugged and kissed by the aunt they barely remembered.

Flora Heffernan was a strong, proud woman and though her general carriage was as stern and practical as her clothes, her face softened into gentility as she inspected her young relatives. Florentine's chin was lifted with one finger until she stared directly into the older woman's eyes. She hoped she would not be found wanting. Flora squeezed her arms and made her twirl slowly. She finished with a nod and turned to Drew, who she gave a long head-to-toe-to-head stare.

'Your children are a credit to you, Rosalie. So healthy and strong. City living doesn't seem to have made them too soft.'

'There's no time for softness,' Rosalie said.

Flora turned to her niece with an enigmatic expression, and Florentine remembered the strangeness of the night and the weird apparition of the trees and their shadows. She felt cold, though the heat from the fireplace filled the room. Her skin tingled and her nerves jarred an unfamiliar path from low in her belly to her constricting throat. Mother and aunt moved and didn't move, spoke and didn't speak; the ghost of others seemed to crowd the women, strange voices maundered through her hearing. Drew pinched her arm and Florentine's attention snapped to the people around her.

'We weren't expecting visitors were we, Mam?'

Rosalie's eyes glowed beneath a deepening frown. She glanced at her son with relief, relaxed, and shook her head.

'They arrived with the gloaming and not a word that they were on their way.'

'We couldna say, Rosie. Twas not safe.' Flora's accent deepened as she spoke her soft apology. Her voice was laced with sorrow and trepidation.

To have Anastasia and her husband show up unexpectedly was a surprise, but Flora Heffernan's unannounced presence spoke of troubled times ahead.

'Why isn't it safe?' Florentine's whispered words dropped like icicles in a room that had always been the epitome of safety. The ladies lounge of the Garden Arms, where women went to chat, and eat and drink tea, sharing stories and experiences, troubles and woes. Under the gentle and determined guidance of Rosalie Ponsonby, a network of support and friendship had grown between the walls of the lounge unlike any place else in Sydney. Florentine had the feeling it was all about to be stripped away.

Rosalie collected herself, confirmed her usually straight posture, and, putting on her Mistress of the House persona, took her relative's arm by the elbow. 'Rest and a meal is in order before any talk. Drew, show Flora to our guest room and then go gather some things. You'll be rooming next to door to the twins for a night or two. Anastasia and John will take your room. Florentine, you can help me in the dining room.' She held up her hand as Florentine started to protest. 'I'll not have another word spoken on the matter until after we've all eaten.'

~

'I want no darkness in here,' Rosalie instructed as she and Florentine entered the dining room. With the arrival of the visitors and staff pressed to the kitchen to cook a larger dinner than usual, the dining room was unattended. 'Light everything.'

Growing illumination bit into the gloom as candles were lit, followed by the gas light above the fireplace and the paraffin chandelier over the hardwood table. Shades were banished to the night where they belonged.

With a deftness of movement from long practice, Florentine opened the buffet doors and started removing the white china dinner plates. Rosalie slid open drawers to collect the silverware and napery. Overhead, floorboards creaked and doors clicked as they opened and closed. Children's voices, high-pitched with excitement, were overlaid by adults soothing, commanding. Men queried, answered, then the thud of heavier tread as luggage was delivered to rooms.

The dinner setting emerged over the gleam of the table as the women worked; knives and forks placed beside plates, glasses above, napkins below, and cork mats lined the centre awaiting the hot dishes to come.

Florentine and Rosalie finished at the same place setting, hands meeting as the last plate was laid with the last of the utensils beside it. Rosalie clutched her daughter's hand as if they had just completed a challenge far more perilous than the setting of a table for dinner.

'Talk to me, Mam. I know something has happened. Drew and I felt it on the way home. We saw ...'

'Shush, child. We'll talk all we need to, but later. I need to find the words for it and I need normalcy for a while longer. We'll not have it again for a good while after.' Rosalie smoothed Florentine's fingers straight, forcing her own to disengage the claw-like grip they held.

Anastasia entered the room, her skirts swishing as she brushed past chairs to reach her mother and sister. 'The bairns won't settle. John will stay with them until they've eaten and then see them to bed with a story. Even the twins seem edgy. Drew has ordered them to behave, for all the good that will do.' She faltered, the anxiety that had driven her from her home in the mountains to her mother's side catching up to her. The road from the gold town of Tambaroora to Sydney was long, arduous and often perilous, especially with winter's cold and icy winds dogging those who dared the passage.

'See to the fire, girls. I'll take care of the twins.' Rosalie gave them each a brief shoulder-squeeze as she left them to reinvigorate the banked fire.

Anastasia hugged her sister and forced her into movement. 'I'll do this, Florrie. You go freshen up. I thought you'd seen a ghost when you first walked in tonight.'

'I think I might have,' Florentine admitted. 'Though not any ghost we've read about in stories. Drew and I were so scared, and then to see you all. I heard you from the street, but you sounded scared too.' Anastasia had paled as Florentine spoke and the younger sister was suddenly placating the older.

'We are frightened, Flor. We're not sure what's happening either and the uncertainty underlies everything we do and say, but we're together now and stronger for it. Go now and hurry back.'

Lucent moonlight split Florentine's bedroom into realms of hidden and partially hidden with a sharp incandescent stripe into the centre of the room. Lace-curtain edging threw a mottled pattern across the bed. The Botanic Gardens across the way appeared the same as every other night, the silhouette of the Palace in their midst etched black across the silvery sky.

Music and voices carried across the expanse as glittering carriages wheeled their way down Macquarie Street and through the ornate iron gates. Men and women in their Sunday best walked the paths, stepping in and out of the sanctuary the gaslights offered from the night. All so dark and solemn only a fleeting time before, the grimness now dissipated to resemble a normal night in the city. Another entertainment-filled evening at the Palace.

Laughter and arguments filtered up from the bar downstairs as they came and went, heading home or to work or to the Palace across the road.

Florentine stood to the side of the moonlight's edge and watched the people passing by three storeys below. The ominous breath of foreboding that had set her hair on edge and her skin prickling as she'd walked home couldn't have been the result of an overactive imagination. It had been so long since she'd been that scared and over nothing. Here in the safety of her room, her nerves still felt stretched with the echo of fading horror.

A burgeoning of sound and light drew Florentine closer to the window as another gaily lit carriage passed below; tinkling laughter and low singing dashed away brooding fear with its effervescence. The noise abraded her senses like a clarion bell. As the celebrating party turned into the long drive leading up to the Palace, the gaslights seemed to burn a little brighter, reaching deeper into the tree shadows. Florentine thought she saw a dark figure, blacker than the shadows in which it hid. In that flash of a moment, the brush of imaginary wings came back to her, then the shade vanished, and Florentine wasn't sure it had been there at all.

A creak from behind, and hall light pooled in to the room, warning her that she was no longer alone. The soft scrape of knuckles on wood as the opening widened indicated the presence of her brother.

'It wasn't our imagination. Was it?' Drew slipped into the room, letting the door close behind him. 'My spine's still tingling. What do you think it was?'

Florentine watched him come to the window to peek out. His face was cast oddly as he passed through the shadows and across the stronger edge of the moonlight, only to blur as he stepped into the shadow opposite her, eyes wide, waiting for her to answer.

'Can we imagine the same thing at the same time?" she offered. 'If we both felt it, then it must have been real. Surely. As to what it was, I have no idea, but it hasn't gone. Not completely.' The tremble in her heart warned her that there was more to fear than shadows on a dark winter's night.

Drew's attention snapped back to the window and he pulled the curtain aside for a clearer view. 'Did you see something?'

'Yes. I think so. I'm not sure. Oh, I must have, but it was so quick. A dot of light where there shouldn't be there in the trees; a vague shape, only it wasn't tree-ish enough'.

'Something or someone? I don't see anything.'

'Someone. A man. Watching us, the hotel, me …' Her arms tightened around her chest, fingers bit into her arms. Her eyes burned with the strain of staring into the night. It was futile. There was nothing there that shouldn't be.

'Well, he's not there now.' Drew released the curtains and let them drop back into place. He reached for the heavy velvet drapes and, drawing them closed as well, disappeared into the darkness of the bedroom. 'Time for some light in here. Don't you think?' His voice was like dry leaves crackling, and Florentine felt the lucidity of the night tilt. She moved at last, released from her stasis by the blocking out of gardens, palace, and night. She opened the door and blinked at the brightness that washed over her. Now able to see, Drew went to the sideboard to light the cold lamp, and the glow grew to encompass the whole room.

'You're okay, aren't you, Flor? You're as pale as a sheet.' Drew paused to chuckle. 'Must have scared the bejesus out of you too, hardly said a word.'

'Tch! You've hardly paused for breath since you barged in,' Florentine re-joined with a smile. She recognised her brother's attempt to distract her from the knot of fear she felt inside. 'Mam wants us downstairs as quick as we can. I'll just take my coat and hat off, and be right down.'

'I'll wait and escort you if you like. Just in case there's anyone else lurking in the shadows. I can throw the lamp at them and lead the way down the stairs if there is!'

Florentine contained a burst of nervous giggles as she unpinned her hat and added, 'Maybe I should keep a hat pin handy too.'

Then she paused with a sobering thought. 'Mam must have known.' Sending Drew along to protect her, she must have known that peril would haunt her daughter's steps. Florentine wasn't used to feelings of vulnerability, she was too young and full of confidence to feel anything other than all-conquering.

She flung her hat onto the bed and unbuttoned her coat while Drew lifted the flickering lamp, his face still caught between light and dark—the uneasiness of what their mam knew and the desire to laugh it all off.

Anastasia was almost at the door to the nursery when it opened and a bundle of children tumbled out of the room, hell-bent on escape. Rosalie's two youngest, Emily and Kate, and Anastasia's toddler laughed and bantered. The ten-year-old twins were playful and mischievous, and little Fiona appeared to be cut from the same cloth.

From further into the room, John's voice sounded harried and baby Evie was mewing restlessly.

Anastasia brooked no arguments as she put on her sternest voice. 'You lot back in that room or no cake!'

The youngsters froze.

Florentine, divested of her outdoor layer and looking almost as fresh as when she first left the house earlier in the afternoon, caught her brother's eye. They couldn't hold back any longer and let their laughter dash away the remaining tendrils of uneasiness. Outside the world might be scary, but inside there was still cake to be had.

The cake turned out to be Apple Charlotte, fresh from the oven, with a jug of warm nutmeg custard.

Conversation over dinner was light: children, education, music, books, Florentine's afternoon visit to the home of the Young sisters, and the mild weather—on the coast, at least. But now, with steaming bowls of Apple Charlotte before them, each of the diners seemed to sense a shift. Time to discuss unexpected arrivals and their meaning, and a certain sense of feyness that each could feel crowding in on the room, collecting in the shadows where gaslight and candles could not reach, congregating among the embers and low flames in the fireplace; an impression that if one could turn their head fast enough they would see, in full, the phantoms haunting their peripheral vision.

The crispness of apples baked just enough to release their natural sweetness once teeth had bitten into their soft flesh, the crumble of toasted bread crust mixed with crunchy sugar, and the spiced goodness of the custard relaxed the family as only stomachs full of good food could.

'I received a letter from home,' Aunty Flora started, dabbing at her the corners of her mouth with the linen napkin. 'Three actually.' She studied the faces of Rosalie, Anastasia, and finally, Florentine. 'They were sent separately, but were held up for one reason or another, and arrived together in the one delivery. I could hardly believe it.'

Rosalie nodded as if to agree with the vagaries of letter delivery, a constant thorn in the sides of people living on the other side of the world from their families. Anastasia fumbled with something papery in her lap and Florentine continued sipping at spoonfuls of custard, the passage of her spoon from bowl to mouth slowing as she listened to the reasons why the older woman had deemed it more expedient to travel all the way to Sydney rather than write herself. She was a prodigious correspondent and the far-flung branches of the family knew each other well because of it.

Bridie entered through the swing door of the dining room backward, managing to bring in a tray laden with tea cups, a sugar bowl, and a small pitcher of milk, with only the slightest rattle of china as she avoided the return of the door and quickly stepped across to the dresser. The soft cloth spread along the dresser's gleaming surface absorbed the impact of the tray and prevented any further clatter.

'Mrs Keogh says to tell you she's made tea and coffee, and there'll be more as well as slice for supper when you're ready, Mrs Ponsonby.'

'Thank you, Bridie. Dinner was lovely as always. I'm not sure how much more we can fit in, but it's likely to be a long night and I'm sure we'll need sustenance before we find our beds at the end of it.'

'The Apple Charlotte is divine, Bridie. Mr Bray and brother Drew here have had two serves already! I hope there was enough for the children. It will be a rare treat for them to taste something so fine.' Anastasia's bowl remained half-full. Her too-thin fingers still gripped her spoon and it seemed likely she would finish dessert even though she'd not been able to empty her dinner plate.

Bridie gave a little curtsy and a wide smile. 'We baked another just for the bairns, Mrs Bray. Our Alice has already taken theirs up. I'll be right back with the teapot and coffee jug.'

'The letters,' Rosalie prompted Aunt Flora.

'Yes, from home. That is to say, from our cousin Sile, in Broadford, who reports of goings on out at Kilmarie.'

'My brothers?' Rosalie asked. She'd left three elder and one younger behind her when she emigrated to Australia from Skye.

'And their children, specifically Mairi MacKinnon, daughter of your eldest brother. She was a wee thing when you left, Rosalie. Do you remember?'

'No more than a babe in swaddling cloth,' Rosalie agreed. 'With a healthy set of lungs as I recall.'

'Sounds like to our Fiona,' John added. 'We'll be hearing her soon enough, though she be on the top floor and we down here. Just as soon as the Apple Charlotte settles, and she decides she wants more.' His Irish accent had not dimmed since coming to Australia and Florentine tingled with the sound of his clipped singsong words. The family had yet to hear little Fiona in full voice though and Florentine wondered if her brother-in-law might be exaggerating.

'You know that she didn't marry and cared for your mother for many years, Rosalie. Before your mother passed, she gifted Mairi her cottage and all her belongings. Not on the grand scale when it came to wealth, but enough for Mairi to lead an independent life not often experienced by women, and to be desirous of not sharing or losing it to a man.'

Rosalie frowned. The greedy and unscrupulous Mr Boseman had tried to use unjust inheritance laws against her after the death of her beloved James. 'Wise thinking. Not every husband is as benevolent as my James was. Many a man would take everything and leave nothing.'

'MacKinnon women are known for their wise ways. My dear Patrick and I agreed on our terms of marriage early as well and our children were instructed on his wishes should he depart this world before I.' Aunty Flora's first husband, Colin Campbell, had died young, leaving her with two young children and little else on an isolated New South Wales property. Her second husband, Patrick Heffernan, hardworking and wily, suited her own propensity for work. They were happy with each other and their extended families.

'And I'm not given to bouts of stupidity either,' John added, keen apparently to stay on the good side of his wife's relatives.

Alice, the housemaid, entered the room ahead of Bridie with the tea and coffee, and began collecting the dishes, now all empty. Drew blushed as she leant over him to reach for his plate just as he lifted it for her. They bumped hands and the teen's face turned a brighter shade of red. Florentine stifled a snicker and Alice smiled, not at all concerned with the touch or Drew's obvious embarrassment.

'Thank you, Alice,' Florentine said as she leant to the side to enable the maid's easy access to her dessert dish. They caught each other's eye for a moment and Alice's eyes widened, bright white above her dark cheeks glowing. She quickly attended to the rest of the dishes, balancing them with some skill on her arms as she moved between table and dresser, filling the tray that Bridie had cleared of teacups, and avoiding the besotted gaze of Drew and the teasing looks of Florentine.

Bridie served the tea and coffee just as efficiently as if the pair had choreographed the routine, and then held the door for Alice and her heavy tray. 'There's plenty more tea in the pot,' she said. 'Mrs Keogh says to ring when you're ready for the slice.'

The door swooshed closed behind her, and for a moment or two only the clink of teaspoons on cups and saucers and the slurp of hot drinks could be heard.

'Back to Mairi and the letters,' Rosalie prompted Aunt Flora.

'There was a gathering of MacKinnons by the loch at *Cill Chriosd*. Not many, but Mairi was among them and so too our Broadford cousin. Some of the old graves in the churchyard were desecrated and the family went to put things right. Apparently, the same thing had happened at Kilmarie.'

Rosalie's expression turned thunderous. 'Were any of the family hurt?'

Aunty Flora shook her head and sipped her tea to avoid meeting Rosalie's stern gaze. 'None even knew of it until by chance one of the lads came past with his sheep. The gravestones were upturned, some broken, and two have vanished.'

'We have similar news.' Anastasia's tea had gone ignored as she fidgeted with the paper in her hand and listened to the growing concern around the table. John laid a hand on his wife's arm as if to calm her, and Florentine could see that her sister was indeed extremely pale and tense.

'While I was lying in with Evie, I had a visitor. A friend of a neighbour who only recently arrived in Australia to try their luck on the gold fields, even though they are past their prime and not much has been pulled from the earth in some time.'

'We had already been talking about returning to the city,' John broke in. 'But we hadn't mentioned it to anyone else.'

Anastasia opened the letter. 'This is a note from that friend, Mrs Jean O'Connell. It turned out that her family live not far from John's in Dublin, and everyone was upset about the ransacking of an ancestor's grave out in the country. Items were stolen, pieces of significant importance. Mrs O'Connell was chatting away telling me all about the ruckus when I came over faint and clammy. The poor lady was perturbed that she'd upset me and suggested I needed my family close by.'

'But my faintness and health are not the issue.' Anastasia handed the letter to John who stood and brought it to Rosalie at the head of the table. 'One of those items surely must be the twin of the box on your side table. When the woman talked about the thievery, I felt as if someone had walked over my own grave.'

'She's had nightmares ever since,' John added. 'And I've never known Ana to miss a wink of sleep, other than by the demands of the children. We've naught to keep us in the mountains so we came home.'

Rosalie read the note and showed it to Aunty Flora. It seemed that the strange tales of grave robbing must be connected.

Flora nodded and continued. 'Our cousin's second letter mentioned more strange happenings at Kilmarie and talk of ghosts. The land was no longer as blessed as it had once been, even with the effects of the blight and the weather had turned sour; bitterly cold during winter, hot elsetimes, and very little rain.

'Steely clouds would gather on the horizon and everyone would talk about a break in the drought, but no easement came. And no word came from the ancient home of the MacKinnon, even though Sile had sent letters and it was usual for visitors from that side of the isle to come to town. She ended her letter stating that she was off to see Mairi the next day and would write again on her return.'

'She did as promised.' Aunty Flora waved the third letter in the air and began reading it aloud.

'Mairi's cottage was deserted and the hearth cold. It was clear that it had not felt flame for some time. The stone was covered in dust and dead ash. Fearing the worst, I raced to her father's cottage on the hill and found none at home. Sharp keening and angry voices carried on the sea breeze, and I knew I would find them at the remains of Dún Ringall. They stood in a circle beneath the branches of the ancient wych elm. The whole family crowding the tree, and between them I could see a strange huddle of cloth on the ground. I didn't want to go any closer, but knew I had no choice. Oh, Flora! Such terrible news. What is it? I cried out. What has happened? And when they parted, saying nothing for there was nothing to say, I saw for myself that the bundle on the ground was not rags but the remains of a woman's skirts and poking from beneath were two stockinged feet, shoeless and unmoving, a shawl tangled between them. I am sorry to appear morbid, to drag this out, but even though I witnessed for myself, putting it down on paper makes it feel so final, like a judge's anvil. It was Mairi lying there; over the sacred grave of our ancestor, as dead as she, her clothes a mess from some great struggle ...'

Rosalie's face was set, not in stoic acceptance but in grief already known. Lines had deepened around her mouth and across her brow, and her eyes gleamed like embered coals. It was clear that she expected sad news, though this did not lessen the bitter gall at hearing of her niece's violent death.

John knelt beside his sobbing wife, clasping her hands as if to share his strength and keep her safe from harm. Anastasia buried her face in his shoulder. Rosalie's grief and growing anger washed over them.

'And the rest?' Rosalie's words fell like chips of ice.

Flora's hands shook as she lifted the letter once more to the light and continued reading in a shaky voice.

'Mairi's father seemed to have aged a century since I saw him last. His back bowed with grief, his very essence gaunt and stricken. The disturbed grave beneath her body told the story. Grave robbers! Though none know why. Mairi lay not only across but in the grave, and the bones of our

ancestor, even the shroud that covered her and that which she was laid to rest with, are all gone. The roots of the wych elm were clear for all to see, white where a shovel struck them. We are all in shock at the rape of the grave and the murder of Mairi. Please tell Rosalie that her brother has written, but no one has heard from her in some time, and we are now unsure of where she may be found. You will know and I have calmed the family with the knowledge that I would write to you immediately.

'*Please tell Rosalie also that her brother believes her to be in some danger and that she should be wary. With Mairi passed, she is the only ward left and it may fall to her to return, though I know not why nor what would be left for her here. Her brother would not say more, only that she would know.*'

'*Flora, I believe that Rosalie and her family are safe so far away from home, but does evil know boundaries? Does it know or care for the great distance that lies between Dún Ringall and the new world? I hear thunder in the distance, Flora. I pray for rain to wash away the stain of the evil things that have been done. Take care, your cousin, Sile.*'

'That is all. That is everything.' Flora's voice sounded flat. 'The three letters, and Anastasia's note, clearly show that great evil is rising.'

'I see now why you have travelled so far, Flora, dear. Thank you.' Rosalie stood and walked closer to the fireplace. The mantel above it, hidden by a length of fabric draped like curtains, held a bowl of seashells the children had collected, vases overflowing with native bush and blossoms, a lamp with a crystal-laden shade, and a carved maple clock. Its pendulum swung from second to second with barely a click to signify the passage of time. Only half past the hour, over two hours until closing time, and four more until midnight; the wytching hour.

'Thank you,' she repeated. 'I've had no word from my brothers for some time now. I had wondered how my letters to them could go unanswered. I have also written to Sile with the same result. Now, I know. They have obviously received nought of my missives. Something, someone, has intercepted our correspondence. How foolish to not read and then forward on. We would never have suspected a thing, and you, Flora, would not have felt the need to come to Sydney. Even so, they have hindered us. Hindered us and yet made us stronger.'

'How so?' Flora asked. 'It appears that whoever is behind this has more knowledge than us and has many arms.'

'Slippery as an octopus,' John added, frowning. 'Are we in danger then?'

Anastasia clasped his hand, her knuckles white.

'This person's machinations have intended to keep me ignorant and isolated. However, we are now all together, are we not? And we are stronger for it. It is a small detail perhaps, but important.'

'What does she mean by ward, Mother?' The room seemed to slip as Florentine listened to the talk, as if the foundations beneath them were lilting. Everything blurred and snapped back into sharp relief so quickly she wondered if she might be coming down with fever. Her skin tingled, stretched too tight over her flesh.

'And why would anyone want to steal some old bones?' Drew's lips turned down at the corners in disgust and his eyebrows formed a deep V over eyes glittering with fascination.

'They are the bones of our ancestor, Drew Ponsonby, and are venerated by all who followed after her. This desecration affects us all deeply, and has ramifications far beyond the ransacking of a lonely grave.' Rosalie frowned at her son.

'But why would someone go to the trouble?' Drew's teacup rattled in its saucer as he spread his hands out in question.

The air in the room was stuffy and smelled of old pinecone and beeswax rimed with the sour tang of the gas fluming out of the heavy chandelier above the table. Florentine gripped her brother's agitated hand to keep it from knocking the china cup off the table, and watched the colour drain from her mother's face.

'A ward is the person guarding or keeping watch over a sacred item,' Aunty Flora explained. 'Your cousin, Mairi, was the ward of the grave. I don't know why someone would take the remains. However, the items our ancestor was buried with were important relics, quite valuable in their way.' She cast a sideways glance at

Rosalie. 'Sile told me about it the night before we left the isle for our new home.'

'The last words I heard from my mother were to keep it secret.' Rosalie's clipped voice was softening with sadness, but Florentine could hear fear in the edges.

Florentine untangled the strands of information from the stories she had grown up with. She created a whirlpool in her teacup with a spoon and stared at the swirls of milky fluid as they folded over each other. She knew about the box by Rosalie's bed, they all did, but it had rarely been opened in their presence. Vaguely, she recalled an old hairbrush and comb, some swatches of fabric: purple velvet, soft lawn, and some yellowing lace. Perhaps something more valuable was hidden beneath the fabric or sewn into the lining of the box.

'Mother?' Rosalie's pained gaze and thinning lips held back secrets; like the innocent looking box, something valuable was hidden from view. 'What are you guarding?'

Rosalie's bones ached with dread; her well-ordered life had turned upside down and her children's future was under threat. She had spent every waking moment working toward a level of comfort she had never known in the draughty old stone cottage of her childhood. Huddled in the narrow confines of the ship that had brought them both from dreary England to sunny Port Jackson, she and James had shared dreams and planned their future. Poverty and a life always on the edge of ruin was not for them. It was the same promise most emigrants swore; that life would be better, fortunes and destinies changed. Such promises kept sanity intact on the long days spent tossed around on leaky old barques with grand names.

Rosalie had the gut-wrenching sensation that her luck had run out and she was now perched on the eve of a new life of loss and suffering to come.

She wished for her mother's presence; for more time, more

stories, more everything. She did not even have the comfort of her husband's calm demeanour and strong embrace. Now, she must give the support and tell the stories, every single one she could remember, to her children; to Anastasia and Florentine.

Beside her, Flora shifted in her chair and stood to fetch the teapot. *When in doubt, drink tea,* was the family motto.

'I'm not sure how much help I'll be, Rosalie. My family have long been separate from Dún Ringall. My grandparents left the old tales and ways behind when they moved to town.' She poured the remains of the brown brew into teacups and passed one over to Rosalie before admitting, 'Most of them anyway. I separated even further when dearest Colin and I came to Australia.'

Rosalie acknowledged her relative's admission, but she heard only strength in the woman's clipped words. She was reassured by Flora's presence, but not in the anxious gazes of her daughters. Florentine chewed on her lip as if she'd not just eaten her fill of Honora's baked dinner and Apple Charlotte; the deep creases of her questioning frown forebode danger, anger, fear, and a thirst for adventure. Anastasia's face, gaunt and drawn over her usually generous mouth, eyes red-rimmed, showed only fear. Worry gnawed at her strong frame. Sometime in the last few months she had become fragile. One daughter impetuous and the other full of timidity.

As her mother had done, some thirty years ago, in the shade of the wych elm tree, Rosalie had a decision to make: which daughter to send into danger and the unknown. Appearances at this moment would suggest Florentine the natural choice. Rosalie had never made decisions based on appearances. Anastasia had the strength of experience and the ferocity of motherhood; Florentine, youth and conviction. Some time ago she'd pondered the veracity of either of the twins. The girls were a force unto themselves. When Anastasia was pregnant, Rosalie's thoughts had turned to grandchildren; to wee Fiona. One of them? Two? Why not all?

The time for pondering had slipped by and a decision had to be made tonight. But not right this instant. Slivers of time may be all that were left to her, but they were enough. She would share her stories first and let the choice come to her naturally, through the sharing.

She lifted her teacup and drained its contents wishing it were whisky instead. The cup clunked in its saucer as she returned it, uncaring of the value of her precious china. She gathered the linen napkin from her lap, dabbed droplets of tea from her lips, and stood. 'We'll take this upstairs now, I think, and let Bridie and Alice finish clearing the table.' Chairs scraped, and dishes clanged as the rest of the family arose from the table. 'Drew, please go light the fire and tend to the candles. Ana and John, why don't you check on your bonny wee bairns first? Florentine, perhaps you would like to assist Flora upstairs?'

Rosalie turned her back on her family. Ignoring the sound of chairs moving, skirts swishing, voices whispering, consoling, questioning, she looked once more at the heavy mantel clock. She had just over three hours to tell her stories and start preparing. The pendulum maintained its steady swing. Rosalie ran one finger along the cool wood of the clock. It had once belonged to William Ponsonby's wife, the only item left from that woman's tortured life here in the colonies. It had been wound every day and never missed a beat. Rosalie dropped her fingers to the catch on the glass door that shielded the clock's working parts. It clicked open easily. She reached in, placed her fingertips firmly on the bob of the pendulum, gave it a firm twist, and disengaged it from the lever. The bob was a plain bronze disc, pointed at the bottom with an elegant swirl at its top. Rosalie clicked the glass door closed and turned away from the fireplace.

Honora stood waiting. 'What do you need?'

'Black salt. As much as you can make. How much dried lavender do we have?'

'Enough to last at least three uses. I'll send Bridie out to cut fresh rosemary as well.'

'Do that. We'll start at midnight. Thank you, Nora. You're my rock.'

'We'll be ready.' The Irishwoman didn't know all of Rosalie's stories, but knew enough—and she had her own. She'd recognised the gathering of shadows in the night. She would do what was needed to protect the family from harm.

Rosalie tucked the pendulum bob in the pocket of her skirt and took a deep breath. Time had caught up with her, it overflowed the moments. Soon it would stop her completely or leave her behind. The next few hours would tell. She left the room and followed her family upstairs to the sitting room.

From the shadows of the trees and iron fence, Clement Benedict watched. To this place his father was drawn, thousands of miles from where he, the ever-obedient son, expected to be, and he still wasn't sure why—not exactly. His father sprinkled out his secrets like grain to starving sparrows, but kept the most important ones closely guarded beneath his steel grey top hat, secure behind his heavily starched collars and tight silk neck ties. Clement suspected that one day his father would choke on the secrets he refused to share. He hoped he would be around to witness the event.

Until that joyful day, Clement was loathe to admit that he was as committed, and ensnared, to the path his father laid before him. Duty and obligation haunted his every breath; they were the iron manacles he fought to free himself from and the trap from which escape seemed impossible. Lord Algernon Benedict's word was both law and compulsion, the binding that kept his son close and, for the most part, biddable. Clement wasn't sure whether he hated the old man or loved him. He knew though that he, and only he, had the man's trust and that behind the stiff collars and trimmed moustache, the permanently frowned forehead and florid cheeks, his father was proud of him.

And so, Clement perched in a low branch of a tree. With his coarse woollen trousers and heavy cotton shirt and vest, worn boots and ex-navy cap, he had the appearance of one of the street cleaners, and should any curious soul wonder at his lurking presence in the garden, they would assume he was shirking his duties. A crew of cleaners were hard at work not far off, scrubbing shit and mud and dust from the wooden road. What was one more, albeit not quite as hardworking as the others?

Music stuttered out from the exhibition building behind him. He thought he might attend the evening concert if all went well. He'd miss the first half, of course, but the program was to be repeated and he was sure to fit it in before more nocturnal chores later in the week. The colonial band of musicians warming up for the night's festivities struck a nice balance between the higher style he was used to and the working class jigs he'd taken a liking to on board the ship out here. A carriage rolled past, a couple of soused men fell out of the hotel across the road, and a straggle of people walked down the path. He ignored the distraction of the music and concentrated on the hotel and the people. He'd sipped a rather fine whisky in the main bar earlier in the evening; his father's interest in the hotel proprietor had necessitated a reconnoitre of the premises. The woman in charge watched over her customers something like a mother hen, or hawk, he hadn't decided which. She didn't appear to be much of an adversary, but the effect she had on the crowd of drinkers couldn't be mistaken. Raised voices softened when her gaze raked that section of the room; rough bantering edged toward gentlemanly conversation as she walked by. No, she didn't look much of an adversary at all. They were the most dangerous kind.

Clement's task tonight, simply to watch and remember, was already growing tedious, but it was one he was particularly good at. He had never forgotten a face, a voice, or a name.

He pulled his pipe and tobacco from his vest pocket, tucked the bit on the end of the aged wooden shank between his lips, and held it in place with his teeth so he had two hands free to pull out a small wad of leaf from the pouch and drop it in to the bowl. He pulled the strings of the pouch tight to close it and replaced it in his pocket. Hands free again he took the pipe, tapped down the tobacco with the tip of his finger, retrieved a packet of safety matches from another pocket, and prepared to light up. The process helped his concentration, and as the match flamed he paused before waving it gently in a circular motion over the tobacco. He breathed in the acrid smoke and let his focus go to the people walking down the incline toward him. They would pass by within feet of his position in the tree, but they were too full of themselves and the night ahead to notice him. Their chatter drowned out the soft draw and gurgle of the pipe as he coaxed it into warmth. He judged time by the life of the pipe. Each life took approximately twenty minutes. He allowed a similar length of time between lightings. By the end of the night, his mouth would be dry and bitter, and his lungs would ache. The next morning his chest would be thick with the need to cough out the poisoned air of the night before. But right here, at the start of the first pipe, he relaxed and enjoyed the taste and smell of the tobacco.

The chattering group passed by. Dusk was fast becoming true night. Lights in the hotel blazed like beacons as men going in to drink and out to wobble home ebbed and flowed like the tide. Clement narrowed his eyes and avoided the bright light to direct his gaze on the dull streetlights dotting the footpath. A lanky teen and young woman had rounded the corner on the opposite side of the street. They were ordinary in the extreme, nearly as chatty as everyone else out and about, until they drew level to the tree where Clement hid, and then silence fell over them. They darted fearful glances into the gardens; the woman appeared to look straight at him, and quickened their step as if they sensed danger.

The woman couldn't have been much older than the teen and it was clear that she must be his sister, though her hair was a dark frame around her pale face while the boy's hair was a sandy untidy mess beneath his cloth cap. The light was too dim to see the colour of their eyes, but the intensity with which they searched the trees was unmistakable. Clement held his breath and cupped one hand over the bowl of his pipe to hide the tell-tale glow of the burning tobacco. The smell would hardly be discernible over the stinging aroma that trailed behind the street cleaners. The boy put an arm around his sister and they hurried past the hotel, ignoring the drinkers and the noise, and sending furtive looks in his direction until they reached the corner of a dark lane. They turned in and disappeared between the buildings.

The buzz of excitement washed over Clement as he drew a deep breath and felt the warmth of the burning tobacco on his face. He'd seen who he needed to see. These were the people they'd been searching for. His instincts were impeccable and, once again, his father was right. Hidden away on the opposite side of the world was the last riddle in the quest that his family had devoted generations to. Now if he could coax his father into sharing the purpose of all this, he was sure he would finally understand what the hell was going on.

CHAPTER 7

The cellar hadn't seen sunlight since the day it had been sealed off from the outside world, buried underneath the hotel. Rectangles of light slashed in through the street windows when the sun was in the right position, but otherwise the dank room was lit only by candles. Risky to be in the cellar for anything other than hotel business, but Rosalie had no choice. She'd dallied far too long, using preparations as an excuse. Her girls, like she, were born canny women.

Candlelight bobbed with each stair she descended. In the cellar, hiding from William Ponsonby and giggling like teenagers, she and James had planned their future together. So long ago now, but the memory still tugged a fond smile across Rosalie's lips. After William's death, they had come down to the cellar to console and plan afresh. The cool isolation of the lonely room provided sanctuary and more.

Rosalie stepped out onto the earthen floor packed hard from decades of use. At the edges of the light, shelves full of bottles, stores, and equipment. She moved away from the working area and further into the little used corners. Behind the dusty shelves was her travel trunk. It had come with her all the way from Broadford on

Skye, a gift from a relative when she'd shown up with very few possessions and nothing to put them in. Other relatives, including the newly wed Flora and her family, had provided Rosalie with dresses, a cloak, and a pair of sturdy boots. Colin, Flora's doting husband, had hand-tooled a leather pouch and embossed her initials into the trunk. He'd been such a thoughtful man. Rosalie could barely remember what he looked like now—thirty years since she'd seen him. A featureless figure waving goodbye from the wagon in which he was carting his family northward, only to be killed a year or so later. Flora was Mrs Heffernan now and Colin's youngsters were all grown up with their own families, absorbed into the large Heffernan clan. Rosalie would not recognise either of them in the street.

The trunk was thick with dust and set in its position half-buried under disused and forgotten household items. She tugged the cracked leather handle, sneezing and trying to keep clear of the muck rising into the air, and eventually could free the trunk enough to open it.

Her mother was a witch!

Florentine sat on the end of her bed, cross-legged and gazing at the silhouette of swaying tree branches through the window curtains. The air was cool and goose bumps spread along her skin. Her cotton chemise and pantaloons were not enough to keep her warm, yet she delayed reaching for her woollen dressing-gown. The happenings of the evening before filled her thoughts. Rosalie's stories had sketched around what everyone had sensed; stories of warrior queens, magic, and old women, shifts in time and location, spells, and mystical objects.

Thinking on a life time spent in relevant ease in warm Sydney, Florentine cast her mind to her mother's early life, much harder than could be imagined. Florentine understood about old stories and traditions, had thought that many of her mother's sayings and habits were quaint and amusing. She had not thought for one minute that the sayings were spells and the habits protections against real harm. She could not believe for one second that her family had magical forebears, did not want to accept that Rosalie was anything but how she perceived her to be: a generous, rather bossy, no-nonsense Scotswoman.

Her mother was a witch!

Anastasia had not seemed surprised, nor had her husband John, or Aunty Flora. Honora, the doughty old Irishwoman, had entered the sitting room with the family carrying, of all things, a small cauldron full of burnt offerings that smelled of lavender and fat from a month's worth of roast dinners. While Rosalie talked, the women sprinkled the crystallised substance by the window and across the hearth, murmuring as she shuffled bent over like an old crone.

Florentine's gaze sharpened and she jumped off the bed, hopping over to the window on feet stinging from "pins and needles". She took a handful of the gauzy curtain and pulled it aside. The window ledge was covered in black crystals. Hanging from the catch was a sprig of lavender tied with kitchen string. Florentine pulled it free and shards of crystal fell into her hand. She smelled them, popped her finger into her mouth and then placed it on her crystal-covered palm. The crystals dissolved a little when wet. She swiped her finger with the softest lick of her tongue.

'Salt?' She stared at her hand. Old wives' tale or magic? Was there even a difference? The blackened salt was liberally strewn across the ledge. She could feel it under foot where it had fallen to the floor. Turning, she noticed a trail of it from window to door, and hanging from the doorknob another sprig of lavender. Her fingers tightened on the poor looking piece of plant in her hand. Its grey green leaves didn't seem to impart any sense of magic and she wondered of its purpose. Protection? They had a whole garden of lavender and other sorts of shrubs in the courtyard. Mother and Honora regularly brought cuttings inside to pretty the place up a little, or so they said. Florentine looked at the sprig. Too early for the pretty purple flowers, but its scent was definite in the cold room and she shivered. It reminded her of her mother too. She hooked the string back over the window catch and went to the coat hook to fetch her dressing-gown. Florentine was not going to let her mother's stories scare her. She'd dress and go help in the kitchen where everything would be busy and normal. She was slipping her arms into the heavy sleeves when a faint tap came at her door. Most of her family would knock loudly and walk right in. Drew would barely even give that courtesy. The tap came again. Perhaps it was Aunty Flora. She was old and probably had a lot more manners than anyone else in the household.

'Who is it?' She folded the gown around her and was tying the sash when the door opened. An unexpected face appeared through the gap. 'Alice? Come in. What is it?'

Alice was a little older than Florentine, but the pair had grown up together; their mothers, while not friends exactly, knew each other. A true native, Alice's family had originally lived by the shores of Camp Cove, and lately at the boatshed by the fort. They moved up and down the coast, lately preferring the growing settlement at La Perouse.

Rosalie had taken Alice into paid employment when she was young on the understanding that the intelligent girl was also educated and trained in skills that would improve her opportunities once she'd reached womanhood. She came and went over the years, but always returned for the winter. Her connection to the Ponsonby family meant they had fresh fish and could offer guests fishing tours, and Alice's family had a source of blankets and shelter when needed.

Most days Alice served guests in the tearooms. Afternoons were spent reading and talking with whichever woman was in the kitchen—all of whom were keen to better themselves and each other. Rosalie had encouraged her daughters to mix in and they were often in the thick of heavy conversations about politics, books, or the latest fashions from England. Outside of the kitchen, each knew their place in society, and this kept them safe from meddling outsiders. Especially Alice. As something of a conduit between her own mother and Florentine's, Alice walked the path between Europeans and natives.

Florentine looked at Alice, as she did Bridie, and saw a friend, one of the few who knew her well. Growing up in the insular world of the Garden Arms had erased outside pretentions and bolstered a relationship that may otherwise never had occurred.

'What happened after tea last night, Florrie?' Alice closed the door with a gentle push and reached up to remove her hat.

Florentine grabbed her elbow and ushered her to the bed to sit. 'Have you only just got in? I found out something terrible about Mother. I'm not sure what to do.'

'I have something to tell you too, but you had better go first.' Alice rested her hat in her lap and fiddled with the brim.

'You won't believe this, so I'll just come right out and say it. My mother is a witch! A bloody witch, of all things. There! I'm sure you won't believe it, but it's true. I saw for myself.'

Florentine waited for some sign of disbelief or shock from her friend and felt her world slip a little more when she realised no sign would be forthcoming. Alice already knew.

'She's not a witch, Florrie. Not like in the fairy tales. They're made up to scare little children and silly old whitefellas.'

Of course, she was right. Rosalie didn't look like a witch at all. For her age, she was quite handsome.

'What is she then? She and Nora cast spells in the sitting room looking for an evil presence.'

'Did they find it?' Alice stood, turning her hat in her hands and averting her face. 'I need to talk to her.'

'I wouldn't know. I don't believe in all that superstitious stuff. What worries me is that they do. They always have and kept it hidden.'

Alice turned, scowling. 'Of course they kept it hidden. You're an educated woman. Look at how you're reacting. Power must be kept hidden or the whitefellas will take it away. Do you think you'd be sitting here worrying over this in your fine bedroom if anyone outside knew? Do you think I'd be standing here talking to you?

Neither of us would be where we are if anybody knew about your mother. It has to be a secret and not just because of what people would think or do.'

'Why do I get the feeling that you know so much more than I? Does everyone except me know? I think Anastasia did, but Drew looked like he'd seen a ghost, so I presume he didn't know either.'

'Flor, stand up.' Alice took her hands and drew her to her feet. The hat fell forgotten to the floor.

'How come you know?' Florentine asked.

'Shh, Flor. This is important. Did your mother find the evil?'

The robe slipped from Florentine's shoulders. She found it difficult to remember past the surprise of walking into the family sitting room and finding her mother standing in the centre of the room. The square table that resided by the window had been dragged over and, instead of the lace cloth and pretty vase of flowers it ordinarily held, it was covered in a large map of the city. Aunty Flora and Drew stood beside Rosalie, hands clasped; Drew's eyes wide and dark. Anastasia and John pushed past Florentine to stand on the other side of their mother.

'Leave space for Florentine,' Rosalie whispered. Anastasia waved her sister over to stand beside her. Everyone shuffled around until they formed a circle around the table. Anastasia's hand felt warm. Her long fingers wrapped around Florentine's and held on tightly.

Rosalie murmured something, and took Florentine's hand in her own, holding on even tighter than her sister, and raising it to her lips.

We are Blessed ...

Florentine shook herself from the memory of her mother invoking strange spirits to the circle. 'I didn't really understand a lot of what she was saying, Alice. I thinking she was speaking Scots. She had a pendant of some sort that she held over a map. She hardly moved but it swung in circles. I'm not sure what it meant. When she was finished though, she said, "We must prepare ourselves." Then it was over, and we went to our rooms.'

'Are you sure that's all she said? Nothing else happened?' Alice frowned, and Florentine wondered what she really asking. She pulled her hands free and walked to the window.

'Everything's a little hazy after that,' she admitted. 'But when I woke up this morning, there was this salty substance everywhere and sprigs of lavender at the window and door.' She tapped the lavender on the latch and turned back to see Alice touching the lavender on the doorknob.

'It's at the back door too,' she said. 'I noticed it when I came in.' Alice let the stems drop to swing against the door and strode to Florentine. 'My mum had a bad dream last night. She said the spirits were warning about something bad. She's been getting a bad head lately too, but this morning, halfway to waking up, she had that awful sensation where you feel like you're falling and when she looked up she was in your mum's room and your mum was in the bed with greyish skin and old, like a crone. My mum's never been inside your mum's room, Flo, but she described it exactly. She says it's a warning. Whatever's coming isn't natural. It's not from here. It's come with the whitefellas.'

Alice's agitation was clear and Florentine's anger at her mother's secrets faded into worry. She didn't believe in magic and evil spirits, yet Alice clearly did. Florence couldn't second-guess herself. Should she shrug it off as fanciful, or was there more to her mother's strange behaviour of the night before than she believed? Was her mother a witch? Or was something else going on? She couldn't bring herself to believe in magic. Surely that was preposterous. But then, that pendant …

The pendant had drawn wide circles in the air above the map and gradually, the circles tightened, until the string was taut and the pendant, hung like an arrow caught just before entering its target over a patch of green watercolour. Florentine was drawn once more to the window. She pulled the curtain wide. Sunshine gilded the trees. It bounced off the windows and dome of the exhibition building in bright flashes as if dancing around the building's turrets. Gaily coloured pennants flapped about in the morning breeze. It was hard to believe such a glorious morning could be hiding anything beyond joy on the first day of spring. Yet the patch of green was labelled in perfect cursive: *Grounds of the Garden Palace.* And the golden pendant hanging from her mother's still hand pointed directly to it.

'It's the Gardens,' she whispered. 'Whatever … it … is. It's in the Gardens.'

Rosalie had a dozen loaves in the oven. The warm aroma of lavender, cinnamon, and butter filled the kitchen. Bridie and Alice were due any moment now. They would start the cleaning and cooking. Honora scrubbed the table. Giggles drifted in through the open window. John had kept the young ones entertained since dawn. Not long now until breakfast. The bread would be ready just in time for eggs and toast. Clambering footsteps heralded Drew's approach. A few minutes later and a more measured tread, and deep voices, indicated the arrival of Mr Sellick and Mr Caro. The pair, travelling salesmen for a Sydney business, would be departing today; one south and one westward. Rosalie was glad they were down at last. It meant she could put off further conversation about the situation the family found itself in.

A serious discussion with Florentine was first on the list of things to be accomplished that morning. Her daughter's reaction the night before had not been as expected. She had the feeling her second eldest had misunderstood events and she wasn't quite sure how to remedy it.

'Mrs Ponsonby?'

Rosalie realised with a start that Mr Caro was standing in front of her trying to get her attention. 'Good morning, Mr Caro. Come in. Come in. I'll pour some coffee while we wait for breakfast.'

Drew was already setting the large kitchen table. Mr Sellick pulled out a chair. Mr Caro nodded and went to his usual place. John was ushering the children in and the smell of bacon and eggs frying meant that Honora, bless her, had started cooking while Rosalie stood in a daze.

'I must have been off with the faeries,' she said as she bustled around to the stove and the coffee pot.

Honora shook her head in admonishment. 'Pull yourself together, lass,' she muttered. 'Let's get through breakfast and worry about everything else once our stomachs are full.'

As if in agreement, Rosalie's stomach grumbled. The frying food and the fresh bread smelled divine. Honora picked up the thick oven gloves and the wooden bread shovel. The heat and the aroma of bread billowed around the room as she opened the door.

Regular guests counted the breakfast smells of the Garden Arms kitchen as one of the main reasons they kept coming back. Sitting at the kitchen table with the family and waiting for one of Mrs Keogh's meals was like being at home. Not the homes they so rarely attended being on the road for most of the year, but the home of their dreams, where meals were excellent, sheets on comfortable beds were crisp and smelled of sunshine, and everyone was always pleasant. Messrs Sellick and Caro enjoyed the homey atmosphere and considered themselves honoured to participate in the breakfast rituals of the Ponsonby family. They waited patiently as the bread was left to cool while the eggs and bacon were piled high onto white china serving dishes.

On cue, Alice and Bridie walked into the kitchen together, aprons and caps in place. The business of the kitchen and dining area became a stage for a choreographed movement of people, chairs, food, and pots of coffee and tea. Alice placed dishes of butter and fragrant peach jam at each end of the table along with salt and pepper. Bridie collected the heavy trays of food from Honora; eggs first then bacon, and placed those side by side in the middle of the table. Mr Caro, sitting closest, held his plate aloft, and it was immediately filled with an ample serving of breakfast. Bridie winked at Mr Sellick in a conspiratorial 'don't worry, you're next' gesture and walked around the hustle and bustle of people settling down to their first meal of the day to serve his breakfast as generously as she had Mr Caro.

Alice was slicing the warm bread and putting some over the grill to toast when Florentine walked into the room dressed as if she meant to spend the day outdoors. Rosalie raised an arched eyebrow at her daughter. Their world might be teetering on an abyss, but there were still rooms to be cleaned, a bar to be prepared, and lunch and afternoon tea to prepare for. At the Garden Arms Hotel, family worked beside staff to ensure a well turned-out and successful establishment. Florentine appeared to be in the mood to test the family work ethics.

'Daddy, where's Mummy?' Young Fiona pulled on John's shirt sleeve. She usually sat between her parents at meals, and having an empty chair where her mother should be was not right at all.

Florentine, not quite as insensitive to her family as she appeared, slipped into the vacant chair and tweaked her niece's ear before John could answer. 'Not to worry, Miss Fee. Mummy's seeing to Evie. She asked if you could bring her up some breakfast when we're all done. We'd better be sure to save her some of Grammy's lovely toast and jam. Do you think she'd like that?'

Sufficiently distracted from her mother's absence, Fiona nodded, causing a mess of curls to flop over her face. 'Mummy loves jam and toast!'

'Aye, she does,' John added. 'But she'll want to know how good everything tastes so you'd better start eating so you can tell her yourself.' He caught a fried egg between his knife and fork and carried it to her empty plate, then stabbed at some bacon and dropped two slices beside the egg.

Alice brought around toast racks full of crispy golden bread and laid a slice on every plate. The untoasted bread waited on yet another serving dish on the sideboard until the hot food had been eaten and could be cleared away to make space on the table. Katie and Emily filled their plates with their favourite breakfast food and squabbled over which topping was the best.

There was no silence while people ate at the Garden Arms'

breakfast table. Conversation and comments on the weather or the latest ship to arrive in port or the museum's latest collection or the spread of the railway around the country filled the room with sound. Rosalie sat at one end of the table between Messrs Caro and Sellick, and chatted between mouthfuls about the journeys each were soon to undertake.

'You see, I can take a train as far south as the Victorian border now with the Murrumbidgee Bridge and subsequent line extension completed last year. I was one of the first to travel the route from Sydney when it first opened and it's quite the journey. I'd be interested to make the trip even if it wasn't for all the new towns the railway has opened up for the company along the way.' Mr Caro, it seemed, was a railway enthusiast, and judging by Mr Sellick's enthusiastic nodding as he munched his way through a second serve of bacon and toast, he was just as smitten.

'It's similar for the northern and western routes,' Mr Sellick added. The edges of his bushy moustache gleamed with the coating of bacon fat each new mouthful of food added. He chewed and swallowed, reached for his coffee to gulp down the rest, and continued on: 'I took my wife on a short trip last summer. She'd not been to visit the sea since she left it behind on arrival so I brought her down for a few days to enjoy the cooler breezes. Our home is at the foot of the mountains, as you know, and the heat was almost unbearable.'

'I imagine that travelling at such speed and with windows open would assist to cool one down as well,' Rosalie contributed. She had yet to catch a train any further than the outer reaches of the city—rattling, cumbersome things they were, noisy and smelly as well. Rosalie preferred a horse and carriage or one of the steam trams than a train. But the speed of travel and the convenience of the railway could not be denied. It was a conversation she'd had with many different people over the years, around the table and in the tearooms. Everyone was abuzz with the excitement of the railway and the potential for travel. The world was indeed growing smaller.

Bridie took away the near-empty platters and Alice replenished the toast racks and served the thick slices of fresh bread. The clink of knives on the jars of jam and butter added to the general melee. Bridie and Alice circled the table with coffee and tea (milk for the children), and chatted pleasantly as they refilled cups. Breakfast was starting to wind down now. Stomachs were full. The sun shone through the kitchen windows, adding a gay light to the room. In a few more minutes, everyone would be up and about to get on with their day, but for now everyone was relaxed and satiated.

Alice poured Florentine some tea and then reached over to pull the cream and sugar dishes closer. 'Have some sugar, Florrie,' she said, leaning in close so she wouldn't be overheard. 'You look as pale as a whitefella.' Alice's lips spread in a wide smile as Florentine turned and glared. 'That's better, put some colour back in them cheeks.' Alice straightened and moved on to John, who shook his head and wiggled his still full mug of coffee. Fiona did the same with her cup and milk sloshed over the edges. 'I'll fetch the cloth, Miss.' Alice said.

Florentine heaped two teaspoons of sugar into her tea, added a drop of cream, and stirred. Rosalie watched as she sipped the sweet liquid and frowned. Yes, she needed to talk to her daughter as soon as possible. She sipped her own tea and fortified herself with a deep breath, girding her loins so to speak, for the conversations needed to clear the air, and the stories that remained unspoken.

Mr Caro pushed back his chair, rubbing his belly as he rose. 'My train leaves in an hour. I'd best get on with packing. I'll be down in approximately fifteen minutes, Mrs Ponsonby, to settle up.'

'I'll do the same if you don't mind, Mrs Ponsonby. My departure is closer to noon. However, I have an appointment with the museum secretary in the meantime. He has a list of items he wants me to collect on his behalf. He's prepared to pay, would you believe it, for any native trinkets I come across. It will make me a tidy profit, I don't mind saying. As I will only have to part with cheap trinkets to fill my bags with the items Mr Sinclair requires ...'

Rosalie watched Alice as Mr Sellick carried on, oblivious, describing the methods he employed to extract the trinkets from their owners. His attitude toward Aboriginals was a commonplace inconsideration for their natural rights and, even though Alice was clearly Aboriginal and within earshot of his prattling, he seemed not to notice that he might be talking out of turn.

'Alice, would you please fetch me some fresh cuttings from the garden?' Rosalie waved the young woman over, ignoring the indignant expression for the time being, to send her outside and away from the departing guests.

'Mr Sellick, I'll have your bill ready for you before you leave for your appointment.'

He nodded and waved at her, ignorant of her stern expression and disapproving tone of voice, and left the room talking about Mr Sutherland Sinclair and the new Technological Museum being installed at the Palace.

'Really, the man has no manners!' Florentine stood, fuming, and started collecting plates.

'Put an apron on,' Rosalie ordered. She turned her back on her family and went to join Alice in the courtyard garden, no doubt taking her temper out on the shrubbery. 'And rightly so,' Rosalie mumbled.

Morning sun found its way through the gaps between the buildings. The day would be warm. Secateurs clicked and scraped as Alice worked. Some of the plants had grown from cuttings various visitors had brought with them from their home countries. The lavender, for instance, had come wrapped in silk and poking out of a lovingly tended pot of English dirt. The bearer had traded the cuttings for meals. A month's worth, they'd received in the end. Alice wouldn't have given them a single meal for a scrap of some plant. It might smell nice, but there were far better growing all around the city, even in the gardens across the road. Heather grew in an old horse's trough filled with soil and kept on the shady side of the yard during summer. They reminded Mrs Ponsonby of home.

Alice understood that anyway. A body needed to be reminded of home, of country, when they lived surrounded by buildings and encircled by paved roads. Some things weren't so different. Other things were the exact opposite and always would be.

Mr Sellick always treated her nice enough. Polite and grateful when she served him a meal or poured his tea. Growing up at the Garden Arms sometimes meant she forgot, a little bit, what people could be like. At the hotel she was protected. Mrs Ponsonby did not stand for nonsense and she did not approve of people acting as if they were better than others. No matter who the others were. And she most certainly did not approve of the way newcomers treated Aboriginals.

It's just like home. Newcomers show up, take over, think they're better, and everyone else who has been in a place forever is shite. I'll not stand for it in my hotel.

The problem was, Alice knew, that the law was not on Mrs Ponsonby's side and it was most definitely not on Alice's side. Police had started rounding the Gadigal up and moving them on. Missionaries came to take them away.

Mrs Ponsonby, head covered by a floppy brimmed hat, moved beside Alice and started dead-heading the blooms that had opened early and were already fading; petals tinged brown and curling into death.

'I'm sorry you had to hear that, Alice. Mr Sellick spoke without thinking.'

'Don't excuse him, Mrs P. I hear words like that all the time. Most people talk without thinking. Without caring.'

'That's true. I know it. Their education is lacking. They hear only what they want to hear and spend their days in ignorance.'

'Why?'

'If I knew that, my love, the world would be a far improved place.'

'My mum says they're scared. Scared all the time. Of everything. They want everything to be the same so they're not so scared.'

Mrs Ponsonby was nodding, but Alice couldn't see her face to see if she was angry, sad, or as scared as all the other white people.

'Your mum is a wise woman. We are all scared.'

'You're not like that though, Mrs P. You took me on when you didn't have to and you treat me fair.'

'But you're only one person, Alice. If I wasn't scared, I'd help a lot more.'

'Mum says you help plenty, and teaching me to read and write will help others later on.'

Mrs Ponsonby lifted her head so that Alice could see under the hat brim. She was smiling, proud of Alice as she was proud of Bridie, whom she had also taken under her wing and educated.

'Education works both ways though, doesn't it, Mrs Ponsonby? I learn the ways of the whitefellas, so I can recognise their tricks and lies. You, Drew, and your Florentine learn the ways of Gadigal, so you know the truth.'

'Yes,' Mrs Ponsonby answered. 'It works both ways. Doesn't make it any easier for you though. And it seems such a little thing matched against the wave of ignorance that steps ashore with every immigrant ship.'

'You're different, Mrs Ponsonby. Mum says it's because you walk between worlds.'

Rosalie tilted her head at that and her expression turned quizzical.

'You can see deeper past the surface of things, past skin.'

Alice stopped cutting the bushes and turned to face Mrs Ponsonby full on. 'Mum reckons the whitefellas would have us all in chains if they could, manacled to the places in society they think we should be. You and your family just as much as the Gadigal and all the others out in country. She says what they think is not important. We must think for ourselves.'

'Well, yes, I suppose. If they knew ...' Rosalie started to say, but Alice had to finish.

She put her hand on Rosalie's. 'There are some Gadigal that would not be friends with you because you are white. Some would turn from me because I count you as friends and allies of sorts. But you are white and the lure of the whitefellas' promises is strong for you. It's your history and your culture but it's not and never will be mine. You don't need to save me. I will save myself.'

Rosalie had tears in her eyes.

'And you must save yourself too. Mum says you are in danger. Something's here, hiding among the whitefellas. It's looking for you. She dreamt of you last night, Mrs P. And in her dream, she heard the clank of iron. They'll catch her if they can, Mum said. And they'll lock her away or worse.'

Alice felt no relief at having finally given Mrs Ponsonby her mother's warning. Mrs Ponsonby would not give way to danger. Alice could see it in the grim thinness of the older woman's lips and the way her eyes had narrowed to dangerous slashes.

'Tell your mum, Alice, that I ran once, a long time ago, and ended up here. I don't have it in me to run further than this.'

Rosalie took Alice's hands and clasped them together. Alice didn't think any white person other than a Ponsonby had ever touched her skin to skin. The dark and the light made a pretty pattern and went well together.

'Maybe you should stay home tomorrow, Alice. I'll give you a month's wages up front and maybe you should go with your mother to somewhere safe.'

'I'll stay if it's all the same. Mum says I'm to watch out for you. And Florentine and Drew.'

'Perhaps I should talk to your mother.'

'Mum and aunties have started singing. They'll send word, but we have to be listening for it.'

'Whatever is looking for me, Alice, it's not from here. It's from Old Country and it has travelled a long way. Look for disruption. Your gods won't like it any more than mine do. But it's good at hiding. We'll start our songs tonight. You can come and listen if you like, but you must be good at hiding too. We will need someone to tell our story when this is over, and I have a feeling that may fall to you.'

A dry shuffle on the back stoop and the flash of movement in the corner of her eye warned Alice they were no longer alone. She stepped back from Mrs Ponsonby and pulled her hands free. She looked to the back door at the same time as her mistress and, whereas she relaxed in relief, Mrs Ponsonby straightened with tension.

'Florentine!' Rosalie said. 'We need to talk.'

Alice collected her cuttings and returned the secateurs to their place on the back wall. 'I'll get started on the rooms, Mrs Ponsonby. Have them done in no time.'

'Thank you, Alice. And would you please let Mrs Keogh know that we're full up for the rest of the week? Any guests can be sent to the Mercantile on King Street. She and Bridie will oversee the tearooms today.'

'Yes, Mrs Ponsonby. Right away.'

Alice brushed past Florentine, who stood as if turned to stone staring at her mother. She had lost all colour from her face now and no amount of sugar and tea was going to fix that.

'It's not what you're thinking.' A poor start, but a good few words for her second eldest—almost a challenge really.

'You can read minds too now, can you?'

A wave of heat swept through Rosalie and she clenched her teeth against responding. She turned back to the garden and continued dead-heading, picking off snails and slugs, tugging at the occasional weed. Florentine would come to her when she was ready and she must be almost there now, otherwise why else step outside when there were plenty of places she could go and things she could busy herself with to avoid a confrontation?

There was a soft rattle of the secateurs being removed again from the hook, click of the blades as they trimmed bushes, and the gentle fragrance of spring blooms as Florentine brushed past the rosebush. The courtyard garden was the family sanctuary; box hedges for frustrations, roses and lavender for peace of mind, herbs and vegetables for encouraging thought and ideas, and a big enough plot to allow for serious digging to soothe tempers and dirt to work hands through and relieve a melancholic mood. It hadn't been planned that way, but each of the Ponsonbys had learned that time working outside alleviated the pressures of living in a busy hotel.

'I can't accuse you of dishonesty as this … situation has never come up before, but couldn't you have at least hinted … no, I suppose not. Family matters need to be kept in the family and you can't very well tell your children your deepest secrets. I've been embarrassed enough times by the twins' mimicry abilities. Children are the last people you'd be sharing this with … which is why I suppose they were put to bed and sound asleep before we went into the drawing room last night. I suppose it also means that you trust the rest of us to know when discretion is needed, and I suppose …'

Rosalie faced her daughter, smiling. There was hardly a need to talk with Florentine at all; she was supposing her way through the whole conundrum.

'Why don't you cut some more sprigs of the native rosemary for the kitchen? We'll have rosemary and herb bread tomorrow.'

Florentine moved to the native shrub and the sharp tang of resin replaced the rose scent as she clipped the woody stems.

The steadiness of working in the garden helped Rosalie clarify her thoughts and choose the words she needed to say. 'Your suppositions are all correct. No doubt you'll eventually land on the main reason for keeping secrets.'

Florentine brought a handful of rosemary to her mother and dropped it into the basket at her feet. 'Which is?'

'Safety. When I left my family on Skye, it wasn't just because of the famine and the clearings, though they affected everyone and still do to this day. No, I could have stayed and married and been a crofter like the rest of my family. Life wasn't easy, but we weren't starving. My mother was a well-respected member of the village. A matriarch, if you like. She wasn't the Clan Chief, but he came to her for advice and … other things.'

Florentine's steady gaze was a little unnerving and Rosalie wanted to take her in her arms and hug the seriousness from her face. Now was not the time for vanquishing a child's fears and Florentine was no longer a child.

'Things along the same vein as your ceremony last night, you mean?'

Fatigue started with a cramp in Rosalie's toes and an soreness in her ankles. The trouble they faced felt insurmountable even here in the peaceful courtyard. High walls couldn't keep the noise of the street outside away and they would never be high enough to keep out the evil that threatened her family. As if on cue, a voice rang out and a horse whinnied as it clip-clopped down the cobbled lane dragging along a carriage. The carriage driver sounded impatient. The horse sounded resigned.

'Mother knew things and was acquainted with the old ways of our people. She felt trouble coming, as I do now, and sent me away to be safe ...'

'You'll not be sending me away!' Florentine's open hands fisted as she straightened in anger. 'I won't go!'

'Rest easy, Florrie. We'll not be running anywhere.' Rosalie hoped that would stay true. In the end, if it came to saving her children, she would run as fast and as far as she needed to. 'It will be easier if you just observe, listen, and do as I say for a short while.' She put her hand out to quell the oncoming protest. 'You will need to understand a great deal in a brief time.' She bent over to pick up the basket. The dull throb in her ankles was travelling upward. Age had always been a minor concern, but today, on this beautiful spring morning in the garden, she felt every single one of her forty-eight years plus some.

'When I left, I also took certain items. The safety of those items was at stake even more so than my wellbeing. It has taken a long time, but I have been found—or rather, those relics have been found.'

'What must we do?'

'Find out what it is we have that has caused such a relentless search, discover who our enemy is, and decide a course of action to safeguard ourselves by any means possible.'

The courtyard was a hold-all for morning sunshine and the temperature was starting to climb, a hint of what summer would bring in only a few short weeks. Soon would come Samhuinn, or it would if they were all back home. Rosalie supposed that just like the seasons the festivals would be opposite here. If she were practising, they would be celebrating the end of winter and the arrival of summer. She wasn't practising though, at least no more than a private nod to traditions, and Beltaine had gone virtually unmarked since she fled Skye. Now was the time for change, if they had time, and she would need to remember every scrap of knowledge she possessed for any hope of survival.

'Let's go upstairs. I have something to show you.' Florentine's hand warmed Rosalie to the core and the tiredness retreated at the touch of youth and vitality.

'I'm sorry, Mother. I'm not sure I understand, but I'm sorry I didn't trust you.' Rosalie tightened her fingers around her daughter's and tugged to bring her closer.

Heads together, Rosalie whispered, 'And I'm sorry too, my beautiful daughter. I should have trusted your strength sooner.'

Rosalie had the sigil hidden deep in the folds of her underthings, warm against her skin. A small ebony box was tucked under her belt. Its lid an artwork of seashell slices carefully arranged into the likeness of the Dún Robin shoreline. It was one of her most valuable possessions, this box, having among its contents her mam's brooch and her granny's carved bone comb. Each of the women had at one time filled it with their treasures.

Her mother had warned her to keep the sigil safe even as she pushed her out the low back door of their stone cottage. The voices and hard footsteps of clansmen could be heard coming along the beach trail, their shoes clunked on the rocky shore.

'*Take the cliff path to the wharf. Dún Scáith will help you. Do not let them find you.*'

'*Mam ...*'

'*Know that I love you, daughter, and will do whatever I can to protect you. Follow our plan and pray for safe passage. Whatever you do, Rosie, keep it secret. We will not meet again.*'

And they hadn't. Not even a letter. Though Flora, her mother's cousin, often heard news and passed it along.

Rosalie couldn't imagine never seeing her own daughters or her son again. It could happen, of course. A twist in the smooth path of her ordered life had already taken her husband. She counted her blessings that her children had thus far remained healthy and alive. Oh, so alive! That too could change at any moment, and Rosalie felt the weight of impending doom and the prickle of hot tears as an image of her children, dead, flashed through her mind. Happiness was so fleeting after all.

In her bedroom, with the windows closed against the cool spring day, the sturdy iron bed covered in a colourful patchwork quilt, she wished for time to stand still, for happiness to be longer lasting, for words to be easier.

'Sit on the bed, Florentine.' Rosalie went to her dresser, ignoring the image of a tired middle-aged woman in the mirror, eyes that reflected dread and horror. From the top drawer she retrieved a brass key. She clenched her hand around it, appreciating the sensation of cold metal on hot skin for a moment, putting off the inevitable for a few seconds more.

She crouched on the floor and reached under the bed, arm stretched, fingers wiggling, until she found the small trunk from the cellar. Craggy with age, the trunk stood apart from the rest of the bedroom. A large room lined with simple furniture, plain except for the patchwork quilt. Each square represented a year in Rosalie's life, a child, friends that had come and gone, her beloved James. Each piece of cloth was a memory, each stitch a joy or a tear.

Rosalie tugged the trunk toward her, straightened and lifted it to her lap. She stood holding the trunk firmly and sat beside her daughter. Florentine was distracted by the quilt, her fingertips brushing a dark square of cloth that sat just below the pillow where Rosalie laid her head each night.

'This patch smells like father.' Florentine picked away imaginary lint from the square of worn fabric that had once been her father's favourite shirt. Striped cotton, soft from wear and age, it was the shirt James had worn away from the public eye, relaxing in the evening with his children or on the occasional family outing. He rarely wore a jacket with the striped shirt; he liked the comfort of going without, preferring an extra under-layer on chilly nights.

Unseen on the quilt, Rosalie had sewn squares of James's night shirt and flannel vest as wadding. Further along, a square of rougher fabric from his coat, another created from his pockets.

A soft tap on the door and Anastasia appeared, poking her head through the narrow gap, eyebrows raised in question.

'Come in, Ana. I want you to see this as well.'

'And Aunty Flora?'

Flora hesitated in the hallway and Rosalie nodded to the older woman to join them. Flora closed the door behind her and remained a standing guard against any intruders.

Seating herself beside Florentine, Rosalie patted the quilt beside her for Anastasia and placed her hands flat on the top of the dusty trunk.

'I was only sixteen when I left home, but you already know that.' Rosalie's daughters huddled closer to their mother. 'What you don't know is that I didn't leave by choice. Witch-hunters had scoured the hills and valleys searching for the daemon-possessed. What some men do to ease their fears is a crime.' Rosalie's knuckled whitened as she gripped the edges of the trunk.

'Mam said it was just an excuse for the Lairds and Englishmen to control the villagers, scare them half to death, and clear the villages. Many of the cunning folk were taken, of course. They were the mainstay of village life. The people you went to for medicine or stories or advice. My mam was as cunning as they came.'

'At the first rumour, Mam started teaching me some of her

spells. Mostly how to prevent illness or bless the hearth, truth be told. Mam was never in league with daemons. But on my last night, she must have got wind of danger close to home. She sat me down at the dinner table and showed me a bundle I'd ne'er seen before. She pulled away layers of waterproofed leather, then an old striped *arisaid*, and lastly a covering of dyed plaid.

'The bundle was just three small items, which she picked up, held to her heart, forehead, and lips, and then dropped into cotton pouches pulled together and knotted with twine.'

Rosalie showed them the brass key before slotting it into the lock and turning. It clicked and a tiny latch opened.

'She also gave me the ebony box to serve as a decoy if I was caught. The pouched items she hid under the folds of my skirt. I was to cover myself with my winter arisaid, belted and buckled, and from that she hung a leather purse. Another decoy.'

Rosalie lifted the lid of the trunk to show a tightly bound bundle of cloth and leather. 'Take the bundle please, Ana, and put it on the bed beside you.'

Anastasia reached in carefully. The bundle was old, the fabric moth-eaten in patches and torn. The leather straps that secured it were cracked and fragile.

'You may not breathe a word of what I'm about to tell and show you. John or Drew may know, but only if necessary and only the bare minimum. Some secrets must be kept between mother and daughter.'

Flora shifted position, doubt and discomfort plain on her face.

'Flora, you have been as a mother to me since we left Skye. I would be honoured if you stayed, but understand if you feel you can't.'

'You honour me in return, dear Rosalie, and your mam as well. I'll stay if only to offer support where I may.'

The bundle trembled in Anastasia's hands. 'What is it?' she whispered.

'As I said, my mam was as cunning as they came. The bundle is another deception. Its contents are important, precious even, but they have no power. Keep them safe if you can, but if they must be given up, do so.'

The trunk was lined with crumbling fabric and trimmed in faded ribbon. Rosalie pulled at a piece of ribbon at the bottom and the whole base lifted to reveal a hidden compartment. Empty. Rosalie wasn't concerned. Cunning ran in her family. The compartment was studded with fixtures that held the lining in place. She slipped her fingernail under one of these, clicked it upward, and a side compartment was revealed. Inside was a leather-bound book.

'Was that your mam's?' Florentine took the trunk from her mother's lap as the book was lifted clear, and put it on the floor at their feet.

There were no embellishments on the leather, no embossed pattern. It was plain to the extreme and stiff with age and disuse. Rosalie brought the book to her heart, her forehead, and her lips.

'Not quite,' she answered at last. 'The book is mine. I wrote every single spell and story Mam told me down on its pages. There was little enough to do on my long journey.'

She opened the book. The writing was spidery, words badly spelled, ink blotches marked the pages. Each spell was accompanied by diagrams, squiggles, and strange markings.

'The spelling is awry and my hand hardly neat and steady while the ship rocked, but it's readable. I was going to copy it all out again once my penmanship improved, but I never seemed to find the time.'

The pages stopped turning on an image of a wild woman atop a castle stronghold, clothes ravaged by wind, legs bare. In her clasped hands a spear. Rosalie caught her breath. She'd forgotten about these drawings. Images from her dreams plagued her as she lay in her cramped bunk praying for calm seas and a gentle breeze to ease the dreadful seasickness she'd suffered once the emigrant ship had left the safety of Falmouth Harbour and encroached upon the dominion of the ocean.

Another page, warped from damp, showed yet another woman

by a grave, patchwork quilt around her shoulders, one hand on a strangely carved gravestone.

'This one I recognise,' she said. 'It's the grave of our ancestor at Kilmarie, near Dun Ringall. The very one that has now been robbed and desecrated by Mairi's murderer.'

She passed the book to Florentine. 'You and Anastasia will need to memorise every single word and drawing in this book.'

Florentine took it with two hands and held it firmly. 'We will mother. And we won't say a word.'

Rosalie met her daughter's wide eyes with a serene calmness. 'The contents can be shared with those you trust as you see fit or as needed must. But only with family. What I'm about to show you is just for us and, when the time comes, for your daughters.' She stood then and turned to face them, hands on her belt unbuckling the small clasp and loosening the heavy woollen material that kept her warm on the coldest of days. She let the outer skirt she wore drop. Underneath was her flannel skirt held at her waist with a cotton sash. The layer of flannel was dropped as well. The girls blushed as their mother stripped.

'Mother, what are you doing?' Florentine gripped the book. Anastasia hugged the bundle to her chest.

Rosalie placed her fingers at the edge of the cotton yoke and pulled free a small pouch. She repeated her action at the back and then lay the pouches on the bed. Her skin shivered with the chilly air in the room and she started redressing.

Florentine and Anastasia looked first at each other, then their mother, hurriedly pulling on her layers.

'There's a third,' Rosalie told them. 'But you're not ready for that one quite yet.'

'I shudder to think where you have it hidden, Mother,' Anastasia said. 'Your concealment of these two items was inspired. Who would think to look among your sanitary towels?'

Rosalie finished buttoning her clothes. 'Not on my person, you can be sure.' She stepped to her desk and pushed up the roll door.

'Bring those pouches and the book over here. We have magic to learn.'

Flora left the room, pulling the door closed behind her.

~

'Magic is not all fire, potions, and words.' Rosalie gathered her daughters in closer. 'Unbutton your cuffs. Remove your shoes and stockings.' She waited. Shoes were laid aside, stockings draped over the top. 'Now, unbutton your shirts and place your hand here.' Rosalie put her hand over her heart.

Florentine and Anastasia did the same, hands pale and trembling.

'We work within the space of our heartbeats. Close your eyes and count under your breath. Listen to your heart.' Rosalie watched as each woman relaxed into their task. She moved behind them. 'Feel the rhythm, the timing. Notice how your breath slows.' She touched their shoulders so they knew where she was. 'Concentrate on your breath and your heart.' Rosalie let down first Florentine's hair, then Anastasia's. 'Let go of restraints.'

'Open your eyes.' Rosalie returned to her spot and took the girls' hands.

'The real power comes from within. It is shaped by our intent. For good or ill, there can only be truth with magic. If our intent is tainted then our magic will become corrupted and unreliable. Corrupted magic causes chaos, and Chaos is the bane of the spirits. We are all part of a grand plan being woven by the Creator. Chaos is like a faulty thread, a stitch out of place causing a wrinkle or buckle in the finished fabric.'

Florentine and Anastasia stared dark-eyed at their mother. Anastasia trembled with cold. Florentine's hands were tight fists by her side.

'Feel the floor beneath your feet. Curl your toes into it. Connection with the land is important. Later we'll go out to the garden, but for now feel the wood and imagine the many times we've walked across this room. Our stories are wrapped up in the skin of our home. It protects us, keeps us warm and dry. It gives us a place to live and play and sleep.'

Rosalie let her mind drift. Memories of each of her children sleeping in the cradle James had made for them, beside the bed so she had only to reach out and rock when they wakened. The times James had lifted them from their cosy blankets and returned to bed so all three could nuzzle in close. Older children wandering in for morning cuddles.

'Our magic draws strength from home and family. Even if we find ourselves adrift, we will always have each other in our hearts and minds. Now, hold hands.'

Rosalie arranged their hands so that their palms were together, fingertips touching the inner wrists, left hand on top. 'You also need to listen to each other's heartbeat. Feel it with your fingers. You may not feel it straight away. It comes with practice.'

'Your heartbeat is strong, Florentine. I feel it already,' Anastasia whispered. 'Do you feel mine?'

Florentine frowned with concentration. 'Almost.' Her fingers searched Anastasia's slender wrist. 'Yes, there it is.'

Rosalie retrieved the pouches that had been hidden in her undergarments and emptied them into her hand. Each contained an engraved disc; one of amber and the other a pale silver metal. She held her hand out flat so the engravings could be clearly seen.

'These sigils are each part of a whole; a lock that draws and holds great power. These are the relics that I, and now you, guard.'

'What do the symbols mean?' Florentine asked.

Rosalie caressed the amber disc, her face softening. 'Sigil magic is complex, steeped with the intention of the originator. I asked my mother the same question. We do not know the exact meaning. We're not meant to. A sigil is created and then given to the spirits. They remember meaning. We let it go.'

'That's vague. If we don't know what it means, how do we know if we're doing right or wrong?'

Anastasia answered for Rosalie. 'Our intention is what matters. We are guarding these relics, not using them.'

'In your heart, Florentine, do you feel that anything we have ever done has been to the detriment of others? Have we tried to exert power over anyone? Have we attempted to stamp our will upon another?'

'No.'

'And we never will. Our intent is pure, so to speak.' Rosalie slipped the amber disc between their hands so that it lay on Anastasia's left palm. 'We may not know the meaning behind the symbol, but we have shared memories that come down to us from our grandmothers. With this relic, we remember to welcome travellers to our hearth, for though they may be strangers to us, they also may be the Creator in earthly form. She who wanders forest paths, climbs mountains, and hopefully for us, swims the Great Seas. My mother told me that this piece of amber unlocks the door to the underworld. With it, we can commune with the spirits of our ancestors. Yet, other travellers can also use this door, so we must be vigilant in who we welcome.'

The amber disc had warmed with the heat of Rosalie's hand; burnished with age, the silver disc remained cold. Rosalie held her hand flat, a faint vibration tickled her palm.

'This relic is something else entirely. It unlocks the mysteries of Scaithaich, a mighty warrior and our ancestor.' She slipped this disc into Florentine's left hand.

Florentine flinched.

'Feel your sister's heartbeat. Listen to your own and concentrate on your breath. Absorb what you are feeling. You have nothing to fear here today.' Rosalie placed her hands over Florentine's shoulders. 'That's it. Relax.'

'We take what the Creator gives us
To grow family and tend hearth
To feed and heal
To share and welcome
We respect the lives that have gone before

And those yet to come.
Our magic is the thread that weaves through the spaces
And joins us together.
Our magic is the breath in the void
The beat in our hearts
The pulse of our life-blood
And the truth of our intent.'

Rosalie circled her daughters, keeping one hand on them and the other on her heart. When she came to the end, she stopped.

'I cannot see into the future. For now, we must expand our knowledge so that we can face what comes. You are not alone. We are united and must stay so. Trust yourselves and each other. Therein lies our strength.'

The silver disc grew hot and heavy. Only her mother's steady voice kept Florentine from flinging it away from her. She listened to the soft singsong cadence of the words, felt Anastasia's pulse strengthen, focused on her heartbeat and breath, and the heat became comforting. It spread from her palm to her wrist, along her arm and throughout her body. The cold floor could have been wood or stone or a green field. Walls and furnishings wavered on the edge of her vision, hazy and translucent. Anastasia's face took on a luminous sheen, pearl-like. Her winter-grey eyes deepened to pools of crystal blue. Behind her, great trees danced in the wind. A eucalypt and an elm grew from seedlings and entwined until they were one behemoth casting shade over the land and blossoms into the air. Rosalie's voice echoed across the skies, others chimed in—so many that Florentine could feel the vibration of every syllable on her skin. She caught her breath on a sob and emotion suffused every particle of her being.

Rivers of feeling surged through her. Kinship over long ages. Soul-joining happiness at new beginnings. Grief of parting. Unconditional trust and belief. All tied to the land, the sea, forest, and mountains; the deep Earth and the fathomless Sky. The bright Sun. The silver Moon.

Florentine awoke knowing this day was her first. Now was she truly born. She rocked on her heels. Anastasia's hands were her anchor, gripping tight. Florentine glimpsed wonder in her sister's face and tightened her own grip in a silent promise. She would never let go.

CHAPTER 8

hin trails of scented smoke curled upward from a
pyramid of wood chips and blackening herbs coated with
tears of resinous myrrh. The brass bowl that contained the offering
was unadorned and glowed with heat and flickerings of flame.
Beside the bowl was another, smaller container overflowing with
damp moss-lined mud. Yet another remained empty. Each bowl was
as plain as the others.

The table the threesome of plain brass bowls sat on was covered
with a deep red satin cloth that reached to the floor where it
bundled like pools of red water on the carpet. With curtains drawn,
the only light in the room came from wall sconces where white
candles dripped wax and an ornate candelabra sitting on the
dresser.

'You may begin.'

Algernon and Clement were dressed in long black cloaks, two
monks about to commit sacrilege, if monks anywhere dressed as
richly as these two or performed dark rites in luxurious surrounds
in the middle of an antipodean night.

Clement leant over the table. The glow of uneven moving light
reflected from the surface of the silver dagger in his hand. Father

and son had performed this ritual several times and Clement knew what to do. The soft litany that his father spoke was relaxing, the performance comforting; one of the few times that the two men worked together.

With left hand over the mud and moss-filled bowl, Clement pierced the centre of his palm with the tip of the blade. Blood welled but did not drip. Clement laid his hand over the bowl and pressed his tingling palm into the cool moss.

Disgust and loathing swirled in Clement's stomach. Desolation threatened as nausea boiled and kicked its way upward. Breath came hard as his chest tightened and his throat burned. Thoughts of bad wine and tainted food slid across his consciousness, though he had consumed only morsels of dry bread and sips of tepid water since the evening before.

His father insisted upon fasting before each ritual performance. A glance and Clement could see that old man looked as grey and haggard as he felt. Good. Adverse physical affects were to be expected, a natural outcome indicating, in an altogether unpleasant way, that Algernon Benedict's magic was working.

Feeling as ill as he did would mean that whatever the purpose of tonight's ceremony, it must be more powerful than the usual attempts at scrying. Clement listened to the ragged liturgy tumbling from his father's mouth and repeated over and over. Most of the words were foreign to him, yet a few were familiar and some were names.

MacKinnon came up often, though spoken with a strange accent, more guttural than his father's usually plummy English ways. Not Scots or Irish either. Perhaps a melding of all three.

His hand throbbed. The moss scratched his skin, bit into it like fire ants. Algernon grabbed it before Clement could pull away and a thin thread of fear started to unfurl. The blade in his father's hand reflected a red and orange glow tinged with muddy grey and putrid green. Algernon slashed the blade across Clement's palm, forming two intersecting lines with the welling puncture wound at its centre. A short cut ran between thumb and little finger, and a longer slash from his middle finger to the heel of his palm, stopping at the edge of the hard muscle.

Clement tried to curse through lips that wouldn't part. He tried to pull his hand away, but his father's strength was unbreakable. What the hell was going on? The multi-hued glow of the blade seemed to explode in flames that licked the hooded men with the hot stink of the grave. Clement weakened. His hand was hot with pain. Blood flowed freely, filling the cup of his hand and over-flowing between his fingers to pool in the empty brass bowl below.

A line of pain circled his wrist, ran up his arm, and stabbed at the tender flesh of his inner elbow. The nausea cramped, an iron band around his stomach, a stake impaling his groin. He doubled-over, knees trembling, vision dimming.

Words reverberated around the shadowy room; commanding, rough, angry. Clement's throat seared. His arm was aflame. Tongues of light spasmed upward, outward from the guttering candles. White light flashed once, twice, and starred across his foggy percep-tions. He fell into a kaleidoscope of sight and sound that he could not understand or protect himself from, an abyss so deep and yawing beneath him that he felt nothing for a time but ice-cold wind whipping through him. Enthralled at the freedom the fall aroused, he nevertheless felt terror that he would fall forever, lost to the world and his own body.

Chimes tinkled in a curling melody, the most beautiful music he'd ever heard. Tears welled within him; if he had eyes he would cry, if he had a mouth he would shout for joy and love. If he had hands and feet he would clap and stamp and dance.

He had nothing. Flesh had fallen away as if he'd disrobed. Tendons and muscle discarded like his trousers at the end of the day, bone and limbs shaken off like a pair of old shoes. The chimes faded. The stars dimmed. He floated in a formless void with only distant thunder, that same rough voice spewing words too fast for him to understand.

Without eyes, he saw forward and back, upward and down. Massive circular shapes loomed over him, joining together to form a cavernous vortex. A figure descended. Shadows and shapes, hard lines and speckled clouds littered his periphery vision, the ghost of a room. Below him, sinewy ribbons of something old and venerable glided, reaching up to entangle and trap him in an ethereal web.

'Focus.'

He grasped at the word, a lifeline to a time gone by when he had a body and thoughts that were his own. It came again, an order for him to follow when all else was impossible.

Before him, the void solidified into a hewn rock face. The figure in the vortex was clear, engorged eyes flecked with crystalline stars of granite, a tongue protruding from lips drawn back into a screaming stricture, swollen fingers held open grotesquely carved female thighs with an opening through which he could see the swirling vortex.

'Reach in.'

Pain returned, as did the heavy sensations of being enclosed by a physical form. His fingers, stained black, flexed and his arm, tattooed with rivulets of blood, straightened as he reached toward the vulgar carving. His hand slipped into the opening and the stone enclosed his fingers and wrist. Sharp stabbing sensations started at his fingertips, shredding his skin, slicing through to the bone. He screamed and tried to free himself. The stone held him firm. Panic gripped, and his heart crashed inside his chest, splintering his ribs like matchsticks. The thunder-voice returned, summoning some-thing he didn't understand, and the stone released him. He pulled himself free only to see that his hand was gone. White bones stripped of flesh extruded from the end of his arm. Tattered skin hung loosely where his wrist should have been.

He screamed again, just once, and everything went black.

Blessedly, black.

CHAPTER 9

Florentine sat in the family sitting room, diligently copying her mother's old journal to a new book. Her mother's handwriting across the page was like a spider's crawl after it first waded in ink. She copied what she could in neat cursive and wished she had at least some of the drawing talent as the rest of her family. The sketches would have to remain uncopied for now and given to Anastasia's care.

She hunched low over the book of faded pages, a nagging ache above her eyes indicating that perhaps it was time to shift her attention elsewhere for a while. One line illegible.

'Perhaps more light?' Florentine took the book to the window and held it up to the sunlight. As she did, she noticed something about the accompanying sketch that hadn't been apparent earlier. The figure held a bowl and was dipping the pointed end of an oversized white quill into it. The sketch below had the same woman waving the quill in the air. A black substance sprinkled from the point, grey shapes appearing out of each droplet. Florentine lowered the book and the shapes vanished. As she lifted the book to the sunlight, they reappeared and shifted across the page to mingle with Rosalie's badly formed letters.

Florentine sucked in a quick breath and blinked several times as the shapes rose from the page and wove a tight pattern, mimicking letters and symbols as it exuded into the air, melting and reforming its way around the sitting room. She turned as she followed its passage, glancing to the journal as she realised that what she'd thought was poor penmanship was a mix of symbols and words she could not decipher. They appeared old to her now, as if she could see their great age sink into the rough paper, older than the woman who had scribed them.

Strange words, in a whisper just beyond her hearing, opened a door in her mind, and she could see what the markings meant. The strange inky mist withdrew, stuttering with decrepitude as it returned to its home, to its rightful time. Rosalie's rushed writing of some thirty years ago shone now as if newly written. Florentine's pen dipped and swirled and marked and danced across the pages of her own journal.

Whispering words sang in a croaking voice as a scene appeared before Florentine; a much younger version of her mother, huddled in the corner of a tight room, writing and sketching as the room rocked. Sea brine wafted across her senses as the floor beneath her tilted as if straddling waves. A rush of nausea filled her. The vision faded and was replaced with a crowded wharf full of nervous people, her mother again, and Aunt Flora. The man beside the ghostly women, solicitous of their wellbeing in the waiting throng, Flora's first husband. Water slapped at the wharf and Florentine shivered with cold. And then found herself standing, though she had not moved from her desk, by the shore of a large body of water that rose and fell as if breathing beneath a warm blue sky.

Pressure on her arm turned her away from the water to a crumbling ruin and a giant tree. Beneath the tree's weighty branches, a ravaged empty grave. An old woman stood waiting for Florentine to notice her, beckoning her closer when she did. The crone's red-lipped smile filled the young woman with warmth and peace. In the sultry air between them, inky symbols appeared. Florentine recognised some from her mother's journal. Others were a mystery. A plume of cold spilled from Florentine's mouth as the temperature dropped. The woman's face had become blue stone, her expression craggy and forbidding. Words speared into Florentine, embedded into every fibre of mind and body. She couldn't move to protect herself, could not forestall the woman's flinty commands.

'Bring it to me.'

The vision vanished in an instant, leaving Florentine exhausted and shaking in her chair, fingers gripping the pen, white-knuckled and stiff. On the page before her, with precise detail, a drawing of a ferocious warrior gripping a sword mid-swing as she fought off demons, a broken spear at her feet dripping with blood and gore. The rock on which she fought her last stand was engraved with a serpentine symbol that wound its way around a simple shallow cup. Florentine dropped the pen with a yelp and stood so quickly the chair fell and the desk rocked. The inkwell tipped, but did not spill. The book jostled and the pages fluttered, each filled with the likeness of the warrior and symbols that spilled over and around her, and then at the end of the book, a detail of her weapons that was steely in its clarity; the spear, a dagger, lastly, a graven cup. On the final page, listed in the strange unfamiliar handwriting from Rosalie's journal:

Spear of Scathaich
Lord of the Wildwood
Keeper of the Way
Traveller of Worlds

A shadow passed over the sun outside, a quickening of light in the room, and for a sliver of time, Florentine saw a pale scared face with silvery eyes, as astounded as she felt, and just as shocked.

The woman's scratchy voice sounded and Florentine could see that the mysterious vision before her could also hear the mysterious words:

Summon those that came before and after.

The voice faded like a bell-tone in her ears. The normal passage of time and light returned, and Florentine was standing, alone, in the sitting room on the third floor of the Garden Arms Hotel. Outside, a dry wind swept through the treetops of the Botanical Gardens, carrying with it an acrid trace of smoke.

Music jangled and beat through the grand hall. Swathes of colour sashayed around the room, feathers dipped and bobbed. Having paid the guinea tickets, despite the personal invitation from Mayor Harris, Lord Benedict and his son waited in the receiving line to the annual St Vincent Hospital Ball.

With dress code of either plain or fancy dress, father and son had opted for formal attire. Clement had considered arriving dressed as the devil, but Lord Benedict had quashed that idea. They were too close to the bone to risk either discovery or temptation of the spirits for a mere whim. Clement had acquiesced without argument, which made his father nearly as nervous as the ridiculous costume suggestion.

Lord Benedict would have preferred to slip into the ball unnoticed, but the Mayor and Lady Mayoress stood at the pinnacle of a welcoming line of regimented stature. Clement chatted to a young couple ahead of them. He looked quite dashing in his black suit and cream satin vest. His son must have been to a tailor. His jacket tails were crisply pleated and his pants striped down the outside in black satin. The jacket lapels were trimmed to match and contrasted sharply with the pristine white shirt. Algernon felt old and drab in the same suit he'd worn several times in London. He harrumphed as if in answer to something Clement said and was met with a glance and lift of eyebrows from his son, who stepped to one side to let his father into the conversation.

The three were involved in vacuous chitchat and Algernon nodded, smiled and frowned at what seemed the most appropriate places. He really couldn't understand the need for women to smother themselves in colourful fabric, face make-up, and scent. The woman he was conversing with was dressed in lurid purple velvet with a scandalous black lace décolletage. Her elaborate skirt was made in alternates of purple and black lace. Rather than be embarrassed by the display, her husband was complicit in a suit with matching purple and black lace vest. Algernon's face burned and he turned away. The woman behind him was dressed in a bright red jacket with oversized cuffs—he couldn't see her hands at all— and a rather plain black skirt. Ostentatious, but at least her breasts were in no way exposed. Further down the line were puffy sleeves in yellows and blues, flowers of all varieties, fans, parasols, masques, and more leather than usually appeared at a ball. He nodded and smiled at the woman in red, and was relieved when Clement nudged his elbow.

'Father. Mayor Harris and his beautiful wife.' Clement bowed to the host and hostess. 'We were delighted to receive your invitation, your Honour. Such a worthy cause.'

Lord Benedict matched his son's bow with a deeper version of his own, took the Lady Mayoress' gloved hand and brought it to his lips. 'An honour to meet you both.'

'How has your stay been thus far, Lord Benedict?' Elizabeth Harris asked. 'Enjoyable, I hope. We've certainly been having some pleasant weather.'

'Delightful!' Algernon replied. 'As warm as full summer at home.'

'Excellent to hear!' Mayor Harris enjoined. 'I've been hoping to meet with you, Lord Benedict. Of course, a ball is not the place for business. Perhaps we can organise something for later in the week?'

'Of course. I shall look forward to it.'

Algernon shook the Mayor's hand and was introduced to the next in line, the Governor of New South Wales, Lord Loftus. His Lordship didn't appear at all congenial. They exchanged banal pleasantries and compared voyages. Lady Loftus asked about his family, London society, and whether they might share acquaintances, but it was clear that Lord Loftus wanted to be elsewhere, and his wife wanted to dance. Algernon left them to their duties with a promise to join their party later, and entered the hall. Clement had already been swept into the throng of dancers, his dark head visible next to a white-blonde vision in aquamarine silk before vanishing in a graceful twirl.

A liveried waiter paused long enough for Algernon to take a glass of sherry, and before he could wince at the noise in the room, he was met by a florid-faced gentleman who seemed to know him and was introduced around to several more men of varying degrees of floridity, all holding never-empty glasses.

Mr Boseman approached the group and imposed himself into the conversation. Conversation flowed around the unseasonably warm spring and the effect of the dry winter on the coming summer. Drought was harsh in the colony and the bush would go up like a torch with the slightest spark. Heads shook as past seasons were remembered. Boseman took the opportunity to bow his head and request a private conversation with the Lord.

Across the room, arches showed the way to side rooms and porticos. They headed in that direction, pausing for a word or two with men and women along the way, dodging others, skirting dancers and entered an area designed for discussion. Chairs upholstered in deep blue velvet circled a collection of low tables where drinks and coffee were being served. The dark wood walls were unadorned except for triple brass sconces lining their length and the steady glow of light emitting from the etched glass shades.

Already guests more interested in talk than dance were filtering in and taking their positions. Voices buzzed around the room. Someone laughed, a high brittle sound incongruous with the low-key surroundings. Faces were a mixture of flushed and happy to fixed and business-like. Boseman ignored them all and made toward a door in the corner lit by a hanging ceiling light and leading to a private portico.

The portico was small yet deep-set. If they didn't lounge over or stand too close to the stone wall between them and the walking path beyond, they would not be seen or heard. The seating here was built into the stone walls, with cushions to soften the hard surfaces. Tall candelabras stood either side of the bench seat, sheltered by the corners of the portico and casting a soft radiance into the space.

A wrought-iron table held a crystal long-necked decanter and two whisky glasses. Boseman poured without asking and held one of the glasses out to Algernon.

'A fine drop this. Imported straight from Scotland. It's a blend, of course, but I find the taste appealing. Opens the mind to thoughts, clarifies questions waiting to be asked and answers waiting to be heard.' Boseman held his glass up to the candlelight so the pale gold of the liquid could be appreciated.

'What do you want, Mr Boseman, that couldn't be discussed at the club?' Algernon had already finished his whisky and reached for the decanter to refill his glass. He wouldn't normally drink a blend, but it sat well with the sherry he'd already consumed, and warmed him against the night.

'The Garden Arms Hotel, your Lordship. Your son is interested in the proprietor. I'm interested in the licence.'

'The hotel is of no concern to me, sir. Get to the point.'

Boseman sidled closer and lowered his voice so that even in the quietness of the portico, Algernon had to strain to hear.

'The Garden Arms enjoys both a prominent location, physically and by reputation. I have plans to take it over, but I need the reputation of the current proprietor to falter so that when I do take over I am not seen as an interloper. Sydney barhops can be loyal and quite physical about that loyalty.'

'You are uncertain then of pitting your reputation against Mrs Ponsonby's? I am not sure how I can be of assistance in the matter. Perhaps you should be speaking to my son.'

'You will no doubt meet with the mayor and his cohorts over the coming days and would likely find yourself in the situation where you could drop a word or two in my favour. And perhaps, if you could enlighten me further on your business with Mrs Ponsonby, I might then be in the position to take advantage of any opportunities that arise.' Boseman put his hand up to forestall an interruption. Algernon's hand tightened around the glass.

'For us both, of course. I can muddy waters for you just as you could for me. You work on the surface and I will dive a little deeper, if you catch my meaning.'

Algernon's chest tightened, anger tinged with uneasiness pulled tight on his ribs. He did not fear muddy waters, but the ugliness they could throw up was another matter. And he did not trust anyone with his secrets. He wondered briefly what Clement might have said. Nothing, he was sure. Clement was as secretive and distrustful as himself. The man was fishing. Information equalled power.

'My business with Mrs Ponsonby is personal and historical. I've not met the woman nor had any dealings with her.' Algernon considered how much line to give. 'I met her mother once. Many years ago, or nearly did. The local healer in the backward isles of Scotland. The whole village stank of fish and sheep and whatever that woman was concocting in her kitchen.' He could see the women backlit in the door of their stone house, his groomsman dead at his feet, as clear as if it was yesterday. 'But whether Mrs Ponsonby dabbles in that sordid business, I wouldn't know. She would only have been a child then and was reportedly in Port Jackson not long after.'

Boseman clapped Lord Benedict on the shoulder and whisky sloshed from his glass to his fingers.

'I'm prepared to support you should any question of your good character come up, Boseman. To a point. I'll not have my reputation tarnished or my private affairs hindered in any way.'

'I'm the sole of discretion, your Lordship. Let's have another nip of whisky to consolidate our understanding.' Boseman poured two nips for each and clinked glasses with a self-satisfied smirk. Algernon had seen the same expression on the face of a stuffed shark once, grey skin deceptively tough, black button eyes glittering with menace, just the hint of pointed teeth in the tiniest of lift between lips. Beside the taxidermy specimen was a skeleton with massive jaw prised open in permanent threat. Even stripped bare, Boseman would give off the same foreboding as that shark. One to watch, but could he be controlled? Algernon suspected not. He would talk to Clement about him. Tonight.

CHAPTER 11

lorentine stood at the edge of the quay. Ships from all over the world filled the harbour almost to overflowing. So many people arriving. And so many leaving. The water heaved, throbbing with the constant swell coming in from the ocean. Even here in Sydney Cove, protected from the dangers of open water, ships creaked, rigging clanged against wooden masts, formless waves splashed against the sandstone wharf and receded upon themselves dragging sand, seaweed, fish, and rubbish along for the ride.

The previous summer, she and Drew often sat here, kicking the damp wooden beams with their heels, guessing at where ships were going, making up stories about the people on board. Drew wanted to join a scientific expedition in the wilds of India or Africa. Florentine yearned for the Alps in Switzerland or France. She wanted clean crisp air and quaint villages that smelled of pine woods and snow instead of disinfectant, horses, and dirt. She wanted to live in a cottage with a garden filled with flowers next door to another cottage and garden of flowers, next door to another—no tall buildings, no drunks, no wool and bond stores or warehouses.

Florentine was used to the smell of the water and wharves, and the noise of men loading and unloading cargo ships. Still the stench of packed wool waiting to be shifted was overpowering even this early in the morning. Her nostrils would be glad when the cargo wharves were replaced with passenger terminals and she could catch a ferry away from the cove to just about anywhere else in the harbour.

Florentine started walking toward Fort Macquarie. The sandstone block edifice stood on Bennelong Point, replacing, as had the wharves and warehouses, the campsites of a large family of Aborigines. A small family was living in the police boatshed. They seemed to be happy, though Florentine couldn't see how when all the land was once theirs and now they lived on the edges. Alice had told her that this was where she was from. Her family considered this their land no matter where they lived or what ugly building squatted on it. Florentine quite liked the concept. It was similar, in a way, to her mother's connection to her island home in Scotland. MacKinnons had been born, lived, loved, and died there for so long, her mother said, that the land and MacKinnon blood were one and the same. Florentine didn't feel it. She had no sense of being connected to a land she had never seen. She wasn't sure she felt connected to her place of birth either, which was only up the road a little from Alice's traditional home.

Florentine left behind the wharves and approached Fort Macquarie, stuck onto the headland below the Governor's House—a folly if there ever was one. Every few years, more cannons were added to justify the glitz and glamour of parade days and soothe worried citizens when wars thousands of miles and many oceans away headlined in the newspapers. She held her skirts a little higher in front to avoid tripping, slipping, or in any other way landing on her backside in the dirt. A few of the workers frowned as she passed, no doubt wondering what a young woman was doing wandering around the docks and fort. Most, though, had seen her walking this path often enough to leave her alone with her thoughts. A nod of acknowledgement here and there, and the occasional 'Mornin', Miss Ponsonby. How's your mam?' was the only intrusion into her morning walk. The Ponsonby family had owned the Garden Arms, just up the road a bit, for years and most people around this part of the city knew who she was.

Drew had once vowed that he would join the army so he could stand guard at Fort Macquarie and be the first to shoot at any invading forces. The likelihood of either occurring was low. Drew enjoyed outdoor pursuits, but was more interested in studying and drawing than attacking and killing. Florentine hurried past the fort, keeping to the cliff that formed a natural 'upstairs downstairs' barrier between the governor and his family, and the working people of the quay and fort.

No vessel was moored at the Man O'War Steps, which was lucky for the men sitting on its edges, legs swinging while they fished and chatted. And no sign of invading forces, if the row of boats tied to the sandstone walls of the fort was anything to go by. It wasn't that Florentine didn't believe Sydney could never be attacked; just that the battles were all on the other side of the world in Europe or Africa. Far too distant to cause her any concerns. Especially today, when she had escaped her mother and the growing demands at home.

Florentine's path eased as she reached the start of Farm Cove and the more natural tree-filled pastures that rolled down from Government House almost to the water's edge. She crossed the road ahead of a horse and carriage clip-clopping along the cobblestones and stayed close to the sea wall. She'd managed to avoid looking at the Garden Palace that overshadowed everything and now she kept it at her back, refusing to acknowledge its presence. They had yet to identify the exact source of her mother's ill-feeling and foreboding. Rosalie Ponsonby had been too long away from her mother's stories, but they all knew it lurked somewhere inside the Palace and its gardens.

Florentine searched for fish and shells in the water, and dragged her fingers along the sandstone wall. In her pocket, a sheaf of papers with her hastily scrawled notes waited for her attention. Over the past week, she and Anastasia had read until their eyes ached, copied out strange words, drawings, and practices on paper, and committed instructions for rituals that would see all of them landed in prison, or worse, if any but family were to read them. Rosalie had ordered everything be memorised and then burnt, but Florentine had happened on something too complex to be easily memorised. A concept she could barely get her head around to find the words to write, let alone share with her mother. She needed time to think.

For now, she was happy to keep her focus on the water and let her mind wander.

The old pasture became the Botanical Gardens from one tree to the next. Cows and sheep were rarely heard nowadays, but not too many years ago, Florentine knew this hill was once the main farm in the Port Jackson area. Settlers and immigrants had flocked to the colony and transformed most of the land into housing and streets, factories and warehouses. Except this portion, which, up until the day Aunty Flora, Anastasia, and John had arrived, had been a peaceful sanctuary amid the bustle of the metropolis. Now it was the epicentre of trouble brewing. Though it seemed that only the Ponsonbys, and possibly Alice's extended family, were aware of the situation.

Florentine strolled by the sandstone gatehouse. Mrs O'Connor, with an apron full of fresh eggs, waved as she exited her hen house. The hens chattered unseen behind her while puppies swarmed at her feet and 'Cheeky Bugger', their nanny goat, bawled waiting to be milked. The O'Connor yard nearly matched the governor's zoo on the hill for animals and noise. Florentine returned the wave, but didn't stop.

'Come visit me later, Florrie. I've some milk and butter for your mam.'

Florentine waved again and quickened her step, unwilling to be drawn any further into Mrs O'Connor's sphere of conversation, which tended to be the distance her loud voice could carry. She passed the First Fleet Steps and reached the end of Farm Cove, rounding the headland and climbing the staircase that led to Mrs Macquarie's Chair, a hand-hewn bench seat cut into massive sandstone boulders that acknowledged the former governor's wife.

Cold seeped through her skirt and underthings as soon as she sat down and as quickly as if she'd been naked on the stone. Dawn light softened the edges of the bay before her, gentling the swelling waters. It would not last. Already the sky was turning that pristine shade of blue that heralded a balmy day ahead. Too early in spring for the heavy heat of summer, but warm all the same and more noticeable as it rose from a chilly night.

Waves lapped the rocky shore below. An early pied-currawong croaked in the nearby trees, a young one calling for its mother. The croak was followed by an impatient caw as an adult currawong flapped its wings overhead and landed with a flourish beside its nest. The resulting conversation between parent and baby birds threatened to become raucous and then subdued to a satiated lowing as breakfast was consumed. Further along the road a kookaburra started up, stopped, started again as if unsure, and finally let out a long, loud laughing call. The sounds of the bush going about its daily routine, even here in the city, were a distraction for tense nerves.

Florentine relaxed into the bench seat and closed her eyes to listen to birds and ship bells, the soft grumble of men starting their day's work, leaves rustling, and fishermen chatting about weather and tides and whether the fish were on or off. Workmen's voices carried up from the wharves, a mix of languages, accents, curses, and slang. Florentine smiled to herself as an image of her mother's disapproving mien came to mind. So straight-laced! She didn't fool anyone. Well, not her nearest and dearest anyway, who had heard many an unladylike murmur in the back rooms of the family hotel. In the front rooms, a frown had more impact than a thousand curse words and the power to change conversations, quell arguments, and attempt sobriety. The frown was the forerunner to suggestions and recommendations that if not followed would promptly result in ejection from the premises.

Florentine wasn't allowed in the public bar area, but she and Drew, and Anastasia before she married, had often hidden in the nook their mother used to keep an eye on patrons.

A smile started in her toes and went all the way to the top of her head as she remembered tucking her five-year old self into a corner of the nook to listen to her father play the piano and sing, and the regulars chiming in on all the choruses with such gusto that the windows rattled in their frames and the glasses jiggled across the bar.

A shadow blocked the light and Florentine slit open her eyes to see her father standing before her, his suit neat though tieless and his head as hatless as always. Just the way she remembered him. The shadow moved. Not her father, of course—how could it be? A somewhat younger, straighter facsimile.

'Hello again!'

'Alexander Ridlay,' the silhouette continued. 'You tripped over my luggage last week.'

Mr Ridlay shifted from one foot to the other and turned enough for his face to be bathed in sunlight for a moment before facing her again in shadow. She remembered him now; the good-looking young Scot she met on her way to the meeting of the Women's Literature and Geographical Society. It seemed like much longer than a week since she had trotted off to the Misses Young's residence on Castlereagh Street, puffed up with her own importance. What an ignoramus she'd been. Time to make up for it and improve on what must have been a horrid first impression.

'Oh, yes, outside the New South Wales Royal Society. Have you enjoyed your first week in Sydney, Mr Ridlay?'

'I have, Miss Ponsonby, though I've been stuck indoors for a good deal of it.' He held up a wooden easel, battered and covered in smears of colour. 'I've managed to escape the scientists today for something more pleasurable.'

Florentine frowned. She didn't recall introductions a week ago.

'Do you mind if I share your view?' Mr Ridlay propped the easel against the sandstone boulder and eased a leather satchel from his shoulder. The easel slipped and Mr Ridlay dropped the satchel on the bench seat beside Florentine. A mahogany box, as battered as the easel, and a hardbound and rather tattered sketchbook fell out.

Florentine caught the book before it went any further and steadied the box. Mr Ridlay opened the easel so it stood, three-legged and self-supporting, and plopped himself beside his supplies.

'My apologies. Again. My property appears quite attracted to causing you mishap.' He returned the box to the satchel and held out his hand for the book.

'You have me at a disadvantage, Mr Ridlay.' Florentine opened the book and started turning the pages. Each was covered in water-colour renderings of the ocean, ship rigging, people, and sea birds.

'How is that?'

'I'm quite sure I haven't introduced myself to you prior to this morning and yet you know my name. How is that?' She arched her eyebrow and attempted a disapproving glare in his direction. She felt mirth rather than annoyance though, so she gave it up before she laughed at his guilty expression and returned her attention to his paintings. 'You, sir, are a very good artist. If this person was as sick as he looks in your painting then I would be worried at his ability to survive a sea journey at all.' The painted figure was crouched over several buckets with shirt and trousers unbuttoned, while a slip of a boy swabbed his sweat-damp brow and did his best to keep his distance. 'Please tell me the poor man survived …'

Mr Ridlay peered over Florentine's shoulder at the watercolour in question and laughed. 'That's Mr George Peat, a rather bombastic personality even when deathly ill. The poor boy is his son. Both survived. I believe Mr Peat is still recovering somewhere out west, as far away from the sea as he can get is my understanding.'

'I'm not sure who I feel sorrier for, Mr Peat or Mr Peat's son.' Florentine turned the page and held her breath at the image of a large sea-bird staring straight out of the page at her. 'Oh, my goodness! Your paintings are wonderful!'

'Thank you.

The next page showed a detailed diagram of plumage—*Albatross: wing span 11', feathers black and grey with some brown shading in parts*—and an examination of its beak—*upper mandible ends in a large hook*—labelled in clear cursive followed by a portrait of Mr Peat's son, *Geo Peat Jr*, staring out to sea, his head resting on his folded arm, the hint of a smile in the corner of his mouth.

'Mr Peat's son is a dreamer!'

Mr Ridlay reached across and closed the book in Florentine's lap.

'Are you a zoological artist or a portraitist, Mr Ridlay? You excel at both certainly.'

'Actually, I'm a botanical artist, but there's a dearth of plant life on a barque bobbing around in the middle of the ocean, so I had to extend my skills. My scientific labelling is somewhat lacking, but these are just for me so it hardly matters.'

Florentine allowed the book to be returned to the satchel and leant back against the engraved sandstone, waiting. Mr Ridlay tidied his belongings and settled beside her.

'I was at the museum yesterday with a colleague being bored to death by a retelling of his adventures in the Indies when you walked in. I heard the doorman greet you.' Mr Ridlay held his hands palm upward to indicate his innocence as it were. 'Unfortunately, my colleague wouldn't stop talking even when I walked away, and as he is also my superior at the Royal Society I wasn't able to make your acquaintance at the time.'

'How fortunate then that we happened to bump into each other this morning. Are you here for an expedition into the wilderness or an exhibition at the museum?' Florentine hoped for an exhibition. She found the young gentleman quite interesting and easy to talk to. His accent was only slightly Scottish so she guessed he must have travelled quite a bit or perhaps left Scotland as a youth, an adventurer as well as an artist.

'An expedition. The London Royal Society has commissioned a set of lithographs of the shore life of Sydney Harbour, Botany Bay, and several other ports and bays along the southern coastline of New South Wales. More sailing, but at least we'll be close to shore and putting in most days.'

'And where have you come from?' Florentine hid her dismay that her new acquaintance would be off travelling again very soon. Things could be worse. If they started in Sydney Harbour she could see more of him before they headed south. And by the sound of it they would be back in Sydney much sooner than if they were exploring the other side of the Great Dividing Range or worse, heading to Tasmania, even further away.

'The Orkney Isles originally. Then a town near Edinburgh and then London. And you?'

Florentine grimaced. 'Sydney born and bred. I've been no further south than Botany Bay and no further north than the other side of the Harbour. I did, however, once make the journey to Tambaroora, in the mountains, to visit my sister.'

'Yet you sound a little bit Scots ...'

'My mother is from Scotland and my father was from Cornwall so I probably sound a little bit like each—depending on my mood.'

Mr Ridlay laughed. 'My brogue broadens as my temper rises, so be warned. If I'm sounding as if I've just stepped out of Stromness then my mood is foul and I should be avoided at all costs.'

Florentine smiled. She liked the sound of that. Not his mood, but that he thought to warn her for the future.

A scrabble of children came down the stairs behind them, all giggles and teasing, and Florentine realised that the morning was getting away from her. She should probably leave Mr Ridlay to his painting and make her way home. She straightened and inched her way to the edge of the stone bench.

'It's getting late ...' she started to say.

'And the peace and quiet have fled,' Mr Ridlay finished. 'May I walk you home?'

'But your painting? I would hate to be the reason you didn't complete another wonderful watercolour in your book.'

'You are not the reason.' Mr Ridlay nudged his head toward the children. 'I wouldn't be able to concentrate with that lot playing games around my feet. I will come back in the evening and capture a sunset for you. And you can tell me again how wonderful I am.'

'I didn't say … I meant your watercolours …' Florentine wasn't used to flushing with embarrassment, but her skin heated just the same. She jumped up and had started to walk away when Mr Ridlay grasped her elbow and held her still.

'I'm just teasing you. Wait while I get my things and I'll promise to behave for the rest of the day.'

'I'm not sure I want your company anymore, Mr Ridlay.' Her embarrassment was already fading into excitement. She liked the young man, a lot, and having his company a little longer was exactly what she wanted. She waited; foot tapping, hands on hips, conscious that there was no need for him to know just how interested she was in his continued acquaintance.

The easel and satchel were collected before the invading family fully arrived and Mr Ridlay was by her side, a wide smile on his freckled face as he hooked one arm over the easel struts, the satchel strap over his head, and repositioned his hand on her elbow in an instant.

'My utmost apologies. Again. How can I make it up to you?'

The two turned their back on Mrs Macquarie's Chair and strolled along the path that led up to Mrs Macquarie's Road. They turned left at the junction and proceeded to take the long way home to the Garden Arms Hotel. Florentine extracted a promise that Mr Ridlay would take her brother, Drew, out for a day's drawing and painting, and Mr Ridlay extracted a promise that from now on Florentine would call him Alexander. She graciously agreed, and because the museum doorman had greeted her with her surname the day previously, informed Alexander that her first name was Florentine and that he could use it in private only.

~

Rosalie had slept light since the night she left her family and home behind in Kilmarie. With the returning threat, she had hardly slept a wink for the last two weeks.

Florentine left her room just before dawn, trying to avoid creaking floorboards and steps in her stockinged feet. No doubt with her shoes tucked under her arm. Rosalie had memorised the tread of each of her children and all the sounds of her home long ago. She knew who was sneaking in and out as soon as the bedroom door swung open and whispered its warning. Sleep clung to her and Rosalie drifted back to dreams of summer walks in the gardens with James until she heard her mother's voice: *This is no day to lay about. Get up!*

Wide awake after that and with not long to go until her usual rising time, Rosalie gave up on any more rest and sat up in bed. Her long hair was held back in a single thick braid that flopped over her heavy cotton nightdress like a rope. This early in the morning, barely light outside, there was a definite chill in the air. Her bed warmer was almost cold. She shivered as she pushed back the blankets and quilt, wished yet again for her husband's warm embrace, and placed her feet on the bedside rug.

The room was quite chilly, so she dragged the hand-stitched quilt to her and slipped it over her shoulders where it could keep her warm and surround her with the scent of her husband. She shuffled to her wash stand. A clean flannel with drops of lavender oil awaited her morning ablutions. For the tiniest of moments, Rosalie considered skipping her routine in order to stay warm, but the thought was gone as soon as it arrived. She could delay it though, and turned away from the stand to fetch her clean underwear, stockings, lilac embroidered shawl, and dark-grey dress. By the time her clothes were ready, she'd warmed enough to drop the quilt on the end of the bed, strip off her nightgown, and return to the scented flannel on the washstand. Scrubbing herself from head to toe, her skin soon tingled from the rough treatment and glowed pink with heat. All that was left was to dress as fast as she could and capture that added warmth in her undergarments.

Within moments her feet were trapped in boots and she was walking out the door, not quietly or sneakily as Florentine had done, but with the determined tread of one who thought it was time for everyone to be up and about their business.

As she made her way downstairs, her mother's voice ghosted in her hearing. *Keep your wits about you, love ...*

Rosalie's preferred fragrance of lavender mixed with the memory of her mother's deep spicy scent of bearberry, and by the time she reached the kitchen she could not get either the thought of her mother or her warnings out of her head.

The family were sitting down to breakfast when the focus of the warning became apparent. Loud thudding on the front door, Bridie's running steps through the corridor, and her flustered announcement as she reached the kitchen made everything clear.

'Mrs P! It's Mr Boseman and a couple of his lads to see you.'

'Well, Mrs Ponsonby, the Garden Arms appears to be doing well under your sole proprietorship.' George Boseman sipped at the breakfast tea Rosalie had poured for him. She held her teacup before her and waited for him to get to the point of his visit.

'Though I've heard you have no paying guests now and have been sending visitors elsewhere ... Not in a bother, are you? It's quite a task, I'm sure, to run a hotel, guesthouse, tearoom, and a family, I'm sure. I do believe my lad, Harry here, saw your Andrew at the billiards room several times last week. Not running a little wild now he's fatherless, I hope ... Lads that age need a firm hand.'

Boseman made a gesture toward the erstwhile Harry.

'Thank you for your concern, Mr Boseman. More tea? No? I have family visiting from the country and our rooms are taken up with them at the moment. Are you sure your lads wouldn't like some tea? Please do take one of the little cakes. Boys, come help yourself to some cake ...' Rosalie waved Harry and the second lad over, and held up the plate of sweet treats Bridie had served with the tea. 'I'm sorry I didn't catch your name,' she said to lad number two—a surly creature, but no doubt hungry.

'Will,' the second lad mumbled, helping himself to two cakes and steadfastly ignoring Mr Boseman's irritated expression.

'Yes, yes,' Boseman scowled. 'There have been other rumours as well. I only bring the subject up as a favour to you, Mrs Ponsonby, as I know they can't possibly be true. Witchcraft to be frank, secret meetings, spell casting and odd lights at odd times.'

Rosalie refilled the teacups, passed one each to Harry and Will, and waited for Boseman to continue. Rumours of witchcraft had to be unfounded. They'd performed no ceremonies or castings since the night they'd formed a circle to identify the source of the brewing trouble. No, Boseman had to be fishing, but to what end Rosalie couldn't discern.

'Gossip and rumours make very unreliable news, Mr Boseman. I assure you that someone is up to no good telling such tales.'

'Well, perhaps it's one of your guests or your servants. You still have that native Aboriginal girl, I presume. All sorts of sorcery is practised in their camps.'

'Mr Boseman, please stop wasting my time with gossip and get to the point. I have business to attend to, as you well know.'

The straight-backed chairs that populated the Garden Arms tearoom were provided for equally straight-backed ladies who did not lounge or slouch or sip tea in any appearance of relaxation. Mr Boseman was better suited to leather wingbacks and club lounges. Rosalie had no desire to make him comfortable.

'Of course. Important business too, no doubt. However, rumours are nothing to be sneezed at in a city like Sydney. We may harbour desires to be cosmopolitan, but at heart we're a country town where everybody knows everybody else's business. For good or bad. Myself and certain friends are quite concerned that our modern reputation may be tainted by old wives' tales and spell-mongering. We're determined to stamp out any such happenings and I'm here to both warn and advise you, Mrs Ponsonby, that we have our eyes and ears on your family, and untoward occurrences on your property.'

Rosalie's fingers clenched in her lap and her lips thinned to a dangerous line.

'For good or bad, Mrs Ponsonby. Rumour or truth. Either can be turned to your advantage or disadvantage with a single word.'

Rosalie stood, fuming. 'Your threats are not appreciated, Mr Boseman. If there's any mongering going on in this city, sir, it is from you and your cronies, stirring up trouble for honest people. Your slithering way of conducting business has been duly noticed by more than just myself, and I do not hesitate to advise that you also are under the glass.'

She pulled her skirts away from the laden table and walked to the door. 'You are not welcome in the Garden Arms and I demand you leave these premises and do not haunt our doors again.'

Mr Boseman pushed back his chair to stand, dropped his napkin beside his teacup, and waited for Harry to step forward with his hat and gloves. Harry, face studiously blank, performed his required duty and puffed out his chest in an added show of threat. Will, blushing, placed his cup and saucer on the table before pulling the chair back for his master. He avoided Rosalie's gaze throughout.

Rosalie frowned at Boseman's insolence and then frowned deeper as she heard Florentine's voice come through from the back rooms.

Where's Mother? With whom? Of all the nerve!

Booted steps followed. The staff entrance door swung open and Florentine was in the room, with John Bray glowering behind her. Boseman glanced in their direction.

'Mr Boseman, if you please. I don't have all day.'

'I'd heard your daughters were as wild as your son, and one married a Dubliner. If I'm any judge, you're in danger of falling hard and fast from the perch.'

'You're not a judge, Mr Boseman. Please leave. Now.'

Boseman walked to the door and out onto the street, placing his hat on his head as he moved. Harry and Will followed closed behind, Harry still attempting his threatening stance and Will blushing. He nodded to Rosalie as he walked by.

'Thanks for the tea and cake, Mrs P.'

Rosalie closed the door on the men and breathed deeply a moment to gather her thoughts. She met Florentine, John, and a young man she'd never seen before halfway across the room. They all spoke at once and Rosalie had to hold her hands up to stop their rush of words.

'Please. Let me think a moment. Mr Boseman was here looking for trouble. We'll use that to our advantage.' She folded her arms across her chest in her usual 'I'm thinking' stance, and then caught the eye of the young man who seemed as offended and vociferous as her daughter and son-in-law. 'Let's start with you. Might I enquire who you are?'

Florentine blushed and took the young man's arm. 'Mam, this is Mr Alexander Ridlay. Mr Ridlay, this is my mother, Mrs Rosalie Ponsonby.'

Mr Ridlay stepped closer and held his hand out to Rosalie. 'Ma'am, forgive my intrusion. I had only intended to walk Miss Ponsonby home, yet we heard a commotion and I thought it wise to accompany her inside in case assistance was needed.'

Rosalie shook his hand and nodded before turning to Florentine. 'You go for a walk to Semi-Circular Quay and bring home a young gentleman?'

'Yes, Mam,' Florentine answered. 'We have met before, though briefly. Mr Ridlay is an artist. We've been chatting about sketching Australian wildlife and scenery.'

More scuffling and voices from the back rooms, and Rosalie peered around her son-in-law to see Alice whispering fiercely into Drew's ear and holding him back with a hand on his shoulder. In the kitchen beyond, Anastasia and Honora were bustling around the breakfast table and seeing to the children. She returned her attention to Florentine's young gentleman.

'Lovely to meet you, Mr Ridlay. Florentine's sister and brother are both artists as well. I'm sure you'll be welcome at the Garden Arms for conversation on the subject in the future. As you are sure to understand, however, we have some urgent family business to attend to.'

'Perfectly understood, Mrs Ponsonby. If there is nothing I may be of assistance with I will take my leave. I'll just collect my things from the courtyard and be on my way.' Mr Ridlay was almost at the kitchen door when a smash of glass was heard, followed by children wailing, astonished screams, and a dog howling.

Rosalie pushed her way past the milling crowd in the doorway to see Anastasia nursing her shoulder, her shirtsleeve stained with reddish mud, and the window in the back door broken, jagged glass poking precariously from the frame and pieces scattered from the doorway to the table. On the floor was a soaking, smelly, cloth-bound lump.

John Bray went straight to his wife. 'Ana, you're hurt! I'll skin the hide off whoever did this.'

Drew was out the door and tearing through the garden to the lane beyond, and with Anastasia's assurance that she would be okay, John followed.

'Honora, take the bairns upstairs. Bridie and Alice, help her. Mr Ridlay, you're still here, good. Please help Florentine check the rest of the doors and windows, make sure the doors to the street are locked. Anastasia, sit! Let me see that arm.' Rosalie's brusque orders were followed without questions and within minutes the kitchen was quiet.

'Who would do such a thing, Mam? The bairns were just about to head outside to play. What if one of them was hurt?'

'Hush, Ana. What-ifs are useless. It's you who's hurt and you who needs attention.' Rosalie pulled away the torn shirt sleeve to reveal the same discolouration on her daughter's skin as the shirt. It smelled of mud and worse. She wrinkled her nose and moved to the sink to collect a bowl of water and some clean clothes. 'There doesn't appear to be any broken skin, which is good. How does it feel?'

'Like I caught a rock in the arm.' Anastasia poked the tender area and grimaced. 'Do you suppose it'd be broken?'

'I hope not.' Rosalie squeezed water from the cloth and gently wiped the muddy mark away. 'We'll bandage it and make you a sling just in case. I'll fetch some herbs in a moment that will help with bruising, and we'll see.'

'I saw who did it, Mam: a lad a year or two older than Drew, cap pulled low over his face. He looked right into my face when he threw the rock, Mam, right into my eyes and smiled.' Anastasia shuddered.

Florentine and Mr Ridlay returned. 'All secure, ma'am. Shall I see to the whereabouts of Mr Bray and young Drew?'

'Thank you. I have no wish to involve you any further in family business, Mr Ridlay. I certainly would not want to make trouble for you seeing how you're still new to the city.'

'And, of course, you don't know if you can trust me. Trust must be earned, Mrs Ponsonby, and I hope that I'll have an opportunity to do just that in the very near future.' Mr Ridlay turned to Florentine. 'Lovely to meet you again this morning, Florentine. I shall look out for you when I next go strolling around the park.'

'Florentine, see him out, please.'

Rosalie ignored Florentine's frown and continued to tend to her eldest daughter. With most of the muck removed, it appeared the arm was deeply bruised. Already it was starting to swell. Rosalie pressed a clean damp cloth to the area and placed Anastasia's hand over it.

'Hold that there. We'll need some arnica.' Rosalie went into the pantry, where there was a cupboard especially for storing medical herbs and bandages. Minor injuries in a working hotel were commonplace, and her children had always been adventurous. She collected a bottle of arnica tincture, a soft cloth bandage, and a larger piece of muslin to use as a sling, and brought them to the kitchen table. 'This will help some.'

Anastasia removed the cloth from her arm. The bruise was starting to show a motley purple on her skin. Rosalie poured a liberal amount of the tincture onto the bandage, pressed it to the bruise, wound another cloth around Anastasia's arm to hold the bandage in place, and started preparing the sling.

'You'll have no choice but to rest this, Anastasia. I suspect your whole arm will be out of action for a few days at least.'

'Yes, Mam.'

'You may need something for the pain, too. I'll have Honora mix you up a tonic. In the meantime, this bandage will need to be changed every few hours as the arnica dries. John can do that for you if you like. I'll give him the bottle and some more bandages. Now, rest here while I see what's happening out on the street.'

'I'll go, Mam,' Florentine said as she walked through the broken doorway, but Rosalie was already shaking her head.

'No, I need to see the lie of the land out there. I want you to stay here for now and look after your sister. Make some tea and see about getting this glass cleaned up before the bairns escape from the nursery.'

'Yes, Mam.'

'And then after that, we'll need to have a family meeting. Our time of preparing ourselves is over. From now on, we will be taking action.'

Rosalie pulled her shirt sleeves down, stepped over the broken glass, and strode along the garden path. Angry with herself for not taking steps sooner and furious with Boseman and his lads for bringing harm to her family, she entered the laneway ready to take on anyone who looked crossways at her. She was greeted by an equally angry looking son and son-in-law.

'I think it was Harry,' Drew informed her. 'I saw him turn the corner when I came through the gate. Right little bastard he is. I'll give him a thick ear next time I see him.'

'He won't have a feckin' ear left when I get through with him,' John said.

'You'll both leave him be for now. We have more important

things to do. You can deal with him, and his master, later.' Rosalie herded John into the courtyard. 'We'll need reinforcement on this gate and fence to keep hooligans out. Go and check on Anastasia first though, John. She'll be fine, but she's in pain and I'm sure could do with some comforting from you. Drew, come with me. We're going for a walk.'

Mother and son did not walk far. Along Macquarie Street to Hunter and down Hunter as far as Phillip Street before crossing over and walking back along Hunter to Macquarie. They stopped outside the Shadler Bakery and Rosalie pulled a penny from her pocket.

'Drew, would you please pop in to the bakery for me? I'd like one of Mrs Shadler's sweet buns. One with raisins, and please let her know it's for me.'

'Mam, you don't eat sweet buns.' Drew's face showed confusion and impatience. 'We're wasting time.'

Their walk was measured and no doubt, to Drew, seemed point-less. Rosalie patted him on the cheek with some affection. 'We'll give it to Anastasia. But for now, just tell Mrs Shadler it's for me and don't mention anything about what's happened this morning.'

Drew took the coin and pulled his cap from his head, no further enlightened about his mother's actions. As Drew opened the door, a bell set above rang out its warning of customers in the shop.

Mrs Shadler was stocking the shelves at the front window with the morning's bread. She caught Rosalie's eye as she turned to serve Drew. Rosalie turned away then to face the gardens at the end of the street, to all observers patiently waiting for her son to make his purchase and return to her side. Inside the store, she knew, Amy Shadler would be reaching to the basket on the counter for raisin-studded sweet buns.

The bell rang again as Drew exited the bakery with his paper-wrapped bundle of buns fresh from the ovens. Rosalie breathed in their scent and smiled.

'She gave me two, Mam. Can I have the other? We never got to have breakfast. My stomach thinks my throat's been cut!'

'Eat it while we walk if you like. I've had time to clear my head. We should be heading back to the hotel.'

They crossed the road, almost bumping into young Will, the second of Boseman's lads, who was twirling his cap in his hands and looking more worried than his earlier surly demeanour gave him credit for.

Rosalie nodded at him and gave him no further mind as they retraced their steps along Hunter Street.

Will followed at a discreet distance. No doubt as ordered. Rosalie wondered if Boseman realised that he had a fox hidden in his little herd of lackeys.

Planks of lumber and a bucket of nails sat just inside the garden gate. John was already busy at reinforcing their battlements. By the amount of wood and nails, Rosalie presumed he had plans for the stables as well. They were so little used nowadays that she'd forgotten about them.

'Would you help John with the gate and stables, Drew? We can't have them completely blocked, but I definitely want them inaccessible from the outside.'

'Yes, Mam.' Drew handed her the package from the baker, now with only one sweet bun, and ducked into the stables.

The kitchen was a hive of activity. Rosalie could hear Honora barking orders and see Bridie and Alice scurrying to obey as she approached. Someone had removed the back door from its hinges and swept the glass clear.

You've been a foolish old woman, Rosalie MacKinnon.

Foolish and fearful.

Putting off the inevitable could no longer be borne.

Today. Now. They must act.

She would need the kitchen.

'Honora,' she said as she stepped in. 'We need the baking and cooking completed as soon as possible. Basics for lunches and dinners today. Alice and Bridie, concentrate on the tearoom and keep an ear out for chatter as usual. Alice dear, don't worry about bedrooms—family can look after themselves. We have a traveller due this afternoon, so please air Room 1 at the top of the stairs.'

'Yes, ma'am,' Alice said. She hurried out of the room to open the guest room's door and window. Nearly a week had passed since a traveller had stayed, and though Alice dusted the rooms every day, they were starting to smell musty from disuse.

'Bridie, would you please take a tray up to Ana and the bairns. We seemed to have completely missed breakfast and I'm sure they're all very hungry by now.'

'Of course, Mrs P. Mr Michaels has arrived to open the taproom. What should I tell him?'

'I'll talk to Mr Michaels, Bridie. We'll keep everything that's happened to ourselves for now, so no chatting in the corridors where guests might overhear. The Garden Arms is business as usual, well almost as usual. I want no one suspecting that things may be otherwise.'

'I don't know what's going on anyway,' Bridie answered.

Rosalie looked at the battered old grandfather clock in the corner of the kitchen. 'We have very little time and much to do all while keeping the hotel running like clockwork. In a nutshell, Mr Boseman has shown his hand rather too well. He obviously has plans to undermine us, Bridie. We must show a united front. There is more going on under the surface, which I'm sure you suspect.'

Bridie cast an anxious glance at Honora.

'We're both behind you, ma'am, all the way. We've not forgotten the old ways and nor are we likely to.' Honora handed Bridie plates of toast. 'Put those on the tray, lassie, and get a move on with the butter and jam.'

Bridie fetched ceramic dishes of each condiment from the pantry, a jar of sugared cinnamon for an extra treat, and a pitcher of milk. 'I'll come back for the pot of tea.'

'I'll bring the tea, Bridie. I want to check on Ana's arm.'

'Yes, ma'am, and what Mrs Keogh said is true. I'm as ready as anyone to do my bit. I'll not fail you.'

'Thank you, dear. Now off you go and let Ana know I'm right behind you.'

Bridie, now holding the fully laden tray aloft, pushed the kitchen door open with her foot and followed the outward swing before it could come back and knock her load from her hands.

'She knows what to do, Rosie,' Honora said. 'Smart as a whip, that one, and knowing.'

'I'm scared, Nora. We're all in danger. I can feel it. I'm especially fearful for Florentine and Alice. Florentine is about to go into battle and Alice's position is precarious. There's been talk of sending the natives to their home districts as if they hadn't lived right here for hundreds of years.'

Honora walked around the table and grasped Rosalie's hands. They were hardened by years of cooking and cleaning. Rosalie held on tight.

'Alice knows what she's about and Florentine has the heart of a warrior. Both are strong with family to support them. There surely is a battle to be fought, but they're not alone. We don't know Alice's role just yet. Fate has plans for her and they're entwined with yours and Florrie.'

'She's not safe ...'

'None of us ever have been and that's the truth of it. What's coming now has been building up for a hundred years or more. Since the time our ancestors were booted from their homes and sent into destitution and slavery. Since our grandmothers were accused of atrocities they didn't commit and thrown into fires or hanged or drowned.'

'Longer even than that, Nora. Longer even than that.'

'You're strong too, Rosie. You're our commander. Florrie, Bridie, Drew, Ana, Johnny, and me, and, I suspect, Alice, we're your army. It's time for us to go to war.'

Rosalie stared at Honora, wondering at her old friend's staunch grasp of the situation, so ready to trust and fight for their shared history and, hopefully, future.

'You're right as always, Nora. I may make you a general though. I'll need someone who can control the troops. When you bark an order, it certainly is carried out to the letter.'

'My first order then is to suggest a meeting in the dining room while I get on with the kitchen. Florrie needs direction and your Aunty Flora has been at sixes and sevens. Put them together. Drew too. Now, when's this traveller expected in then? He can have his meals in the guest sitting room. I'll take care of all that, with Bridie's help. You'll have enough to do with everything else.'

Honora was right. Everything else included her usual duties of overseeing the bar and tearooms.

'When will the kitchen be cleared?'

'I'll keep a pot of stew on the heat. We'll close off the back section of the tearoom and keep the cakes in there. We can take tubs of water in too for washing. We'll need the stove for hot water for the tea and coffee, of course, but everything else can be done from there.'

'This evening, then?'

'Aye, but it'll be risky.'

'Everything we do from here on out can be considered risky, Nora. I'd prefer to leave it until tomorrow when at least the taproom is closed. But we need to get started. I'll go and see Ana. I have a sweet bun for her from Mrs Shadler. I can talk to Florrie and Aunty Flora and Ana while the bairns eat. Drew is helping John, so I'll leave them to reinforce our borders for now. Our overnight guest is travelling down on a packet from Newcastle. It's not due to dock until three pm. I'll send Drew down to meet him and help with his luggage. That's still quite some time away. This would be easier if we didn't have guests to worry about, you're right, but there's nothing to be done. By the time we're ready to start, our overnight guest will be fed and either tucked away or in the taproom.'

'The business will be a distraction from what's really going on. If only this weren't the driest September we've had in years. A good storm would send them all scurrying for home. You get that treat up to your child, Rosie. She's all skin and bones as it is, and terribly worried about her little ones.'

'Thank you, Nora. You're the voice of reason as always.' Rosalie smoothed the paper that covered the bun. Honora cackled with laughter as she returned to the cooktop.

'You put that on my headstone when it's time. His Lordship will double up with laughter and we'll have storms a plenty that year, that's for sure.'

Rosalie left her friend to get on with the day's cooking and pushed open the kitchen door, only to nearly knock over both Bridie and Alice in the process.

'Mrs P, you forgot the teapot. You go on up and I'll fetch it. Won't be a minute.'

'Thank you, Bridie.'

Rosalie shook her head. Forgetfulness was not something she needed right now. All her wits were what she was wanting, plus some. Hopefully Aunty Flora and Florentine would provide the extra she needed. She walked up the stairs, dreading and antici-pating the day to come.

Dim corridors of overcrowded shelving, dry dusty air, and a world of titled spines, gold-tipped pages, and mountains of journals. This was the world of Ina and Douglas Bell, booksellers on Castlereagh Street.

Mr Bell, a small man with a wealth of slicked-back hair and spectacles perched rakishly on his nose, was glorying over a trunkful of books, just arrived in. Mrs Bell, tall and quiet, noted prices on the inside cover of each addition and strolled the shelves to find their perfect position.

Rosalie found their store peaceful and enjoyed the endless liter-ary-themed conversations. She'd also discovered that if any piece of information was wanted, no matter how esoteric, then Bell's Bookstore was the place to come.

The front door was open promptly at ten o'clock each morning, Monday through Friday, and closed at six o'clock in the evening. On Saturdays, they closed at midday and spent the afternoon wandering through parks and visiting friends.

On the Saturday that Rosalie chose to visit, they were wiping down the counter and polishing the cash register. The grandfather clock in the corner was about to start chiming the seconds down to noon.

'Good morning, Mrs Bell, Mr Bell. I realise you're about to close, but may I speak with you a moment?'

Mr Bell draped his polishing cloth over the cash register and shuffled past Mrs Bell and around the counter with a low 'Excuse me, my dear,' and then 'Excuse me, Mrs Ponsonby' as he stepped past her to the door. He closed and locked it, and pulled down the blind to indicate they were indeed closed for the rest of the weekend.

'I'll go make a pot of tea then, shall I?'

'Thank you, dear,' Mrs Bell answered. 'Is everything all right, Rosalie?' Ina was a pale Irishwoman who had emigrated, with her husband and several crates of books, some ten years previously. The Ponsonbys were regular customers since the first day of the store's opening and friends not long after that.

'Ina, I'm worried. We've had many a conversation about history and the old ways, and such. I know you come from a similar background to myself, but we've never actually acknowledged where we stand now on the subject.' Rosalie felt a little ill, anxiety rippled through her body from her pounding headache to her upset stomach and trembling hands.

'Come through to the kitchen, Rosalie. You look a little pale. Let's talk over a cup of tea. Has something happened?'

They moved through the bookshelves to the back of the store and into what was once a small dining room, but now served as a reading room and office. Every corner was piled high with books and papers. The women moved around two desks set up in the middle of the room; one desk held bookbinding equipment and the other a set of neat ledgers, pencils, and a stack of books waiting to be priced and put out for sale. Rosalie held her skirts close to her body to avoid bumping into any of the precious stock and equipment, and followed Mrs Bell through to the kitchen.

Like the Ponsonbys, Mr and Mrs Bell spent a good deal of time in the kitchen. Rosalie had shared many a pot of tea in its cosy environ. Mr Bell was just pouring the boiling water into the teapot; cups were already laid out, and the room smelled of the rich Irish tea leaves the couple habitually used.

'Sit. Sit. This'll be only a moment longer. Would you like me to stay or go? I don't want to intrude.'

'Stay please, dear,' Mrs Bell answered. 'I'm sure Rosalie will welcome your views as always.' She nodded in an assuring manner to Rosalie and gestured for her to take the closest chair before sitting down beside her. 'You know, of course, Rosalie, that Mr Bell's family and mine originated in the same village in Ireland not far from the Giant's Steps, and that our grandmothers were cousins. Mr Bell's grandmother was a talented healer and my own was considered something of a wise woman, isn't that right, dear?'

Mr Bell placed the pot on the table with an iron trivet underneath to protect the tablecloth and wood below. 'That's exactly right. Very talented, as are you, my dear.'

But Mrs Bell was shaking her head. 'Not nearly as gifted. However, I inherited enough to know, Rosalie, that you too share this power, though you have a deep need to keep it secret. We respect you far too much to intrude.'

Rosalie sipped her piping hot tea and let some of the tension ease. 'You are correct. I have had to keep secrets, even from you. Something indeed has occurred and the time has come when I need to share my story. But first, I must ask your permission to share it with you. It's larger than just us three in this room, larger even than this whole city and the world we live in. Knowledge can be a burden and a danger.'

Mr Bell sat opposite Rosalie and Mrs Bell. He held a hand out across the table to his wife. 'Rosalie, my dear. We are your staunchest friends and allies, and up to any task or challenge.'

Mrs Bell took her husband's hand and squeezed. She placed her other hand on Rosalie's shoulder. 'You have our permission, Rosalie. Douglas and I stand firm in support of you and against whatever has you so worried.'

Rosalie's eyes burned with unshed tears that threatened to spill over. She replaced her shaking cup in its sauce with a clatter. She pressed her lips between her teeth and took a deep breath.

'My family can trace its origins to before the Scotland and Ireland that we left behind. Before the MacKinnons or the Fingans and the people before that. Our roots are buried deep in the land, in the island of our birth. We are not faery, exactly, but we know faery. We lived beside them in harmony in the days before they hid in the forests and the caves, and under the earth. Our people survive by assimilating, but we never forget our roots or our stories, or our purpose on this earth.'

'When the enemy came, we hid in plain sight as simple folk. Our treasures were buried. Our stories became secrets. Our history became myth. We thought we only had to survive the dark years, as long as it took.' Rosalie's mouth and lips felt dry. 'We were wrong. There are some who know our secrets, or suspect. They hunt us down, rape and murder us, steal our relics and our power. We have been weakened while they grow strong.'

Rosalie closed her eyes, remembering the storm-lashed night she'd fled her village, leaving behind her family and friends.

'They came to my village in 1850. They are here now.'

Lord Benedict took coffee in the tearoom opposite the Botanical Gardens. He generally preferred tea in the afternoon. However, his hostess had ordered on his behalf, and as she was the Lady Mayoress he thought it diplomatic to acquiesce.

'There are many coffee palaces, of course, your Lordship, but the Garden Arms have a delightful selection of cakes and tarts that you must try for yourself. And excellent service. Such a quaint room and so close to the Gardens. I do hope you enjoyed our stroll?'

'I did indeed. An interesting collection of plants and with such an agreeable vista. I look forward to writing to my wife as soon as I can. She'll be most envious.'

He looked about him at the furnishings and the women who milled around them. There were one or two gentlemen, but for the most part the tearoom's patronage was female. He sniffed. He would have much preferred to retire to his rooms at the Union Club, however, the afternoon walk was tiresome and the weather warm. Refreshment was in order, and the chance to see inside the Ponsonby woman's establishment an enticement he couldn't resist. The room was quaint enough, he supposed, fashionable in a country-ish sort of way and certainly handy to the tavern next door. The clientele was a step or two above some of the other tea and coffee rooms. They were, after all, neighbours to some of the richer residents on this side of the city.

A dark-skinned waitress wove her way in and out of the tables, serving tea and coffee from two large pots and flashing a brilliantly white smile. He was mesmerised by the way she managed the pots, bobbing to the customers, murmuring questions and answers, and pouring without spilling a drop. Every now and then she'd place the pots on a side buffet and take a tray of milk and sugar around. Another lass came in and out with three-tiered trays of sweet treats, handing them out with the silver service one would expect from a high-class hotel in London.

A woman at the next table greeted the cake-bearer enthusiastically and requested a strawberry-chocolate cream tart and complimented the waitress on her baking skills. The Lady Mayoress ordered the same, and as Benedict bit into the confection he had to admit that the tart was exceptional—sweet and creamy and crumbly. He was halfway through the treat when Mrs Ponsonby walked into the room and, looking around her with an expression that seemed to suggest her customers were guests in her home, came toward them.

'Lady Mayoress, an honour as always to have you with us today.'

'Mrs Ponsonby. I was walking in the Gardens and could hardly pass by without stopping in for one of Bridie's tarts. Allow me to introduce you to Lord Algernon Benedict. He's been locked up in meetings with the mayor all morning and I felt it my duty to whisk him away for some fresh air and exercise before they reconvened and talked the rest of the afternoon away.'

Lord Benedict nodded at Mrs Ponsonby, unsure, for once, the custom. Surely he wasn't meant to stand and greet the woman as an equal. She was the proprietor of an hotel.

'Lord Benedict, a pleasure. Welcome to the Garden Arms. I hope you enjoyed your sojourn with Mrs Harris?'

He let habit and good manners take over and stood to give a perfunctory bow, though it galled him to do so. Mrs Ponsonby, at least, did not hold out her hand. Neither did she seem in the least bit intimidated by him.

'Indeed. A pleasant stroll. Your tearooms are in an excellent location to welcome strollers and the like.' He sat down, unsure of himself and a bit confused that he should be so.

'Especially when Sydney is experiencing such a warm and dry spring. I do hope you enjoy the rest of your stay, Lord Benedict. Mrs Harris, lovely to see you again.'

Mrs Ponsonby moved on to the next table and the next, greeting her guests, sharing a few words, circulating around the room as practiced and graceful as the waitresses who fanned out around her.

'I understand Mrs Ponsonby is also proprietor of the tavern,' Benedict said. 'That's unusual, is it not?'

'Not really, Algernon. There are a fair few businesswomen around town. They are left widowed. Husbands go off to the goldfields in search of fortune, or just go off. Families still need to be fed, so it is the wives left behind that must do what they can. Many, of course, are well-acquainted with their business before they take its charge.'

'Mrs Ponsonby is a widow, is she not?'

The Lady Mayoress paused to take a sip of her coffee before answering. Benedict could feel her inquisitive gaze.

'Indeed, these past twelve months. Her husband James was the proprietor before her. In legal terms, anyway. They had run the Garden Arms together for close to thirty years prior to his death. Mrs Ponsonby's standing in the community is exceptional.'

'I'm sure it is,' Algernon placated his hostess. 'Such a novelty though. I don't believe we have women in charge of taverns in London.'

'Or perhaps you do and you just aren't aware of the fact.'

'Perhaps. My wife will be most amused to read how different colonial society is.'

'Indeed.' The Lady Mayoress peeped at a fob-watch that hung from a chain around her neck. 'My goodness, it's getting quite late. The mayor will be anxious as to our whereabouts.' She took a final sip of coffee and patted her lips with a napkin. 'Time to be on.'

'Of course.' Benedict stood and moved to assist Mrs Harris, but was too slow. The Lady Mayoress was already on her feet and pulling on gloves. 'After you.'

Rosalie watched Mrs Harris and Lord Benedict step out into the sunshine, pondering her reaction to the meeting. She felt sick to her stomach when the lord stood. Something about this pompous man left her uneasy. She'd heard of his arrival with his son, and that he was staying at the Union Club. She needed to know more.

A stiff-looking fellow entered the tearoom, and Rosalie put aside her concerns about the lord and his son. Mr Wilson Kent was a dried up, humourless man whom Rosalie preferred to have nothing to do with. He was also an inspector for the Licensing Court.

'Mr Kent. Good afternoon. Are you here for pleasure or business this afternoon?'

Kent ignored Rosalie as he took in the busy tearoom. He made to move past her and, without paying her any attention, stated, 'Business. The room is not usually partitioned off, I believe. What's going on behind those doors?'

Several people followed Kent's line of sight and whispered to each other. Rosalie frowned and fought to remain calm. Wilson Kent was the most irritating man. Two nights ago, he'd inspected the taproom and issued a fine for the street light above her door not being lit. There was no point arguing that some stray breeze must have extinguished the fixture. Rosalie recognised a trumped-up charge when she saw one. And now he was here. By the tone of his voice, a new fine was in the offing.

'Would you like a cup of coffee or tea to take with you on your inspection, Mr Kent?'

Kent stepped around waitresses and customers as he moved toward the glass doors. He peered through and could see movement, but nothing more. Lace curtains formed a discreet barrier between private and public spaces. He made a move to open them.

'The door is locked, Mr Kent. If you'd like to use the staff door, you may, of course, go through and see inside for yourself. We are merely undergoing some renovation.'

Kent gave Rosalie a disdainful look, to which she stepped aside and showed him the swing door that led into the restricted areas of the hotel.

'I don't believe the magistrate is aware of renovations at the Garden Arms, Mrs Ponsonby. Have you submitted plans?'

'Not yet. They'll be submitted in due course. The magistrate and I discussed them when he was in for coffee this morning, Mr Kent. No doubt he has yet to inform you of his private conversations for the day. Perhaps you can ask him yourself. After your inspection. Shall we start? I'm eager to hear your opinion on wallpaper. I have several sample books we can peruse ...'

'I'm here on business, madam, not to waste time on frivolous matters of décor.'

Alice appeared in front of him then with a cup of tea and a plate of sandwiches. 'Tea, sir? The sandwiches are lovely and fresh …'

Kent grunted and pushed past the waitress, nearly knocking a cup from the hand of Miss Scott, who was taking tea with her mother, regular customers at the tearoom.

'How rude! Who is that vile creature, Mrs Ponsonby?'

'An inspector, Miss Scott. Here to inspect the premises. He's quite passionate about his work. I'm sure his intention was not to cause you or Mrs Scott distress.'

'His manners are appalling. I should put in a complaint if I were you,' added Mrs Scott. To her daughter, she said, 'You should mention it to the magistrate on Friday evening, Rose. Mrs Ponsonby takes great care of her customers and this inspector is nothing but a bully.'

'Excuse me, Mrs Scott, Miss Scott. I must attend to Mr Kent. I'll have Alice bring you over some fresh tea.'

Alice was already on her way to the pot. All the waitresses were trained to have a constant supply of fresh tea and coffee on hand to ruffle feathers and ease nerves.

'Keep an eye on him,' Miss Scott said. 'I don't trust his countenance at all.'

Rosalie followed Mr Kent through the swing door and took charge of the inspection. 'This way, Mr Kent.' She led him into the closed-off section of the tearoom. 'We're hoping to open the courtyard area early this year. The season has been so warm that the garden has left its winter drabness behind and will soon be ready to seat customers. We'll be refreshing this end of the tearoom to match and making minor repairs on the French door into the garden. We're using the space to provide extra cakes and sandwiches to our customers. We've been quite busy with the fine weather, but having this area assists us to maintain a high level of service. Would you like to see the garden, Mr Kent?'

The tables were piled with the tiered cake trays, some empty, some full, and the sideboards were loaded with platters of sand-wiches covered with a sheet of muslin to help keep them fresh.

Kent grunted again and walked out. Rosalie steered him toward the dining room.

'The dining room is next, Mr Kent. Our overnight guests have the choice of eating their dinner here, in the guest sitting room upstairs, or in their rooms.'

Quite empty, the room appeared as it always did to the casual observer. Mr Kent was no casual observer.

'It doesn't appear to have been used recently. How many guests do you have now?'

'Just the one. His meals have been served upstairs.'

'At his request?'

'Naturally.'

'If you've finished here, I'll show you to the kitchen.'

'I would like to inspect the guest accommodation next, Mrs Ponsonby.'

They left the quiet dining room and headed toward the stairs. Voices could be heard in the kitchen and from the bar as Mr Michaels, the head barman, entered the corridor and headed toward the storeroom. He scowled at Kent as he passed, but said nothing.

'This way, Mr Kent, if you please.'

That evening, the tearoom closed and the kitchen quiet, Honora, Flora Heffernan, and Rosalie shared a few quiet moments. Their relief that the inspector had not wanted to see the kitchen was mingled with the obvious targeting of the Garden Arms. After finding nothing untoward on the first floor and signs of habitation in Room 1, Mr Kent had inspected the ground floor storeroom and the taproom. Michaels had not been impressed with the inspector's acerbic comments on cleanliness, service, and staff. Nor with his pedantic concern over the most minor of details.

He complained about labels not showing properly, glasses not lined up perfectly, and smudges on the tap handles, for chrissake! He was a right pain in the arse when Mr P was around, but he's worse now.

Michaels was not one to mince his words and only his respect for the Ponsonbys kept him from sharing his true feelings about the inspector. Rosalie knew this and understood how frustrated he must be feeling. It was his last words that worried her.

You watch yourself, Mrs P. He's gunning for you. I can tell the way his beady eyes poke into every corner. He's looking for an excuse to write you up.

Rosalie knew that as well. She suspected Kent was in Boseman's pocket. She was on friendly terms with the magistrate, so Kent's feverish concerns with misdemeanours didn't come from that direction.

'What will we do if that inspector decides to visit again? How much trouble can he make?' Flora Heffernan was fast learning the ins and outs of running a hotel, lending a hand wherever she could in the kitchen, behind the scenes, with the children.

'A lot of bloody trouble if he sets his mind to it. Right bastard, that one. Pardon my language,' Honora said. 'Little understanding outside his book of rules, though. We can set things up to appear normal and he probably won't notice.'

'I agree. He made a mistake this afternoon being rude to Miss Scott and her mother. I wouldn't be surprised if he'll be reined in and soon. Rose Scott is not one to be trifled with.'

'That could make him more dangerous.'

'I'll have a word with Mr Michaels and John, Aunty, but we'll all have to be on guard. Someone else came into the tearoom this afternoon who I think could be trouble. Lord Benedict. Recently off the ship from England. A pompous man, by the look, but no fool. I came over all queer when I saw him.'

'We'll keep an ear to the ground then. See what we can find out. Mrs Shadler's delivered the items we need to get started. We should get a move on before the others arrive.'

Rosalie sighed. Her feet ached and she had a thumping headache, but Honora was right. With John watching over the taproom and the children safely ensconced upstairs, it was time to start.

~

The kitchen table was festooned with branches of wych elm and wattle and laid out with earthenware bowls, mugs, and wooden spoons. A cast-iron cauldron stood in the centre of the table beside a platter of seed cakes. The fire in the stove was banked to keep the pots above it at a low simmer.

Tapping at the door announced a cautious Drew. 'Mrs Shadler and Mrs Bell are here, Mam.'

'Amy. Ina. Welcome,' Rosalie greeted her friends.

'Drew, please go see if John needs any help before dinner service starts in the bar. Remember to stay out of sight. With that inspector lurking around, I want no accusations of underage drinkers or workers in that taproom.'

'Yes, Mam.' A table was set in the hall just outside the kitchen, stacked with bread, tubs of butter, plates, bowls, and utensils. Drew was to come into the kitchen only to fetch the pots of stew as needed or to provide warning of unwelcome visitors.

'Is anyone else coming tonight, Rosalie?' Amy Shadler placed a basket of baked goods on the kitchen bench and started removing her coat and hat. 'I've brought some soda bread to share.' She hooked her outer garments by the door and brought the bread to the table.

'And I have a pot of native bee honey.' Ina's coat and hat were divested and her gift placed on the table beside the basket of bread.

Honora poured tea into everyone's cups and ladled hot water into the cauldron. The women stood behind their chairs until she was ready to join them and then they sat, ready and waiting.

'We are here this evening to open our hearts, minds, and hearths to our ancestors,' Rosalie began in a soft voice. Her bowl was full of beans; stems, curly runners, and flowers still attached. She took a handful and dropped it into the cauldron.

'They have far to travel, but what is distance to a dweller of the spirit realm?' said Honora. She placed a handful of herbal tea leaves from her bowl into the cauldron.

'They lived long ago, but what is time to the magic of the faery queen?' Amy Shadler dropped a bundle of basil leaves into the pot.

Ina Bell sprinkled anise seeds over the top. 'They seek only peace and respect, but what are these when kith and kin are threatened?'

Rosalie stood and stirred the concoction with the ladle. Each of the now empty bowls were handed to her to fill with the soup, which she did in silence, thinking of her mother and grandmother, her niece murdered trying to protect the grave of their ancestor, and finally Ethne M'Kynnon, whose resting place had been ransacked, her bones taken. She felt hot; grief and fear were melding, anger sparked deep within.

Bowls filled, each woman took a piece of soda bread and a seed cake, and broke them in half. In a low voice, Rosalie recited:

'O Grandmother old across the seas
We entreat of you your aide
Queen of the hills and Queen of the waves
Queen of the breeze o'er the faery mounds
Your daughters need your wisdom
O mother let your voice be heard
By those who have sore need.'

Chunky pieces of soda bread were added to the cauldron. Rosalie continued:

'O spirits of the Land
We have no wish to conquer
Our Queen seeks no harm but to those
Who bring fell deed and wish to these shores.
Our Grandmother seeks to aid kith and kin
Our Mother seeks to protect her daughters
O Spirits of this Land, we beg of you, forgiveness.'

The seed cakes were added to the soup.

The woman held hands across the table. They were not related by blood, but by heart. The imprecations were sent to ancestors shared by story and song, by bonds hidden deep beneath the veneer of their colonial lives.

'It's time to feast with our grandmothers,' Honora said. She dipped her spoon to her bowl. 'The herbal tea was dried last summer and contains lavender, rosemary, and some local tea-tree leaves that Alice has been helping me to grow. Its essence is the combination of that lore which we left behind and that which we now know.'

'It smells divine, Honora. Thank you for sharing with us,' Amy said. 'The soda bread is an old recipe of my mother's. I baked it this morning, just this one batch, for us and the ancestors. It goes particularly well with basil and will help to protect and purify our space, within and without.'

The women smiled and sipped and dunked the bread into their bowls.

Ina Bell was not known as a cook. She did, however, have a keen interest in bees and honey. When she wasn't busy with books she could often be found in her back garden tending several hives.

'The honey has been blended with star anise. I recommend trying it on the seed cakes when we've finished our soup. I hope it will be a lovely blend of heartiness and sweetness. We will be both protected and open to the arrival of our ancestors.'

'I'm sure it will, Ina. Very thoughtful. The seed cakes were a gift from Alice's mother to help connect us to this country. The honey will be just the right addition. To the soup, I added beans from our garden. We all feel the need for protection in many ways. Tonight, we take steps to protect ourselves from manifestations of evil from both the physical and spiritual realm. We are right to do so.'

Amy and Ina hefted the cauldron from the table and held it between them. Rosalie lit a candle and led the way from the kitchen to the dining room.

They passed Drew, who was busy cutting bread and smothering it with butter. The dull roar of male voices talking, boasting, laughing filled the dark corridor each time the door into the taproom opened. The men were waiting for their dinner.

'Ask John to help you with the stew,' Rosalie told her son. 'We're finished in the kitchen for now.'

Drew dropped his greasy knife and ducked into the rear of the taproom to talk to his brother-in-law. John Bray peeked into the hallway and then ducked back behind the door, muttering to Drew that the customers could wait one more minute.

Rosalie entered the dining room. Standing on either side of the fireplace was Anastasia, her bruised arm still in a sling, and Florentine, bristling with barely constrained energy. The young women appeared to alternate between courage and near panic. When the glowing light from the fire cast their inconstant shadows, Rosalie saw the soul of the guardian in her eldest daughter and the warrior that lived inside the younger. Up to this point, she'd remained uncertain of which daughter she'd be sending into the fray. The life's purpose of each was etched into their souls the day they'd been born.

Rosalie felt the last vestige of tension drain away. With the homely ceremony she and her friends had just performed, and her new understanding of the future, she felt hope for the first time. Success or failure didn't hang solely on the outcome of the next few days and weeks, but also on knowledge, understanding, and acceptance. She and her family would fight on as they always had.

Rosalie placed the candle on the mantelpiece, cleared away now to reveal fine shallow carvings on the wood surface; swirls, interconnecting lines, circles within circles. Anastasia made space to allow her to stand between her and the fireplace. Amy and Ina stepped forward to place the cauldron in the fire, and they all made way for Honora, who laid the tray of cake and honey on the hearthstone. Standing in a semi-circle around the offering, they held hands and stared into the fire as it blazed around the cauldron, searing the iron and seeming to reach in and taste the thick soup.

Rosalie pulled a small notebook from her pocket. Each page held a single design of wriggles, dots, and short sharp lines. She tore the top page free, handed it to Anastasia beside her, who passed it down the line. Each woman touched the paper briefly before Florentine, last in line, gave the paper to the flames. Six pages in all, each design different, each consumed by the fire, the last in a conflagration that licked out to scorch the stone surround and came close to catching alight the women's skirts.

None moved.

A sweet earthy smell carried upward on wisps of silver-grey smoke. Tendrils of black exuded, ghost-like, around the still figures, encircling their bodies, caressing exposed skin; hands, throats, faces, and trailing away into the dark corners of the room.

Faint vibration came through the floor like the earth awakening or shifting to make way for something new. The glass chandelier above the dining table tinkled. The candle flame stuttered. For a moment, the smoke appeared indecisive in its exploration, seemed to withdraw, brittle against an unseen barrier, and then embers popped, wood cracked, the cauldron glowed red hot, and the soup bubbled. Smoke gushed out, thick and black. One of the women stifled a cough. Tears streamed down Rosalie's cheeks; she could barely see for the sting of acrid soot.

They waited.

The punishing entity of vapour redrew, satisfied it seemed, accepting. The softer tendrils also returned to the coals until only ordinary smoke lingered. The women all coughed then, eyes streaming, noses running. They would taste the smoke and remember its hot menace in their raspy voices for days.

'Did that really happen?' Florentine asked.

'It seems we have permission to proceed.' Honora knelt warily on the hearth and, using her skirt to protect her hands, retrieved the blackened plate of offerings and the honey jar.

'For now,' Rosalie added. 'Amy, would you mind fetching two bowls from the kitchen? It's time Ana and Florrie shared in the ancestor's feast.'

Amy clasped Rosalie around the wrist. 'Tread carefully, Rosalie. Spirits are easily offended.'

Rosalie shared a grim smile with the baker, her friend and sister for some ten years or more. 'Clean your face while you're in the kitchen. But only your face. When you get home tonight, scrape the soot from your hands and neck, and keep it in a kerchief. It will be a small protection, but a protection nonetheless, from any retaliation or rebound of magic. We will all do this. It may be the only assistance we will receive from the land whose territory we are encroaching upon.'

Amy nodded and left the room. While they spoke, Ina had placed the serving tray on the table to shield its surface from the hot plate and retrieved a broom from the corner of the room. She started to sweep cinders, soot, and a fine layer of speckling sand toward the hearth, murmuring all the while an old Irish song. Rosalie recognised some of the words from her many years of listening to Honora sing as she worked. The broom glided across the floor in time to the bookseller's lilting voice. Rosalie could almost see faeries dancing around the sweeping woman, invoked by ancient words, and the plea they'd sent out into the night.

Amy returned to the room with bowls, spoons, and the ladle, passing them to Honora who filled the bowls to the brim with broth and vegetables. Anastasia and Florentine were already seated, eyeing their meal suspiciously.

'Are we allowed to ask what's in it, Mam?'

Amy passed her a spoon with a chuckle. 'Vegetables and herbs with a dash of spice. The floating bits are bread. It's quite delicious. We've all had some.'

'And when you're done, eat some of that seed cake with honey. Whatever is left we'll put in the fire,' Honora added.

Florentine didn't look impressed and Rosalie couldn't blame her. The seed cake was quite charred.

'If we're done, Rosie, Ina and I will head off.'

'Yes, of course, Amy. Thanks to you both. We're beholden …'

'No, Rosalie. You are not beholden to anyone. Don't ever forget that. It is our privilege to offer our assistance whenever you have need.'

To Rosalie's embarrassment, Amy and Ina bobbed a secretive

curtsy and departed. Ina's cheeks and forehead were still quite sooty.

Rosalie watched Honora usher the women out.

Where would I be without Honora?

Honora and Amy had boarded the same ship bound for Australia, and prior to that were guests at the same orphanage on the West Coast of Ireland. They'd shared dreams, gossip and recipes ever since.

Sisters of the heart, Honora had often told Rosalie. The Irishwoman was witness at Amy's marriage to Anselm Shadler and godmother to all their children as she was the Ponsonby children. The circle of family and friends around the Irishwoman was tight.

It was Honora who set up the coded requests for help between the Shadler Bakery and the Garden Arms Hotel, and she who now prepared the way for Rosalie to step away from safety and into danger.

As the women's voices faded into the kitchen, Rosalie realised the taproom behind was quiet. She glanced at the hall clock, astonished to see that hours had passed since tea time. She rubbed her hands along her arms, smoothed her skirts and then, just to keep them still, pushed them into her pockets. Her feet wanted to move, stamp the floor, run away. All the while, the clock hands crept their way toward midnight.

The scrape of furniture and low baritone of male voices told her that John, Drew, and Mr Michaels were busy cleaning and putting the bar back into order. She ought to go in, see how the evening went, at least make an appearance, but the thought alone caused a heavy sensation to settle deep inside her. The men didn't need her checking up on them.

Anastasia and Florentine waited in the dining room. She could see their faces, knew every line and dip as well as her own—better. Concern for them crescendoed inside her. The heaviness of a moment ago tightened like a vice in her ribs.

What if they're hurt? Worse, what if they die? No. She refused to give in to her fear. No matter the cost, she and her daughters had to keep moving forward.

The kitchen door creaked. A soft touch on her arm …

Rosalie unclenched her hands and pulled them free of her skirts, straightened her back, squeezed her lips between her teeth, but she couldn't bear to look at Honora right now, to see the worry and compassion in her face. To do so would crumble her willpower and waning strength. She longed to be held and comforted, but time, it appeared, was furtive.

'The girls need us.'

CHAPTER 12

Clement contemplated the display of weaponry on the walls
and in glass cases around him. Quite a collection, though
somewhat meaningless. Where were the references to religion?
Where were the representations of the black man's beliefs? What
did he do when he wasn't off making war or defending his women
and children? If the curator of this museum thought this was all
there was to the local natives then he was seriously misguided. He
rubbed his wrist and flexed his aching fingers. There was always
more.

The mistake the curator, and his supply of collectors and thieves,
had made was in not looking past the surface meaning of power.
Power to them was in weaponry, strength of arms, and shows of
physical superiority. *Fools!* They were as children in the face of the
true, deep-flowing meaning of power.

It rankled like any insult to intellect would, but it was their loss.
He, who understood the hidden depths, would take control and
they, facile ingrates that they were, would be his puppets to play
with as he saw fit.

Clement and his father had made this journey to lay claim to the last of the items they needed to control old powers, take back that which was theirs, and change the direction history seemed intent on sending the world.

These people are as foolish as those we left behind, his father had told him. *They seek power through the paper-thin halls of government, making up silly rules they believe will save them from the past.*

As Clement learned more from his father about what the past entailed, he was wholly inclined to agree. The ancient powers of the past may have been sleeping for millennia, but the time was fast approaching when he and his father would have the strength and tools to waken them and use them for their own advantage.

Clement paused at a roughly built canoe. Its thick bark sides appeared weak compared to the sloops that sailed on a constant rotation between Europe and Australia, but what need did the natives have for masts and rigging? Their interests and purpose lay in fishing, and navigating bays and rivers rather than vast oceans.

Greed, it seemed, was an affliction that riddled European culture alone—greed and a sense of superiority. He'd used it to his advantage many times. Understood that this was the base of his desire, yet aware that power and strength could be fleeting. Hadn't his family lost it and fought to regain it for several lifetimes?

He believed that his father's motivation was revenge for all the family had lost. He wondered sometimes, as he watched the elderly man repeatedly tend to the relics they'd recovered thus far, if he really understood what it was they were trying to regain. If Lord Benedict really knew the meaning behind the items and the ceremonies and the words.

A memory came to him of a gaping toothless mouth with insane eyes and a bulging nose. His flexing fingers clenched into a tight fist and he shuddered with revulsion. For that moment he felt defenceless, stripped bare by a figure he did not recognise or understand, and left helpless by a father who was playing with powers even he was ignorant of.

Clement walked away from the canoe and the pronged spears,

and soothed his raging thoughts with the Art Society exhibition: landscapes, flowers frozen for eternity on canvas, semi-naked women nibbling grapes from a cornucopia of fruit. He strolled through gathering himself, calming his mind. By the time he'd crossed the room, he was planning his next move. Relics were easy to find up to this point. They knew something was here, in this city, perhaps in this oversized museum, but not what or where.

George Boseman had traced the MacKinnon woman to the Garden Arms Hotel, but how much she knew was still a mystery. Did she have the strength to stop them in their tracks?

Boseman was about his trouble-making ways. If anyone could be a distracting source of nuisance, it was Boseman. Hosting him in the Union Club bar while they laid out their plans to invest heavily in Sydney property and businesses to the preening man was an unavoidable irritation. Lord Benedict had given the impression of favouritism to Boseman, but the civility had covered a thin layer of patience.

Neither Lord Benedict nor Clement cared at all for investing in Boseman's interests. He was merely a fly sent out to distract Mrs Ponsonby so Clement could investigate the woman's abilities and depth of knowledge without being seen.

Clement entered the long hall and stopped as if he'd come against a wall of ice. He shivered. *So, power is here. How interesting ...*

Voices carried toward him from the cross intersection of this hall to the north-south nave.

'Miss Ponsonby, you seem to know exactly where you're going, while I am repeatedly distracted with the items on display. Have you actually seen an animal like this in real life?'

'Not often, Mr Ridlay. Wombats and cities do not go well together, I'm afraid.'

'They're nocturnal, you know. Perhaps they only come out when you've retired for the evening.'

'Perhaps. Now I do need you to hurry. Mother has requested a likeness of Queen Victoria's face. Do you think you could manage it even though the queen is set so high?'

Clement watched as Miss Ponsonby guided Mr Ridlay away from the taxidermy specimens and toward the statue that held pride of place under the Great Dome. It seemed that he may have to keep a closer eye on the young Miss Ponsonby, and as he had an appointment with Alexander Ridlay later in the day, he knew how he would go about it. He doubted Ridlay would spy for him, but he might be encouraged to share information under the guise of a friendly conversation and with the aid of a fine single malt or two.

The buggy bumped along the poor streets of Sydney's wharf area. No wood-paved roads cleaned nightly down here. Cobbles and mud populated by filthy dogs, raggedy children, hollow-eyed men and grey women. The children appeared happy enough playing their games in the laneways. What did they know of secret evils? Clement noticed one girl, her dress hanging limply to her calves, bare feet streaked with dirt. Her face between child and adult, fairy tale and whimsy into hard-edged reality.

He pulled on the reins and brake and his horse came to a clacking stop.

'I'm looking for Market Wharf. Do you know it?'

The girl's bright blue eyes flashed on him, raked him from top hat to polished leather boot-tip, but she didn't answer.

'I have an artist friend down there. Very nice chap, you may have seen him. A Scot with light hair. Wanders around loaded with cases of paints under his arms and paintbrushes poking out of his pockets.' He imitated Alexander Ridlay on an artistic mission and the girl giggled.

'You don't look half silly,' she said.

'I assure you that is exactly how he walks around.'

A withered face appeared in the window behind the girl; knuckles rapped on a loose pane of glass. The girl half-turned, frowning at the interruption, and gave the figure in the window a dismissive flick of her hand.

'Is that your mother?' Clement asked.

The girl nodded and sighed. 'I'm supposed to be watching the littl'un.' She hooked a thumb in the direction of the laneway where hoots of laughter and the occasional ball rolled out. 'They're so annoying.'

'Well, I don't want to get you in trouble so I'll be on my way.' Clement dipped into his change pocket for a few coins. 'Here's something for your trouble. The quickest way from here is?'

The face had vanished from the window and he had the distinct feeling the front door would open any moment. He dropped two coins into the waiting hand and whispered, 'One for you and one for your mother.'

The girl's smile widened as she hid one coin in her pocket and closed her hand on the other. 'Follow this street along two more blocks then turn left and right straight away. It's steep at the end, but you can leave your horse and buggy outside the butcher down there and they'll be safe enough. The butcher's boy, Jack, is my brother. Tell him I sent you and he'll keep an eye out for you. He's probably seen your funny friend too. He's out and about all the time making deliveries and such.'

The door opened and the face from the window emerged as a full-bodied irritated mother.

'Who's this gent then, Polly? You don't have time to stand around shootin' the breeze.'

'Thank you, Polly.' Clement smiled, took Polly's hand and gave a slight bow. 'No need for concern, madam. I was just after some directions. I won't take up your daughter's time any further.'

Ten minutes later, he was easing into a vacant spot outside the meat market under the suspicious gaze of a young lad with Polly's bright blue eyes.

'Would you be Jack, by chance?' he asked.

'Who wants to know?' the boy said.

Clement ignored the rudeness. 'Your sister, Polly, said you might keep an eye on my horse and buggy.'

'It's safe enough. We're not all thieves and robbers.'

'Of course not. But I have business to attend to and would appreciate the service. I would pay you something for your efforts. Say, two bits now and another when I come back?'

'We don't get many toffs this end of Market Street.' The boy stared with suspicion.

'All above board, I assure you.' Clement dipped into his pocket. 'Have you seen Alexander Ridlay the artist yet today?'

The boy took the money as Clement knew he would. 'Saw him earlier. Drawing seagulls. Messy bloody things, but he likes birds in all settings, he said. So he's set up with an umbrella so he don't get shit on him and tidbits to attract them. Like a seagull needs attracting. He's probably got half the birds in the world flapping about his head by now.'

Clement had to admit, the thought of Alexander with an umbrella up and birds flapping around him was amusing. He doffed his hat to the butcher's lad, and headed in the direction of the wharf and the raucous squawking of a hundred seagulls.

'Taken by force. Given willingly.'

Lord Benedict pressed the dulled point of a bone spear head into the bowl of blood-soaked moss.

Clement waited for a sign other than the renewed throbbing of his hand. It had hardly stopped hurting this past week, the knuckles seizing during sleep and cracking with every waking movement of his swollen fingers.

A dark green stain, brackish with the taint of blood, impregnated the near invisible fissures in the spear tip, bonding the unstable relic like glue. Benedict removed the spear head and submerged it in the grey ash in the fireplace. Ash became glowing embers, and spurts of fire licked the spear as if hungry for the taste of bone and blood.

Clement waited. The spear was an odd shape: shaft mostly gone, either struck off or broken in some battle, only one hand's width long endured. Wood and bone had fused into a singular petrified mass, its edges puckered and ridged. The bone strengthened in the fire and the irregularities became tooled slits, sharp barbs designed to rip and shred any flesh it was withdrawn from. A killing weapon.

His father pulled it from the fire and balanced it on the flat of his palms. His skin blistered and burned, and was ignored.

'Secrets hidden will reveal.' The old man spoke without trace of discomfit; the fire-hot bone of the spear head did not seem to affect him at all. Clement's hand, however, was heavy with pain.

'Take it,' he was urged. Clement reached out. His skin was so tight it shimmered, as if any moment now the skin would peel back to reveal a flayed and useless hand. Veins pulsated a shadowy blue-green below the heel of his palm. His lifeline traced black across his palm, leeched into the corresponding creases, deepened into impossible gullies. He closed his fingers around the fused shaft and bone of the spear and pain seared into every joint of every finger, raced along the sinews of his arm, burst into his shoulder, and lanced through his neck into the base of his skull.

The laughing gorgon that had swallowed his hand appeared before him, a shifting phantom, gurgling with delight as it grinned lewdly. Sharp teeth gnashed and chomped. The beast flickered in the shadows, there and not there, seen and not seen, and drifted, inexorably closer, licking oily lips that dripped like melting wax. Clement couldn't move. Panic threatened to tear his insides to pieces. Hot liquid gushed between his legs. The beast placed stumpy hands on Clement's heaving chest. He couldn't seem to catch his breath. He watched the beast open its awful mouth wide, sink its teeth into his ribs, his heart, and gnaw a passage through to his spine. It slipped inward, stretching itself thin so that every part of him was touched from the inside out and Clement became a glove over the ruinous remnants of the beast.

A gush of steaming vomit burst from Clement's mouth, staining his white shirt with streams of blood and gore. His father smiled beatifically, and in that stretch of lips, Clement saw for the first time the stain of madness. A stain that now infected him.

'And so, you have a voice to the gods,' Lord Benedict intoned.

Soft mewling in Clement's ear calmed him, soothing sounds that countered the evil possession clawing his soul. He spared a glance at his chest, whole and sound, and listened to the multitude of voices inside his head and out.

His father turned to a shrouded table and lifted the flimsy material with a flourish. 'These are the relics I've collected, with your help, of course,' he said, carrying on as if nothing untoward had occurred. 'With just these few, our power has increased. We've joined with forces that will help us change the future of this world.'

On the table were several cleaned bones: fingers, some teeth, the skull Clement had stolen from the Dun Ringall grave, and the empty shallow dish they'd taken on their first visit together. There were items his father didn't know about. Items that weighted his pockets: a brass circlet, an amber disc—and Clement knew there were more bones than his father had on display this night. Enough for two women; a third still to find.

Benedict was nodding, his fingers a hairs-breadth from fondling the brittle bones. 'The woman has the missing piece of the cup. I'm sure of it.' He pointed to the indentation in the centre of the shallow bowl. 'This is a cup of welcome, but it won't welcome anyone until it is complete.'

'Something lays hidden in the Palace, Father,' Clement rasped. A wavery image of a stoic face superimposed by the gorgon's visage. 'Inside the statue.'

'We need the cup restored first. You will have to take their willing gift.'

Clement didn't want to speak. Sound bounced around inside his skull. He blinked back an aching mass behind his eyes. 'It will show me the way?'

'It will be your guide to the inner spaces, Son. With her help, this woman and her ilk will bow before you. The gods will fall over themselves to assist us.'

The inner voice didn't sound as helpful as his father implied it would be. He had the sick feeling that they may have been duped. He opened his mouth to say so, to give warning, but the voice dropped low, filled his mind with shadows, caressed the worry and the madness away.

You will bow before the Mistress of the Dark and tremble ...

ellow pools of light lined Macquarie Street. The occasional twinkle from porches and black windows cast no strength into the black velvet of the night. Midnight had trailed away. Dawn idled on the horizon. Each building was a grey frontage guarding against the night-time mysteries of the Botanical Garden on the opposite side of the street.

Only a few hardy sleepless souls were out. The evening had turned cold early; bitterly so and frost limed the paved road. Smoke dwindled from a thousand chimneys, blanketing the city in a wintry fog that eddied and rolled down pathways and lanes, over fences and walls, coating all with the slime and grit of spent coal.

Clement gripped the spear head hidden in the folds of his cloak. The porch light over the door of the Garden Arms Hotel had been snuffed out. He kneeled by the front stoop and touched the top of the spear to the worn sandstone, letting free the sense of roiling disgust he'd kept bottled inside all night. The sour taste of old vomit and the foul smell of disease. His stomach cramped, his groin scalded, knees fused to the stone, skin and flesh rotted away. All of this sickness flowed from his thoughts to the spear. Lines of loath-

some will filtered through the soft rock and into the building, encircled windows, sizzled as it seeped through gaps in the frames, vined
through every join and brick, peeled the paint from the iron railings, and loosened the roof tiles.

Before him the Georgian-style building appeared to shudder and
sink in on itself. Windows rattled, clouds of mortar drifted down
like snow. Clement felt empty, a used vessel tossed asunder like
refuse, and then the voice sounded and strength flowed in. He
stood, back straight, arms strong. He tilted his head to the sky and
breathed in the smoky air. Every part of him tingled, every hair was
on end. He never felt as alive as this moment.

He could hear the groan of the building, the protections
surrounding it turning to cinder as the power of the spear washed
over them. Street lights blinked out and he was plunged into darkness except for the faint greenish glow of the hotel. No sign of life
came from within. No hastily struck lantern or anxious voice. The
subtlety of the evil Clement had injected would remain disguised
until morning, until the light of day illuminated the damage he had
caused. He wrapped the cloak around him and vanished into the
night, one more shadow in a sea of such. Only the trees of the
Gardens witnessed the attack; they shrank back with a low voiceless
moan, and as dawn leaked across the harbour, withering branches
hung low in despair.

Rosalie woke with a start, head throbbing and eyes burning with
strain. She had stayed up late reading and scribbling notes. Trying
to work out a plan of defence against what she still didn't understand. Every joint ached with fatigue, protesting with sharp stabs of
pain as she attempted to sit.

Something had happened in the night. Her bedroom looked old
and tired, curtains bedraggled, rugs threadbare. Even her hand-
stitched quilt, full of the power and energy of love, appeared faded.
She forced herself to move.

Feet on the floor brought the sensation of rocks inside her heels, loose bones grating against each other, calf muscles so tight she could hardly stand with feet flat. She tiptoed, as tremulous and unbalanced as an age-struck crone, to her dresser and stared horrified at her reflection. That same crone: hair in wispy strands around a face sunken into her skull, eyes blood-rimmed, lips slitted over a cavernous void of a mouth. Her nightdress hung in tatters over her skeletal frame; breasts hung loose and flat on her creviced stomach.

Rosalie screamed, a sound of soul-shriving agony that split her skin to hang as tattered as her clothing from parched bones that dried and crumbled and ground to dust until nothing remained but a mound of ash-like sand on the floor, each grain and flake dissolving into the rotting floorboards, long forgotten; not even a memory of the home that had once stood in this place lingered …

Florentine and Alice were in the kitchen when Rosalie came down. They stood clasped in each other's arms, tears in their eyes.

'What is it?' Rosalie croaked.

Florentine took one horrified look at her mother and sniffed her tears into submission. 'Mother … you?' Her mother's hair was braided but uncombed, face pale. Her dressing-gown haphazardly pulled on and tied. Her feet poked blue with cold from beneath the thick folds.

'I didn't sleep well. A cup of tea and I'll go back upstairs and change. What has happened that you're both weepy and white-eyed?'

Florentine wasn't sure how to explain it. Their beautiful spring garden was dying. Black rot marked all the leaves, flowers drooped, petals dropping with every sway of breeze, white mould crept up trunks and curled around delicate branches. She pulled her mother by her loose dressing-gown sleeve to the back door. Rosalie looked down at her feet, at her toes scrunching the gritty wooden floor.

'Mother, the garden …'

'What is this on the floor?' Rosalie asked before finally turning her attention to the courtyard. Rosalie stepped outside flanked by Florentine, who held onto her elbow, and Alice guarded the rear.

Together the women stared at the wreck of their oasis. 'It's some kind of infection,' Rosalie whispered, kicking at dirt-covered paving usually swept clear.

'And Mother, look at the hotel. Touch the bricks.'

Rosalie lay a hand on the cool sandstone, dragged her fingers along its surface. Her hand came away covered in a layer of pulverised stone; flakes separated from the large bricks and dropped to the ground.

'All of them are the same. Alice and I have checked the whole back wall as far as we can reach. Drew is checking the rest. Bricks don't rot overnight!'

'Magic has been used against us, to draw us out. Call Drew back in and wake the others. We'll need to check the beer and food. We may need to order in new stock or stay closed today.'

'Alice, start in the kitchen. Has Honora not come down yet? And no sign of the bairns? No one ever sleeps late in this household. I'll head upstairs. Florentine, come straight up once you have your brother.'

Alice darted into the kitchen and started opening and closing cupboard doors, pulling out small packets of sugar and dried herbs, and placing them on the table to be thrown out at the end. Weevils squirmed through everything.

Florentine, torn between staying with her mother and doing as told, opted for the latter and raced to the back gate and the lane beyond. She slipped on the old cobblestones. The whole lane was covered in a carpet of brown and grey sticky slime. She had no desire to step in the stuff, but her brother was not to be seen.

'Drew! Dammit!' Florentine held her handkerchief to her nose and mouth. The laneway really did smell awful and she swore fluently into the piece of linen as she ran and slid all the way to Macquarie Street. She poked her head around the corner and waved at her brother standing across the road, mouth agape, staring at the front of the hotel. 'Drew!' Ignored, she hurried to his side to berate him and drag him back inside if she had to. Following his stupefied gaze as she tugged on his arm, her mouth dropped open, stunned at the sight of the building. The windows looked as if they'd been crying black tears that stained the cream-coloured sandstone as they dripped to well on the footpath in puddles of the same sticky grey slime that covered the cobbled lane.

'Mother wants us inside now! I have a terrible feeling we won't be opening for business today.' Florentine renewed her tugs on Drew's arm. 'Come on.'

'I have a terrible feeling we won't be opening ever again,' Drew said. He hurried after Florentine.

In the park behind them, a cloaked figure watched and waited.

Mr Alexander Ridlay arrived just as Anastasia, John, and their young girls were shuffling around the backyard inspecting the decaying plant life. Florentine met him as he strolled in with a confused expression on his face.

'Mr Ridlay. This really is a terrible time for you to be here. Something awful has happened.'

'I see that. Your hotel and garden both look as if they've been struck by the plague. There surely hasn't been enough rain to result in all this damp mould?'

'None at all. Mother is looking into it, but we're frightfully busy. Can you come back another time?'

'Wait!' Rosalie called from the kitchen. 'Bring your young gentleman in please, Florentine. I'd like a word.'

'I'm not sure if I should be pleased or not, Florrie,' he said quietly. 'To be honest, your mother doesn't look at all happy to see me.'

Florentine blushed at his diminution of her name. Her whole family called her Florrie, but from Mr Ridlay it sounded familiar in a way she hadn't experienced before. 'I'm not sure you should be pleased either. We've had a terrible night. It looks like we'll have to stay closed today and Mother is in a frightful mood.' Florentine could hardly come out and say her mother was in the middle of preparing spells and potions to combat whatever it was that had so sneakily attacked them during the night.

Honora, woken from a deep sleep, slurred her words as if she'd been drugged. Aunty Flora stayed in her bed with a migraine. Anastasia and John were soothing their weeping children. Even the twins, usually precocious and brave to the point of harmful behaviour, were subdued into docility by the strange mood that infected them all. Florentine was scared and torn between wanting Mr Ridlay to stay and help, and wanting him tucked away safely in his room at the Royal Society. She held his hand firmly for a second and then pulled free to guide him to her mother.

'Well, I have that drawing you requested of Queen Victoria, should I need a sweetener.' He held up a flat wooden case. 'My da always said bearing gifts was a good way to start.'

'Your da must be very smart then.'

'He was indeed, in his own way.' Mr Ridlay paused in the doorway to remove his hat.

The kitchen table, cleared of turned food, was now cluttered with bowls, a pestle and mortar, new white candles, and brushes made from branches of wattle and elm. An unusual oval platter held a colour palette of grainy clay-based paints.

Rosalie waved him in. 'Don't mind us, young man. Meddling in old wives' tales and kitchen help recipes. Careful you don't get flour on your coat there.'

'Mrs Ponsonby, good morning. Has that chap been causing you problems again? Fl— I mean, Miss Ponsonby was telling me that things are out of sorts here today.'

'Not this time, sir. Not this time. Nothing we can't see right, now we know what we're dealing with.'

Florentine nudged the hand holding the case. 'And I brought along a sketch I've been working on for you, Mrs P. Florentine mentioned how much you admired the statue of our beloved Queen Victoria installed in the Garden Palace, and I've drawn her likeness for you.'

Honora grunted and mumbled something about young men

courting. Rosalie stopped what she was doing and wiped her hands on her apron. 'How considerate, Mr Ridlay. Let's go into the dining room, shall we? You can show me your drawing while we chat.'

Florentine tried not to let her nerves get away from her when Mr Ridlay was so familiar with her mother. Really, what was he thinking? But he seemed to have fallen into the pattern of intimacy and affection that came with long-held friendship. It suited him somehow and she had to admit that she too felt as if they'd been acquainted much longer than a few short weeks.

She followed them through the kitchen and into the dining room. The room showed no trace of the ritual and ceremony performed there only two nights previous. The table was covered in a pale-yellow cotton cloth embroidered with tiny rosebuds. A dried native arrangement stood in the centre. The fireplace was stacked with wood waiting to be lit. Above it, the mantelpiece clock stood silent and still.

Mr Ridlay placed the case on the table and opened it. The sketch of Queen Victoria lay on top; her face rigid as bronze and soft as a woman should be. Her eyes stared straight out as if no mere slip of paper could ever truly contain her.

Florentine had no words to describe how proud she was of Mr Ridlay's talent at that moment. To speak would break the spell. Her mother clearly agreed as she remained silent, tracing the lines of the queen's face and smoothing the paper on which she rested.

'I've also included a drawing of the full statue and a detail of her hands holding the laurel and sceptre.' Mr Ridlay lifted the top page, handing it to Rosalie, and took the next two to lay out on the table.

'They are excellent likenesses,' Rosalie said in a quiet voice. She returned her attention to the box and the pad full of sketches, notes, and loose dried plant samples. 'What's this?' she asked. The top page was covered in strange symbols, curving and twisting, interlocking in places, and at the centre, the image of a grotesque face, tongue protruding large and deformed.

Mr Ridlay hurried to hide the dark image, pulling out lower

pages that contained his more usual subject of botanical art, but Rosalie held the page and pulled it from his grasp.

She stared at it, expression hardening. 'I ask again. What is this?'

'I was given permission to view the statue from the base of its pedestal. It is positioned on a stage. The symbols are carved around the outer edge and the face is in the centre. It's not an uncommon carving, adorns quite a few of the older churches back home, but I've not seen it in this context before.'

'One does not often observe the base of a statue,' Rosalie murmured.

'An excellent location for secret symbology though. Once planted, a statue is often a near-permanent edifice. I wonder at the sculptor's religious practices. It is an odd place for a carving most often seen above a church door and used for requesting fertility.'

Rosalie looked up sharply and seemed about to say something, but her lips twisted on the words, realising perhaps that the young artist had not yet been shown as friend or foe. Florentine wasn't sure either. She wanted to trust him with every secret she knew. He'd shown no deeply ingrained prejudices or religious fervour of any kind, and mild disdain whenever politics was mentioned.

Florentine could see in her mother's searching expression that Mr Ridlay may be sincere, but he had still to prove himself. The face had figured in her mother's journal—just once, near the end, in the bottom corner of a page filled with a description of wild seas and howling winds. Hiding in the journal as it hid on the statue.

Biding time.

Whatever words Rosalie had intended to utter, what came out was, 'Florentine tells me you have an excellent portrait of an albatross …'

Mr Ridlay seemed a little surprised with the abrupt change of subject and cast a glance at Florentine before smiling broadly. 'I do indeed. However, I don't have it with me today. I would be happy to return with other pieces this afternoon.'

Doors banging open and closed, and heavy footsteps on the

stairs reminded them all that outside the calm of the dining room, events were unfolding.

'Florentine, would you please go help Anastasia while your young man and I chat some more about art?'

'Mam, I don't think ...' Florentine started to protest and stopped. Arguing with her mother had never got her anywhere and even less so today when everything hinged on Rosalie's ability to command and that her knowledge be trusted was paramount. 'Yes, Mam.' She gave Mr Ridlay's hand a squeeze, smiled, and left the room.

'Now, Mr Ridlay. Tell me about your mother ...'

Mr Ridlay's answer was muffled as the door closed on the dining room and Florentine was thrust back into the crisis of the rest of the hotel.

Alexander Ridlay walked from the laneway beside the hotel straight across the road and through the open gates of the Gardens. His drawing box was tucked tight under one arm. Clement watched him pass by from the shade of a young casuarina tree. Their conversation the previous day, punctuated by seagull cries and droppings, had let him to conclude that young Mr Ridlay was quite enamoured of Miss Florentine Ponsonby.

'Who is that?'

'That, m'dear, is the gent I want you to distract.' Clement pulled his gloves tighter over his hands and tugged on his jacket sleeves. The woman he'd hired came with glowing references: discreet, smart, and beautiful. Clear blue eyes that sparkled when she laughed and pale pink lips that were entirely kissable. Her drawling accent with a touch of London and the occasional perfectly pronounced Parisian edge was enchanting, and Clement knew that he was in danger of being distracted by Adelaide Blum himself.

'Alexander, did you say? Scottish? A passionate people; strong and determined. And earnest. He appears quite earnest.'

'He is. The type that would most certainly put himself in harm's way should a situation warrant it. I want him out of harm's way.'

Adelaide raised an eyebrow. 'Mr Benedict. How altruistic of you. And how you raise my curiosity. I did not realise you had such a selfless side. You must be close friends, or perhaps more?'

'We are acquaintances. Nothing more. However, he is becoming involved in something I wish him away from. Also, having him … distracted … will assist in unsettling the opponents in a little game I'm playing. Do you think you can manage it, Miss Blum?'

Miss Blum twirled her dainty parasol and lifted it to provide a modicum of added privacy to their tête-à-tête. Her smile transformed from innocent pout to lusty beam. Clement's body answered. He leant forward, legs softened in their stance, head lowered. His hand on her elbow pulled her closer.

'Yes, Mr Benedict. I can manage distraction very well.' She let his lips come so close to hers, he felt their warmth, and then they were gone. 'I can manage it, control it, and shape it to any form I choose.' She laughed, twirled the parasol again, and stepped away, adjusting her hat and patting her hair. She lifted the edge of her skirts enough to allow her slippered foot to peek out from the filmy fabric. 'I don't have my walking shoes on, but they should suffice for a stroll through the gardens. It's such a glorious day after all, and you never know who you might meet.'

Clement straightened, caught out by the woman's skill in manipulation. 'I believe you.' His gentle touch on her arm hardened, trapping her by his side a moment longer. 'Be careful who you play your games with, Miss Blum,' he warned.

Her gay expression did not change, but Clement could see the steel hidden deep within her. 'I charge extra for bruises, Mr Benedict.'

Clement's fingers tightened a fraction more. This hard version of Miss Adelaide Blum set his blood on fire. 'We'll come to a suitable arrangement at a later time. For now, set your charms upon Alexander. Keep him away from the Garden Arms Hotel and his attention on you. Do not mention me.' He released her then and watched her saunter along the path Mr Ridlay had taken. She disappeared around a bend and into a forest of she-oak and eucalypts. Clement almost felt sorry for Alexander. He was a nice chap after all and did not deserve the dilemma and temptation about to fall upon him.

The heat of the moment took longer than expected to dissipate, so Clement bided his time in the shade of the tree. He had two options now. Return to the grand exhibition building or pay a visit to Boseman's office by the quay. The building dominated the gardens with its arches, columns, pennants, and sheer size. The thought of entering its vast halls again sent a wave of lethargy through him. His gaze blurred as he looked out from half-closed eyes, his arms and legs cumbersome with dread. A quick walk down to the water was more preferable and his demeanour lifted as the lure of the sea-going ships and river cruisers tied to the wharves beckoned him.

Decision made, he left the protection of the casuarina, avoided looking at the Garden Arms Hotel to hide his intense interest in its condition, and went to find George Boseman.

The strain of the rituals took their toll on Lord Benedict. He watched his son grow stronger while he shrivelled. His hands shook with palsy and his knees weakened. Outside his room, the plush hallway of the Union Club was hushed. Dust mites danced in the warm air lit by plumes of diffracted radiance. The stained-glass window that overlooked the hall and stairwell took the sunshine and turned it into an artist's palette of light.

He'd closed the door on the desultory air and the noiseless club with the distinct sensation that he had forgotten something, that someone somewhere was laughing good and hard at his foolishness. His head pounded as he crossed to his chair by the window and thrust aside the heavy curtains guarding against the day. He opened his mouth on a gasp for air and realised he'd been grinding his teeth so hard his jaw felt like it was being pried open. He ran his hand over his face and forced the muscles to relax. They ticked and jumped, and spasmed with a life of their own. The window reflected an insane grin, wild darting eyes, and a scattering of white hair standing on end over a pallid skull. Benedict turned to see who had entered the room unheard behind him and saw only the heavy furniture and his unmade bed. Not even a ghost skulked in the gloomy depths.

He was tempted to inspect his collection of relics. Without the spear head, the objects seemed to have decreased in importance. The energy he sensed within them receded. The bones they'd stolen from Ireland and Scotland lay hidden in gauze and wadding, nothing more than gruesome evidence of his growing turpitude. And he'd cursed his son with the same degradation.

Clement had not been able to fully describe his experiences during the ceremonies. Algernon had visions of hideous monsters, murky and opaque figures that lurched through his memories, but nothing more. The monsters passed him by, unaware of his presence, on their way to meet with his son.

He poured himself a brandy and felt the smooth taste of cinnamon and sweet toffee relax his grimacing face. The gentle aroma of the liquor helped settle his thoughts. He walked to the box that held his treasures; perhaps the vitality of the bones would return if he freed them from their confines. Sipping the brandy, he reached out and undid the catch. He started with surprise as the lid popped and a trickle of dank air escaped with a hiss. A low moan set his teeth on edge and he clamped his mouth closed, only to feel the vibration of the sound swell in his throat demanding to be released. He pressed his lips tight and flung open the lid.

Just bones.

Then he realised that the grey of the ancient bones, long-buried, had bleached white, and that each piece appeared reconnected by ghostly cartilage and spider-silk tendons. A skeletal hand, one finger missing, sat nestled in the remains of the protective wrapping. A part-hand made from the remains of two different skeletons. Skin, dried and withered by death and time, spread over the knuckles.

Benedict clapped his hand over his mouth as the moan locked inside became a scream and his lips parted to let it out. He backed away from the box and the table, and sat heavily in his chair, brandy spilling over the edge of the glass, his fingers creating bloodless craters in his cheeks as he fought to keep the screams in.

CHAPTER 14

The Garden Arms Hotel had once gravitated toward genteel respectability for all that it was a hotel. A week after the invisible night-time battle, it was as scarred and jaded as any wharf-side pub. Scaffolding was installed and cleaning was in process, but Rosalie doubted whether it would ever look as it had. Every day since the attack, something else had gone wrong. Beer had gone flat and soured. Food had turned rancid. Even the coffee in the tearoom tasted burnt; the dainty cakes and sandwiches stale and unappetising. Custom had dropped. Money owed had risen. Staff were reporting harassment by the few customers they had left, or worse, in the street. People knew who they were and where they worked and wished to punish them for their loyalty. One week was all it took to bring their reputation and their luck tumbling down in ruins around them.

Rosalie stood in the doorway, arms crossed, face stern, foot tapping a staccato rhythm on the step. Former customers, former friends rushed past or crossed the street to avoid her dire mood.

Boseman had visited with a shark-eyed gleam and offered to buy her out. She'd given him short shrift and warned him not to darken her doorstep again. The odious man scented victory, but she was not beaten. This aberration in fortunes was a breathing space between old and new. Her plans needed time to come to fruition. Her spells needed to sink their roots into the land and their energies into the skies. They had far to travel and much to negotiate.

Across the road, one of Boseman's lads loitered. When people passed by, he affected a smirk that masked his face. When he was alone on the street, the mask slipped and his indecision was plain to see.

'Will!' Rosalie called out to him. He blushed, ducked his head, slanted a nervous look to his left and right, and slouched across the road. Rosalie stepped back and Will walked by her and into the hotel. She cast her own suspicious gaze up and down the street, and then went inside as well, closing and locking the door behind her.

Mr Kent shook hands with George Boseman, placed his hat on his head, buttoned his coat and strode away from the clandestine meeting without bothering to check his surroundings. His steel-tipped cane tapped his steps out on the cobbled lane and faded into the street noise of the busy road beyond.

'He's an arrogant man,' Clement commented from the shadows.

'Detestable,' Boseman agreed. 'But he's useful. And he's done more to speed along the Garden Arms' decline than my lads have been able to. Sneaky as they come, is Kent. My boys are capable, but obvious. These things have to be handled with some circumspection or we'll have the local constabulary up in arms, or worse, the loyal clientele.'

'As you say. I'm not concerned with the finer details of your sabotage. Confusion and chaos, no matter how its gained, is the outcome I require. Consider the scraps your reward for faithful service.'

'What are you getting me into here?' Boseman faced Clement with a look of distaste. 'Are your secrets going to get me hanged?'

'It is merely a matter of ownership. Mrs Ponsonby has something that belongs to my father. My aim is to return the item to its rightful place and our family to its rightful position in society.'

'Send in a thief then. Why all the games?'

'The games make it more enjoyable and increase the value of the item.' Clement tired of the conversation. Kent was long gone and their only company in this isolated lane were shadows and the occasional prostitute with her customer.

'Have it your way,' Boseman responded, shrugging. 'I'll send my lads in tomorrow. See if they can't add to the chaos for you.'

Clement ignored him and walked away in the opposite direction to Kent, down to the water.

Fresh air rarely found its way into the dense atmosphere of Dickens' Billiards Hall. Cigar and pipe smoke competed with low-slung oil lamps dropping light over each table. Conversation flowed, less rowdy than pub-talk, just as consumed by current affairs, gossip, and solutions to the problems of the world.

Drew slipped in past the doorman into the main room of spectators, players, and staff. Tables stood in two straight lines down the middle of the room. Some empty and quiet—it was only mid-afternoon—others ringed by men with rolled-up sleeves, suspenders, and caps sitting cock-eyed over intense faces. The game was all important. Flow. Strategy. Technique. Concentration overruled conversation.

Behind the players stood the waiters—chatty, expressive as they caught up on all the news, and the watchers—eyes narrowed as they followed the click and clack of balls. A few men nodded as Drew strolled past. Clancy Dickens, owner of the billiard hall and an old friend of James Ponsonby, stopped his passage with a hand to his shoulder.

'How's your mam, young Ponsonby? Heard you had some trouble at the Arms.'

'Well thanks, Mr Dickens, and nothing we can't handle. Mam reckons larrikins on the piss …'

Clancy cuffed the back of Drew's head. 'Sure, an' that isn't what she would have said.'

'Near enough.' Drew shrugged and tried not to gag on the old man's tobacco breath as he leant in closer.

'You let your mam know from me that a few of us are getting together to keep an eye on the place. Your da was a great mate and we'll be takin' steps to prevent any more mishaps. We'll be in tonight to square things up with John too. Jim set a lot of store in that son-in-law of his.'

'What do you know about what's happening?' Drew squirmed as Clancy's fingers bit harder into his shoulder.

'Enough to know something's not right. We're from the same country, boy, same traditions, same lore. It doesn't get spoken about because it's not safe, but it doesn't need to. We know your mam. We know cunning folk when we see them. Now, what business are you about this afternoon?'

'No business. Had some time, thought I might watch a few games.'

Clancy frowned. 'I've known you since you were in swaddling clothes, boyo. Don't be trying to pull the wool over my eyes now.'

Drew considered his weak excuse. Da had always said that Clancy Dickens was a lot smarter than he looked and as reliable as the sun starting and ending each new day. 'Will Downs,' he said.

'End table on the left.' Clancy nodded in that general direction. 'Mind your step though, Drew. He's with Harry Whistler. Mean temper, that one.'

'I can look after myself,' Drew answered.

Clancy patted his shoulder before giving him a push. 'Mind yourself all the same. No point courting trouble.'

Drew walked the length of the room. All he wanted to do was catch Will's attention. He had no plan to get close to Whistler.

Splotches of colour filtered through high stained-glass windows. The architecture was from an older time, when the billiard room was home to Dickens Theatre. When the theatre had closed its curtains on the final show, Clancy Dickens had demolished the stage to make way for a competition billiard table of solid carved oak. The auditorium seating had been ripped out and replaced with a sturdy floor and several everyday billiard tables. The former dressing room doors were labelled Reading Room and Smoking Room, and had sharp-eyed doormen stationed at each.

The last table on the left took up the corner where once a piano had sat belting out dramatic music. Will Downs was bent low over the green felt, lining up his shot. His final for the game if he touched cue to ball just right. Drew hung back to avoid distracting Will and gaining the attention of Harry Whistler. Will's eyes narrowed, lips thinned, and with the barest of movements nudged the white ball to the black. A little bit of steel in that nudge, the clock of the balls was audible. The black ball travelled true, slowing as it reached its destination, pausing at the lip of the corner pocket and dropping in to secure a victory.

Will stayed motionless as if unsure and then a broad grin crossed his face and he straightened, flushed with pride. His beam didn't falter as he saw and winked at Drew, and turned to a sullen Harry.

Of all the lads that worked for George Boseman, Harry Whistler was the most chancy: hard-bitten and mean. His ratty hair was hidden by a flat-topped woollen cap he'd stolen from a Polish immigrant. Boseman's lads haunted the wharves looking for gullible new arrivals and a chance to steal and cheat. Drew was no fool. Will Downs wasn't of sterling character and his trustworthiness had still to be decided, but his mam had drawn him in and believed he would be useful. Loyal remained to be proven.

Drew didn't hang around. He stepped between tables, weaving around players and, following the wall to the main door, paused behind a coat rack until he was certain the doorman's attention was elsewhere. While the man was busy talking with a customer, Drew ducked across the street beyond to wait for Will to join him.

Dusk dropped a greying curtain over the harbour. In summer,

there'd be streaks of unforgiving light; early spring too weak to put up a fight. Blue skies faded and day became night with an unhurried air of acquiescence to the natural order of things. Here and there, patches of gold lit up treetops or glinted from windows, and then they too faded. Men and women pulled their coats and collars tighter against the cooling temperatures, hats came down tighter, steps were short and rushed, keen to reach home and warming fires.

George Boseman had left his office at the start of dusk, the wings of victory flapping at his heels, his chest puffed, shoulders back, and a haughty expression crossing his face whenever someone dared to halt his journey. Customs House, a short walk from the Boseman & Hinckley Lawyers and Custom Agents office, waited his arrival, holding its breath and expelling stale air, along with its many clerks, at five pm. Boseman walked in on the inhalation in time for his daily meeting with several of the agents who worked within.

Drew followed Will Downs into the building that housed Boseman's offices and up the stairs. From the outside the building was covered in ornate, gothic elements of architecture that gave the façade a haunted, looming appearance. Gargoyle faces peered over the balconies, guarding the path below. By the chimney, another with stone wings outstretched waited to take flight toward unsuspecting pedestrians.

From the first step inside, Drew could see it was all a pretence. The forbidding stone façade was just that, a façade. Behind the veneer of sandstone, the building was wood and probably as rickety as its less salubrious neighbours. Office doors on the ground floor were closed and dark, not a hint of the type of business that went on behind them. Will jogged up the stairs to Boseman's office and unlocked it with a key he'd kept hidden in his pocket.

'Who's Hinckley?' Drew asked. The name was lettered alongside Boseman on the door.

Just enough light reached in through the windows to show a small neat desk guarding a filing cabinet and a glass-doored bookshelf. To the right, the inner door to Boseman's sanctum appeared much stronger than the outer. Will had the key to that one as well.

'There is no Hinckley,' Will said, waiting for the key to click in the lock before gently pushing the door open. 'I'm not even sure there's a Boseman.'

'What do you mean?'

'No one notices, because he keeps his shirt sleeves rolled down all the time, but he's got a convict tattoo above his wrist. Right there.' Will pointed to a spot half to his elbow on his left arm. 'Skull and crossbones with a name underneath—not Boseman. On his chest,' he lay his hand flat above his heart, 'a woman on a gibbet. Right gruesome, he is.'

'How do you know it's a convict tattoo?'

'Did it himself, you can tell. The skull and crossbones anyway.'

Drew wasn't sure what to make of the information. One or two of his da's friends were ex-convicts. Maybe he could ask them if they knew Boseman. They might know what he'd been sent away for. Not much he could do about it now, so he shrugged and pointed at the key ring in Will's hand.

'Does he know you've got those keys?' Drew asked. They went into an office cluttered with paperwork. Every wall was lined with bookshelves fat with journals, papers, and shipping registers. Broadsheets were stacked in one corner and over half the desk. The chairs were old and well used. Only a low square table by the window was clear of papers. 'Is it always this messy?'

'No and yes,' Will answered. 'He keeps his important papers locked away. I have a key for that too.' Will's grin was on the demonic side. He jingled his key ring and chose a small key from the collection.

Drew went to the cleared table. It struck him as odd that there'd be one organised surface when everything else was covered in paper. Beside it, in a compartmentalised case, were rolls of papers, some bound by string, others in leather cases.

'That's his map table,' Will said. He'd removed a pile of folders from one of the locked drawers and was rifling through them.

Drew nodded, already unrolling a map of the east coast of Australia. Pencil and pin marks covered the sheet of paper; lines from one point to others, notations on conditions, a list of barques and their captains. Drew rolled it again and put it away. A sheaf of smaller maps had caught his attention. He smoothed them out and saw that they were street maps. The top page provided a key, colours and abbreviations for construction type in the main. Turning to the next page, a whole city block in vivid pinks, yellows, and blues detailed whether buildings were business or residential, and the number of storeys of each. Drew stopped at the third page. It didn't need the street labels to declare itself the same block that the Garden Arms Hotel was situated. Multiple circles of ink looped around the plot. The blank area that Drew knew was the Botanical Gardens and the Garden Palace was covered in deranged hand-writing and inkblots. His mother's name was mentioned several times above a hastily scrawled plan to rip out the tearooms and turn the whole bottom floor into a giant saloon. Scribbled notes indi-cated plans for the top two storeys, but Drew had stopped reading. Across the bottom corner of the page was written: *Ponsonby out. Boseman in!*

'I've found something,' Will said, and Drew quickly removed the page from the collection, folded it, and stuffed it down his shirt before turning to the desk. Will was scanning lines of type with his finger, lips moving as he read. He looked up, face shining as if he'd won a round of cards or billiards. 'See for yourself. It's a report on your mam. Boseman's really got it in for her.'

Will moved so Drew could sit down. The type was easier to read than the untidy handwriting on the street map, but no more palat-able. Boseman knew far more about his mother than he should; when and where she was born, when she came to Australia, all her business dealings were listed, her friends and business acquain-tances, her children. Unruly handwriting on the last page contained accusations of witchcraft. Drew was sure they were all fabricated. Boseman seemed of the opinion that being female and in business was enough justification to warrant suspicion. Still, he leant over so

Will couldn't read over his shoulder, and closed the report with a slap when he was finished.

'Pinned to the folder is the name of the man he compiled the report for,' Will said. He walked over to the door and peered out. "Have you heard of a Lord Benedict?'

Drew opened the cover and read the details of the transaction: *Report compiled for Lord Algernon Benedict. 24 August 1882. Copy provided.* Someone else was after this information?

'No, but this explains some things. We thought someone was watching the hotel and this confirms it. It was Boseman all along, or one of his lads.' He cast Will a suspicious glare.

'Not me, mate,' Will said. 'Maybe Harry though. He's a sneaky bastard and keeps things close to his chest. My parents'll go green when I tell them. What are you doing?'

Drew was unbuttoning his shirt and pants so he could slide the folder under his clothes. He rebuttoned his pants, hoping the now snug fit would hold the papers in place. 'I have to show my mam. Put everything back in place so he can't tell we've been here.'

'He'll notice. This might look like a mess, but he knows where everything is.'

'I have no choice. At least he won't know who took it.' He pulled out two more folders. 'Here, take these too. Might help to throw off suspicion.'

'You're a sneaky bastard too,' Will said. He took the folders and layered them between his undergarments and his shirt in a similar fashion to Drew. 'We better get out of here then, seeing how we've taken to thieving as well as snooping. Boseman'll throw a fit and I don't fancy being around when he does.'

They made sure the drawers were closed and locked, and papers were where they were meant to be. The plans of the city were rolled and tucked into their slot. The boys left with some haste. Dusk was descending into night and they couldn't risk a light where there was not meant to be. They reached the ground floor and hightailed it out the front door without noticing Harry walking down the path on the other side of the street.

CHAPTER 15

The paper was cheap, thin, and the writing so scrawled in parts, Rosalie needed a magnifying glass to distinguish letters. The content was damning. George Boseman had been spying on her. He knew everything, or thought he did. Two thirds of the report were factual, dry reading. Boseman, or his secretary, must have combed shipping and business records, copying out pertinent facts that could have related to anyone arriving in the colony.

It wasn't until he'd uncovered records from England that he'd found any links between herself and the MacKinnons, and they were tenuous at best. Rosalie suspected that he'd only continued because he wanted the Garden Arms Hotel. At any cost. Several pages referred to another woman of about the same age, and even Aunt Flora had been considered, and discounted.

That the report had been conducted under instructions from Lord Algernon Benedict underpinned the sickening sensation she'd had when in his presence. An untidy reference to a Clement Benedict made her nervous. She hadn't heard of this gentleman. Knowing there were two connected by blood explained the ferocity and personal nature of the attack.

But she didn't know the Benedict family or their connection to the MacKinnons. Her suspicion grew as she came to the end and the fresh-inked accusations of black magic. Boseman, whether he knew it or not, was under the influence of Chaos. He certainly made a good subject.

Rosalie read through the report another two times before putting it aside to think. Emphasis had been placed on the date of her arrival in Port Jackson. The Benedicts had been searching for an arrival in either 1851 or 52. Specifics on identification had included female, surname MacKinnon, and hailing from Broadford, Parish, of Strath. A general description that could have fit hundreds of women. Had their only solid lead been based entirely on Boseman's animosity and greed? She would never know and it hardly mattered.

They'd found her, and to be looking in the first place, they must be connected to the night she'd fled her home. If they knew who she was then they must also know or suspect what she had in her possession. It stood to reason these were the same men responsible for the grave robbing. And Mairi's murder.

The mystery was, why? Why had Lord Benedict come to her village all those years ago and why was he still searching for her? The relics had to be the answer, but to what purpose?

Rosalie dozed in her chair, nodding off when exhaustion claimed her, jerking awake with the sensation of falling into an abyss. Several times she thought she heard voices, someone walking about their room, another crying out in their sleep. Until dawn came, and with the light enough peace to drift into dreamless slumber.

She awoke an hour later, the twins standing in front of her, staring at their mother asleep in her chair instead of in bed. Their curious expressions ripped through her. She'd neglected them the past two weeks. Shuffled them off with Aunt Flora or to their rooms, keeping them out of the way and protected.

'Mam, why're you sleeping in the chair?'

'You'll get an awful sore neck.'

'Good morning, my lovelies. Aren't I a silly old thing?' Rosalie held out her arms and the twins bundled onto her lap.

'You were snoring!'

'I'm very tired.' Rosalie hoped she hadn't been drooling. The twins were certain to notice and tell everyone.

'Is everything all right, Mam?'

Rosalie's heart clenched. How she missed her rambunctious twins.

'Aunty Flora wants to go home and wants us to go with her for a holiday.'

'She says they've got sheep and cows and kangaroos.'

'And so many galahs, the sky turns pink and grey every time they fly past.'

'Can we go, Mam? Can we?'

Rosalie knew that Flora's thoughts were turning to her own family. Her northern home would suit the girls and they would stay safe to be their mother's vanguard, should events in the city not go well. Now was a good time for travelling with the worst of winter behind them and summer not yet here.

'It sounds like an adventure.' Rosalie squeezed them tight. 'I'll miss you awfully. Will you promise to write? And send me drawings of all these birds and animals?' The twins nodded. 'Well, I'll talk to Aunty about it today.'

The twins jumped up and ran out of the room squealing with delight and imitating the hordes of animals they were going to see as they ran back along the hallway.

Flora had put her to shame taking care of her children's safety when she should have thought of it sooner. She needed a large pot of tea and time to think.

They needed occupants in the guest rooms. Their last guest had departed complaining of evil odours and strange noises. He'd refused to stay long enough to eat breakfast on the day everything turned sour. Rosalie couldn't blame him. But her anger at the situation boiled.

When Will arrived, scared at his own bravery and the likely

response from Boseman, Rosalie had him sign the guest book under a pseudonym and sent him up to Room 1. And then she'd signed in several more fictitious guests and sent Drew off to make the rooms appear lived in.

Rosalie went downstairs feeling as if she had the upper hand. The Benedicts had been exposed as the master puppeteers. They were behind Boseman's stubborn refusal to go away, the awful Mr Kent's relentless inspections, and had used magic to deface her hotel and spoil food and drinks.

She put the kettle on the stove, thinking of George Boseman, and her ace-in-the-hand, young William Downs. A larrikin to be sure, but one with a sliver of conscience and a growing hatred of his boss. Will had informed her of Mr Kent's alliance with Boseman. The inspector she would handle herself. She would send the boy back to Boseman to spy and cause havoc. Now he'd committed his first acts of defiance he was only too willing to commit more.

Her strategy ready, Rosalie thought next of her family. Aunty Flora would return to her northern home, taking the twins with her. She wanted to urge the same precautions for Anastasia and John, but knew they would never leave. Instead, she'd talk to Amy Shadler about taking them in. They'd stay close by, yet removed enough to feel their children were safe. Anastasia would be needed in the fight ahead.

That left Florentine, Drew, Honora, and the staff. Bridie had family in Parramatta. She could send her home with a full purse and a glowing reference for her next employer. Honora would stay by her side until the end. They'd already discussed it, and Rosalie was glad for such undying support. Alice was her next problem. Her position at the hotel was no longer tenable and she feared for her future with every minute that she stayed. Alice too would be provided with compensation and a reference.

The kettle whistled on the hob and Rosalie removed it from the heat to fill her teapot, almost dropping it when she saw Alice's mother, Edith, in the doorway.

'We're leaving the city. There's better fishing at Kamay and my cousin wants some help with her guiding. Alice will come with us for now.'

Rosalie placed the kettle back on the stove. She wanted to hug the woman, but knew it wouldn't be welcome. 'Will you and the others be safe?'

Edith nodded. 'Some'll go to Kamay, some Wreck Bay ...' She hesitated before passing Rosalie a small parcel. 'The spirits have been talkin' to the aunties. They say to listen to the silences and the land, and not to fear fire. It is rebirth, a good thing. The land rejects the new evil, remember that. The fella who brought it is sick.'

Rosalie started to pull at the string wrapped around the package. Edith stopped her. Rosalie was surprised to see tears in her eyes. 'Edie? What else have the aunties seen?'

'This is not for you to open, not for now.' Edith handed her a banksia seed pod. Its golden bristles had been burned away in a bush fire and replaced by thin strips of soft possum fur. Each seed cavity contained a shell polished to a fine gleam. Two of the cavities held black stones. Below the stone setting, the pod had been carved and the smooth interior painted black. It reminded her of the face that Alexander had drawn and the small hiding figures in her journal.

'I made this for you as a gift because our families are linked. It is not lore, but I have ...' Edith paused, appearing to choose her words carefully. 'I have prayed over it. You will travel into the depths, and this will show the way back. Be careful. Only one of you can use it. The other will have to stay.'

A cold shiver scrambled from her neck to the base of her spine. A tingle of energy passed from Edith to Rosalie with the sharing of the seed pod token.

'And watch your boy. They're planning to use him against you. Alice and me both seen this.'

'Please keep Alice safe. She's special. We'll miss her terribly. And thank you. For these.' Rosalie held up the satchel and pod. 'And for trusting us with Alice. She will do wonderful things in the future. I can feel it.'

Edith turned away and left. The garden gate squealed as she opened it and clicked closed behind her. Alice was already gone.

~

The sharp burn of fresh-cut onions pervaded every corner of the kitchen. Anastasia stood as close to the open kitchen window as she could get, chopping and dicing her way through a whole bag of bulbs. Her eyes were red-rimmed as she worked on, filling one large bowl with the vegetable cut in half, skin still attached, another with clean chopped pieces to go in a hearty soup later, and a small bowl full of finely diced for Honora.

Honora worked the last of the dried juniper berries in the mortar and pestle, grinding each husk against the side of the mortar in short, efficient movements until she had a granulated powder, to which she added two drops of vervain oil and the finely diced onion. The juice of the onion brought tears to her eyes, but she was well used to that and worked on, letting her tears fall into the mix. The dark purple sticky paste that resulted would form the protective base for various recipes, giving them the depth they needed to perform the magic Rosalie required.

Anastasia let her onion tears dry on her face and called John in from the garden to help deliver her bounty around the hotel. The black salt had to be cleaned away and replaced with a half onion, cut side up, in every fireplace, above every door, and on every upstairs windowsill.

Rosalie and Florentine continued a task they'd been working on for several weeks. Labelling herbs and oils, noting potency and toxicity, uses and lore, until Florentine's fingers cramped on her pencil and her vision blurred. The urgency of these last few days compounded with the vast knowledge she was trying to memorise made her breathless with worry. She worked on as she knew she must, as did they all.

A shadow passed by the window, and a few moments later Drew joined his sister and mother.

'Will's talked to his dad about Boseman,' Drew said. 'They'll keep an ear to the ground. He's not happy that he didn't know about the Englishman, but he knows now and will do what he can. Will's mam sent this over.' Drew handed Rosalie a bulky rolled cloth bundle tied with coarse string and smelling of sweet wine. 'She said that it's been grown here, but its mother was from the old country and that all the right prayers have been said and it's safe for you to use.'

Rosalie took the bundle and placed it on the bench between herself and Florentine. 'This will need a whole page of your note-book to itself.' She turned to her son and stepped forward to give him a hug. 'Tell Will to pass on my thanks. Is everything else in place?'

'Yes, Mam. Mr Kent is on his way over. We watched him leave. Will is searching his office now. I followed the old geezer halfway, then took a shortcut. He won't be far behind me.' Drew frowned at the array of items on the benches and hanging from the ceiling. 'All this is bound to make him suspicious. The whole hotel stinks of onion.'

'We're ready for his visit, Drew. Mr Kent sees the world in black and white. He won't see or smell anything other than what he expects to see or smell. We are cooking, that is all. Now, I have another chore for you. Would you please go upstairs and help your Aunty Flora with the twins? Their train is first thing tomorrow morning and I need their trunks downstairs tonight to load onto the cart.'

Florentine kept her concerns to herself. She was already under instruction to keep her notebook on her person. Rosalie's old journal was hidden away in the cellar and the few tools they'd been using were everyday items. Not a hint of the arcane would be found in the Garden Arms Hotel.

Kent passed under the onion-laid lintel of the front door with a sniff, a sneeze, and a flourish of his yellowing handkerchief. Floren-tine mumbled a polite *bless you*, and followed him through each of the rooms as he made his inspection. His sneezing continued and from the back of his throat came a congested wheeze whenever he opened his mouth to speak. Fortunately for Florentine, he ignored her presence and spoke little.

He did not appear to hear at all the low muttering that filtered down from the top floor of the house and sprung like surprised butterflies every time he opened a door. On the second floor, a faint scent of burning coriander lingered, and on the stairwell, between the guest accommodation and the family rooms above, tiny lights splashed against the walls and railings. He held his head as if dizzy and, though one foot was already on the stairs leading up, turned and made his way down instead.

Honora welcomed his arrival in the kitchen with a grunt, and spooned salt and black pepper into onion soup. Along the top shelf of the dresser were lined a row of glass vials full of her special seasonings. They were always there and the inspector had seen them many times before. Today he paid them no attention whatsoever. His interest was piqued in the pantry by the crate of wine on the bench and the single bottle left open to breathe. He read the label and was offered a taste, but he declined and left with only a glance at the pantry shelves. They too appeared as they always did. His knowledge of herbs was minimal at best and he saw nothing that he did not expect to see.

Tiny words quivered in the air all around him. He sniffed and sneezed. When Honora opened a jar of pickled radishes, he paled and escaped to the garden to speak with Rosalie.

'My goodness, Nora. That smells disgusting. Put the lid back on quickly.'

Honora laughed, popped some of the radishes into the soup and returned the lid to the jar.

Florentine covered her nose and mouth with her hands and fled the kitchen after Mr Kent.

Her mother was in the garden and started chatting with Mr Kent about spring plantings. She recommended salt-water gargle and chicken broth for his cold, and plenty of rest for his aching head. Indeed, Mr Kent's health seemed to decline with every breath of fresh air and, as he had nothing much to berate the hotel for, decided to go home to bed at once.

'Shall I send Mrs Keogh around with some soup?'

'No need,' Mr Kent replied, pressing his handkerchief to his mouth. 'I'm not happy with the condition of your taps,' he started to say. 'Been hearing all sorts of stories about your ale. You have one week to get it sorted.'

Invisible words pecked at his head. He flinched at their ferocity though he neither heard nor saw their presence. Florentine was sure he had more to say. All that came out was a groan and a cough, and he shuffled away, back humped like a camel, without even a 'good day'.

Florentine met her mother's gaze and smiled at the silent 'good riddance' she mouthed from across the garden beds.

'The garden is looking much better today. When have you found the time for all this gardening?'

'I haven't. Aunty Flora's been hard at it, bless her. We'll have herbs for summer now and be well established before winter comes around again.'

'We'll miss her when she's gone,' Florentine said as her mother approached. She didn't want to mention the twins leaving as well. They'd been beside themselves with excitement at the prospect all morning. That was the kind of hurt that suggested she may never see them again. To speak too much about it felt like she was tempting the fates.

'She has her own family to see to and its better she travels before summer hits. Especially as she's taking the twins. Flora will have enough to contend with, travelling with those two bundles of energy.' Rosalie's smile appeared fragile and her eyes glittered. Florentine took her hand and squeezed her cold fingers.

'Time for some tea,' Rosalie continued, with only the tiniest catch in her voice.

Honora had a tray laid out with cups, sugar, and teapot, and was just adding a jug of cream to the arrangement when Florentine and

Rosalie walked in. 'Gone then and none too soon. Prissy busybody, that man, for sure. Go on up. I'll be right behind you.'

Rosalie, still holding Florentine's hand, led the way further into the hotel and up the staircase to the family sitting room. The scent of burnt paper mixed with sage, bay, and juniper grew stronger with every step.

They paused at the top of the stairs. Rosalie held Florentine's hand to her chest, kissed her fingers. 'I do miss my bonnie wee lasses and our walks through the park. Do you remember? Your father and I would hold your hands and swing you between us while Ana chased ahead after butterflies.'

'How could I ever forget? I felt like I was flying so high I tried to reach the clouds with my toes. I miss those days too. And Father, I miss him the most.'

The two women touched their heads together and Florentine put her free arm around her mother, willing energy into shoulders that had always been strong but today looked anything but. A shudder ran through Rosalie and then she straightened, face firm, her moment of weakness gone. She let go of Florentine and took the last few steps to the sitting room with growing stature.

The candelabra on the centre table was lit, wax dripping down the candles. Mrs Bell stood by the table pressing a thick bob of dried herbs tied with string into a plate of ashes. With each press, tiny embers of fire lit the herbs as if woken from a deep sleep and died out just as quickly. The hum of words seemed to hover in the air, caught by trails of scented smoke coming from the bob in Mrs Bell's hand.

Anastasia walked a slow circle around Mrs Bell and the table, a scorched taper in one hand, eyes half-closed as if to keep out the smoke, lips moving on a silent liturgy.

Florentine wondered at the quiet Mrs Bell's apparent proficiency in folk remedies and spells. But she wasn't surprised. She'd learnt far too much about the need for secrecy from her mother. People that knew the ancient crafts kept such knowledge to themselves for good reason. Her sister's aptitude for the subject was equal to her own, and watching her now, Florentine realised that it really must be in the blood. Her aversion to her mother's true nature and her own heritage had not lasted long at all.

Rosalie moved to stand beside Mrs Bell, indicating Florentine to stand opposite. Neither Mrs Bell nor Anastasia paused in movement or whispered incantation.

Honora came in with the tray, placed it on the table, and removed its contents. When the tray was empty, she eased it in front of Rosalie. Mrs Bell stopped, holding the smouldering bob of dried herbs in front of her. Rosalie lifted the plate of ashes and sprinkled them onto the tray and, taking the bob, started to draw lines across the tray's surface. With each line, she recited:

'And so we banish ill from our home.

We call on the ancestors to bless this sanctuary.

Peace be in your hearts,

And in your minds,

And on your lips.'

Anastasia stopped walking, re-lit the taper from one of the candles, and pointed to the centre of the five-pointed star. The ashes flared.

'So mote it be.'

CHAPTER 16

Mrs Macquarie's Chair sat on its headland overlooking the harbour and Fort Denison, as it had for decades now. Mrs Macquarie was long gone. Her chair, as resolute as the rock it was carved in, a lasting legacy. That and the road behind, planned, according to the chair, by Mrs Macquarie. Why would a woman plan a road? What sort of woman could she have been? Brave, no doubt. Intelligent. Compassionate. Florentine wanted to be all these things. Most especially brave. She sat on the chair and tried to imagine how Elizabeth Macquarie had coped with all the things she'd faced being married to a governor and living so far from home.

Was it any different to her own mother, after all?

Florentine's gaze fixed on the Martello tower that had been built on top of Pinchgut Island. It was not really much use as a fort. It had guns and a cannon that were rarely fired, and quarters for a small garrison if needed. The foghorn was useful on days when Sydney was blanketed in thick white clouds. Not today. Florentine turned her gaze to the sky. Today was clear and blue. Fog would have suited her mood much better.

She'd followed Mrs Macquarie's Road every morning. Visited

the museum every other afternoon. The gardener in the park across the road had taken to giving her a friendly wave, she walked by that often. And she was sure old James Cook squinted down on her with a wry expression, his finger pointing to the sky waggling occasionally at her foolishness.

Sneaking away from the tempest that was home was not easy. So much to do and learn. So many worries. Anastasia's arm was healing. John was busy with Mr Michaels keeping the taproom operational. Florentine wasn't sure about their matching stern visages and tendency to browbeat customers, but it seemed to be working. Aunty Flora was rarely seen as she took the twins on constant day trips to explore the city and surrounds to keep them out of the way.

Drew was either helping the men or off on secret missions with his friend Will Downs, which their mam appeared to be instigating. Florentine didn't like the harder side of her brother's artistic bookish temperament. She'd like to blame the influence of Will, but there was a certain Scots demeanour she recognised in her mother and more than a little of Rosalie's temper had been passed down to her son.

What really bothered Florentine was the absence of Alexander Ridlay. Not a word since the day he'd brought in his drawings.

Mam had denied any collusion. She thought well of him, she said.

But he'd not returned or sent a note or been in any of their usual meeting places. She wanted to hear him laugh, listen to his cheeky stories, see his smile, and feel his hand on hers as he showed her how to get the perspective right in a painting. His warm breath on her cheek as he whispered about light and lines, shape and structure. Florentine's eyes closed as she remembered her last painting lesson right here at the Chair. Fort Denison's tower bulged and leant where it shouldn't, daring to defy gravity. Mr Ridlay—Alexander—had laughed and said other than that slight discrepancy the technique was quite good. She'd blushed, pleased at the praise.

She blushed again, remembering, missing his presence even

more. A bird cackled overhead and she had the distinct feeling it was laughing at her.

'Enough,' she said and stood. She'd never been one for sitting around feeling sorry for herself and she was not about to start now. There were more important things to do. She twirled and strode to the staircase. If he would not come to her then she would go to him.

All the blood drained from Florentine's face when she found Mr Ridlay. She felt it go; a flood of emotion pooling in her toes. Arm-in-arm with Miss Adelaide Blum and chatting like old friends as they strolled down Hunter Street, chatting to Adelaide the way he chatted to her. Here was the reason for his lack of presence in her days.

How dare he!

The flood turned back on itself and surged through her in a tidal wave of hurt and anger. She'd been on the brink of telling him everything. Her mother had certainly shared something with him; she'd hardly seen him since and had blamed her for interfering. Rosalie's plea of innocence in the matter had fallen flat, but her mother had been true. She'd only been trying to find out something of his background and his perceptivity to the truth. Rosalie had given nothing away or said anything to cause his absence.

This woman had been the sole reason behind his sudden defection and the cause of his perfidy. Florentine stood on the footpath unable to move, ignoring the complaints of the pedestrians around her, waiting for her beau and the other woman to reach her.

'Miss Ponsonby. Whatever is the matter?' Adelaide was the same age as Anastasia. They had gone to school together and had once been friends. Florentine did not know what had broken the friendship, but she did know that Anastasia refused to speak or hear the other woman's name.

'I wasn't aware that you and Mr Ridlay had formed an attachment.'

A tiny dot of pink diffused in Adelaide's cheeks. 'We're acquainted. Why? Do you have an attachment with him?'

'Florentine … it's not what you think. At least, I don't think it's what you think. What do you think?' Alexander's words were as flustered as he appeared.

'I thought we were friends.' Florentine hissed the last word and narrowed her eyes. 'Yet, you've not bothered to call on me once.'

'Excuse me, Miss Blum.' Alexander dropped Adelaide's arm and took Florentine's, pulling her gently away from the centre of the footpath. 'Florrie. I've been south for the past few days. I sent you a note to explain. Miss Blum and I really are just acquaintances.'

'I didn't receive a note.'

'Please believe me. We've bumped into each other as I was heading to the hotel to visit you.'

'It's true, Florentine. I promise. Of course, I am interested in Mr Ridlay's company and I have been attempting to lure him away for an afternoon in the park,' Adelaide said, rather too coquettishly for Florentine's liking. 'You promised to paint my portrait, Alexander, and the weather is so lovely today.'

'If you recall, Miss Blum, I did say I was rather busy.' Alexander had flushed bright red.

A morsel of regret crept into Florentine's heart. Adelaide reclaimed Alexander's arm and leant against his chest. When she rested her head against Alexander's shoulder, Florentine's anger stamped it out.

'Well, don't let me keep you,' she said. 'Miss Blum, you're getting far too much sun. We wouldn't want you to be red and blotchy for your portrait. Mr Ridlay will, of course, need to return to his room for his paints and brushes.'

Florentine turned on her heel and left the couple where they stood.

'Florrie, wait!' She heard and ignored him. 'Miss Blum, will you please let go of my arm?'

She didn't wait to hear any more; quickening her step she darted through the Sunday crowds and turned right instead of left at

Macquarie Street. Trumpets and horns reverberated from the bandstand in Hyde Park. Noise would drown out her dismay and distract her from her anger. She rubbed tears from her eyes with the back of her hand and ducked her head to avoid people seeing her distress.

∼

Discordant sound thrummed through the trees. He was too far from the bandstand and too many people walked and talked around him to pick up the melody. Heart beats tripped over themselves, jumping to a new tune. Face grimaced around clenched jaw, he forced his mouth open to drag in more air.

A running child bumped into him, knocked him into an older couple. He swirled to apologise, berate, but no words came out.

'Are you all right there, young man?' the woman asked.

Clement couldn't respond. He didn't know. He lurched away, legs heavy and wooden, a puppet with no strings. Heat radiated from the centre of his body, prickled across his skin, itched its way through hair and armpits and groin. He loosened his tie, unbuttoned his blazer, swept the hat from his head, clawed his fingers through his hair.

He heard sails in the wind, an albatross calling. A shady hand reached out to him. He looked up to see he was standing in the shadow of the Garden Palace. Flags and bunting flapped wild. A dull-eyed bird stared down at him, beak clicking. Its throat swelled with sound as it put its head back and fluffed up its black and white plumage.

A door opened, waiting. Wind ripped at his coat, his loosened tie flapped like the flags on their poles. A dark stillness beyond the open door beckoned him in.

The long hall was empty of people. Exhibits were scarce, most packed away, empty glass boxes and naked shelves left to gather dust until the next collection arrived. A white sheet billowed, exposing a slim marble leg. Another outlined the features of a huge animal, cerement for a hidden beast. Changing light filtered in from windows high above, clouds scattering across the sky deflecting sunlight, giving the effect of movement around the inanimate objects in the room.

He wandered through, touching display units, leaving finger marks in the dust, and dragging veils. His eardrums rang with the echo of strident trumpets until the door slammed closed, and outside became a distant memory.

Footsteps tapped a new beat. He paused, waiting for someone to show themselves, realised the steps were his own and he was alone in the vast chamber, an odd buzzing emanating from the walls.

Jaundiced light at the far end was the only hint of colour in the monochrome room. The painted walls appeared bleached without artificial light to give them substance. He walked to the light, paying no heed to the click of the door opening or the soft pattering tread of someone trailing behind him.

Queen Victoria waited in the light, standing in the centre of a hovering platform guarded by stony-faced lions, fangs dripping with blood and gore. Ghostly creatures, pale skinned and dressed in grave clothes danced around her. Rings of pulsating energy rippling with sickly shades of yellow travelled from her crown to her feet. A figure glided past; a waltz of spirits. The buzzing sound came stronger here, rising from a void of startling blackness, an abyss of nothingness, beneath the platform. Close to the fissure, Clement discerned whines and moans. Something moved. Distorted, it grew, sucking in the blackness until it had shape. Spats from the sceptre fed the growing form; eyes, a mouth, pointed dagger teeth, the monster that haunted his dreams. It rose above him, opened its yawing mouth and swallowed him whole.

'I'm telling you, Florrie, Clement Benedict was acting strange in the park, so we followed him into the exhibition building. When he got to the statue he just froze, white as a ghost. Then he keeled over in a faint.'

Drew had walked over to the Gardens with the twins, escorting them so they wouldn't go too far and stay out too long, allowing his mam and Aunt Flora to finish the packing. The twins nodded their heads in agreement from either side of their brother as he spoke to Florentine.

'Did he say anything?'

'Not a word. Not a sound except his body hitting the floor.'

'He fell straight back,' Katie said.

'Straight as a cue stick,' Emily added.

'Then what happened?' Florentine asked. The urgency in her brother's voice and face pushed thoughts of Mr Ridlay to the back of her mind.

'Someone threw water in his face and he sat up spluttering. I think he said some rude words,' Emily said.

'He said something, but it was nonsense. Didn't make a lick of sense,' Drew said.

'What about the statue? Did it do anything?' Florentine was trying to decide if she should go in and look for herself.

Drew stared at her before saying, 'Aye, it danced a jig and winked at me.' The twins giggled.

Florentine returned his look, unblinking until he relented with a shrug of his shoulders. 'People moved around. Some were sitting. The statue was just a statue.'

'And there was the shadow,' Katie said. 'Like the clouds over the sun.' She pointed down to the dappled light on the grass.

'And the man looked so scared.'

'And the shadow sort of floated in the air, right up to his face.'

'And then he fainted. We thought he was dead. Didn't we, Katie?'

Drew looked from one to the other. 'I didn't see a shadow.'

'We saw it, but the shadow was only on him. No one else.' The excitement on Emily's face faltered until Katie pinched her arm, gleaming, and the two mirrored each other's sense of foolhardy adventure.

Florentine had to think, pull together the conflicting emotions and thoughts bouncing around inside her head. 'Did he see you at all?' She peered at each of her sisters and her brother. Mam would be furious when she found out that the twins had been this close to danger. She needed to come up with a plan. If she sent them home now while she and Drew went inside the building, the twins were likely to elaborate on the story and concoct something ten times worse. If she kept them with her, she could be taking them back into danger.

'He didn't see us, Florrie. I don't think he saw anyone even after he came to. He was a mess. Tie almost falling off, no hat, and his hair was on end. People were moving out of his way.'

'You're certain it was Benedict?'

Drew squirmed uncomfortably. 'Will pointed him out to me yesterday. We've been following him around town. Him and his da are staying at the Union Club. And before you ask, no, he didn't see me then either.'

'Just be careful, Drew. Will is a known larrikin. I wouldn't want you tarred with the same brush.' Drew gave her an odd little smile, and she feared her warning was already too late. 'Is Mr Benedict still inside?'

'He ran out,' Emily said.

'Went down to the quay.' Katie pointed past the stables and Government House.

Drew, frowning, said, 'Will sees him down there a lot. Watching the ships.'

Safe to take the twins inside then. 'Let's go in and you can show me exactly what he did and where he did it. I'm sure the statue is important. I want to give it a closer look.'

Brother and sisters walked in through the main door. They each had annual passes to the exhibitions and had visited so many times the ticket collectors knew them by sight. He waved them through and continued straight to the statue.

Queen Victoria appeared as she always did, serene and unmoving, anchored in bronze. The lion fountainheads below her spouted cool water into circular ponds.

'He walked right up to the railing. About here.' Drew stopped in front of the statue. 'People were sitting on those empty chairs there and others were milling around talking.' He stood at the formal guardrail, not touching it, and peered down to the base of the plinth and its watery setting and then upward. 'I think he was looking at the lions rather than the queen. Then he came over all scared, stepped back as if he were falling, and then did fall.'

'And this shadow you saw,' Florentine asked the twins. 'Did it come from the statue or the lions or just appear?'

'Just appeared,' they said in unison.

'But it's not here now, is it?' Florentine could see no trace of anything out of the ordinary.

'No. It followed the man when he ran out.'

'Let's take the twins home and figure out what to do next.'

'We should come back when there's no one around,' Drew suggested.

'Perhaps, but let's not discuss that in front of Katie and Emily. Where did they go?'

'In Egypt, Britain's generals have been playing at war. While here they fluster about pretending that Europeans or Arabs or whoever are making ready to attack. Bored generals can be dangerous men.'

'I'm not sure I follow, Mam,' Anastasia said. 'What do armies on the other side of the world have to do with us?'

Rosalie tightened her shawl around her shoulders. They were in for a cold night. 'Bored generals hound our footsteps, practising their rapier skills on our backs, dispensing orders that hang us, battling for hills and valleys as if their flags speared into the earth gives them ownership.' Rosalie watched the street below from the balcony. Two men leant against the iron fence, talking and watching, smoking. One had a newspaper curled under his arm, the other a lunch pail. They finished their conversation, and newspaper-man departed. The man left behind crouched down, scratched a light from the sandstone base of the fence, and lit his pipe, watching the people that walked by with squinting, smoke-crusted eyes. Dickens' men watched over the hotel as he'd promised.

'Men like those generals feel entitled. They take what they want.' She watched another man, thick coat buttoned tight, a woollen scarf wrapped around his neck, gloved hands covering his mouth, catching coughs that wracked his shoulders. 'Other men, like poor Mr Turner down there, give their all to improve our lives while their inner light flickers and fades and dies away.'

Anastasia looked over the railing. 'Is Mr Turner dying? I hadn't heard. How sad.'

'He sang last night when he should have been home in bed. Overtaxed his voice at the opera. A singer without a voice does not last long in the world. He may turn his hand to other things, but inside he'll be dying, one failed note after another.'

'You're very melancholic, Mam.' Anastasia moved closer, put an arm around Rosalie's shoulders. 'You are the island to which this family clings, but you don't have to be strong all on your own. Florentine and I, and Drew, even Emily and Kate, are here with you.'

Rosalie patted her daughter's hand. 'I'm merely thinking things through, speaking aloud thoughts that need to be aired so they don't take hold. Negative thoughts undermine us ...'

'And what every spell requires to work is our belief that it will work,' Anastasia repeated her mother's mantra.

'And our strength,' Rosalie added. 'To bear the consequences.'

'You're fidgety tonight, Son,' Algernon commented. He'd watched Clement stir his soup three times, lift his spoon twice, and plonk it back in the bowl, splashing broth and vegetables onto the tablecloth. Chunks of ripped bread sat on his plate, crumbs scattered beneath, and the linen napkin had been screwed in a ball, wrung, and twisted.

'I'm not feeling well, sir.'

Benedict could see that. Pale and drawn, his clothes and hair tidied, but not fresh or particularly clean, he suspected Clement was not sleeping, and by the way he toyed with his food, not eating either.

A tap on the door, and two waiters brought in the next course. A simple roast beef and vegetables with gravy. One of the waiters cleared the table with a soft 'Are you finished with the soup, sir?' Benedict waved him on and the bowl and bread were taken away, a fresh napkin laid across Clement's lap, and the second waiter served dinner.

'Eat up,' Algernon said when the door had closed again on the waiters. 'You need your strength.'

Clement cut into his roast beef and put a small piece in his mouth, chewing with all the enthusiasm of a cow on its cud. He put his knife and fork down again. 'Father, do you know who or what these spirits are that you called to aid us? Can they be trusted?'

'Of course,' Benedict answered between mouthfuls of juicy meat. 'I first met them, or it, on the Isle of Skye. I've told you this, surely? The spirit told me to seek wisdom and help would come. And it has. I feel my hands have been guided ever since.' Benedict had not doubted his course since that night, nor the truthfulness of the soft words that came in his dreams, telling stories, giving instructions, providing answers.

'But how do you know this spirit is guiding you truly? How do you know it doesn't have some other agenda? That it won't betray us?'

Steam curled from his baked potato as Benedict cut through the crisp skin. He reached for the silver gravy jug and flooded the creamy flesh with thick brown sauce. How could he explain the inherent trust that filled him? The satisfaction he felt when he followed his dreams?

'Father? Answer me! I swing between feeling like I'm king of the world and the lowest denominator in some demon's machinations. This morning I was ready to explode with the most fantastic energy and this afternoon I fainted in the main vestibule of the Garden Palace. I need assurances.'

Algernon didn't know what to say, wasn't sure he had answers. He'd not experienced the spirit in such a manic, demanding way. Doubt crept into his mind, followed by guilt. He would need to ask for advice on the matter. In the meantime, how to assuage his son?

'I do not have the answers you need, Clement. Perhaps this is a transition period so to speak. You came to the spirit along a different path to my own. It has been rushed. All I can think of is that you were unprepared for the full impact, unknowing as we are, of the intricacy of the powers we are invoking. I do know you must keep up your physical strength, however, so eat. I will seek guidance on the matter this evening and watch over you while you rest.'

'You trust in this spirit as a child does its parent. I fear for the day when the spirit reveals its full self to you and you realise, as any child does, that your guiding light is not as worthy of the trust you have bestowed.' Clement stabbed a slice of beef with his fork and brought it to his mouth. 'I ask for answers, an anchor to hold me in reality, and you tell me to eat. Very well, I shall do so. Each bite is like ashes in my mouth, but I shall force it down while you sit there, guileless, and you may pray over my sleeping body, but I will not be resting, sir. I hear not pretty voices but tortured screams. I see not beautiful visions but horrifying monsters. I will need every prayer you can think of, Father, for I fear I will wake from my sleep babbling with insanity in purgatory!'

Shocked, Algernon watched as Clement forced forkfuls of meat and vegetables dripping with gravy into his mouth, swallowing only when he could fit no more food in, then jamming in more, chewing and swallowing. Juices from the meat mixed with globules of gravy oozed down his chin. He finished his meal and gulped down red wine.

'Clement! Control, please! Do not give in to your doubts and fears. We will rise above them. We will conquer them. Together. Tell me what's tormenting you. We will find a way to ease your mind.'

'We? I do not know how we can do anything when you do not have answers to a single question I ask. You operate on blind faith,

Father. I am not able to do that. You see kindly spirits. I see demons. My fear is that we are seeing the same entity.'

'The power we invoked is bigger than either of us. I could not possibly contain it. You, on the other hand, younger and stronger, can. It isn't easy for you. I see that. You must learn control. Over yourself if not the power residing within. We are close, are we not, to achieving our end goal? The woman is faltering. Her home and security is wavering. She will give us that which she has in her possession to save her family. We will have all that is needed to focus the power and appease the spirits. When they are released, you will know a measure of peace.'

'I am a vessel for a demon queen and you talk about destroying a family to appease spirits.' Clement swiped his napkin across his face and dropped it on the table. He took a last drink of wine and stood, tottering as if drunk. He met his father's confusion with a dulled, resigned expression. 'I will continue along this path you have set. I have no choice. Your ideals fill me with a desire to see them achieved. I cannot deny it. This thing inside me—power, demon, vengeful spirit of a thwarted ancestor—whatever it is, I can only hope it does not destroy us in the process.'

He lurched from their private sitting room into his bedroom, standing as if dazed by the bed. Algernon cut his beef into neat squares, forked potato and beans, and scooped them into his mouth. He sipped his wine, dabbed his lips with his napkin, and watched as his son came to life, washed, changed, and returned to the sitting room, adjusting his cravat.

'I'm going to the theatre, Father.'

'Shouldn't you be resting?'

'I need some frivolity. To distract me if nothing else. Stay here and pray if that is your wish. May God bestow some knowledge if He chooses.' He buttoned his coat and collected his hat, gave a short bow, and left.

Algernon lifted his glass. 'What does God have to do with this?'

At the Union Club on Bent Street, men wandered in and out at all hours. Each time, a doorman pulled the doors open, bowed, and greeted them with a polite good evening or good morning as the time of day warranted. Clement arrived not long after the day shift started, eyes bleary and lips parted in a relaxed smile. He smelled of spring flowers and smoke. The doorman on duty greeted him as any other. Not for him to judge what the lord's son got up to.

'Morning, Fredericks, old man.'

'Morning, sir. Have a pleasant evening?' His name was not Fredericks, but what did it matter?

'I did indeed. Everyone is so friendly in this city.'

The doorman's smile was practiced and did not reach his eyes. 'We do our best. Would you like some breakfast sent up to your room, sir?

Clement stopped to think, blocking the doorway.

'Extraordinary! I'm suddenly ravenous for bacon and eggs, and those little sausages if you have any, and toast with orange marmalade, and a gallon of coffee to wash it all down.'

'Very good, sir. I'll see to it straight away.' The doorman waited, still holding the door. 'Was there anything else, sir?'

'No … Yes! Double that order, would you? It occurs to me His Lordship might enjoy a hearty breakfast as well.'

'Of course, sir.'

Clement shambled off to the staircase, paused, and then jogged all the way to the top. The doorman couldn't be sure, but it sounded like he jumped and clicked his heels at each landing. He shook his head, closed the door, and went off to wake up the kitchen staff.

Adelaide Blum lay in her bed, silk sheets tangled around her limbs. She'd had the most glorious night making love; gentle one moment, rough and firm the next. Her lover's late night visit had been unexpected, spontaneous, glorious. She rolled over, reaching for the pillow he'd laid his head on, and imagined his lingering warmth. 'Glorious!' she repeated, out loud this time. She'd relive this moment for hours, days, weeks. She was on her lover's mind and planned to stay that way. Adelaide rolled over to daydream of strong arms, warm hands, and long legs.

Teenagers loitered outside the entrance gate to the Union Club. Ever mindful of his duties, the doorman trotted down the stairs to send them on their way.

'You there! No loitering here, thank you. Get yourselves off to school!'

The boys shared a surly demeanour the doorman recognised, trouble in the making for sure. He stood over the smaller of the lads, using his bulk to appear as menacing as he could.

'I'll have none of your shenanigans around here so just be on your way.' His gruff voice could be heard up and down the quiet street.

'Is he in?' asked the lad, hiding his question behind a scowl and a smirk.

The doorman nodded. 'Don't give me any trouble now.' The second lad laughed, turning to watch the street, and shielding the quiet conversation taking place.

'I'll send word when he leaves, but I doubt it'll be before noon. He's not long in and has a lot to sleep off.' The doorman maintained his threatening stance, but dropped his voice.

'You know Charlie and Peter Tasker?' the short lad asked. 'They'll be loitering all day.'

'Right then, that's enough of that. Be on your way before I call the bobbies.'

The boys ran off and the doorman returned to his post.

The Garden Arms Hotel was closed. Doors locked tight. Staff paid off. Sheets covered the tables and buffets, the bar had been draped in old curtains. A sign in the window stated a reopening date two weeks hence, when renovations had been completed.

James would be disappointed the hotel couldn't open. Rosalie whispered apologies to his memory. Renovations, at least, were not a lie. John and Mr Michaels would start soon on clearing pipes, cleaning spouts, replacing rotting wood and weakened floorboards. Honora and Bridie, who'd refused to leave, were in the kitchen, cleaning.

Thudding on the staircase brought Rosalie from her reverie. She hadn't been able to shake off the melancholia of the night before. Today, Flora and the twins were leaving. She'd put on a brave face, hoping it might seep through to the rest of her. If only she didn't have this nagging feeling that she would never see her impish girls again. John appeared carrying Flora's trunk; Drew dragged the twins' luggage behind him.

John glanced at Rosalie and spared her a lopsided grin before disappearing into the kitchen and out into the yard. Drew looked despondent and didn't acknowledge his mother's presence. The hotel was too quiet already. Without Katie and Emily, it would be a mausoleum. A crypt full of bare bones and ghosts wandering around wishing life could be restored.

The girls came running down the stairs. 'Mam! Aunty Flora said she'd teach us how to ride a horse!'

'And make damper like the drovers do!'

Aunty Flora followed them down at a more sedate pace. 'And billy tea,' she added, one hand on Rosalie's crossed arms. As the twins raced out into the sunshine, Flora put her arms around Rosalie. 'They'll be fine, I promise. When this is all over, why don't you come fetch them yourselves? Then I can show you around the farm and you can meet Paddy. The children would love to see you again. They don't live too far away. We could have a little family reunion and share a toast to dear Colin. Remember on the ship, how he used to drag you up to dance when the band started playing?'

Rosalie returned the hug. 'Music and dancing made that whole journey bearable. And your Colin, of course.'

'And your James too. Such handsome young men.'

'I miss him so much, Flora. Sometimes I think he'll be home soon, just gone for a walk in the park or down the wharves. He'll be back all smiley and cheerful.'

'It will take time, Rosalie. A lot of time. That feeling will fade, but your memories won't. We always have our memories.' The women hugged tighter. 'Be brave, Rosie. Your family needs you. We all do.'

'And if I fail? What then?'

'Then I will tell your daughters every single story I remember and I will raise them to be wise women just like you, warriors like Florentine, and protectors like Anastasia. They will follow in your giant footsteps with love in their hearts and the memory that their mother never gave up.'

Rosalie sobbed.

Flora held her shoulders until Rosalie looked up with teary eyes. 'I make this promise to you, Rosalie MacKinnon, daughter of Rhona MacKinnon. I borrow these children of yours to keep them safe, yes, but also to give you time and space to do your work. You have battles to fight and they are too young to be warriors just yet. For all that, they each have a warrior's soul within. Stand up straight and put away those tears. Your children rely on you to do what must be done. You will not fail.'

'Thank you, Flora.'

'Now, come away with me and let's get these goodbyes over with. We have a long way to travel on this rattletrap. Trains may speed things along, but the distance remains the same.' She held up her hand to stop Rosalie speaking. 'Your Mr Michaels will deliver us to the railway station and see us off. It's all organised, Rosie. Goodbyes are better from home than in some dusty rail yard.'

Rosalie had misgivings about that. Saying goodbye at the rail yard would give her another half hour with her babies. As Flora had said, it was all arranged. She gave her cousin one more hug and went out to the yard to spend a final few minutes with the girls.

By afternoon, the hotel rang with the sound of hammers, wood-sawing, and voices. Some voices gave orders, others pleasant conversation. John Bray sang Irish ditties in a deep baritone, sawing new floorboards in time to music only he could hear. The doors and windows were flung open to let in fresh air. Passers-by caught the heady mix of sawdust and onion filtering out from the windows and smiled.

A corner had been turned. The women's protective spells had taken hold, seeping into the fabric of the building, giving it the strength to hold firm, renew its integrity, and reaffirm the life-soothing energy that flowed through every brick, plank of wood, and pane of glass.

Rosalie sat on her bed, the Gift Stone cupped in her hands. She'd given Florentine and Anastasia a disc each to guard. Rosalie wasn't sure of the Cailleadch's intent in giving her the stone, and the time left to discover its purpose was short. She wasn't sure how to go about it. It had no outer markings, was neither perfectly formed or smooth. It made no sound and did not appear to contain any magical energies. As far as rocks went, the Gift Stone was particularly rockish. Today, like every other, it remained a mystery. Rosalie put it in the bowl of shells that had been collected by various members of the family and went to find her remaining daughters.

Anastasia was in her room packing a suitcase. Little Evie was fast asleep in her crib and Fiona was collecting clothes and toys from drawers and piling them on the bed. Anastasia held two straw dolls in her hands. She looked up as Rosalie entered, a wavering smile on her lips.

'I made these last night. The girls can play with them and be protected at the same time.'

Each of the dolls wore a plain linen dress with a dyed felt pinafore, ribbons around their waists, and a cotton bonnet on their heads. Their hair was braided straw and silk threads, faces made of tiny buttons and painted smiles.

Rosalie remembered making similar dolls when Anastasia and Florentine were little. She held one to her nose and breathed in lavender and rose petals. Embroidered in the pinafores were the flowers she could smell. Her thumb rubbed on a knob of thread on the underside. She lifted the flap. Tiny sigils in the same colour as the felt.

'The discs we carry are carved with sigils, so I thought I'd do the same with the dolls. No one knows what they mean but me and I'm giving them away. I'm hoping that's enough.'

'Every bit helps,' Rosalie said, placing the doll on top of the folded clothing.

'Fiona's already given them names. This one is Ana and the other is Florrie.' Doll Ana joined doll Florrie in the suitcase.

'They'll be fine with Amy,' Rosalie said. She waved Fiona over and picked her up to sit on her hip. 'They'll have so many sweet buns to eat they'll come back roly poly.' She tickled Fiona's stomach and gave her a squeeze. 'Amy will give them as much love and care as if they were her own.' She passed the little girl to her mother.

'And they'll only be five minutes away and I can go visit when- ever I like. I know,' Anastasia said. 'I think I feel guilty more than anything, Mam. My bairns are so close but the twins have been sent far away.'

On the bed beside the case lay a soft knitted blanket embroi- dered with bunches of roses and sprigs of lavender. Rosalie picked it up and held it in her hand, smoothing it out, holding it close. 'The twins are of an age where they cannot be contained as easily as a babe and a toddler. And you know what they're like. First sign of danger and they'll run toward it. I could not bear for them to be hurt and we can't be worrying about what they're up to.'

'Still. It's hard, isn't it?

'The hardest thing I've had to do to-date,' Rosalie agreed.

Anastasia folded her arms around her mother. 'You still have us and we're full of common sense.'

Rosalie laughed. 'Well, at least, the sense to tell the difference between complete folly and rational action, and hopefully the wisdom to pause long enough to work out which is which at the time.'

It's all I can hope for.

In the belly of the dome, Florentine and Drew huddled together in the pale wash of moonlight filtering through the windows. Sunlight had glittered gold in the dome as the sun set and brother and sister were mesmerised. With the sun and any traces of its warmth gone, the pair shivered. Reflections, tinged with the blue of the stained glass, gave off an eerie watery effect.

'I'm freezing. Let's go,' Drew said. He looked over the railing of the narrow maintenance catwalk and gestured for Florentine to join him. 'It's like we're among the stars.'

From their lofty position, the lower levels were cloaked in dark- ness. With intermittent lanterns and the slow patrol of the nightwatchmen giving off pinpricks of light, it did indeed appear as if they were part of the universe.

Florentine joined him and took his cold hand in hers. 'And the earth is asleep below us.'

'Have you ever been this high before, Drew?' Florentine had her back against the slope of the dome and peered over as far as she could without being seen.

'Sure. Me and Charlie Tasker snuck up to the top of St James' spire last Christmas. He and his brother are choirboys there. He pinched one of those white dresses they wear for me as a disguise.'

'How did you manage that and not get caught?' Florentine's amazement at her brother's daring bordered on admiration.

'Who said I didn't get caught?' He laughed and nudged her with his elbow. 'Billy said I was a new boy and I had to sing psalms all afternoon.'

'You're lucky Mam didn't find out.'

'Worth it,' Drew said. 'Being high like this is like being on top of the world. I want to put my arms out and fly like a bird.'

'More like drop like a rock.'

'Don't you ever wish you could be a bird, or fly like one anyway? Go wherever you want as far as you want, in the clouds and free of the earth.'

Florentine cocked her head and stared hard at Drew. 'That's not possible, so why bother wishing for it?'

'The impossible is possible if you use your imagination. I know you've got one, Florrie. I've read the same books you have. Don't you dream of travelling to other countries, other worlds like in Jules Vern's novels?'

'Just because it's in a novel …' she started to say, and then paused, reminded of something else. 'What other worlds would you travel to?'

'Ha, I knew you had an imagination!' Drew sat down in the corner, stretching his legs in front of him. 'I'd travel to the moon in a heartbeat. Fly around the universe discovering new stars!'

Florentine nestled beside him. 'What about time? If you could, would you travel through time?'

'Sure. I'd go back in time to see da again.'

'Not the future?'

Drew shook his head. 'No, that's too risky.'

'What do you mean? If we went into the future we could find out what happens.'

'But what if what happens is not good? It's easier to face what's coming if we don't know what happens after.'

'And what if we could find out something that could help us now? What if that's what we're meant to do?'

Drew looked at her. 'What do you mean?'

Florentine had read her mother's journal several times, copied it out, and added notes. She'd been to the library and Ina Bell's book-store, and read everything she could find on Old Traditions, old wives' tales, and magic. It seemed to her that they all ended at a point just short of miraculous discovery. Especially her mother's journal.

'I don't know what I mean. It's just a feeling I have that there's something more.'

'More than what?'

'More than all of this. More than Mam's magic and Honora's spells. More than whatever scared Mr Benedict half to death yesterday. More. Just more. I can't explain it, but when you mentioned flying, I had the sensation that we could fly through time. I've never thought that before.' She banged her head with her fist. 'So much new stuff in there that it gets all mixed up. There's something else and it's more than this. That's all I can explain it as.'

Drew had chocked open the door earlier. With no people around to absorb sound, any click or scrape or unwise step would be echoed around the grand hall. They tiptoed down the stairs until they reached the gallery and, using the shadows and columns to stay hidden, peered down to the ground floor.

A section had been closed off and converted to offices. Lowered blinds glowed yellow, silhouettes moved like shadow puppets from one window to another. Voices grumbled like distant thunder echoing around the chamber. The nightwatchmen had left the door open and a lantern hooked outside.

'Good. We'll need to keep an eye out, but looks like they've gone in for a nice long visit.'

Midway down the next flight was another landing. Drew stopped there and said, 'I'll go ahead and check the way is clear. Wait here.' He darted off and Florentine was left with the statue of Queen Victoria for company. Bathed in a sheen of light, the last shining down through the glass dome and catching reflections from the few lights left on, Florentine could see how the statue might have inspired Mr Benedict's hallucination. If that's what it was. She recalled the vision she'd experienced when copying her mother's journal. To anyone else, that would have been called an hallucination too.

The queen's draped gown seemed to catch a breeze and move with its ebbs and flows. Her arm looked as if it were soft flesh, and Florentine imagined the shadowed face turning toward her.

Drew reappeared and gestured for her to follow him down the stairs. She tiptoed after him and tried to avoid looking at the statue as they went past.

'It's really dark down here,' Drew said as they left the partly lit staircase behind and stepped into a wall of blackness. 'There's a light around the corner, keep going.'

Florentine held her skirts tight against her so they didn't catch on any unseen objects. During daylight hours, this was the refreshment area with many tables and chairs spread around. To trip here would most certainly make a racket and alert the guards. The lack of light was starting to get on her nerves when she turned the unseen corner and caught up to her brother, waiting beneath the dull lamp.

'Looks like they're doing some work down here. You can just see some scaffolding around the fountain.' Drew pointed to a spot in the dark room. Florentine couldn't see anything until her eyes adjusted to the lack of light. A faint structure could be identified, but whether it was scaffolding or tables, Florentine could not tell.

'How are we going to see anything?' she asked. 'If only we could have brought a lantern with us.'

'Next time we'll sneak one in under your skirt,' Drew said. He started fumbling in his coat pockets. 'For now, we could wait for the nightwatchmen to come along and borrow theirs. Or …' he pulled his hands free and flattened his palms to show two candle stubs and a packet of matches with flint, 'we could use these.'

'You are scarily well-prepared for sneaking around where you're not meant to be,' Florentine said.

Drew struck a match against the flint. It sputtered and went out before he could touch the candlewick. He tried again with better luck, grinned and said, 'You stick to magic and spells and I'll do all the sneaking.'

'Deal,' Florentine agreed. 'Just be careful.'

'Always, dear sister. I'm the soul of carefulness. Come on then. Enough chit chat.'

They walked to the fountain. During the day, the cascade of water from above made for a pleasant natural backdrop to the elevated level of noise in the restaurant and helped to cool the room. Even in winter, with the number of people that gathered for refreshment, the room was warm. After hours, and with the fountain turned off, it was cold and silent.

The scaffolding formed a narrow bridge over the basin of water from the outer rim and under one of the arches. A ladder led up to a higher internal section that held the inner workings of the fountain.

Drew went ahead. The door, left unlocked by the maintenance crew, opened with ease. He held his candle up and climbed into the fountain's control room.

'Drew?' Florentine whispered. 'Drew?'

His pale grinning face popped through the opening. 'Come on up, Florrie. There's not much room and it's a bit smelly, but I think we've found something.' He put a hand out to help her up.

'Take this,' she said, passing him her candle. 'I can manage a ladder.'

By the time she was in, Drew had placed the candles either side of the room on plain brass candleholders with sconces to protect the wooden beams of the walls from the flame, and glass jars to slip over the candles to protect the workers moving around the confined space. Grey stalactites of solidified wax had formed at the edge of each dish. Oil lanterns had been hooked to other beams.

The small room was lined with copper piping that travelled from a main pump and spread like golden strands of cobweb over the beams and struts of the walls to the outlets for each fountain-head. The floor was damp, but not puddled. The pump's bronze lever was switched to 'Water Flow Off'. On the floor beside it sat a toolbox.

'What are the chances a workman will appear?' Florentine asked. 'They wouldn't be working in here during the day while customers are eating right outside, surely.'

'It's all very neat and tidy. Perhaps they're working on the outside, not in here. Let's hurry up anyway. The place gives me the creeps,' Drew said. 'Look up.'

Four of the pipes went straight up to the lion head water spouts. The ceiling of the room was far above. 'This whole structure is hollow. Sandy must have climbed to the top.'

'Sandy?' Florentine asked. She could feel her cheeks grow hot.

Drew shrugged. 'Your Mr Ridlay. You know, he's really very nice and likes you a lot ...'

'This is not the time and place to be discussing Mr Ridlay and his feelings,' Florentine hissed. 'I need to see the symbols he drew and I want to know if they're connected to Mr Benedict's strange behaviour.'

'This other woman is not a contender for his affections, at all! You do know she is a ...'

'There's a ladder here,' Florentine interrupted. 'I'll climb up. Perhaps you should go check on those nightwatchmen. Make sure they're not right outside listening to you rattle on.'

Drew's expression was a mix of earnestness, over-zealousness, and realisation cast over by the poor light and shadows. 'All right, but it's your turn to be careful. Wait for me before you do anything rash.' He took the remaining candle, ducked through the door and landed with a soft thud on the scaffold. Florentine listened to his footsteps and tried not to think about being inside the fountain with only her candle for company. She climbed the ladder into the narrowing space until the walls became slabs of stone. Above her head the four pipes, not so golden this high up, entered the stone. She had reached the lions' heads.

The ceiling formed the platform the statue stood upon and, even though the candle's flame barely penetrated the gloom, she could make out faint lines. She took another step, breathing light and fast, as her shoulders touched the walls in the cramped confines. She recognised the unknown symbols in the corners and the nightmare face in its centre. Every line and curve of the face had been carved into the surface. A protruding tongue, fat and rough, pointed to a hole below, held open by deformed fingers. Florentine ignored the sounds of Drew climbing the ladder beneath her and touched the edges of the hole with her fingertips. The figure was ugly in the extreme and exposed itself in a way that confronted her sense of decency, yet she knew that here was a mystery from the past. A doorway straight from the old world her mother had left behind to the new.

'What do you think it is, Florrie?' Drew had reached her feet and had kept climbing the narrow ladder. He could go no further than her waist and twisted to see around her arms, grunting when she elbowed his head.

'I don't know. There's a hole in it though and I think something may need to be inserted. Let me down and you can have a look for yourself. I warn you though, its ... disturbing.' Florentine shifted aside, clinging to the side of the ladder as Drew came up, and lowering herself down two steps so he could squeeze into the cavity.

His whistle was low and soft as he reached up to touch it.

'Don't,' Florentine said, gripping his kneecap. 'Let's go.' She squeezed his knee harder when he seemed inclined to ignore her warning, and pulled down on his leg. 'I mean it, Drew. It's not for you. Leave it and let's go.'

'Did you see the guards?' Florentine asked when they had their feet back on firm ground.

Drew shook his head. 'No, but I could hear them. They were heading to the north side of the building. If we head to the service door on the west side, we should be able to get out without their noticing.'

'Lead the way then.'

They closed the trap door behind them and hurried along the scaffolding to the stairs. They could bank on the fact that there was a lot of building for the nightwatchmen to check, but not on where they would start or whether they would stay together. A dash to the western door was risky, but they could hardly go out the front door.

The night had deepened while they'd been inside the fountain, and Queen Victoria's imposing figure joined with the other shadows in the hall. Florentine and Drew rounded the staircase and headed to the service door on the far side of the building, ducking behind displays and columns, weaving around tables and glass boxes. Every now and then they paused to listen for the guards. When they reached the door, Drew pulled out a heavy key from his satchel, while Florentine crouched in the alcove keeping watch. A swinging light appeared in the distance. A single guard.

She turned to warn Drew, who was fumbling with the lock. 'They've split up,' she said. 'One is heading this way. I have no idea where the second guard is.'

'I've nearly got it,' Drew said, giving the key a hard twist. The lock clicked and Drew turned the doorknob. 'Got it. Let's go.'

They slipped out and ran toward the gardens and fence along Macquarie Street.

CHAPTER 18

'I do not like what I'm hearing from Mr Boseman, Clement. He has sent me a note that indicates the Ponsonby family are preparing for a confrontation. The hotel has closed, ostensibly for renovations, the children have been sent off to relatives, and two of the family have been spied at the Garden Palace on a number of occasions acting suspiciously!'

Clement stood by his washstand in his vest and drawers. Hooked over a nearby chair was a pair of moleskin trousers and a checked shirt, a brown woollen waistcoat and navy-blue jacket were folded over the armrest.

'I have everything in hand, Father. If you want them to willingly give you the last relic you need, then they must be brought out, tempted into action. They will not give us anything for nothing and I plan to offer them fair trade.'

Algernon picked through the clothing. 'What are you up to? You need to keep me informed of your comings and goings. I've been paving our way in the spiritual world. I do not want your grand plans in the physical to get in the way.'

Clement picked up the trousers and resumed dressing. 'As you keep me informed? Where were you this morning, Father? I ordered breakfast for the two us and you weren't anywhere to be found. And then gone again tonight. Have you found a woman? A man? Some errant spirit, perhaps?'

'All questions I could ask you, Son.' He handed him the jacket.

'True, but disappearing into the night is a habit I've picked up over a lifetime. Whereas you are usually as predictable as a tree. This bout of unpredictability is disconcerting to say the least.'

Benedict turned away, hands clasped behind his back.

'I have my challenges, as you do yours. I am bound to this task. It has guided me my entire adult life.'

He ignored a scoff from Clement. He needed to trust his son. The undercurrent of duplicity, the strengths and weaknesses that warred within the young man, fuelled his doubt. Yet no evidence for doubt and distrust was apparent. Clement's many machinations moved with one purpose, collecting the relics that would see his family restored.

'We are all bonded to this task from birth,' Clement said. 'I, as much as you, have had my life mapped out for me by the path our forebears chose to take.' Clement came to stand beside his father.

'True,' Algernon paused. 'I find I have grown tired of waiting. I need action.'

'We knew that drawing the woman out would take time.'

Benedict looked at his son, so like his mother. Perhaps it was this streak of difference that caused his doubt. His wife did not support his life's purpose, thought it folly and the result of an overly inflated sense of entitlement. She who had never known the sense of injustice that coursed through his family.

'Age is catching me up, Son, but it does not ease my worries. Time rushes past me and I can no longer muster my usual patience.' He held a hand up to forestall further interruption from Clement. 'Every particle of my being seeks to be doing, not waiting. Yet wait is what we are forced to do.' He took a deep calming breath. 'And so, I have been satiating myself in the arms of a skilled courtesan.'

Clement's blank expression changed with the widening of his eyes and a slow shake of his head. Amusement made him cruel.

'Sex? You've been sneaking off for sex?' He laughed. 'If I'd known you had such an itch, I could have introduced you to any number of women. No sneaking about required.'

Algernon straightened his back and shoulders. Yes, just like his mother.

'You haven't said yet where you're going.' He eyed Clement's utilitarian outfit. 'And why the disguise?'

'The disguise is to avoid watchful eyes. I'm meeting one of Boseman's lads. See if we can't hurry things along for you.'

'Watchful eyes?'

Clement nodded. 'Yes, but don't be concerned. If everything goes to plan, we'll be putting a stick to those eyes tonight.'

'Does Boseman know about this?'

'Yes. He's offered the services of his boys to deal with the matter.'

Clement could disguise his outer self, but not the secrets fluttering at the corners of his lips. Algernon bit down on his tongue. He had his own secrets to hide.

'Be careful, son. We're nearly there. Foolhardy actions could set us back days if not years and we're so close.'

Clement put a hand on Algernon's arm. 'I won't let you down, Father. I promise. We'll have what we need by week's end. You look after the spirits and I'll take care of everything else.'

Algernon shambled away. What was it about his son that drained him so? He stopped at the door into their private sitting room. 'An equinox is almost upon us. We'll have a direct connection to the spirit world. If we miss it, we could be waiting months. I do not wish to spend a summer here, Clement, nor give Mrs Ponsonby time to recoup losses.'

'Now or never, Father,' Clement said. 'I'll make sure of it.'

Clement left his father thinking about his indiscretions and exited the room. A plain door at the end of the corridor led into the servant's stairwell. It opened without sound and he slipped through, jogging down the narrow way until he came to the bottom level and two more doors. He put his ear to one and heard the clash and bang of plates, pots, and pans. He'd explored every door and every level of the club since his arrival and knew this was the scullery. The second door opened to the yard, and from there a passageway and footpath that came out on Bligh Street. He'd have to walk by the gardener's house, but it was close enough to the servants' quarters for him to pass himself off as having come from there.

He was being watched. He'd seen two boys loitering in the mouth of the lane that ran beside the hotel on the corner earlier that evening. Their sudden busyness when he'd walked out the main club doors was obvious, so too their clumsy attempt to follow him and continued presence on his return. He waited by the corner of the cottage, watching them, bored now and bickering. Time to go. He crossed the road, slouched, hands in pockets, a workman heading to the pub. They paid him no heed.

Whether they were members of Boseman's group of young thugs or someone else's remained to be discovered. He would know soon enough.

Spring moved fast on this side of the world; each day longer than the next, but come six pm, it was as if God had turned out the lights. The gloaming period seemed inordinately short. Clement met up with Harry Whistler at the right-of-way between Elizabeth and Phillip Streets, opposite the fire brigade. Whistler leant against a light pole, watching the firemen putting their harnessed horses to the wagon. The docile horses were held by a young lad while another clipped the pole chains. An older gent in full uniform, from his sparkling helmet to his polished boots, came out to grumble and complain about tarnished buckles and slipshod workmanship. Whistler spat on the ground, turned on his heel, and headed down Phillip Street.

Clement followed. Neither spoke until they were clear of the police station and yards. The Alfred Street wool stores were busy even at night. Storesmen loaded wagons, wagoneers tied off loads, warehouse foremen belted orders; all worked toward making ready for first light when they'd harness skinny horses and head out of the city with their loads. Sailors wandered by, leaving behind the wharves and their ships or boats, to drink the night away or find a bed at the Sailors Home.

'The boss says you're responsible for what happened to the Ponsonbys' hotel.' He kept his head down and face averted. He looked up enough as he spoke for Clement to see red and bruised cheekbones. 'He's pretty impressed. Takes a lot to impress old Boseman.'

Clement didn't answer. Whistler tilted his head and they resumed walking at a stroll. 'Stinks down here,' the lad said. 'Worse once it gets warm. You'll wanna be well away by then.' He stopped again at the end of the street and waved Clement closer. He smelled of sweat and blood.

'Boss says I should do whatever you say. That's fine. I'll do it. But when you leave, I want to go too.'

'Are you asking for a job, Mr Whistler?'

'Shhh, call me Harry. No one down here says that mister shit.' He spat again. 'Yeah, I am. Before you say anything, take a look in here.' They were at the door of a dilapidated shed held closed with a heavy chain and lock. Whistler leant over and stuck a brass key into the slot. He caught both lock and chain before they could fall and pushed open the door. 'I haven't told the boss yet, but his star boy is a turncoat. Come in.' He reached up and pulled a lantern down from a shelf. 'We use this shed for storage.'

Clement waited in the doorway. Whistler smelled of this room. The stench of blood was so strong he wondered how no one else could have noticed it. How could no one have seen the blood on Harry Whistler's hands. The lamp flared. Crates were arranged along one wall, canvas piled on top. In one corner, white coils of rope. In the other, luggage stacked from floor to ceiling, and in between, curled up on itself, a body. Whistler walked straight to it. Lifted up the head. 'Was a turncoat,' Whistler added.

Sightless eyes stared their death's gaze at Clement. 'Who is this?' he asked.

'Will Downs. Terrible at billiards, lying, and loyalty.'

'You did this?' Something welled inside Clement, urging to be released. Not bloodlust. He felt no particular satisfaction in Harry Whistler's murderous claim. No delight in seeing the torn and broken remains of Will Downs.

'He got pally with Drew Ponsonby,' Whistler was saying. 'I saw them come out of Boseman's office. Followed them right back to that bloody hotel. Then Downs went to Mr Kent's office, searched it. He's been in and out of the Garden Arms like it's his second home.'

'You killed him?' Clement's hands tingled, his skin itched. At the edge of his vision, stars gathered, a sparkling array blinking a strange dance of sorrow and joy around the dead boy.

'I don't cotton to traitors,' Whistler said. 'He was going to meet Ponsonby again tonight. They were planning to sneak into your club. Someone inside's been helping them.'

'Two boys have been watching me,' Clement said. 'I take it not friends of yours.'

Harry spat again. The wet sound sickened Clement. The stars pulsed and went out, snuffed like candles, except for one miniature supernova hovering between dead eyes.

'What next?' Clement asked. His voice was tremulous. The dead eyes leaked tears like shards of glass. Stars emerged as an underlay to the fatal scene, hesitant to intrude.

'What do you mean? I found a traitor. I dealt with it as proof to you of my loyalty. Proof that whatever you want done, I'm up to the task.'

Clement dragged his gaze from the ever-young Will Downs, saw again the dark and dreary shed full of stolen goods and contraband; the crooked, disturbed, indiscriminate figure of Harry Whistler.

'What of Drew Ponsonby? He will come looking for his comrade.' Clement couldn't tell if Whistler's face, void of expression, was feigned or genuine. A yellowish gleam lit deep in the dead eyes. It kindled a fire, foretold an alternative ending to a story that until this moment had seemed writ in stone. 'The journey to England is long. What do you know of the sea?'

Harry Whistler grinned a shark's grin, and Clement knew that here stood a weapon of infinite possibilities.

'He and his witless sister are at the Palace.'

Shock like cold water slapped Clement in the face. Will Downs became the epicentre of a swirling tempest of starlight, a hole in the fabric of reality that reached into Clement and, with agonising slowness, opened a door through which the cold face of the future shone.

For that sliver of time, Clement understood the potential of all possibilities. He had only to open the door wide and step through. 'Cover the body and lock up,' he ordered. The Palace was a short distance away. He needed to stand before that great dome and divide the children from their mother.

They arrived as two figures clambered over the fence. Harry lifted a finger to his lips and held up his hand for Clement to stop where he was in the darker shadows away from street lights. He pulled a cap from his pocket, nestled it low over his head, and stepped into that pool of light from which Clement hid. He stood straight, cocky, and confident—as unlike his usual slouching self as possible—and gave a low breathless whistle.

The first of the figures, nimble without the restrictions of dress, was on the path helping the second down. He glanced toward the sound and then back to his present task.

Clement saw the brother and sister clearly, faces pale in the low moonlight as they each looked in the direction of Harry Whistler, shadowed as they turned away to whisper fiercely, the sister not happy with the brother even as he pulled away, drawn by the call of his friend.

Harry shifted to the edge of the night, moving further in as the brother approached, luring him away from his sister and the safety of the Garden Arms Hotel.

Clement remained motionless, daring to breathe only in shallow whispers of air for fear of alerting the sister to his presence. One word from her so close to her home could change completely the path he hoped to travel down tonight.

Drew Ponsonby walked past him, following Harry into the darker cluster of shadows. Florentine, torn between returning home as she may have been instructed and following, stood indecisive on the path. Clement leant toward her, called her in his mind to come, come away. She looked toward the lights of her home, hesitating, then came to a decision. And followed her brother.

CHAPTER 19

Despite every instinct that she needed to seek out her mam, Florentine followed Drew away from the warmth and protection of their kitchen hearth and into the chilling dark that was already swallowing her brother whole. She felt the bite of winter not yet passed on her cheeks. Her eyes watered. The circle of safety the street lights offered reached a few feet and no more. The rest of Macquarie Street, like Drew, had been devoured by the night.

Florentine came to a stop beneath the light pole. She sensed something menacing that set her hair on end. The monsters were real. They waited for her, barely two steps away. Sounds of a scuffle, Drew's voice surprised and angry, the pounding of fists on flesh, and stumble of boots and dull thud of a body landing on the paved road, and a low wicked laugh.

Voice and thought and fear left her as she rushed into the vacuum that was the night to defend her brother. The deadness that enveloped her was far worse than any monster-filled cupboard in a child's bedroom, worse than the most heinous of nightmares. Light and life were sucked from this space as if they never were. She could not see or hear or speak. Her lungs were emptied of breath and though she gasped to refill them, no air drew in. She was drowning in emptiness as effectively as if she were under water.

Momentum dropped her out of that barren chasm even as her lungs screamed for succour and her desperate heart beat its last. Frigid air burned her throat and filled her chest, her wild pulse clamoured and settled, still fast but now steady as her body realised that death had been avoided. Florentine stood straight, trembling with fright, breath ragged as she looked for Drew.

A hunched shape wavered over a lump on the ground. Silver slashes of light crossed her vision, cracks in the blackness where the moon forced its way through, and she could see enough to recognise her brother on the ground. She charged at the horror that was reaching out for him, shoving it with such force that it faltered and staggered. She rushed it again, hitting and punching, kicking when it fell at her feet until it stayed still, curled up on itself like a slug in the gutter.

'Drew,' she screamed. 'Drew!' Hearing his groan in answer, she dropped beside him.

Crystallised flickers of light suffused the strange night sky. Drew's face was alabaster except for a streak of wetness across his brow and the pebbles of jet that were his eyes. He blinked sleepily, confused, and struggled in Florentine's grip, though without her hands to hold him he would be as helpless as a newborn.

'Drew.' His eyelids closed and he sagged, mouth soft, head relaxing against her.

A shift of shadows in the corner of her eye warned her of something hidden in the darkness. The form she'd pushed away from Drew squirmed, but otherwise remained where it lay. Something else was here with them, watching, yearning. It went to its fallen comrade, dragged it across the footpath and propped it against the Garden's fence. Florentine heard its deep castigating voice and the smack of a hand against slackened cheeks.

'Are you murderers of children?' she accused. 'Cowards!' She pulled Drew tighter to her and attempted to stand. She hooked her hands under his armpits and started to move him away.

The forms by the fence found their feet, one unsteady, and moved toward her. They didn't speak to her, didn't acknowledge or rebuff her accusations, yet she could sense anger and recrimination between them. One took Drew from her arms, his face visible as he leant over, and recognisable. Florentine did not know his name, but was certain she'd seen him slouching around the wharves like a vulture. The false curtain of night obscured the second face, and for a tremulous moment she thought he might be an evil spirit or, indeed, the half-forgotten monster under her bed. Then she felt the strong grip of a man on her arms as she was hoisted upright, and smelled the scent of sweat and tobacco, and knew that he too was no monster, just another thug.

'You'll not get away with this,' she said. 'I'll see you in prison yet, hanged if you've killed my brother, flesh stripped and bones ground to dust when I'm done with you.'

'Witch,' the deep voice said. 'I fear you not.'

Harry Whistler lumbered down Macquarie Street, limping from the deep bruise he could feel deadening his calf muscle. Florentine Ponsonby didn't look much, but she could kick like a furied mare protecting its young. His ribs creaked and flashed with pain every time he breathed or moved or was bumped by the deadweight that was her brother as he lugged Drew to the locked shed and the corpse of Will Downs. He had no regret for anything but his pain and the humiliation of being foiled so easily by a girl.

A moan came and he wasn't sure if it was his own or Ponsonby's until Drew's head attempted to rise, his feet trying to take some of his own weight.

Behind him, fighting every step, Florentine was being pulled. She railed and accused and called for help, but the night had them trapped in a cell of isolation more confining than any prison. In the whole of this dark world there was only the four of them; their movements and sound absorbed into the shifting wall of shadow that surrounded them. Behind her cries, Harry could hear guttural murmuring that triggered the start of something like fear inside him. He understood without knowing that the almost inaudible chanting came somehow from Benedict, and that Benedict may have called Florentine a witch, but he was something far worse.

Pain alone kept Harry sharp, kept him from thinking past the immediate task of reaching the shed, and doing Drew Ponsonby in like the little bastard deserved.

Pain alone pushed him onward like it always had, the only feeling in his days that he could rely on to guide him true.

Whistler pushed the brother into the unlit shed and without the conscious sense to save himself, Clement heard the boy drop, a lifeless bundle, to the floor. A scrape and a scratch and a snatch of burning oil in the air, and Whistler had the lamp alight.

Clement stepped into the centre of the room, forcing the girl in with him. 'Let me go,' she demanded, staring at her brother's limp body. 'If you've killed him, you'll die a thousand deaths …'

Clement gave her a shove and she landed beside Drew. She gathered her brother to her, hands fluttering over his pallid face, probing his head, his chest, feeling that he still lived, and when he groaned and flinched, laying him on the floor to jump up and meet her gaolers face to face, ready to defend herself and her brother to the end if necessary. Clement could see the fire deep in her eyes, the formidable strength that foretold of battles to come.

'You!' she said, recognising him as he did her. 'I demand you release us!'

'You can only kill me once,' Clement said, enjoying the confusion his answer engendered. 'And that may happen, but not tonight.'

'What do you want? Why are you doing this?'

Clement reached out to touch her pale face, grasping her head in his hand when she recoiled from him, pulling her close enough to feel her torrid breathing on his lips.

'Your mother has something I want. I have no desire to hurt you or your brother ...'

'You're a lying bastard,' she accused, struggling to break free.

'I am neither lying nor a bastard,' he said. 'Needs must, however. You will take a message to your mother and she will obey or your brother will be forfeit. Do you understand?'

Florentine's expression hardened, and Clement knew he was in danger of being the victim of every threat the girl had hissed at him. Here was the person capable of thwarting everything he planned and hoped for. While he had her brother, however, he had control.

'Do you understand?'

She spat in his face. She understood.

'On the eve of the spring equinox, your mother will bring me the relic she possesses.'

'What relic?' Florentine asked. 'I don't know what you're talking about.'

Defiance and truth marched across her face in equal measure. He tightened his grip in her hair, dug his fingers into her neck.

She gritted her teeth and repeated, 'I don't know what you're talking about.'

'I don't believe you. Regardless, your mother will.' Clement's gaze slid from her face to Harry Whistler, who had removed the tarp from Will Downs and was pulling awkwardly on Drew's arm, moving him across to join his dead friend against the wall.

Florentine renewed her struggles and slithered out from his grip, turning on the instant and freezing as she took in the wretched tableau of a murderer arranging his victims.

'What have you done? Will! Drew!' Drew's eyes fluttered open, but consciousness was temporary. The streak of blood that marred his forehead was fresh, dripping down his face. His ear was bloodied as well, though it could not be seen if this was a separate wound or an extension of the gash in his scalp. 'Drew! Drew!'

Clement wrapped his arm around her waist and lifted her from the ground. She screamed and punched and kicked, but could not free herself. 'That's enough,' he said, words harsh in the enclosed space. 'Stop screaming. No one can hear you.'

Her voice lowered to a hoarse whimper.

'He is still alive.' Clement nodded at Whistler, who poked Drew to elicit a groggy movement in return. 'And he will remain so until the equinox. If you and your mother do as you're told, he will be released.'

The girl's body sagged in his arms, defeated for now.

'And Will?' she asked.

'I'm afraid there's nothing to be done there. Mr Whistler has his own demons to appease.' He placed his free hand on her head, palm to temple, and closed his eyes. The spirit within him rose up, rattling his bones and gouging muscles with an urgent need to free itself from his mortal body. A spectral brume leached from his skin, met the innate force that protected Florentine, and gently caressed her hair, cheek, brushed her lips with a lover's touch. She slumped, unconscious, and the spirit retreated to the cavern where it dwelled, deep in Clement's soul.

CHAPTER 20

*D*awn had stretched its first foray into the night when Florentine awoke, cold and cramped inside a stable that stank of horses. No amount of lye could disguise the stench of manure. It rankled in her nostrils and made her eyes water. She coughed and choked, until she was awake enough to crawl to the door and push it open.

She turned, hoping against hope that Drew was with her and cried when she saw she was alone. Using the doorframe as a crutch, she pulled herself to her feet, staggered for balance, and lurched out into the rear yard of the Garden Arms Hotel.

The kitchen door was wide open, spilling yellow light and a hubbub of voices into the morning. Florentine walked the short distance as if to the gallows, her heart quaking with the message she had to impart, and the magnitude of its meaning if not followed.

Rosalie sat huddled in the embrace of Honora and Anastasia at the kitchen table. No one had slept. Each was as miserable as the other, faces grey with fatigue, arms and legs heavy with the exhaustion of having spent the night searching for Florentine and Drew. They'd returned to the hotel to warm themselves and seek strength in hot tea and a scant meal. John Bray had stayed out with Clancy Dickens and Alexander Ridlay determined to find the errant Ponsonby children and return them to the fold.

Rosalie heard his bellow from the yard and feared what that sound might mean. She squeezed her eyes closed on tears of despair as her son-in-law's running steps came to her, and opened them in surprise when she realised he was laughing and Anastasia was pulling away from her, crying and laughing. Wrapped in John's bear-like hug was Florentine, bedraggled, eyes red, hair all over the place and skirts muddied and torn, but Florentine it was. Honora stood, poured tea into an empty mug, added spoons of sugar.

'Let the girl breathe, Johnny. Let her breathe,' she said, pushing the mug of tea into Florentine's cold hands, tracing her fingers over her wrists, and rubbing her arm. 'Come and sit, girl. I'll get you a bowl of soup. You look half done in.'

Rosalie sat and watched, hope a fragile thing in her heart as Florentine crumpled into sobbing. Anastasia rescued the tea before the mug fell. John, still holding his young sister, helped her to the chair beside her mother. Rosalie held her tight, her own tears flowing free.

'Shh, child. You're home now. Tell us what happened.'

Honora plonked a bowl of soup on the table. 'Let her eat first. She needs her strength.'

Rosalie nodded and lifted Florentine's dirt-streaked face, wiped away the track of tears and cradled her cheek. 'Honora's right. Have some soup. Drink some tea. Is Drew with you?' Rosalie's heart quelled when Florentine shook her head, misery etched into the poor girl's every feature. She put a finger on her lips to stop her from speaking. 'Just a mouthful. You look as if you'll faint without something to nourish you. Please, just a mouthful.'

She lifted a spoon of hot broth and vegetables. Florentine took it and began to eat. Half the bowl was emptied before she stopped, dropped the spoon, and reached for the tea.

'Drew and I went to examine underneath the statue of Queen Victoria. Mam, it's just like Mr Ridlay drew it, only … not worse, but more than his sketch could show.'

As if her mention of his name caused it, Mr Ridlay appeared in the doorway. 'Is that Florentine? Is she found? Is she hurt?' John stood aside to let the young man in. His flushed face showed the worry he felt when Rosalie and John had first gone to his rooms looking for her and Drew. Despite the apparent cooling of their friendship over the last few days, it was clear to all that the artist was enamoured of Florentine. He'd joined the search party immediately and led the small contingent that had climbed the fence into the Gardens. He came forward, sat beside Florentine, and held her hands in his as if he'd never part from her again.

'I'm not hurt,' she told him, and turning back to Rosalie, said again, 'I'm not hurt. Just tired and cold and scared. We left the Palace without anyone seeing us. Or so we thought. The gates weren't locked, but the nightwatchmen were about so we climbed the fence. Just across the road, so close to home. Will Downs was down the street a bit, he whistled and beckoned to Drew. I tried to get him to come home first, mam, to tell you about the statue, but he wouldn't. He said something about Will and some of the other boys having been following Mr Benedict and that Will must have something important to tell him, so he went.' Florentine paused, swallowing hard. Mr Ridlay let go her hand long enough to pass her the tea and urge her to drink.

Grateful for the interruption, Rosalie wrestled with her desire to know what had happened to her son and the dread that was uncurling itself in her belly. *Not Drew …*

'He didn't want me to come and I wasn't going to, but something didn't seem right. Drew walked under the street light and then vanished in the dark as if he'd stepped through a doorway. I could feel the night closing around us so I followed him and … it wasn't Will at all. It was one of Boseman's other lads, the mean one, and he hit Drew again and again.' Florentine started crying.

Rosalie clenched her hands so tight, her fingernails cut into her palms. She forced calmness. 'Take a moment, Florrie. Sip your tea. The story is there to be told without you needing to torment yourself.' She dug around in her pocket for a handkerchief and, ignoring the spots of blood from her hands, wiped the ravages of the night from Florentine's face.

'My blood boiled, Mam. I was so shocked and so angry. I pushed Drew's attacker away and punched and kicked him until he fell. Drew was on the ground, not quite conscious. I tried to drag him to safety, but he was too heavy for me.' She took Rosalie's hand. 'Then Mr Benedict came out from the shadows. He took my arm and the other regained his feet and took Drew, and I'm sure we were walking down Macquarie Street, but it was so dark, Mam. I screamed and screamed, but no one came. Then we were in a shed and a lantern was lit and Mr Benedict was talking, and I heard Drew so I turned around and the other lad was dragging him across the floor, and then I saw that it never could have been Will calling Drew on the street.' She gulped and Rosalie knew what was coming. 'Will Downs is dead. Murdered. Drew's okay,' she rushed to say. 'Hurt. I think badly, but alive, and Mr Benedict said he'll stay that way for now. I'm so sorry, Mam, but it all happened so fast.'

'There's nothing you could have done, Florrie. I sensed something was going to happen and when you didn't come home, I knew our enemy had made a stand. We fought and searched the whole night through. My poor babies. You have nothing to reproach yourself for, child. Not a thing.'

'I'll have that Benedict!' Mr Ridlay said, each word sharp as a knife. Fury etched a mask over his face of formidable strength and determination. Benedict would pay for what he'd done, if not by her hands then by Alexander Ridlay's. Rosalie saw a similar expression on John's face. Anastasia and Honora too were ferocious in the plainly writ need for revenge.

'What is it that Mr Benedict wants, Florrie?' The poor girl had taken as much as she could for one night, her misery and fear were palpable.

'He wants you to take the relic to him on the eve of the equinox. Drew will be safe until then.'

Rosalie nodded. 'Did he happen to say where?'

'He's staying at the Union Club with his father, Lord Benedict,' Alexander interrupted.

'I hardly think they want me to come there.'

'Lord Benedict's not involved, surely?' Alexander looked anything but convinced. 'He's old and does nothing but drink sherry and eat.'

'Lord Benedict is more than what you see on the surface, Mr Ridlay. He is the master, and his son the apprentice.'

Rosalie knew the location of the meeting. The coming battle would be lost and won under the belly of the great dome, at the feet of the queen; the crossroad where time and distance, land and spirit met and became one. A shiver crept across Rosalie's skin as the echo of an ageless voice rang in her ears.

Anastasia stood behind her, hands on her shoulder. Florentine sobbed into Honora's shoulder. John and Alexander were by the door, muttering dark words that boded ill for the Benedicts. The men were going to war and it would be bloody and merciless unless she stopped it. Time had passed while she sat daydreaming.

'As you were, gentlemen.' Rosalie stood to put the kettle back on the hob. 'Drew is safe for now. We will not risk that for fruitless revenge. Clement Benedict wants a relic.' She looked at Florentine. 'He doesn't know what it is he asks for though, Florrie, now does he?'

Florentine shook her head and sniffed. 'He wasn't specific, Mam.'

'And we do not know why he wants it or what he intends to do with it. Therefore, on the eve of the spring equinox, we will give him a relic and we will watch and wait. I need to know his plans and to save Drew at the same time. He and his father have dark power at their fingertips. We have an army.'

The men glowered, not ready to give up the instinct of savagery that came with having loved ones to protect.

'Sit,' Rosalie ordered. 'This battle cannot be fought with angry fists.'

John said something about getting his hands on some weapons. Rosalie glared at him until he came away from the door and pulled out a chair. An arched eyebrow in Alexander's direction and he followed suit.

'Honora, let's start breakfast. Anastasia, please set the table.'

'Mam …' she started to say, surprised perhaps at this sudden return to normalcy when her brother lay injured and captive.

'Have no doubt,' Rosalie responded before she could get her words out, 'Clement Benedict has drawn a line, which we will cross, armed not with clubs or rifles, but with knowledge and the power of our ancestors in our hands. That knowledge and that power starts right here in this kitchen. Sit while we make breakfast.'

That Benedict knew of Alexander's connection with the Ponsonby family was in no doubt. He'd waxed lyrical on several occasions. Thinking back on those conversations now, Alexander blushed on realising that Clement had encouraged the direction of each exchange with chatty observations and remarks.

Clement's surprise visit to watch him draw and paint down at the wharf just a few days ago had ulterior motives that he'd been too flattered to see. He'd been such a fool! Clement had flicked through one of his sketch books, seen a few of the sketches of the Queen Victoria statue. Alexander hadn't needed much prompting to tell the traitorous son of a bitch all about it. He skited about how he'd coaxed the guard to let him in before opening, cajoled the fountain engineer to show him the inner workings of the fountain. He'd thought he'd been so clever about the whole thing, all the while Clement Benedict was playing the same ploy to get what he wanted. Information.

He helped Florentine upstairs, noting how quiet and dark the lower floors were. They should have been bustling with a life that was being sapped out of the Ponsonbys. It occurred to him halfway up that Florentine had said she'd received no note from him over the last week. He'd sent several. Heat suffused his cheeks, less embarrassment than pig-headed temper. How far had Benedict's manipulations gone?

Florentine turned the doorknob to a room at the top of the stairs, and pushed the door open to reveal the family sitting room.

'I'll light the fire,' he said, ushering her to a plainly upholstered settee. He fetched a cushion from another chair, plumped it up, and spread a knitted throw over her legs. She had yet to say anything further and he didn't want her to endure any more exertion. Soon enough she'd be back out on the frontline with her mother and sister. For now, peace and quiet and warmth were needed.

The previous night's fire had long since burned away. The remains of the logs were fragile ashes. He collected kindling from the log caddy and a taper and set to work. By the time the cook had come up with a pot of tea and more soup, the fire was crackling away and Alexander was by Florentine's side, rubbing warmth into her hands and murmuring gentle platitudes and apologies.

'Thank you, Mr Ridlay. I'll take care of her now. I believe Mr Bray is after seeing you in the yard as soon as you can.'

Alexander recognised a hardness in the Irish woman that he suspected ran deep in everyone connected to this household. They were by no means cowed by Clement's brazen attack. The more they hurt, the more they showed how tough and determined they could be.

Benedict had crossed them to his own detriment. Alexander hoped he would be there when they took up arms against him.

Rosalie escaped to the dining room to think, fighting through a growing numbness that started in her belly and inched its way to her groin, her thighs, her breasts. Her hands and feet roared with the fire of frozen appendages thawing too fast. Her head throbbed and her throat constricted. She swallowed down bile, clenched her teeth, and blinked back hot tears. *Drew is alive.* She repeated those three words, over again. On the table was Mr Ridlay's book with his drawings of the statue. One page had come loose and poked out, marking a place in the bulging pad. She took it in a pincer grip and pulled it free.

The Cailleadch stared out at her from the lines of the queen's face, her lips blue, eyes tinged with red, a furrow of chagrin across her brow. Rosalie put her fingertips to her own face, felt the tight lines, the damp cheeks. She had to pull herself together. She touched her fingers to her lips and then to the picture.

Keep him alive!

She walked out, ready to take command.

John Bray lived for his family. Marrying Anastasia Ponsonby had come with a set of unspoken rules. First and foremost, family was everything. With his own brothers and sisters back in Dublin and his parents deceased, he'd taken to the Ponsonbys as easily as they to him. To hurt them was akin to hurting one of his own; they were his own.

He shared a similar sentiment with Honora Keogh and sensed the same in the young artist.

When Ridlay came out to the yard, the softness John had seen in the man's face earlier had been replaced with a simmering anger. Good. He would need that to bolster his strength in what was sure to be a bloody and vicious encounter. Florentine would need that too.

Each spring morning thus far had been warmer than the one previous. Except today. A cold snap and frozen dew to the bare bushes in the garden, icicles dripped from the windows and the path crunched underfoot. John and Mr Ridlay had talked but a few minutes in the yard before walking into the stables, John's arm on Mr Ridlay's shoulder.

Rosalie debated on bringing them to rein or letting them commit carnage on the Benedict heads. They had two days until the eve of the spring equinox.

Even though it tore through every instinct, she would have to stop them. The yard felt particularly lifeless without Drew. She commanded an iron will and kept the blubbering tears at bay. The men's voices could be heard but words not distinguished until she opened the door.

'She said down Macquarie Street so we'll head in that direction and search every building we come to.'

'If we talk to her again, she might remember more of the room. If we know what sort of room he's being kept in, we might be able to narrow down the search,' Mr Ridlay suggested.

'Aye, clever idea, but she'll need some rest and we should be out straight away.' John thumped the blunt end of an old axe in his hand. His fingers closed around the rusted metal, feeling for the edges, before he thumped it down again.

'I'll talk to her,' Rosalie added. The men started and turned toward her, squinting to see her shaded face. She stepped through the doorway. 'Mr Ridlay, you're a friend of Clement Benedict?' He blushed and frowned, lips straightening in an angry line. 'I want to know everything you know about him and then I want you to go back to your room at the Royal Society.

'I'll be helping to search for young Drew,' he interrupted. 'I would never have taken Benedict for a kidnapper. It's partly my fault that this has happened …'

'Don't be ridiculous. The fault lies with Mr Benedict alone.' She softened as she went on, taking his hand and patting it with affection. 'I need eyes where mine cannot reach. He has worked to keep you apart from Florentine this past week has he not?'

Mr Ridlay looked shocked, but nodded. 'I suspect as much. I sent notes to Florentine, which she did not receive. I had no desire to be separated from her. Why would he interfere like that?'

'To distract Florentine from her task, perhaps. Or perhaps for the sheer enjoyment of manipulating the people around him. That I do not know. However, we will use that to our own ends. You must pretend that you know nothing of what has happened. I want you to go to the Union Club. See what you can and report back to me.'

He was set to argue. Rosalie held his hands firmly. 'To be a spy is a dangerous task. Will Downs has paid a price I do not want anyone else paying, but even more wicked, he was used as bait to lure Drew and Florentine in. You, sir, will also be bait. You will need to be at your most observant, most careful.'

'If I show up at the club, he'll be suspicious, surely. I'm not a member and I've only been in by invitation previously.'

'That will be taken care of. Go and wait in the kitchen a moment, if you please. I'll have a word with John in private.'

'Of course.' Alexander left, closing the door behind him.

Rosalie liked this young man. He fit exceedingly well into the family. She turned to John, waiting patiently with his axe. 'Put that down, John,' she said. On the wall hung a basket full of gardening tools. Rosalie went to it and retrieved a piece of wood shaped at one end to accommodate a hand, clubbed at the other for pounding herbs and nuts and roots. 'This will fit much easier under your coat.' She handed it to him. 'Less threatening. Less blood. Just as deadly if it needs to be.'

John took the club with a grin that did not bode well for anyone who got in his way. 'They'll not be getting away with this,' he said.

'No. They won't. But listen to me, John. You are searching. Find Drew without arousing suspicion if possible. We need him safe, but without Benedict knowing his trump card has vanished. I expect you'll find that Harry Whistler is the culprit doing Benedict's dirty work. Confirm that if you can. Again, on the sly. He's as dangerous as Benedict and too ready to commit violence. Will Downs was as much a friend as he's ever likely to have had, and he murdered him or stood by while Benedict did the deed.'

'Yes, ma'am. Shall we go chat with Florrie now?'

Rosalie nodded. 'We also need to talk with Ana and Honora. Protections must be put in place.'

∼

The kitchen appeared as it always did, a hive of activity. The rest of the hotel might be waiting for use to return, but the heart beat was strong as ever. If walls could hold memories, floors absorb the tread of familiar step from baby to adult to aged, then this kitchen was a storybook, an encyclopaedia dedicated to the Ponsonby family. At this table, babies had been fed and sung to, children instructed on the business of family affairs, adults joked and cried and shared news. At this stove, countless meals had been cooked, kettles boiled, soups stirred.

And now, with the culmination of every story ever told within these walls about to be reached, Anastasia worked the magic she had been born to. Every hob on the stove was lit with a pot bubbling away above it. Anastasia wove a wooden spoon through the air like a maestro conductor, singing as she worked. Her free hand sprinkled herbs and petals, spices and crushed berries, or used a second spoon to stir and fold.

Words danced around Rosalie and John as they entered, settled on their heads and shoulders, welcomed them into Anastasia's bounty. The aromas from the pots strengthened resolve, straightened shoulders, and brightened faces. Intention, Rosalie had taught, and Anastasia had listened. She would be the steel in her mother's step and the backbone in her sister's resolve.

She met John's gaze and saw there the controlled anger and force that would find Drew and bring him home, and then mete out the appropriate punishment. His knuckles were white, fist strong around the club in his hand. Anastasia smiled. John had come from a troubled family in a troubled neighbourhood where brawling was a part of every day. He'd left that behind the day he signed up for emigration. Today, it all came back and her peace-loving husband was ready to step to the front to defend his family.

'Nora is seeing to Florrie. She took some warm water up not ten minutes ago. Breakfast is almost ready. What do you need?'

Rosalie sniffed at the aromas vying for attention. 'From what I can tell, you've thought of everything. Protection and strength, good. Mr Ridlay will need a Concealment. He's going to do a little spying. I don't want him found out. John is to go looking for Drew so he'll need an Unearthing potion.'

Anastasia reached for the wax-sealed bottles above the stove. Her song turned its focus toward the tasks the two men had been assigned.

'I'll go to Florrie,' Rosalie added. 'We'll be down soon for breakfast. We'll eat and then she should be ready to talk.'

Anastasia waited until her mother had left the room before turning to John. 'I'll check on the children while you look for Drew.' John came to her and wrapped his arms around her waist. She leant into his body, felt the tremor of his emotions and the tight control he exerted.

'Be careful,' he whispered, his lips grazing her earlobe.

Anastasia turned her face to his. 'You too.'

The shifting of a chair at the table reminded them of Mr Ridlay's presence.

'If you and Mr Ridlay would like to set the table, I'll fill your plates now. You'll want to be on your way before the day grows much older.' Her hands shook as a vision of her brother, battered and bruised and alone, came to her. She feared for him. She feared for her wee ones tucked in their beds above the bakery. She feared for them all. A rush of steam from behind her drew her attention back to breakfast and potions. She blinked back tears, sprinkled coarse salt over the frying potatoes, and stirred a thickening brew.

Sounds of eating, knives and forks being pushed around plates, tea being drunk, and mugs refilled filled the kitchen. Faces sombre and

strained, each person concentrated on the meal as if it were their last.

As the plates were emptied, Bridie started clearing the table. Honora went to the pantry to fetch a basket of herb-filled muslin bags and Anastasia returned to her potions simmering on the stove.

Rosalie had brought down a roll of paper from the sitting room. She unrolled it now and lay it on the table in front of John. She had already talked to Florentine about what had happened and hoped that going over this map with her son-in-law would jog a few more details from her tired mind.

Mr Ridlay had placed himself beside Florentine the moment she'd returned to the kitchen. If they could get through the next few days, Rosalie could see a long future for the couple. For a fractional moment, an older version of the two superimposed over their youthful faces and Rosalie took heart. She may be a sentimental fool, but she would take hope wherever she could find it.

'This is the most up-to-date map of the city there is. There've been a few changes by the wharves since you and Anastasia left for Tambaroora.'

John leant over the map. 'I've noticed,' he said. 'Some of the wool stores are gone and there's some new construction on the water's edge here.' He pointed to a spot on Circular Quay where work had started on converting the wharves and buildings to ferry terminals. He looked up at Florentine. 'You went down Macquarie?'

She nodded as Alexander's arm went around her shoulders. 'Definitely. There was no mistaking the steepness of the hill and I remember smelling the governor's stables, but I don't think we went as far as the water.'

'So not by the fort then?' John asked. Florentine shook her head.

Rosalie stood behind John and pointed to a narrow lane. 'Do you recall crossing the street or turning a corner?'

Florentine closed her eyes, pressed her lips together in a tight line. Her brow furrowed as she tried to recall. Rosalie wished she could take this horrible night from her daughter as Florentine's face paled. Honora placed a cup of honeyed herb tea in front of her and as steam wafted upward, her face relaxed. She opened her eyes and sipped the hot tea before speaking.

'Drew was being half-carried, half-dragged by Harry Whistler. I remember seeing his face now. His hat slipped back and there was just enough light to recognise him. We'd been on the garden's side of the street and they tripped on the opposite gutter, then we stepped up behind them, and the buildings were close by my left side. We crossed again, I remember stumbling from the path and then cobbles underfoot. We didn't walk on the footpath again.'

John double-tapped the map. 'Definitely this right-of-way then. Any further and they'd be by the wharves. Its uneven, there's no paths, and plenty of back doors to hide behind if you have the key.'

'I don't remember how long we walked. It didn't seem any time at all, but the whole night was unnatural.'

'What do you mean?' Rosalie left the map to rest a hand on Florentine's shoulder. She cupped her face and lifted her chin until their eyes met. Rosalie searched for evidence of misdeed in her daughter's tired gaze, a trace of lingering magic that might still cause harm.

'Time, Mam. We would have been home for supper, I'm sure. And I don't feel we were in that awful room for long, nor in the stable where I woke up, yet the whole night passed by.'

Rosalie watched the fear rise once more, tinged with shame, and she smiled. 'This Benedict has some power. You are not to blame for what happened and neither is Drew.' She glanced at Mr Ridlay. 'You were all tricked.' She smoothed an errant lock of hair from her Florentine's cheeks. 'But remember how you feel now, my daughter. You will need this to fuel your own power, to anneal your birthright. Soon you will realise that within you is all you need to follow your path.' Rosalie blinked away a gritty tear. Florentine's face swam before her, hard with appalled puissance, and faded as light fades on sleep and the night takes hold.

'Mam? Are you all right?' Florentine pulled away, red marks on her skin where fingers had squeezed.

Mr Ridlay had pushed back his chair and started to stand. Anastasia had dropped her spoon into a pot with a clatter and rushed to grasp Rosalie's shoulders. 'Mam, what is it?'

Rosalie shook her head and wiped her face with a trembling hand. 'Nought to worry about.' She patted Anastasia's arm. 'A glimpse is all. Not enough to make sense. Florentine in a temper. Nothing unusual in that.' Rosalie caught Honora's steady gaze from across the room. She forced a smile to her face and turned away.

'Time to be getting on, I think. Are you ready, Mr Ridlay? John?'

The right-of-way formed a casual passage bounded by Macquarie and Phillip Streets through a slab of vacant land between the Treasury and the Water Police Courts. Shanty huts huddled together along its length, an extension of outhouses that serviced the courts and police station. Sheets of iron were nailed over wooden frames that stored anything from spare hoses for the fire station at the Phillip Street end to extra bonded storage. Outhouse Lane was dark and dismal even as the sun spread across the harbour and into the city.

Mr Michaels and Clancy Dickens waited in the stables. Honora had sent Bridie out with tin mugs of hot tea and slabs of bread with eggs and bacon. They were just finishing off when John Bray walked in.

'Michaels. Clancy. Your boys still out?'

Clancy wiped bacon grease from his mouth and swallowed before answering. 'Aye. I've sent word for them to come back here. We heard the lass'd returned. No sign of the boy then?'

'That she has. Drew's being held.' John spat on the ground. 'Bastards have given him a good beating, but he's alive. Not so for young Will. Florrie says they've done him in.'

Michaels growled, shoved the rest of his sandwich in his mouth and washed it down with a gulp of tea. 'We best be moving then before they do the same to the boy.'

Clancy nodded. 'Aye. Jim and his boys have been searching 'round the Rocks. He'll be devastated. Do you know who's responsible yet?'

'Florrie recognised Harry Whistler and a toff in town who's been causing the family trouble.'

The three moved out into the alley.

'Whistler's a right little prick. One of Boseman's lads,' Michaels said. 'Who's this bloody toff?'

'Name's Benedict. Mrs P's handling him. You know Florrie's young fella?' John said, and when Michaels nodded he continued, 'I want someone backing him up. He's going into the Union Club to see what he can find out. He's pretty green.'

Michaels swiped his cap from his head and slapped it against his thigh. 'I'll do that myself. Good man, that. He still inside?'

John fished in his coat pocket and pulled out one of Honora's muslin bags on a long leather cord. 'Take this. Mrs P says take no chances. Stay invisible. This Benedict bastard is not what he seems.'

Michaels took the bag and hooked it over his head, tucking the bag under his shirt to rest against his chest. 'I won't act unless the situation warrants.'

The two men shook hands and Michaels returned to the stable to wait.

John and Clancy walked fast along the alley and broke into the spreading sunshine on Macquarie Street.

'We need to get down to Outhouse Lane on the quiet as well. We think Drew and Will might be locked in one of the sheds. Do you know if Boseman owns one of those?'

'Owns most of them,' Clancy said. 'Rents them out and keeps a couple for his personal use. They're all chained and locked, and stronger than they look. Breaking in won't be quiet, 'specially this early. Residents'll get shirty.' One of his boys appeared on the street ahead of them. Clancy waved him over and sent him to fetch Jim

Downs. 'If we wait for Jim, we can get his boys to form a net around the lane to see what they can catch, maybe create a distraction while we search the huts.'

'That'll do. We haven't got a lot of time. I want Boseman caught in that net as well as Harry bloody Whistler, but we can't close in on them straight away unless there's no choice. Something big is happening tomorrow night and Mrs P needs to spring Benedict's trap without him knowing until the last possible moment.'

'We'll do what we can. Won't be able to hold Jim back though. War'll break out as soon as he knows. Boseman and Whistler are as good as dead.'

When the men had gone, Rosalie sent Bridie to Bell's Books with a message for Ina Bell, and Anastasia to the bakery to check on her little ones and pass a message to Amy Shadler.

'I'm scared,' Florentine said. 'For Drew, for Alexander, for all of us. Mr Benedict is evil, Mam. All the way through. I can feel it.' She waited for Rosalie to say something to make her feel better, something that would ease her worries.

'I'm scared too,' Rosalie said. Not at all what Florentine was hoping for. 'As soon as the others get back we'll start on our next move. Until then, we need to talk more about the relics. You have the disc I gave you?'

The disc had been warm against her skin since her mother had given it to her charge. She dipped a hand under her blouse and pulled out a long leather thong that ended in a pouch. Similar to the muslin amulets Honora had been working on all morning, Florentine had designed this one with an embroidered circular emblem. When Rosalie arched an eyebrow at the bold pattern, Florentine gave a lopsided grin. 'The design came to me in a dream. Don't worry. That's the decoy.'

Rosalie emptied the pouch onto the table and a round creamy-white shell slid out.

'I found that the day we all went for a picnic to the beach. Do you remember, Mam? Drew and I spent hours fossicking at the waters edge while Ana and Johnny walked up and down the beach and da taught the twins how to swim.'

'I remember. It was teach them how to swim or watch them drown when the raft they made broke into pieces.' Rosalie shook her head. 'Aunt Flora surely has her hands full with those two, they haven't changed one bit.'

Florentine opened the top of her blouse and exposed her chemise beneath. She loosened the ties and slipped her fingers into her brassiere and, this time, when she pulled them out, she held the metal disc she guarded.

The morning sun stretched fingers of warmth into the kitchen and burnished the metal with a deep gleam. Her palm tingled as the weight of the disc grew heavier in her hand.

Rosalie closed Florentine's fingers over the disc and pushed it back. 'Keeping it over your heart is appropriate, but nowhere is safe from Benedict. Remember that.'

'I will, Mam.'

'The disc you hold is the key to unlock a great weapon. I don't know what the weapon is, nor have I ever seen it. It was lost long ago. The story is that it belonged to an ancient grandmother who was such a warrior she could tame the hounds of hell, leap across oceans, and conquer armies.'

'We could do with a little of that now,' Florentine said. 'And the other disc? The one Anastasia has?'

'Have I told you about the Cup of Welcome?' Rosalie paused to refill her cup with tea. 'We have one on the mantelpiece in the dining room. We use it when we have a visitor from home.'

Florentine knew that meant anyone from Scotland. Other than Aunty Flora, no family from the Isle of Skye had ever come calling on them at the hotel. The one in their dining room was silver steel with an intricate pattern in the base.

'The tradition is that you offer your best whisky in the cup and each visitor, and yourself of course, takes a sip. Such a cup was buried with our ancestor under the wych elm tree outside our village.'

'The grave that was ransacked?'

Rosalie nodded, turning her teacup in her hand. 'Yes. I now believe that Mr Benedict is responsible for that reprehensible act. The magic he uses, that I can smell in the air, is palpable. A pall over the city. He has taken something he has no right to and corrupted the energy within.'

Florentine thought for a moment. 'But it's the intent not the tools that are corrupt, isn't it? If we were to take this cup and whatever else he stole back, we could, I don't know, purify it somehow. We have the right of use, don't we? Whatever manifestation we created would not be corrupt.'

Rosalie stared at her, eyes widening. 'That would be true. However, Ethne's Cup is used for welcoming spirits. Through it we can call on the spirit of our ancestors to assist us in times of need.'

'Just our ancestors?' Florentine asked. Something niggled at the back of her mind. She needed to see her copy of the journal.

'That I don't know. I've not seen or used the cup. Times of need is generally held to be a major catastrophe or world-altering effect and I don't recall any such time occurring. But to get back to the disc. It also is a key. The cup cannot be unlocked without its key.'

'And the weapon not used without its key? Do you think Benedict has that as well?'

Rosalie stood and took her cup to the kitchen door.

'Do you think he's found a way of using them outside of their true purpose? How? Why?' Florentine joined her mother and the two women shared a quiet moment of repose looking into the dew-damp garden.

'Mam, why would the Benedicts do all they have done? What do they hope to achieve?'

'So many questions, Daughter. Why have they murdered and pillaged, pirated themselves for a power they cannot possibly hope to understand? We would need to ask them. No doubt they follow their own stories. Life in Kilmarie was not always idyllic, even though I prefer to remember it that way. Perhaps through the eyes of a child it was. I was only sixteen when I left. Close enough to childhood to see life around me and, up until that last night, think it was good.' Rosalie took a deep breath.

'Story has it that every generation or so, a strange man would come to the village, sometimes quiet and full of shadows, other times raving about evil witches. Such a man came when Ethne was a young woman. It is she who was buried with the seeds of the wych elm at her head. She was one of three sisters. One married an Irish chief and left for that wild country. Of the two left behind, Ethne was already married with bairns at her ankles. The third, Lilas, fell in love with a man who came to the village. One of the quiet ones. He could speak Scots well enough, but had a strange accent. They were betrothed. Not long after, on the cusp of winter, he was out walking in the hills and was caught in a storm. Too close to the faery mounds, it was said. Outside when he should have been safe inside. He returned days later, unshaven and unwashed, hair wild, raving. He raped his betrothed violently, viciously; he took from her what was not his to take. Of course, he was found and caught.

'There's an old fort at Kilmarie. A ruin now, and even then not habitable, but it had some rooms that could be used. He was locked in the fort while the villagers decided his punishment.'

'What happened?' Florentine asked.

'It's not known for sure. Blood was found on the ramparts one morning, a pool of it on the rocks, but no body, and Lilas' arisaid flying flag-like from a branch growing halfway down the cliff.'

Florentine could not find a single word. Cold, ragged breaths rent her throat. A woman on a rocky cliff, face tortured with horror, her wrap fluttering behind her. Below her the sea. Above, pulsing stars in the night sky. Florentine could feel the wind on her face, betrayal and loathing in her heart. Her hands, slick with her lover's blood, gripped a dagger. She plunged it into her chest, leant forward. And fell.

Rosalie grabbed Florentine's arms and held her upright, helped her to a chair. 'What is it? What did you see?'

'I didn't see anything, Mam. I was her. I killed him with some kind of dagger. I loved him so much, hated him for what he did. I killed him and then myself. Or she did, but I was there, inside her. The dagger, Mam. She used the ancient weapon outside of its true purpose without the lock and with hatred in her heart. How could she?'

'No one knows the story of her last moments. Except for you, Florentine. You have become her witness. Be careful with this knowledge. It's not complete. Neither that dagger nor Lilas were seen again.'

'What has any of this to do with the Benedicts?'

'Somehow they know the power of the relics. They've collected enough to use them, partially. Having the key to the cup will give them access to the ancestors, and through them will they learn the secrets to bend the world to their will. The very reason the relics were hidden in the first place.'

Florentine jumped to her feet. 'How can we hope to stop them?'

Honora stayed in the yard hanging out the wash, picking herbs, waiting for Anastasia and Bridie to return with Amy and Ina. Rosie needed time to talk with Florentine in private. The girl had suffered a shock, but it was nothing compared to what was coming. Honora could feel it in her waters, and see it in her oldest friend's eyes. Worse was yet to come.

Voices filtered through the fence from the lane beyond. Women discussing weather and fabrics and food. Honora swung open the gate to admit the chattering women. She met the gaze of each as they walked by, the conversation faltering as they acknowledged the brevity of the situation. Amy lagged behind while Honora closed and bolted the gate.

'Will we few be enough?' she asked.

Honora and Amy had been friends a long time. The Irishwoman held the baker back, let Anastasia and Bridie enter the kitchen ahead of them. 'Aye, we are enough. Three and three and three.' Amy raised her eyebrows and Honora finished. 'Rosie, Ana, and Florrie. You, me, and Ina. Bridie, Johnny and, I suspect, Florrie's young gent may be the last. We'd have Mary Downs, but for her son's murder. She sent over a prepared mandrake last week.'

'Who knew quiet mouse Mary knew mandrake lore? I'd have not thought Jim would hold to the old ways.'

'He must do. Such lore requires a lot of effort and can't be hidden so easily from one's husband.'

Amy nodded. They let the subject drop as they walked into the kitchen.

Six women filled the kitchen with their circle. The closed door and blind down at the window kept the sunshine at bay. Candles lined the table. At one end were unstoppered bottles and dishes of herbs. Stove hobs extinguished but for one, kept low, under a cast-iron cauldron. Another cauldron placed on the floor, filled with hot, sweet-smelling water.

Either side of Florentine stood Amy and Ina, then Anastasia, Honora, and Rosalie at the head. Bridie tended the stove.

They held hands and started to sing. Their voices, soft at first with welcomes and introductions as they assured the spirits of their intentions, harmonised as they rose in a melody that overflowed the room and sought out the chosen recipients; infusing John Bray and Clancy Dickens with courage and stealth, and with increased perception. Hands still clasped, Rosalie, Anastasia, and Florentine took one step forward and dropped the tone of their voices to a deeper chorus that underlay the melody with soothing words of healing and strength for Drew.

Hands released, Rosalie turned to Bridie, now stationed beside the table, and took from the young lass's hand the first of the narrow bottles and a glass dropper. She dipped the delicate pipette into the bottle and withdrew one drop of distilled essence. Bridie held up a saucer of mint leaves. Rosalie selected one and knelt beside the cauldron. She squeezed the rubber bulb and the contents plopped into the hot water. Using the mint leaf, she stirred.

We implore you to bring stealth and concealment to the footsteps and actions of Alexander Ridlay and Mr Michaels in their quest to uncover corrupted magic and motives.

The leaf wilted and a cloud of mint-flavoured steam rose into the air. Harmonic sound rang out as the women added their voices to the plea.

Bridie passed down a ceramic bowl filled with dried juniper berries.

We implore you to gift wiliness and strength to John Bray and Clancy Dickens.

They search for the victims of corrupted magic.

Your grandson, hurt. His friend, murdered.

Rosalie added another drop of the essence and a handful of berries. Their sharp peppery scent bit into her nostrils, her eyes watered. She leant over the cauldron and blinked her tears into the potion. Bridie took the bottle and bowl, and stood ready with the wooden spoon used to stir the soup.

We offer you succour and a place in our hearts and that of our children for all eternity.

We offer you the bounty of our kitchen and the warmth of our hearth.

We offer you the purity of our intentions to protect and serve.

Rosalie stood and joined the circle. While Bridie clapped a slow beat, the women danced in simple movements, voices and hearts uplifted, thoughts on the men and the boys, the quest and their safety, love of their ancestors, dedication to traditions, gratitude for their welcome to a new land, and their honouring of that land's spirits and stories.

In gradual breaths of time, the steam thickened, crystalline stars grew, took shape, formed a phantasm of being. Rosalie and Honora lifted their arms to allow Bridie to slip into the circle. In her gloved hands was a plate holding slivers of mandrake root. She lifted a piece with a pair of wooden tongs and placed it gently into the centre of a swirling whirlpool of water and steam. The growing shape snapped upward, hit the ceiling and spread in a smoky cloud looking for a way out of the room. It disappeared in wisps through cracks, reached the walls and slid downward, flushed through the gaps in the windows. Bridie ran to open the door. The entity raced into the daylight, stretched so thin now it appeared as no more than a trick of the light, and divided into two shades. One rushed toward the harbour where John and Clancy searched the huts. The other to Alexander Ridlay in his room, trying to think of a way to sneak into the Union Club.

Voices a low hum around them, Honora, Ina, and Amy prepared to lift the cauldron.

'Take it upstairs to the family sitting room. Start the fire, but keep it banked,' Rosalie instructed. 'Bridie, I'll need you to check on this throughout the day. The potion needs to stay warm. Take some of the berries and the rest of the mint. One leaf, three berries, and a good stir every two hours should keep it active.'

'Yes, Mrs P,' Bridie said. She bobbed a quick curtsy, picked up the leaves, berries, and spoon, and moved to open the door into the corridor.

'What will we do, Mam?' Florentine asked.

'We have talismans and more potions to prepare. I want you to do these in the pantry away from the others for now. You'll need the journal, paper, ink, and a quill each, and some pencils for practising before you create sigils.'

'I'd rather help find Drew.'

'Leave that to John and Mr Dickens, Florrie. Mam needs us here and no one else but us can help with the magic.' Anastasia pulled on her sister's arm. 'Come away upstairs. I have plenty of paper and pencils and the like. You fetch your copy of the journal.'

Rosalie felt a dead weight press down on her shoulders when her daughters left the room. She'd rather be looking for Drew as well, but Ana, wise as always, was right. Only they three could do what needed to be done next.

Honora could be relied on to take care of the family while she worked with Anastasia and Florentine. Amy and Ina would offer every support they could. Rosalie glanced outside at the bright sunshine filling every corner of the garden. John would be back with Drew soon, and poor Will would be with his parents as well. She whispered a prayer for Will's soul. That he perished while serving her cause, out of loyalty to his mother's beliefs, provided no ease to her regret and guilt. She hoped he found his true path in the next world.

CHAPTER 23

*N*oon crackled in the sky by the time John Bray came into the garden carrying Drew Ponsonby in his arms. The boy was groggy and begrimed, but alive. Rosalie cried with relief and renewed fear for her son, and slammed out of the kitchen to meet them. Florentine was a step behind, ignoring the tears streaming down her cheeks.

'Let us go in out of this sun,' John said. 'He needs shade and water and a bath to wash the stink of that hovel from his skin.'

Rosalie put a hand to Drew's forehead. 'He's a fever. Quickly. Straight up to his bedroom. Florentine, start boiling water for his washstand. We daren't risk a bath right now. Have Anastasia warm some broth. The soup'll be too rich.'

Florentine held the door open for them and bundled in behind. Anastasia had already started on broth and water. Honora went to the pantry for a herbal poultice and lavender-infused cloths for his head. The making of talismans and spells was put on hold while Drew was cared for and Florentine had little to do in that regard. Her brother had more than enough people fussing around him than he needed or would want. She quashed the guilt and the uselessness that lingered and decided that time had come for her to take some action. Alexander needed her. She could feel that as strongly as she knew Drew did not.

But she would be recognised by Benedict and couldn't risk that. She gazed out the window at the clothes hanging in the breathless air. The thought came swiftly and was acted on immediately. She went to the line, removed the pegs from a pair of Drew's trousers and one of his shirts, and returned to the pantry, closing the door tight and pulling the blind to change.

Once dressed she poked her head out into the kitchen.

'What are you doing in there, Florrie?' Anastasia asked. She turned from the stove and hid a smile behind her hand. 'What on earth?'

'Everyone's busy with Drew now—as they should be,' she hastened to add. 'I thought I'd go for a walk.'

'Disguised as your brother?' Anastasia forced a frown. Florentine wasn't fooled for a second.

'Yes, well, as a man, anyway. I don't want to be seen. What do you think?'

'I think you look like a woman in man's clothing. Drew's old shirt and trousers are tight where you don't want them to be.' She wiped her hands on her apron and went to the coatrack by the back door. 'Here. A coat to hide your curves and a hat to hide your hair.' She paused, hat twirling in her hands. 'Unless, of course, you're planning to cut all your hair off, then you may not need the hat.'

'Don't be silly.' Florentine slipped her arms into the coat sleeves and fastened the buttons. 'It's too big. Who owns this one?'

'Honora does. She likes it too large. Something about plenty of room to breathe. This is her hat too.' Anastasia pushed the hat down on Florentine's head. It hid her hair and half of her face. Anastasia giggled. 'You look a right goose.'

'I don't care. I need to get out. You won't tell Mam, will you?'

'Of course I will. But not until I see her. Are you going to see Alexander? Do be careful and stay out of Benedict's reach.'

'How did you know?'

Anastasia piled some old bread and a few books into a basket.

She slipped in a muslin pouch that smelled of juniper and mint and covered it all with a cloth. 'I'd do the same if it were John. Take these. You'll look like you're making a delivery.'

She handed it to her sister. 'I'm serious, Florrie. Be careful. Benedict's already attacked you once. You may not get off so lightly the next time.'

'I won't take any risks, I promise,' Florentine assured her sister.

'I don't believe that for a second. Off you go and be fast about it. I need you back here to finish the talismans.'

Florentine took the laden basket and walked out the door. She'd have to walk the long way in case the hotel was being watched, and sneak between the buildings at the end of the lane rather than go out to Macquarie Street, but she could walk fast. She'd just make sure Alexander was okay and then she'd come straight back. She heard singing as she walked through the yard and, from the corner of her eye, thought she saw a crystal-edged shade following her. She certainly hoped that's what she saw as she dashed out the gate and to the rear of the lane.

Sydney's streets seemed busier than usual. Florentine bumped into one person then another. Were there always this many people out of an afternoon? Businessmen in their black crow suits, heads down and in too much of a hurry to make their next appointment to care who they barged past. Workers in stained overalls lolling around with laughter and pointed comments ready to fling. Women strolling, taking in the unseasonal warmth while protecting their faces with flimsy parasols and oversized gardens on their heads. Florentine pulled her own hat down to further cover her face and held the basket to her front with a white-knuckled grip.

The Royal Society was not far. Florentine dodged a tram, wagons, and a pile of manure in the middle of the road and reached the Society's front steps without mishap. Her stomach knotted and she had the fleeting image of landing on her backside in the street after being thrown out for daring to trick the distinguished scientists and other learned gentlemen. She pushed open the door and peered in. The entry hall, dark after the bright sunshine of the street, was empty. No scientists. No learned gentlemen. Not even a doorman. She stepped in and saw a lobby desk with mailboxes behind it. Each box had a name and a number, and being still the newcomer, Alexander's was on the top row. Room 9.

That must mean something. Mam had always said nine was a lucky number. Down the hall, a door squeaked on its hinges. Voices tumbled out from the room. Florentine took quick steps to the staircase and went straight up. The building was narrower than the Garden Arms Hotel but had two more levels of stairs to climb. Room nine was on the top floor at the end of a ragged corridor. She knocked, jiggled the doorknob, and knocked again. No answer or sound of movement.

Florentine retraced her steps. The lobby desk was no longer abandoned. She readjusted her basket so the books could be seen poking out from under the cloth and tried to look disinterested. The doorman looked up as she stepped from the staircase to the lobby floor, but said nothing and went back to sorting mail into pigeon holes. City air never felt so sweet as when she left the building and trotted down the stairs. Her first foray into deception a success. She could barely keep the smile from her face.

The Union Club was another matter entirely. The building was something of a crumbling edifice on its way from old and romantic to decrepit with startling speed. Florentine stood opposite and watched as the doorman greeted visitors, opened doors, bowed, talked to everyone that came close. Her disguise would not get her past his attentiveness. She reached into the basket for the amulet Anastasia had given her and tried to remember the words her mam had spoken earlier. Something about concealment and wiliness, but that was for John or Alexander. She squeezed the pouch and brought it to her lips.

'Please,' she whispered. 'I need to know Alexander is all right. I need to go inside and see the seat of the evilness that has come. Conceal me.'

Florentine hoped that the blurriness in her vision was the concealment she pleaded for. It thickened and then stretched around her, a thin layer of air that made her skin tingle. A sharp crack rent the air as a wagon loaded with produce passed the drive of the Union Club. The wagon lurched. Horses whinnied and the driver cursed. Produce came loose from its bonds and spilled to the ground. The doorman walked over to see what the fuss was about.

'You can't leave that here, mate. Get it cleaned up quick.'

The driver stood, hands on hips. 'This pile's going nowhere fast. Damn tail shaft's snapped clear through.' He whipped his hat from his head and crouched down. 'Look at that. Beats me how that happened.' The doorman leant over to look. Florentine, already inching her way to the other end of the drive, saw her chance and walked across the road and along the narrow lane between the club and a worker's cottage.

With insides quivering, Florentine crept along the side of the building, trying to look as if she belonged rather than the edgy interloper she was. The basket hitting her across the shins warned her to slow her pace. The sweat trickling down her neck and the pound of a headache told her to breathe, relax. She forced her breathing to a regular pattern and blinked away the tightness around her eyes. By the time she walked into the rear yard, she had her unease under control.

The yard was not pretty. A vegetable garden to one side appeared well tended, but the rest was marred by the steady foot traffic of staff crossing between buildings. Hard-packed dirt created an organic pattern that ate into the ground. Florentine had no idea where to start so followed an outer path that circled the yard and took her by most of the buildings. She clutched the pouch in her hand tighter with every window she peeked in and every door she creaked open. The path led her to the side of the main building and two doors. She put her ear to each. Kitchen sounds from behind one, silence the other. The doorknob turned easily and the door swung open without a sound to reveal a short narrow walkway and a set of stairs.

Eyes, she could feel them, grazed her back with an unflinching stare. She froze, waiting for a challenge, twisting her head when none came to see the yard was eerily empty. Not willing to risk someone walking out and catching her, she tiptoed through the doorway and up the stairs. She held the basket in front of her as a shield. It was an encumbrance in the cramped space, but still useful in case of confrontation either as a disguise or a weapon. She hesitated at the landing, closed her eyes, brought the pouch upward, and breathed in the herbal scent, thinking of Alexander all the while.

Upward. The word formed in her mind as an urge to keep climbing until she reached the top landing.

She cocked her head to the side, sidestepping around a heavy door and darting glances up and down the wide corridor. She fought the desire to flee, concentrated on her breathing and relaxing twitchy muscles, and took a step. The floor was covered in a plush floral carpet that muffled her approach. No inner voice came to her here; no hint of which door would be the right door.

Further down the hallway, voices raised in argument, a thud, the sound of glass breaking, and a door being flung open against the wall. Wide-eyed at the swift escalation of violence in the rarefied atmosphere of the gentlemen's club, Florentine stopped moving as a body flew out of the room to land in a heap, jumped up, and threw himself back into the fray. Florentine moved to the wall and sidled along until she was close enough to hear some of the altercation.

'You feeble, dim-witted fool! How dare you presume to contradict me.' That voice shook, each word bitten off as if the speaker swallowed heat and temper. It didn't sound like Mr Benedict so it must be his father, the lord.

A soft scrape followed by a high-pitched ring of metal on metal and Florentine forgot fear and stealth and ran to the room, pausing long enough to peep in to see what was happening before standing legs wide and basket ready. Her voice came out as a roar, straining her vocal chords with unexpected ferocity. Lord Benedict, startled, allowed the blade pointed at Alexander's chest to drop. Mr Michaels, struggling with Clement Benedict, kicked his legs out from beneath him and pushed him to the floor. Alexander stared at Florentine, apparently surprised into immobility.

Mr Michaels advanced on Lord Benedict and Alexander. The blade started to rise, its point digging into Alexander's clothes. 'Don't move!' Lord Benedict ordered.

Michaels slowed, circling now. Clement, halfway to standing, shook his head, wavering and unsteady.

Florentine reached into the basket once more, pulled out a loaf of bread, and threw it at the old man's head. She followed with another and then a book, then rushed into the room as Michaels pushed Alexander aside and pounced on the lord, ripping the sword from his hand and throwing it across the room. Florentine swung her basket over her shoulder and clobbered Clement Benedict, hitting his back and connecting with his head. He fell like a tonne of bricks and stayed still.

'Run,' Florentine yelled. 'Leave them and run.'

Alexander pulled Michaels away from his attack on the older man and followed Florentine out into the hallway. Doors were opening, questions were being asked. Florentine led them to the servant's entrance, down the staircase, and into the yard.

They were halfway down Bligh Street, well past the broken-down wagon, before they slowed enough for Alexander to ask between great gasps of air, 'Florentine, is that you?'

Rosalie sat in the darkened room by her son's bed, a bowl of lukewarm water in her lap and a moist flannel in her hand. His face rested in sleep, damp hair curled at his temples and stuck out at angles over his forehead.

Downstairs, Anastasia and Bridie carried on with the tasks that were hers. Florentine was still not back. Honora moved between kitchen and bedroom with bowls of soup, potions, and an aching heart. Rosalie could feel that as if it were her own. She sighed and Drew stirred, tossing his head and frowning against bad dreams. Her boy looked so much like his father and so young. He winced as his bruised temple pressed against the pillow.

'Shh, now, Drew. You're home.'

His eyes opened a crack. 'Mam? I can't find Will. I thought I saw him, then he was gone ...'

'Will's with his own mam, Drew. Safe. Where he can't be hurt anymore.'

'Hurt?'

Rosalie dabbed his cheeks with the cloth. 'Shh now, back to sleep.'

A soft knock at the door and Honora was back with a bed-warmer wrapped in an old bath towel. 'I've put just a few coals in to keep his feet warm. Florrie's back with Mr Ridlay and Mr Michaels. John's busy giving her a piece of his mind.' Honora chuckled. 'Makes a mighty fine father does that young man.'

Rosalie rose and placed the bowl and cloth on the bedside table. 'Little does he know that those daughters of his will have him wrapped around their baby fingers well and truly by the time they reach Florrie's age.'

Honora tugged at the blankets at the end of the bed, lifted them, and pushed the warmer under Drew's feet. 'I'll keep an eye on his temperature and move that away if he gets too hot. Off with you now. I'll sit a spell here.'

Rosalie did not want to go. Inside this room was peace and quiet and the chance to care for a son who had not needed much caring for of late. *Children grow up too fast.* She could stay in here and pretend the boy was her wee bairn once more, or she could go outside where evil lurked in every corner waiting for her to make a mistake. She sighed again, patted Honora's shoulder, leant over the sleeping Drew, and wiped a ringlet of hair away from his eyes. He needs a haircut. *How could I have not seen how long his hair has grown? How tall he'd become? Too skinny though, still ...*

'Call me if he needs me,' she said. 'We nearly lost him today, Honora. I couldn't bear losing another, so call if he needs me. Every minute is precious.'

'I will, Rosie. Now, you have a job to do. Go do it and leave Drew to me.'

The women hugged. Honora wiped a tear from Rosalie's face. 'Go now,' she said again. 'I won't leave his side. Send Bridie up when you can.'

Rosalie walked with heavy feet and heart to the door, turned for a last look at her son, and went down to the kitchen to hear about Florentine's latest escapade.

~

Chaos reigned in the kitchen. Anastasia stood between her husband and her sister, one hand on his chest. Florentine, flushed with defiance, pointed her finger at him, angry words on her lips. Rosalie was glad she missed that argument. Alexander leant against the sink, coffee in his hand, smiling as he watched the heated discussion and interjecting with proud comments on Florentine's bravery and outrageousness.

She looked outrageous too in Honora's old coat and Drew's trousers. Rosalie folded her arms and waited.

'Mrs P,' Mr Michaels said. 'Coffee?'

'Yes, thank you, Mr Michaels.'

The room became quiet. Florentine, head raised, eyes flashing, did not look at all abashed by her mother's presence. Rosalie accepted the mug Mr Michaels handed her and sat down.

'Now then, let's start with Drew and then Alexander's visit to the Union Club. Bridie would you start dinner, please, while we talk? And I'll need you to check on our invalid throughout the rest of the afternoon and evening. Honora will stay by his side from now on, but even she will need a break occasionally.'

'Yes, Mrs P.'

'Right then, back to our invalid. Drew is sleeping. Not peacefully. He is, however, doing well. Thank you, John, for finding him so quickly and bringing him home. Did you see Jim Downs?'

John rested his hand on Rosalie's back and sat down beside her. 'I did. I've never seen a man so close to fainting one minute and ready to raise blue murder the next. He set a lot of store by that boy of his. Boseman and Whistler will pay ten-fold for what they've done.'

'Good.'

'It won't be quiet though, Mam. Jim will tear down houses to get his revenge and Benedict will know it.'

'He knows already,' Mr Michaels said. 'Our visit uptown didn't go as smoothly as it could have.'

Rosalie cast a suspicious glance at Florentine.

'I'm afraid that was my fault entirely,' Alexander admitted. 'I was

so worried about the younger Benedict that I forgot about the elder.
I don't think I've seen him before today. Quite a force in his own
right. I saw firsthand the obsession that rules them, father and son,
equally.'

Florentine shifted to Alexander's side. 'How could you know?'

'I may not be experienced at subterfuge, but I'm no fool either.
Not usually, anyway.' He leant toward Rosalie. 'The Benedicts have a
suite with a private sitting room separating their sleeping quarters.
Michaels and I searched and found evidence of ritual ceremonies
taking place. Candles and the like …'

'Not to mention the stink,' Michaels interrupted. 'Found a
possum once, it had fallen in the wall cavity, been there a month
before we could get to it, wrecked the walls trying too.' Michaels
leant out the door and spat into the garden. 'Never smelled anything
as awful as that until today.'

Alexander nodded. 'Dead things. Yes. I shudder to think what
they've been up to.'

'Would you be able to sketch some of the items you've seen?
They might help identify who and what sort of spirits they've called
to do their bidding.'

'Of course.'

'Did you see a dagger of any kind?' Florentine asked.

'No. There was a locked chest covered with a rich cloth and on
the table a brass bowl with a dank liquid and a black candle upright
in the centre.'

'What happened that you weren't expecting?' Anastasia asked.

'We checked the bedrooms. Clement's room was empty. I knew
it was his from a suit hanging on the valet, and the scent he wears
reminds me of home. We found a similar bowl with liquid and a
candle, but this one had what looked like black moss.

'Any particular smell?' Rosalie asked.

Alexander shook his head. 'No, but I touched it with a handkerchief and it came away dark red.'

'Blood. Probably his own,' Rosalie said.

'I was worried about how long we were taking so I left Mr

Michaels there to go through the cupboards and I went to start on the second bedroom. I didn't even think, just barged in. I'm afraid your Concealment amulet is no match for stupidity. Lord Benedict was sitting by the window with a small wooden box in his lap. The only benefit of the fiasco is that the box fell to the floor when he jumped up and spilled its contents. It looked like bones—a hand—in pieces, not wired, though it may have been displayed as whole and connected in its compartment.'

Rosalie reached across the table and took his hand. 'Think, Alexander. Was there anything else in that box?'

Alexander closed his eyes to concentrate. 'Bones, linen, and some gauze. That's all. No, a stone was on the floor with the bones.'

Rosalie leant back in her chair. She could hear her heartbeat thrashing in her ears. She swallowed on the lump in her throat. Lord Benedict was using her ancestor's bones to pervert magic, but where was the cup? Surely it wouldn't have been filled with moss and blood.

'What about elsewhere in the room?'

'I really couldn't say. Lord Benedict moves fast for an elderly gent. He came at me with a sword.'

Mr Michaels spoke up: 'Vicious bastard he is too. Unbalanced, I'd say. Nearly skewered Ridlay. I ran out to see what the commotion was about just as the lad dodged the old man's rapier. He came at him again. I was going for the candlestick holder on the sideboard to fend him off when the young one came in. Must have heard his old man hollering 'cause he was straight into it. Next thing you know, Florrie here was standing in the doorway yelling and throwing loaves of bread around. Best thing I've seen in an age and shocked the hell out of everyone. I got the better of the young'un and Ridlay got clear of the old geyser when a loaf of bread hit him in the noggin'.' Michaels paused to laugh. 'Rosie, m'love, you got yourself a handful!'

'No need to look so pleased with yourself, miss,' Rosalie said to Florentine. 'You didn't learn your lesson last night sneaking off without a word—you do it again today. What am I going to do with you?'

Florentine was speechless. Anastasia wasn't. 'You were busy, Mam. She told me and I agreed she should go. If you're going to be angry with someone, it should be me.'

Rosalie turned to her eldest. 'Don't think that I'm not.' Anastasia flushed and this time Florentine spoke in defence. 'Mam!'

Rosalie put her hand up for quiet. 'However, we need to be informed. If foolhardiness is how we learn, then foolhardiness it is. I can only hope Mr Benedict didn't recognise you, Florrie.'

Florentine bowed her head. 'I don't think so, Mam. Mr Michaels knocked him over and when he got up again, I whacked him in the head with the bread basket. I'm sorry, but I think I broke it.' She fixed her gaze on the dented basket near the sink.

'His head or the basket?'

'The basket. And the books are lost too.'

'More's the pity,' Rosalie answered. 'Keep your disguise on then, girl. You can go out again tonight. Paul,' Rosalie gave Mr Michaels a pointed look, 'you think she's so brave, I'd feel obliged if you went with her. Feel free to take more bread if you think you'll need it.'

Mr Michaels grinned.

'Where to, Mam?' Florentine asked as John said, 'I don't think that's a good idea,' and Alexander chimed in with, 'I'll go!'

'It may not be a good idea, but Florrie knows what she's looking for and this time she'll have Mr Michaels to watch out for her. Alexander, thank you, I need you here to sketch as much as you can possibly remember of the items in the Benedicts' rooms.

'Anastasia. You and I will work in the family room. John, would you be so kind as to take a message to Clancy and bring back news of Jim Downs' activities? I'd like someone watching the Union Club if it can be organised.'

'Yes, Mam. I'll go now before dinner.' John went to the bureau for pen, ink, and paper, and placed them on the table beside Rosalie.

'Florentine, would you please fetch some of Drew's drawing

things for Alexander? I don't think he should go back to his own rooms for now.'

Florentine beamed and ran out of the room before Rosalie could give her an admonishing 'behave yourself' look.

'Bridie? How's dinner coming along?'

Almost midnight, and the living room on the third floor had taken on some of the familiarity of the kitchen. The polished oak table had been covered with a thick cloth to protect its surface from the chopping boards, knives, jars, bowls, and assorted roots and berries. The frigid air bit into Rosalie's back despite the thick woollen coat she'd put on and the scarf wrapped around her neck. Anastasia stirred the cauldron that contained the mandrake, juniper, and mint potion, no coat or scarf needed so close to the only heat source in the room.

Rosalie worked on regardless, washing and slicing the mandrake, pulping berries, and shredding more mint leaves. She'd already pulverised some dried linden leaves and had only to de-stem the remaining sprigs of lavender.

With a pencil in his hand, Alexander had remembered more of what he'd seen at the clubhouse. The Cup of Welcome had been sitting on the sill beside the old man when Alexander had walked in on him. In Clement's room, he'd seen what may well have been the mysterious dagger. Rosalie had her suspicions about the dagger. The power and possibility these two items contained and their being in the possession of the Benedicts had her quaking every time her thoughts wandered to the drawings. All the Benedicts needed now were the discs. With those, they would have access to unlimited power. She still suspected that they might not understand the depths they would be falling into if they unlocked those doorways. But that was not her concern. Keeping those doorways locked tight was.

John had returned from Clancy's billiards hall with news she'd hoped and feared to hear. Harry Whistler had not been found, but Boseman had and had been dealt with. Jim Downs had a vile temper when riled and the death of his son had pushed him over the edge.

Rosalie had sensed stirrings of power and, knowing they did not come from her hearth, and could not have come from the Benedicts, understood that Mary Downs was also exacting revenge. Harry Whistler may never be found.

Clancy had advised that his ragtag group of watchers were covering the Union Club and that the building had been infiltrated. The doorman was cousin to Clancy's wife.

Ina Bell had come around to help care for Drew and provide some extra protection if needed. Honora was exhausted and grateful for the opportunity for rest even if that rest was only on the other side of the room from her charge.

Anastasia and John had gone to visit their children and fill in Amy Shadler on everything that had happened.

Florentine and Mr Michaels were stationed inside the Garden Palace with orders to watch only, and not interfere with anything that might occur.

The bewitching period would start precisely at the stroke of midnight.

'Are you ready?' Rosalie asked Anastasia. 'This doesn't need spells. Once I add the new ingredients to the pot, we become observers.'

'Observers to what?'

'The spirit world. We're going to the other side.' Rosalie brought a loaded tray to the fire and knelt beside her daughter. 'This is no exact science. I'll put everything in at once while you stir then we'll see what we will see.'

'Are you ready?' Rosalie asked again. Anastasia nodded and turned the spoon with more vigour. Rosalie tilted the tray and pushed every piece of herb into the cauldron. The water bubbled and popped, hissed and rippled. Anastasia removed the spoon. The potion spun in its container faster until it tumbled over itself and splashed over the side to sizzle in the fireplace.

Rosalie took Anastasia's hand. 'Breathe in deep and relax. Remember we are observers only.'

'Yes, Mam.'

Steam plumed from the cauldron and gathered in a roiling cumulus above their head. The temperature rose until droplets of sweat formed on their skin. They breathed in unison, taking in great lungfuls of the steam, giving way to the sensation of falling. The candles in the room guttered and extinguished. The fire flared, embers popped. In the hall outside, the clock struck twelve.

Anastasia walked barefoot across a dusty plain. The earth, warm beneath her feet, caressed her skin like soft silk. She kicked at the ground and the dust billowed around her legs. She knelt, dug her hands in to her elbows, wallowed in the creamy nebula. A giggle distracted her, and then another. She turned and saw she was being watched by a young girl.

'Fiona?' The girl was a spectral version of her daughter, old and young, smiling and grimacing, laughing with joy and screaming with pain.

The phantom rose and danced around Anastasia, leaning over to kiss her forehead and skipping away to join other children playing by the stream nearby. The silky soft dust turned to thick black mud, squelching when she moved, threatening to suck her in and hold her forever. She relaxed, stretched out, tried to be a leaf settling on the surface, carried with the current, yes, but not drawn down into the depths. She rolled on her back, mud covering every inch of her body.

The giggle, moist and full of youth, became dry and old. The girl had become a crone, crooked and leaning on a gnarled cane. The old woman crooked a finger and Anastasia rose to follow.

'Do not speak,' the crone commanded. 'Unless you wish to stay in the barrows forever, hold your tongue.'

Anastasia bowed acquiescence and the two walked a winding path along the banks of the stream.

'Your mam is wise, but not all-knowing.' A serpent undulated beneath the surface of the water. Its skin glistened in a rainbow of droplets and air bubbles. 'She has sought permission from the spirits of this land.' A figure on the far bank gathered strange animals around her and sang a song of such exquisite beauty, Anastasia wanted to swim across and join the crowd. The crone did not stop walking and the figure and her audience soon became nothing but specks in the distance. 'It is right that she should do so. We are far from our country and local customs must be observed.'

She stopped at a point where the stream thinned and fought its way past boulders and weather-beaten logs; strong tree roots clawed the ground searching for water at the very spot where the stream reached a bowl-like indentation and fell hundreds of feet in a white freefall of water that vanished in a cloud of steaming spray.

The crone stood, toes curled over the ragged lip of the crater, and pointed to an island in its centre. 'Someone from our country has come, forced their way into the spirit world of this country, and torn the tapestry that weaves all worlds together.'

Anastasia stared so hard her eyes burned and her head ached, but she could see nothing but her own tears. A hand fluttered before her face. Her vision cleared, and though these new figures were many miles away she could see every detail. An old man and his son dressed in black robes chanting words she didn't understand around a fire pit that streaked blue and purple flame into the void above them. A cruel and twisted phantom writhed from the fire, yowled in anger and pain. The son held out his hand. To placate, Anastasia thought, like a child with a kitten. The phantom bared sharp-pointed teeth, sniffed at the son's fingers, opened its mouth wide and bit the hand from its wrist.

Anastasia nearly spoke, nearly screamed at the gruesome scene, blood spurting from the stump, the son falling to his knees, his face frozen in a stricture of agony. The crone slapped her hand over Anastasia's mouth preventing sound, holding her upright, forcing calm into her head. Anastasia breathed in an earthy smell of heather and gorse and rich rain-soaked loam, and let the horror leak from her mind.

'They are releasing spirits into the world that should be kept hidden away. Powers that have been moulded by warped minds and shaped by old stories that have never been told. Your mam knows this.'

Rocks and broken tree roots burst out into the chasm. The stream became a torrent, a river that filled the crater, a lake that whirlpooled and buffeted against itself; a body of water that stretched from Anastasia's toes to the horizon.

'You and your mam will fight this vile bane in your world. Your sister and her daughter will fight in the other.'

A raft floated toward them, paused out of reach. 'You must be strong,' the old woman said. 'For all of them.'

On the raft lay a body in perfect repose. Skin like alabaster, hands folded neatly together on her chest. Anastasia cried great tears of hot gushing grief. Her voice could no longer be kept still. She opened her mouth wide and keened the song of death.

CHAPTER 25

*N*ight became day in a slow gradation of light over Sydney Harbour. Thin cloud cover blocked the blue sky and dissipated the sunrise. Florentine watched from her bed, too tired to close the curtains on this ominous day, too awake to let sleep come, confidence and cockiness deflated.

The midnight shift at the statue and fountain had been a waste of time. Nightwatchmen had completed their rounds like clockwork. Nothing to upset their routine, no strange mists, weird occurrences, hallucinating fiends. Nothing.

She'd returned to the hotel at six am, after the last inspection before the day guards began their shift, with only the times the nightwatchmen visited the fountain and the path they took on their rounds. Important information, Mr Michaels had reminded her several times. The balance between success and failure could be tipped by the inopportune arrival of the unexpected.

No chance of that happening. Florentine pulled the blankets higher and nuzzled under to avoid the encroaching day. *I need rest and then I'll get up and have breakfast and put Drew's clothes back on and see about finding something better to defend myself than a basket full of bread and*

*talk to Mam about Mr Michaels and go visit Fiona and Evie, and see Alice
…*

Florentine fell deep and sound into slumber.

~

Trembling and gaunt, Rosalie moved around the hotel like a ghost, listening to the sounds of her family as they began to stir. Soft murmurs from Anastasia and John's room, Drew fussing against Honora's ministrations, stairs creaking from below. She met Alexander on the landing, sleepy-eyed and hair on end, shirt free of trousers and suspenders.

'I heard Mr Michaels snoring. They're back then? Is Florentine all right?'

'She sleeps,' Rosalie said. 'All is well.' Her words sounded false in her ears.

'Are you all right, Mrs P? You don't look like you've slept for days.'

Rosalie heard a whisper from James. *Eat. Rest.*

'Come down to the kitchen. I'm a whiz at bacon and eggs.' Alexander started tucking his shirt in, pulled his loose braces up to his shoulders. 'Come on, Mrs P. Wandering the halls does you no good.'

Rosalie followed him down. *James?*

Alexander pulled out the comfy wingback chair in the corner and plumped the cushion. 'Take a seat.'

She sat, leant back into the chair, dizzy and faint. Alexander lifted her feet and pushed the footstool under. He disappeared for a moment and came back with one of Honora's crocheted blankets. It seemed like only moments more that he brought her over a cup of tea and plate of buttered bread.

She stared at it, willing her arms and hands into motion, and closed her eyes instead.

'You need to eat.' Alexander crouched beside her with the cup and the plate in front of her face. 'Sip, then bite.'

Her mouth moved like an automation as the cup was pressed to her lips. She sipped. The cup was taken away and replaced with a thin slice of bread. She bit into it, chewed, swallowed, and started crying. The tea and bread were whisked away. Alexander took her in his arms and let her cry on his shoulder.

'It's all right, Mrs P,' he said. 'A good cry before breakfast never hurt anybody.'

Rosalie sobbed out raw emotion, her walls no longer able to keep the fear and worry inside. Alexander rocked and patted her back, making soothing noises that she latched onto, her sanity needing such an anchor. It came in waves this pain; an overflowing dam of grief and regret. She pressed her head into his shoulder, sniffed, and took the handkerchief he offered her.

'You're a good man,' she said. 'Florentine will need your strength.'

'And I hers,' he answered. 'And all of us yours.'

Rosalie held on to his words like a lifeline and breathed in deeply. 'I'm so sorry. You're right, I haven't slept or eaten enough, but I already feel a little better. Thank you for the shoulder.'

Alexander rocked back on his heels, searching her face for the truth in her shaky voice. He nodded, apparently satisfied, and stood. 'Let's eat then. I'm famished.'

Lord Benedict had been in a rage all night. Yelling at the steward, the doorman, the poor maid sent up to clean, and his son—though the latter was in the next room being tended by a doctor. Lord Benedict yelled at him too.

Clement, woozy and unsteady, rose with daybreak to find his father slumped on the chaise lounge. The exhausted doctor, packing his portable apothecary away, looked up and put a finger to his lips and waved Clement back to his room.

Seeing his father was still alive, Clement nodded and went to his bed. He'd had a dream that his father had been stabbed through the heart with a stake and thrown into a raging river. Silly, really, he knew, but anxiety ravaged his nerves and set fire to his skin. He'd needed to check.

'Now then,' the doctor said as he came in. 'That bump on the back of your head is not serious, but you'll probably have headaches for a few days until the swelling goes down. Avoid touching it if you can, no straining or lifting. I recommend the same for you as I did your father—bed rest—and I can offer you the same medical aid as well if you feel the need.'

Clement started to shake his head and thought better of it. 'No. I'll be fine. How long will father sleep for?' He hadn't planned on physical retaliation and he'd sorely misjudged Alexander Ridlay's temperament. This wouldn't do at all.

'Not long. A few hours at most, I'd say. I'll order him a light lunch as I leave and if you have any concerns this afternoon, send word.'

'Thank you, sir. Did Father say anything … untoward? He's had a lot on his mind lately, not sleeping well. I'm not sure the climate here agrees with him.'

'He rambled some, but not to worry. His age, the long journey— all taken into account. I'm surprised he hasn't needed a doctor before this.'

Clement peered at him. The doctor looked like not much would surprise him at all. 'Very well. Thank you, again. You won't mind if I don't see you out.'

'Not at all. I know my way well enough.' The doctor gave a short bow and walked out.

Clement pulled his shirt over his head, wincing as the tight muscles in his neck and shoulders stretched. Bed rest was the last thing he'd be seeking today. He needed to search out Harry Whistler and George Boseman, arrange for the next stage in his plan to be executed, and prepare for tonight. The day had come, at last, to collect the remaining artefacts and meet the future full on.

Today he was still Clement Benedict, and his father a minor lord. Tomorrow they would be men to be reckoned with.

Algernon turned, restless and awkward on the lounge. His eyes slit open and he frowned, not recognising where he was. Curtains had been kept drawn on the dark room. A fire crackled in the fireplace to little effect. No warmth spread from the marble hearth.

'Clement?' he called. 'What the deuce is going on?'

When Clement didn't appear, he sat up, rubbing his eyes and looking about him at the furniture he recognised, but did not at all seem familiar. He stumbled to the window and pulled at the curtains. Bright sunlight flooded in, filling his head with pain and regained memory. He turned back to the room, the unsettling feeling of being displaced gone as he remembered the intruders and the violence, and Clement falling to the floor.

'Clement!' He crossed the room and pushed the bedroom door open. Clement's suit from the night before was on the floor in a tumbled pile. The workman's disguise gone, as was Clement. Algernon kicked at clothes strewn around the room and approached the unmade bed. Blood on the pillow and stained bandages on the side table attested that his son had indeed been injured. Not seriously enough to stop him going out. The fool!

A tremor ran through his hands and he cursed. After tonight, this ague would afflict his body no longer. The youth and strength of his son would be his as well. After tonight, he could have anything he wanted. He turned away from the bed and the bandages. His legs moved as if his bones were loose inside, not quite connecting where they should.

Then he remembered the scattered bones on the bedroom rug and ran on stiff feet to his room. The bones were not there. For a heart-stopping second, Algernon knew the deep-down panic of someone about to lose everything they'd worked for and built up over a lifetime. Bile cramped his stomach. His head pounded. He tottered into the room, reached for something to steady him, and saw on his dressing table his old thuja box, linen cloth neatly folded inside, and resting on a lace-edged handkerchief was the carved stone from Loch Slapin.

Relief washed over him, a king tide of emotion, as with trembling fingers he pulled aside the layers of linen to see the skeletal hand in its proper place. He lifted the box and the stone and carried them back to his seat by the window. He dropped the stone in the ancient cup and retook his customary position, the box of bones in his lap.

Boseman's office was locked tight and Clement did not know where he lived. He approached an old man sitting on a low stool, polishing shoes.

'Do you know where I might find George Boseman?'

The old shoe black squinted up at him. He pushed at a tin sitting on the path at his feet. Clement fished for a few coins in his pocket, brought out a handful of pennies, and dropped them in.

'He's gone to ground. Jim Downs is after his head. And when Jim Downs is after something, he gets it. No one crosses Jimmy and gets away with it.'

'I have business to discuss with Mr Boseman. Might you know where he'd go to ground?'

The old man raised an eyebrow and glanced at the tin. Clement dropped in two shillings. 'I'd find someone else to do business with if I were you, but if you're determined, you might try down at the quay. He had a permanent room at the Paragon. Interest you in a shine?'

Clement dropped another coin in the tin. 'Not today. Don't tell anyone I've been asking questions, ey?'

'The sole of discretion, that's me,' he sniggered and held up a shoe. 'Get it? Sole.'

Clement grimaced at the stupid pun and the man's gap-toothed grin. He knew where the Paragon Hotel was. They'd met there a few days ago, when he'd requested some physical help and Boseman had recommended Harry Whistler. He left the man to his box of polish and brushes and headed down toward the wharves, not noticing the shadow that detached itself from the doorway the old man was positioned near, or the brief exchange between shoe black and shadow that ensued.

Watson's Paragon Hotel was famous for its hospitality and sporting connections. Its licensee, Mr Richard Watson, was active in political circles and one of many voices shouting down the spread of the Temperance Society. The former Canadian could not have known of Boseman's character, opposite in nature as they were, nor could he have been wise to the shady business deals. Not that any of that was Clement's concern. He'd met Mr Watson only briefly at the St Vincent's Ball and had found him edging toward bombastic.

He approached the guest reception area, forgetting his outer appearance, and asked to be announced to Mr George Boseman. The butler looked Clement up and down and asked who was calling before deigning to order a bellhop to run a message up to Mr Boseman's room.

'I have business with Mr Boseman,' Clement said. 'I called at his office, but he's not there and we had a firm appointment.' Even in lower class attire, Clement could impress his own importance. The butler flicked a finger at the bellhop and the boy sprinted up the stairs. Back within minutes, the bellhop advised that Mr Boseman was not in his room. The butler looked surprised and Clement suspected that Boseman would probably never be in his room again.

'I'll catch up with him tomorrow,' he said, backing away with the unhappy sensation that his plans had gone awry. He needed to find Whistler and check on the Ponsonby brat. If he'd been rescued then his hand had been reversed and he'd lost his bargaining chip. He left the hotel trying to think how he could contact Whistler without Boseman. He tried to remember every conversation they'd shared and recalled the billiard hall. Too much of a risk. No doubt the dead lad had frequented the same haunts. He had no choice but to go to the lane where they'd left Ponsonby and see firsthand whether the boy remained a prisoner or had been found.

Clement searched the street around him. There seemed an inordinate number of sullen youth lurking on corners, men in groups of two and three talking in angry whispers. Across the way, in the middle of the busy promenade separating harbour from city, a group of women huddled over a wicker basket. Boat masts pendulumed through the air, rigging swinging and clanging as choppy waves crashed against hulls. Seagulls screamed overhead, fought for scraps on the ground. Clement pulled his jacket tight and his cap low against the wind at his back as he walked along Alfred Street. He cut up Phillip Street, passed the Water Police Courts and turned into the passage known as Outhouse Lane. The emptiness of the poorly cobbled lane was as much a warning as if it had been full of people. In the middle of the afternoon so close to a bay that thrummed with activity, this lane too should be populated. Clement stood in its mouth, waiting for a movement, for a sign, anything to say the hidey-hole remained secret. He caught a movement in the buildings behind the huts, a curtain or someone waving, he couldn't be sure. Someone walked behind him and he jumped. Wagon wheels ground against the street and he swerved to avoid being hit. Horse hooves struck rock and the sound cut through him like a knife. Outhouse Lane remained empty. The only soul brave enough to penetrate the gauntlet stood quivering on the corner.

The wind gusted and the iron sheet walls screeched in protest. A ghost moved beside him. *What are you waiting for?* Another materialised from a hut halfway along the lane. It beckoned him forward. *Come, we await you ...*

Hands pulled at his coat, his scarf, tugged at his arms. A dark voice inside his head urged him forward. *Come, I await you ...*

Clement walked along the lane. Stopped at Boseman's hut. The lock and chain fell apart as he reached for them; the door creaked opened. In the corner, a tattered tarp lay spread over something lumpy, something with a boot very much like his own and a leg clad in dark blue moleskin. He leant over, took one corner of the stained covering, and pulled it free until he could see the corpse beneath.

Then he screamed.

~

The next time Florentine woke, afternoon sun had replaced morning. Energised, she whipped back the blankets and sat up, ready at last to face the enemy and battle demons. A fresh pot of tea and some sandwiches had been left by her bed and she dove on them, ravenous. She poured some tea and turned to her window to look out on the street while she ate.

A gentle cough from the corner brought her attention to company in her room and she nearly choked on the bread when she saw Alexander perched on her desk, sketchbook and pencils in hand.

'What are you doing in my bedroom? Were you drawing me while I slept?'

Alexander pointed to the teacup. 'Everyone else is busy with other matters so I took it upon myself to bring your refreshments up.' He smiled and turned the sketchpad around for her to see. 'I've only been here long enough for a rudimentary sketch, but I can do the rest from memory, or make sure I'm here again tomorrow morning ...'

Florentine stood in front of him and inspected the page. Only a few lines, but enough to capture her likeness, soft and peaceful in repose.

Alexander lowered the book. 'I'm sorry to have woken you, though I must say you sleep like a log! I've been in, nearly dropped the tray, poured myself some tea, and half-eaten my own sandwich, and I did drop my teaspoon, all before you even stirred.'

Florentine had never had a gentleman in her bedroom before. She wondered that she didn't feel in the least embarrassed. She took another bite of her sandwich and grinned at him, happy to see a rosy blush in his cheeks.

'Of course, now that you're awake, I'll leave you to eat your lunch and, um, dress.' He fumbled with his pencils, flicked the sketchpad closed, and started to stand.

'Stay,' she said. 'Let's finish lunch together, in private. I have a feeling that once we leave the shelter of my room, we'll have none of that for a while.'

'Well, I wouldn't want to tarnish your reputation or cause your family any concern.' His hand had found her face, cradling it in his palm. She licked her lips, caught the rough edge of his thumb as it wiped away a stray crumb, turned her head and nestled her face in his fingers, breathing in his scent: graphite, ham and cheese from his sandwich, and a rich aroma she would remember until the end of her days.

'Will you marry me?' she asked. 'One day when this is over, will you be mine and I'll be yours? And you can bring me tea in bed and sketch my portrait every morning.'

His hand slipped around to the back of her head, pulled her closer to him. He brushed her lips with his and asked in return, 'Will you promise to always rescue me when I need rescuing and carry loaves to defend me with?'

The teacup kept them apart. He took it from her hands, tasted the milky liquid, offered her a sip, then reached down for his sandwich, offering her a bite.

'With this cup and this sandwich, do I promise that I will be yours and bring you endless pots of tea.'

She nibbled at the bread, swallowed and said, 'And draw my picture.'

'I'll fill countless sketchpads with your portrait. Every expression, every muscle, every inch of skin.'

Florentine blushed. 'And I promise to throw a loaf of bread at anyone that even looks at you cross-eyed.'

Their lips brushed once more before they stepped apart.

'I would like nothing better than to spend the rest of the day here, but your family need you, so drink up, eat, and this time I really will leave you to change.'

Warmth radiated throughout Florentine's body. Her skin tingled. She wanted to dance and spin and keep Alexander to herself a little longer. He laughed, lay a hand over his chest and bowed, then blew her a kiss and walked to the door, opening it with an unsteady hand.

She rushed after him. 'If you can ...' she whispered, 'Later, if we can, if there's time, come to me?'

His eyes were bright and glossy as he stood in the doorway. 'I'll never leave your side again.' He stepped through and started to pull the door closed behind, then stopped, poked his head into the room, and said, 'Except for now, but I'll be just in the kitchen brewing more tea, and after that I'll not leave your side.'

Florentine giggled and pushed the door shut, leaning against it with a sigh. She imagined herself in a white flowing dress with a bouquet of lavender and golden wattle, and a veil crowned with miniature roses, and satin slippers. She spun away from the door, twirled on the rug, and danced a jig across to the window. The looming exhibition building across the road, its dome glistening in the bright day, reminded her that happiness would not be hers until the Benedicts had been dealt with. She had a job to do and she would not fail her mother now. Holding the thought of the wedding dress a moment longer, she put it aside and went to the wardrobe for a clean skirt and blouse. Laying it on the bed, she quickly washed and dressed.

She would look in on her brother first.

Drew sat up in bed, flipping through a book. He looked relieved when Florentine entered, a sneaky grin in the corner of his mouth, that didn't reach his red-rimmed eyes.

'You know everything then?' she asked, sitting on the edge of the bed and folding her hands in her lap. 'I'm so sorry, Drew.'

He put the book down and looked away. 'There's nothing we could have done. That bloody Harry! Some mate he turned out to be, to Will anyway. Turned on him and bloody murdered him.'

'We don't know for sure it was him.'

Drew folded his arms across his chest. 'He was there. He could have stopped it and didn't so he's responsible as much as anyone else. More so. Coz they were friends.'

Florentine rubbed his arm. 'He's already paying the price for what he did, Drew. Will's dad is seeing to that.'

'Won't bring Will back though, will it? We were making plans to travel to America and Canada. We were going to be trappers and get rich selling fur pelts and have adventures.' Drew wiped his face. 'Now, I'm to stay here. Can't even help tonight, even though I feel fine.'

'Find another way to help and have your adventures then. Moping in bed will get you nowhere. You may not be able to come, but there's other things you could be doing.'

Drew didn't look convinced.

'Get dressed and come down. Mam needs everyone tonight whether they have a lump on their head on not.' She combed hair from the white bandage wrapped around his head.

'Ana told me you put on my trousers and rescued Mr Ridlay and Mr Michaels from the Benedicts.'

Florentine couldn't help the smile that beamed from within. 'I arrived just as old Mr Benedict threatened to run Alexander through with a sword while Mr Michaels and Clement Benedict wrestled on the floor.'

'Alexander, is it? About time. I thought you two would never get past the polite formalities. I'm glad for you, sis. Sandy is a top bloke. He's been showing me how to draw eyes so they look real. And he showed me the drawings of all the strange symbols and such he saw at the statue. I don't think he saw all of them. I'm sure there was much more when we were there.'

Florentine leant in close to her brother and kissed the top of his head. 'Perhaps the three of us can go on an adventure together and make discoveries and draw everything we find.'

'You can't draw for quids, Florrie. What will you do?'

'I'll make sure you're both safe. Now, get up and get dressed. I need you outside.'

'Thanks, Florrie. And if you want to wear some more of my clothes, go ahead. Any time.'

~

Time crawled and sped by at the same time. Rosalie longed for an end to the day and dreaded its climax. Equinox Eve was upon them, and though Drew was no longer Clement Benedict's bargaining chip, it didn't negate the meeting required to take place at the foot of Queen Victoria's statue. The symbology beneath it had been carved into the stone long before Drew's kidnapping, long before Ethne M'Kynnon's grave, or that of her sister in Ireland, had been ransacked. The meeting tonight had been planned, not by the Benedicts, but by those that lived in the spirit world. For what reason, Rosalie didn't want to guess. She knew though that it could not be avoided. She would take her eldest children into the mouth of evil and hope that their destiny was indeed to prevail. Anything else could not be borne.

Ina Bell and Amy Shadler had brought around satchels for amulets and talismans. Mr Michaels, Alexander, and John, now armed, would guard their backs as best they could, but they couldn't come to the fountain. Rosalie wouldn't allow it. Blood only could make the final approach. The daughters of the Cailleadch, at the start and the finish.

Dusk deepened into night. Honora inked symbols onto paper and threw them in the fire. Each curled and crackled, consumed by the flames.

'Your friendship has been a blessing to me,' Rosalie said.

Honora looked up from her writing desk. 'And yours to me as well. I have prayed that you will come through this unscathed, Rosie. I hope it's enough.'

'We can only hope so. I don't know what to expect or what will come with the dawn. Win or lose, tomorrow is a mystery to me.'

'The morrow is always a mystery, for how can we tell the future? And if we could, would we want to?'

Rosalie sat her satchel on the table. The only item left to be packed was her gift from the Cailleadch. The decorated banksia pod lay resting among the packets of herbs, a natural boon to be used as a last resort. She didn't understand the magic it contained, but trusted its source.

'Clancy Dickens and some of his men will stay on guard around the hotel so that you, Amy, and Ina can do your work undisturbed. There'll be no need to hold back or go quietly. Not tonight.'

'We'll give our song full voice and we'll not stop until you return to us.'

The door from the backyard creaked open. Amy and Ina.

'Well timed as always, sisters,' Honora said, standing and going to them. 'How go your families?'

Amy shrugged out of her coat. Her dark blue dress glittered with the reflection of the candles that lined the shelves and benches. 'Anselm and Douglas are keeping watching over the children,' she said.

'I'm not sure if it's the children or the menfolk who're in charge at the bakery tonight, but all will be safe,' Ina added. 'We sealed them in with a circle of protection.'

'Bring your things up to the family room. We'll have an almost unobstructed view of the Palace from there.' Honora took their coats and lay them over her desk. The women bustled through the kitchen, each stopping by Rosalie to give her a hug and a kiss on the cheek.

'May the path you follow be blessed,' Amy said.

'And may you show those fools what for!' Ina added for good measure.

'Thank you, sisters. May your words be heard and your dedication be rewarded.'

'All the reward we need is for you and yours to be back here safe and sound, and that other lot be gone for good.'

'If only it were that easy, Amy,' Ina answered as they walked into the hallway and over to the staircase. Mumbled words from Amy mixed with the boots on the stairs, and then Ina said loud and clear,

'I don't think evil spirits can be despatched with a load of pellet.' Their voices continued chatting as they made their way to the third floor, growing louder as they met with others on the landing.

John and Ana, judging by the deep rumble of her son-in-law's voice. Their footsteps went unheard in the stairwell as Rosalie closed the door and went to sit at the kitchen table. Anastasia entered first. Changed into her riding dress with its thick woollen skirt and cotton shirt. She'd put a leather vest over that and had tucked gloves into her belt. Her hair was caught back in a single braid that wound over her shoulder, and over her arm, a sturdy leather coat. John, dressed for stealth and warmth, wore grey trousers and shirt, a sailor's jumper, and a heavy navy coat that hid the sidearm he had concealed in its deep pocket. He carried his wife's satchel and a smaller dagger. She looked defiant. He looked unhappy.

'Alexander and Florentine will be down any minute,' Anastasia told her mother. 'They're just working out a few things.'

Drew walked in before Rosalie could digest what Florentine and Alexander might be working out. He looked washed out, but otherwise none the worse for wear. Honora fetched him a bowl and filled it with stew. 'Eat.'

'You're to stay here,' Rosalie reiterated.

'Yes, Mam.'

'In bed, preferably.'

'Yes, Mam. I will.'

Rosalie watched him eat, evaluating every movement and mouthful. 'If you feel up to it, you may help Bridie.'

'I'm pretty tired. I'll probably just go back to bed.' Drew concentrated on his stew.

'I don't believe that for a minute, laddie. Mind yourself and don't be taking no foolish chances. That head needs to heal.'

Drew gave his mother a long look. 'Yes, Mam. Really, I'll be careful.'

Rosalie wanted to go to him and ruffle his hair. She settled for resting her hand on his hand and smoothing it instead. 'I'll be cutting this hair when I get back. You look like a regular larrikin.'

Drew ducked his head and didn't answer.

Florentine joined them in a rush of long legs and excited movement. She'd changed into Drew's clothes again, this time better fitting, and thrown on a long brown coat over the top and a scarf wrapped around her neck. Her face was bright, flushed, and her cheekbones appeared higher than usual owing to the biggest smile Rosalie had ever seen on her daughter's face.

'Are we ready to go?'

'What are you wearing?' Rosalie asked, holding open the coat to reveal not only her brother's clothes but also a vest like her sister's and leather straps criss-crossed over her chest, and a long leather sword-filled scabbard hung from her waist. Her wrists were adorned with leather guards. 'And where did you get that sword?'

'Well, there's not really time to learn how to shoot so I thought this was the next best thing.'

'You have other weapons at your disposal,' Rosalie said.

'True. Consider this back-up then. Just in case.' Florentine walked over to shelter behind Anastasia and blocked her face from her mother's gaze as Alexander walked into the room.

Too late. Rosalie recognised the flash of adoration in the parted lips and the twinkling eyes. Alexander managed to remain composed even though the whole family stared at him.

'Mr Michaels said he'd meet us at the Garden's gate and Dickens has doused the porch light. Not much he can do about the street lights, unfortunately. He'll keep watch and let us know when it's safe to cross the road.'

Rosalie chose not to address her daughter's guilty glances. That could wait until tomorrow.

'Very well. It's dark enough now and it could take some time to fight through any barriers the Benedicts may have put up. I'd like to reach the statue ahead of them, so let's be off.'

Honora came to her and squeezed her hands. 'Be careful, Rosie.'

Clancy Dickens had managed to do away with the street lights. Macquarie Street lay in a blanket of night. A gentle breeze came up from the harbour and wafted around them, inviting them to attend the Garden Palace. Mr Michaels stood in front of the gate, barely discernible in the shadows.

Rosalie's heart lurched when she saw the heavy chain and lock on the gate. 'Please tell me you have a key, Paul.'

But the gate was not locked. Michaels twisted the bolt and unwrapped the chain from the bars. 'Hurry, all of you. I'll rig this so it looks locked again once we're in.'

They went through the gap one at a time, waiting under the trees on the other side for the gate to be closed.

Rosalie took the opportunity to remind everyone to be careful and for the men to stay back.

'We're simple folk, not warriors and not murderers. Think before you act. Stay together as much as possible. Under no circumstances are you men to come to the fountain or the statue. Do you understand?'

They nodded. As convincing as Drew had been while eating his supper.

'I'm familiar with the grounds and know how to be quiet', Alexander said. 'I'll scout ahead.'

'Take Florentine with you. If you come across anything supernatural, she'll be able to deal with it.'

Alexander and Florentine took each other's hand and slipped into the night, running on the grass to avoid the grind of the gravel drive underfoot.

'Anastasia, you and John go next. Paul and I will hold up the rear. We'll follow along shortly.'

When they were alone, Mr Michaels turned to Rosalie. 'It appears we've arrived first at the scene. Might you be planning a little welcome for our guests?'

'I don't much like surprises, Paul. If indeed we are first, then a warning is what I'm planning. Hold this.' Rosalie passed him a small box from her satchel while she pulled on a cord around her neck. Hidden beneath her underthings and between her breasts was a thin tube. She twisted it and it separated into two pieces. Inside was a twig of elmwood. It had been rubbed smooth and soaked in the essence of rosemary oil. She pulled it out with her fingertips. 'Now open the box.' When he'd done so, she dipped the end of the twig into the finely chopped mix of herbs. 'Stand back. I've not done this before.'

Michaels took two steps away and waited.

Rosalie held the elmwood high and chanted, 'By the power of the three, maid, mother and crone, ward this path against those who would do us harm.' She drew a five-pointed star in the air. The wood in her hand grew warm, a tingle of energy leached from its tip. She drew the star again and was amazed to see the trace of light emit a pulse of energy. 'By the power of the three …' She crossed the path, touched the wood to a tree. 'Ward this path.' Leaves sizzled, light tracked a path along its branches, burned through its veins of the tree and lit its roots. The ground beneath throbbed. Rosalie crossed the path to the trees opposite. 'Ward this path.' As soon as she touched the second tree a curtain of light burst into existence and then faded to invisibility. 'That should do it.' She turned to Michaels. 'Let's go.'

He fumbled with the box lid, passed it back to her when closed, and said, 'I would not have believed that if I hadn't seen it for myself. You've got quite a talent there.'

Rosalie lifted her chin and gave him a knowing grin. 'I've not used it like that before tonight. I don't know how strong it will be. At the least, I'll know when it's been broken.'

They turned their backs on the gate and the invisible cloak of energy that guarded it.

Florentine and Alexander approached the Palace building with caution. When the Great Exhibition had been on, the building was surrounded by temporary pavilions. A broad expanse of empty land remained, which they needed to cross.

'We could go around to the rear and gain access through the halls,' Alexander suggested.

'That would take too long and we'd be following the night-watchmen on their rounds. If we use that side door we'll only need to worry about them on the hour.'

'Can you tell if anything supernatural is out there?'

Florentine slumped. As far as she could tell, everything looked normal. 'No, I can't.' She bit her lip and tried to think what to do next.

'I'll make a run for it and if nothing happens, you join me,' Alexander said, rising as he prepared to sprint.

Florentine looked at him, horrified, and pulled him back down. 'Don't be an idiot!'

She opened her satchel. It had been filled with all sorts of things and she wasn't sure what everything was. Mrs Bell had said to trust her instincts and gone over, once more, the amulets and talismans, potions that supported an action, powders that caused a reaction.

She'd been working on this for days, tucked away in the pantry; everything had been neatly laid out and labelled.

'Trust my instincts,' she whispered and dipped her hand into the bag. Her fingers sorted through the packets and pouches until they found one item that was cold to touch. She pulled it out, a small glass bottle with a perfume dropper for a lid, cold like ice in her hand. She smiled. This one she remembered.

'I'll try this.' She pulled out the stopper and flicked droplets of the liquid in front of her. Snowflakes floated in front of them, each dissolving as it touched the ground, leaving a trail of twinkling purple-edged slime.

'It looks like a snail trail,' Alexander said. 'Is it safe to go in?'

'Yes, I'd think something would have happened if it wasn't.' Florentine pointed forward. 'And look, not all of it remains.' She dipped the dropper into the bottle again, stood, and flicked droplets in a wider arc. A definite path appeared on the short grass. 'Someone has placed a ward around the building, but, unknowingly or not, left a back door.'

'Let's hope it's unknowing. I'd prefer no one be waiting for us inside before we even make it to the statue.' Alexander touched the back of her hand with his fingertips. 'Let's wait for the others to catch up.'

Florentine looked back at the gardens. Anastasia and John were coming out of the trees. Further back toward the gate, red embers sparked above the tree line. She returned to a crouch, pulling Alexander down with her.

Anastasia and John ran the remaining distance and crouched beside them.

'Florrie's found a path we think could be safe,' Alexander told them.

Anastasia looked at Florentine for confirmation.

'Magic has definitely been used here.' Florentine twisted to point out the start of her sparkling trail. 'I'm hoping this will lead us right to the side door. I've only gone a few feet though.'

'Excellent work, Florrie,' Anastasia said. 'You, Mam, and I can follow this and the men can create a distraction out here. That way we should be able to sneak in undiscovered.'

'Unless it's a trap,' Florentine said.

'How can we tell?' John asked. 'I don't fancy letting you walk right into an ambush,' he whispered hoarsely to Anastasia. 'I think I should come with you.'

'We'll wait for Mam and see what she thinks.' Anastasia spread her hand out over the ground and moved it from the sparkling area to the unlit. 'I can't sense anything at all. What did you use, Florrie?'

Florentine looked closely at the bottle and then sniffed it. 'It smells like nutmeg, bay laurel, and soap.' She passed the bottle to her sister, who held it to her nose.

'Yes, and angelica root. We can trust what it's showing us, but that doesn't mean Lord Benedict or his son won't be alerted as we go in.'

Rosalie and Mr Michaels joined them within minutes. 'I've put a ward across the gate. It should buy us some time. Have you found something here?'

Florentine explained the pathway and their conclusions. Rosalie was nodding. 'Trust yourselves always,' she said. 'You've made these potions and they are imbued with the manifestation of your intentions. They will do what you need them to. Now, Florentine, you keep going forward. Anastasia follow her in. I'll take the rear and put in some safeguards.'

'It's a big building with lots of hiding places. Perhaps we should go in as well?' Michaels suggested.

'Not yet, Paul. We'll need you out here to watch. I don't want anyone coming inside but the Benedicts. If any other should come with them, distract or dispose of them as you see fit.'

Florentine shivered when Mr Michaels smiled at her mam's instructions. Whatever she said would be carried out to the letter, and Florentine didn't think their head barman had distraction in mind.

'It's too dangerous,' John protested.

'We can look after ourselves when it comes to magic, John. We need you three to take care of everything else that may come at us unawares. If we need you inside, we'll call for you.'

'I don't like it,' he insisted.

'Do as Mam says, John,' Anastasia scolded. 'It will be even more dangerous if someone sneaks up on us from behind while we're working. Florentine, get started.' Anastasia shook off her husband's hand and stood to follow Florentine.

Rosalie took John's arm. 'This is our outer circle. It must be guarded. You all have your amulets, you'll know if we need you inside.'

Florentine turned away from them, not daring to look at Alexander, whose hand had tightened on hers as the others talked, and reluctantly let go as she raised the bottle before her and prepared to go in. 'I'll be careful. I promise,' she whispered to him.

She sprayed the air with potion and followed the magical path igniting before her. The path was not wide. Hidden shades seemed to close in on her with each step, hovering overhead, pressing against the paper-thin wall of magic that surrounded them. Behind her, Anastasia held a hand to her back and muttered words she couldn't quite understand. She glanced back as she reached the door and saw her mam zigzagging a thin wand through the air behind them, a strand of energy winding away from her like thread on a needle. Anastasia held on to her mother's dress to guide her along the sparkling trail. The shadows crowded at her mother, but with every gesture she made they vanished, held away by the wall of power she stitched.

She turned as they stopped moving, face grim. 'I can't tell if this magic is from the Benedicts or something else. It feels heavy, don't you think? Like a thick fog.'

'What else could it be?' Anastasia asked.

Florentine didn't want to know. The Benedicts were at least flesh and blood. They had magic, but so did she. A mysterious something else could not be good news for them.

'They're men dabbling in women's magic. Who knows what evil they've created or attracted to themselves.'

'Demon possession?'

Florentine dearly wished Anastasia would stop asking questions.

Rosalie nodded and Florentine's hands shook with cold.

'We are three and so they must be as well. Focus, daughters. We are not dabbling, nor do we corrupt with the magic we use. We can win out, but we must focus on our inner thoughts and on each other.'

She reached for their hands. Florentine took her sister's. 'I'm scared,' she admitted.

'Me too,' Anastasia said. 'But we can do this.'

Rosalie pulled her daughters to her in a fierce hug. 'We are MacKinnon women, born from a long line of canny and wise MacKinnons before us and before them, those who walked in the footsteps of the fae. We will have every one of our ancestors fighting on our side in the spirit world. Do not doubt the strength we each contain and the power of our line.'

'Yes, Mam. We love you,' Florentine said.

'And I you. Now, it's time for us to go in. Open the door, Florentine.'

Something else was at play. It had to be. On first entering Boseman's hut, he'd come face to face with his own dead corpse; skin turned white and blue, eyes gone, mouth tongueless, arms cut and blood-less from fingertip to elbow, one hand ripped from its wrist. A brown cloud billowed like morning mist in front of him and he'd strangled his scream, though the horror was imprinted in his memory, a visitation of his nightmares in broad daylight. The cloud attached itself to his body, real and imaginary, a threatening veil of malevolence. When it cleared and he could see, the corpse on the floor remained and Clement knew the reason he'd been unable to find George Boseman.

The Ponsonby boy was gone and so was the body of Will Downs.

Though the mangled mess in the hut would not be identified as Boseman, Clement knew.

Carved into the headless torso was a promise of retribution and revenge. Crushed ribs beneath torn skin, white bone exposed in the centre of a crude spiral, three deep gashes crossed the abdomen below. And from the bone, a length of bloodied twine with three knots, caught in each a grisly object: an ear, a strip of flesh, and in the last, a finger that pointed at Clement. He'd been cursed. He felt it pierce his chest and cover his skin in its brown slime.

A voice laughed, another soothed, a third whispered in his ear: *Only the damned can release the damned.*

His legs buckled. The demon in his head unwound itself from the dark recesses of his mind and flexed its power. Memory and action blurred. The door slammed closed. He tripped on the uneven road. Squeezing between huts, he came out into a vacant slab of land and walked around piles of debris and rubbish, past weedy shrubs, until he reached the roadside. He straightened his back, lifted his head, and blended in with the ordinary people who'd never experienced evil, and whose minds were not tattered and unravelling.

He awoke on the floor of the sitting room he shared with his father, in the centre of a circle of black candles dripping wax onto expensive carpet. His father stood over him intoning garbled prayers, his words falling like dirt into a grave.

Clement couldn't move at first, couldn't see much past the barrier the beast in his head had built around him to preserve the threads of his sanity. His body released its tension. The coldness that had gripped him faded as his heart expanded, filled his chest with a warm glow, and he felt something akin to happiness and relief.

His father's words started to make sense.

In the name of the Gods of the Underworld
Whose wish is our command
In the name of ancestors
Whose suffering is ours to avenge

In the name of those we serve

Break this Geis and return my son to this world.

A dry voice in Clement's head chuckled. *So be it …*

'Father,' Clement said. 'Stop. I'm here.'

His father paced, recited his incantation, unhearing.

Clement forced himself to stand, shaky at first, then growing stronger; the warmth in his chest spread to his face and out to his hands and feet until it suffused his entire body with a welcome vibrancy. He stepped out of the circle and into his father's path.

The old man bumped into him and staggered. Clement caught him before he could fall.

'Son?' Algernon appeared confused. He looked at the floor as if unconvinced of Clement's revival. 'What happened?'

'Thank you, Father,' Clement said. He had no wish to relive the macabre discovery in the hut or the settling of the curse over his head, and he couldn't quite remember his return to their rooms. 'Our factor, Boseman, is dead. Events have come to a head.'

His father was already turning to his box of precious relics. 'It is already night. The spirits call on us to make good our promises. We must hurry to the meeting place.'

'Father, wait. What do you know of this meeting place?' Clement had shared his knowledge of the fountain and the statue, of the symbols found within. 'Have you seen it?'

'Of course, Clement. I've visited the queen many times. She speaks to me as a favourite, as her champion in this world. She calls me now to her side, to be her consort.'

Worry caused a chink in the afterglow of Clement's revival. 'Consort? Are we not avenging our ancestors and regain that which was taken from us? Power and riches that are rightly ours? Who is this consort?'

Algernon paused and stared at the box in our hands. 'She is the mother of our forebears. She is to whom we owe a blood debt. Her power shall be our power, her minions ours to command.'

That dry voice in Clement's mind sighed, *I await thee.*

An image of broken bodies and clawed hands stuttered across

his memory, a gawping mouth that slavered and drooled, the sacrifice of his hand and his soul to a god who would fill him with the energy of countless years. Finally he recognised that he had given himself freely to a power he didn't understand on a promise that was as meaningless to the gods as it was all-encompassing to him.

He had no choice but to go forward. The seed of doubt that ran through him vanished, the lurid images dimmed, and the wealth and sovereignty he desired came to the fore.

They left the candles burning.

CHAPTER 27

The queen rose from the floor, unrestricted by the tether of stone and metal at her feet. The fountain on which she stood a mere lily pad in the pond of her reality. Rosalie could see it now. The statue's cross-purposes of queen and goddess, ruler and manipulator, in this world and countless others.

'We must be wary of every thought, word, and action here,' Rosalie said. 'Much is hidden from us.'

'Mam.' Florentine grasped her elbow. 'I'll just go check on the whereabouts of the nightwatchmen.'

'Also, Florrie, place wards across the passageways to keep them from returning to the nave.'

Florentine kept to the walls and columns as she went off into the darkness to lay a protective line of energy across the long nave.

'Anastasia, place five poppets on the floor evenly around the statue. I want to lay the way for our ancestor, welcome her first if possible and if not, hamper the path for anything else waiting to come through.'

'Yes, Mam.'

Rosalie appreciated the willingness of her eldest daughter to follow her instructions. She followed Anastasia around the railing, placing candles beside each poppet of herbs, lighting them with a flint and breathing the sacred words of welcome to her ancestor.

A soft shift in the air, a glimmer of blue haze around each candle, and Rosalie knew that her ancestor had heard.

'Quickly,' she said to Anastasia. 'We must protect this space. Sprinkle salt-ash on the floor here.' Rosalie pointed to the archway that stood between the nave and the grand entranceway. She held her hands in the air. 'We seek to waylay only. Stay to my left.' As in the park, a shimmering curtain of magic spread from Rosalie to the archway, falling to the floor where it sizzled as it touched the salt-ash.

'Now we must call our ancestor. We don't have time to wait for Florentine to get back.'

They stood facing the queen. 'Repeat each line so that no silence falls between my voice and yours. I'll squeeze your hand on the last word so you know when to start.'

Anastasia nodded her understanding.

'Ancient mother, we welcome you to our hearth

Return to your granddaughters' aid

Beware the coming of evil to this land

And the corruption of the Mother's pure flame.'

They repeated the song two more times, voices growing urgent as they sensed the arrival of Lord Benedict and his son.

A crash of doors and yelling voices, the detonation of magic rent apart. Rosalie glanced to the main entrance of the Palace and the two men that stood silhouetted in the grand doorway. Anastasia fumbled for her hand.

'Ancient Mother, grant us power in your name

We will fight for your honour

And by your side

As you wish it

So mote it be.'

A ring of fire connected the candles. An old woman stooped down from the plinth.

'Your voice is special to me, your need paramount in my heart,' the old woman said. 'I once gave you a gift. Do you have one in return for me?'

Rosalie bowed her head. 'Yes, Grandmother.'

The crone rubbed her hands together in glee. 'Then let us begin.'

The nave filled with dazzling light as Rosalie's protections were attacked with bolts of fetid green light. They fell with a resounding clap of thunder. The impact stunned her and whipped away the apparition of the crone. Anastasia pulled on her arm as the candles guttered and extinguished one by one.

Florentine came racing back, brandishing her sword and throwing rocks. She stood in front of her mother and sister, and met flashes of magic from the intruders with a torrent of her own, screaming words that forced a shield of intensity between them.

'Downstairs, Mam!' Anastasia yelled above the growing cacophony.

Florentine walked backward, holding her shield firm until they reached the start of the staircase.

'Now, Florrie!' Anastasia yelled again.

Florentine held a rock in her hand that glowed with pulsing energy; red then blue. When it reached white, Florentine hurled it toward Lord Benedict with a curse that would have curled the toes of any ordinary man. She turned and dashed down the stairs.

At the fountain, Rosalie stood with her back to the pond. 'Anastasia. Florentine. Get behind me now.'

Florentine had her sword to the ready. Anastasia had filled her hands with vials from her pouch. A shadow darted from the stairwell to hide behind boxes, peering around the edge long enough for Rosalie to see it was Drew.

'Drew! Get away from here!' she cried.

Too late. Clement Benedict followed Rosalie's stricken gaze to the boxes. They blew up in a shower of burning paper and knocked the boy against the wall.

'How fortunate,' he said, walking over and grabbing Drew by the hair to drag him back, kicking all the way, to Lord Benedict.

The lord's mocking smile froze Rosalie to the spot. The very situation she'd hoped to avoid had now occurred.

A third shape separated itself from the Benedicts, nebulous, then taking a more solid form.

'This is it,' Rosalie said. 'Anastasia. Florentine. Take guard. Whatever this demon is, we cannot let it take Drew as it has taken Clement Benedict.'

Lord Benedict laughed. 'Our queen is not interested in a slip of a boy. He is but a pawn.'

Clement raised Drew in the air, dangled him high so that his toes skimmed the ground, and pointed the tip of his ancient spear head into his cheek. The black shape reached out and touched Drew's face. He fell still and the shape started to take on colour, become something almost substantial in the gyre of shadow and light.

Lord Benedict sat a box down on the floor at his feet, crouched over it, and opened its lid. He pulled out the ancient Cup of Welcome and revealed a neatly displayed hand of bones, knitted together in gauze and desiccated skin.

A swirling mist, tinged with blue, collected around Rosalie's feet. Florentine stepped to the side and raised her sword. Anastasia was poised to throw her vials, each glittered with power.

The demon had arms and legs now, a flowing rag of a cloak, armour of rust and bone. Its face remained ill-defined. Rosalie sensed a flash of recognition between the blurred figure and the blue mist now creeping up to envelop her.

Lord Benedict, standing again, held the cup out to Rosalie.

'Do you know what will happen?' she hissed at him. 'Do you care at all about the suffering you will cause?'

'You have the key,' he said. 'Our queen cannot fully enter this world without it.' He sneered at the blue mist wavering in the air between them.

Clement lowered Drew to the floor, preparing to change his grip. Florentine struck, her sword arcing downward as Clement looked away for a fraction of a moment. The blade glanced off the spear head as Clement dropped the boy and raised his hand to defend himself. He pushed the thin metal aside and reached for his human shield. Drew, not quite as unconscious as he appeared, had started crawling away. Clement grabbed his leg and then had to bring his weapon up again as Florentine's sword swung on a trajectory toward his head.

Give them the key ... The blue mist had reached full height, coalescing into the body of the crone, crooked and rheumy-eyed with age. 'Granddaughter. Give them the key. Not everything to be welcomed here tonight will be bad.'

Rosalie hesitated, wincing with every clash of sword and dagger. 'Your boy will be safe,' the crone said.

'Mam?' Anastasia said. 'I beg of you, no. Do you not feel the evil that is this demon? We do not want her type in the real world.'

The crone turned toward the young woman. 'She is already here, child.'

The demon laughed, cruel waves of hatred that pummelled Rosalie. 'Welcome all of your ancestors, woman!' The pall of shadow had fallen away to reveal a tall woman with long black hair and fiery red eyes. 'This old crone is nothing, a wisp of illusion.' The demon waved her hand and the crone wavered and vanished.

Clement caught Florentine's arm and pushed back until she stumbled and fell into the half-empty pond. He raised the spear head, two-fisted in the air, ready to plunge it down.

A tinkling of breaking glass at his feet, and threads of silver and gold spun outward and up his legs, binding him in position and freezing his momentum. Florentine shuffled away, regaining her feet, back against the wall of the fountain.

Anastasia threw another vial, this time at Lord Benedict, hitting him in the face and smattering him with shards of glass. He tried to shake it off, flinched as he breathed in particles of herbs crushed to a fine dust. Sneezed once, twice, and then eyes wide, started to choke. His face reddened, lips turned blue, and he was on the verge of collapsing when his demon queen leant in and kissed his greying temple. He staggered, drew in great gulps of air, and glaring bitterly at Anastasia drew his sword.

'No!' Rosalie yelled. She reached toward her daughter and ripped the leather cord from around her neck. The pouch holding one of the two discs came free from her bodice. Rosalie held it high. 'Put down your weapons or I will destroy the key.'

'She bluffs,' the demon snarled.

Rosalie touched the pouch with her wand. Heat came off the tip of the wood in waves. 'Florentine, get out your disc. Take it into the fountain to the mouth of Sheela.'

The demon woman screeched. 'You dare?' She waved her arm at Lord Benedict and the sword fell to the ground.

'Mam, no. You can't,' Anastasia pleaded.

'Trust and intent, Ana. Remember? Clear your thoughts now and be ready.'

Anastasia's struggle with the situation was clear on her face. She glanced at Florentine pushing through the water and climbing up to the door that would take her inside the fountain; she closed her eyes and let calm descend.

'Take the disc from the pouch.'

Anastasia took the pouch from Rosalie and undid the knots that held it closed. As the knots came free she said a prayer to the Grandmother, followed by an admonition to take care. Rosalie stood guard, watching the demon and Lord Benedict, who stood frozen eyeing every movie of Anastasia's fingers. She lost sight of Clement Benedict for a moment, but caught a gesture from Drew huddled in a corner, and turned her head just enough to see Clement stepping into the water.

'Stop right where you are, Mr Benedict,' she said. 'Or I will order my daughter to give over her relic.'

Clement stopped moving. Rosalie noticed a glint of green spreading through the pond. She was running out of time.

Anastasia pulled out the disc and held it on the flat of her palm. Rosalie lay her hand over it and the two gripped each other.

'You will need this,' she said, handing her the wand. 'Trust me?'

Anastasia nodded.

Rosalie kissed her forehead and whispered, 'Place the disc in the cup and lock it into place. I must go into the fountain. When you see me move, grab the cup and follow.'

'I will.'

The women parted. Anastasia walked with slow reverence to Lord Benedict and the cup. The old man's hands were shaking, his face lit with elation. When Anastasia inserted the round key and twisted it into place, a rippling sheet of blue light stretched outward.

'No!' the demon yelled.

Rosalie turned, climbed into the pond, and ran for the fountain. Anastasia stole the cup from Lord Benedict's hands.

'You fool!'

Rosalie heard the demon's anger and ignored it. The water was not deep but hampered her progress, soaking her skirt and causing it to tangle around her ankles. Clement was on her within seconds, wrapping his arms around her shoulders to wrestle her down. She kicked and wriggled, grabbed the strap of her satchel and swung the bag at his head. It hit with a satisfying thud and he loosened his hold enough for her to get free, but not before he could strike again. He plunged the spear head into her side and she fell to her knees. She nearly fainted when he pulled it out and warm blood gushed from the wound. He was about to strike again when a flash of movement from behind caused him to half-turn and then stumble. Drew had jumped on his back and locked his arm around his neck, forcing him to defend himself and giving Rosalie the time she needed to regain her feet. She balled her skirt up and pressed it into the deep wound to staunch the blood, then started climbing the short ladder of the scaffold up to the door that led into the fountain.

She heard Anastasia scream for Florentine and saw her younger daughter appear before her. Florentine helped her the last steps, lifting her onto the narrow platform, then jumped into the water to assist her siblings. A rush of stifling air behind her and Rosalie knew the demon approached. She turned to see Anastasia, now halfway up the ladder, tossing her knife to Drew on his back in the water, and Florentine with her sword fending off both demon and Clement Benedict.

'Go,' Anastasia yelled. 'I've got the cup. I'll be right behind you.'

Rosalie left as a flash of lightning jumped between Florentine's sword and the demon woman.

The sound of combat carried into the work room, came closer as it followed Anastasia and Florentine in. Rosalie drew on all her power to focus on what she had to do next, reach the Sheela on the ceiling above. That meant another ladder, and with her wounded side Rosalie doubted her ability to manage it. She called out for help, and beneath the clash of arms and yelling outside the room she heard a new sound; the low hum of voices singing. A sensation of fortitude and vitality filled her. The wound in her side numbed. Still she couldn't climb while she was holding it. She searched around and found a short length of knobbly rope coiled over the top of a toolkit. Using it as a belt, she tied her makeshift bandage to her side, and with both hands free she started climbing.

Rosalie had climbed only three steps when Anastasia fell into the room with the cup. 'Place it in the centre of the room, Ana, and create a circle around it.'

Rosalie continued her climb, glancing down to check the position of the cup when she reached the crude carving of the Sheela-na-gig. Florentine was in the room now, keeping the others out with parries of her energised blade. Drew could not be seen and Rosalie prayed that was only because he was on the other side.

Rosalie held on to the ladder with one hand and reached into her satchel for the stone egg with the other. She felt its warm smoothness and pulled it free, marvelling for that moment on its luminescent blue sheen, before lifting it above her head and embedding it into the Sheela's cavernous mouth.

A column of light spat from the stone straight down to the cup where it ignited in flame that licked at Anastasia's feet and singed her skirt, but did not burn. Losing her handhold on the ladder, Rosalie fell to the ground in a bloody heap.

Mist trickled from the Cup of Welcome, covering the floor in thick fog that lapped at Rosalie's body, seeped over her prone form. Rosalie felt the cold touch and opened her eyes. Anastasia stood over her, hands outstretched to help her to her feet. Her smile was so welcoming, so loving, that a tear formed in the corner of Rosalie's eyes. How she loved her children.

Florentine took her other arm and between them her daughters pulled her to her feet. The demon filled the doorway with menace and loathing, her eyes flecked with corrosive green light. She moved forward even as the old crone rose like a spectre from the mist and froze her into place.

'Circle the cup and hold hands.' The crone's hand in Rosalie's was insubstantial, a filmy veil of light and life. As the women took each other's hands, a wall of fire connected them, circling out and around. It reached for the demon and wrapped a tender arm of flame around her waist.

'It is time for the Giving, Granddaughter.'

The demon woman raged as the flame covered her body and consumed her.

Rosalie broke from the circle and stepped forward, taking the banksia pod she'd been gifted from her satchel. The crone took Anastasia's hand. Sound coiled around her, the crone's husky voice incanting peaceful welcomes and farewells, the demon struggling in her fiery bonds, her daughters and her friends singing her strength, Clement Benedict's raw ugliness as he drew on his corrupt power. Then a new sound, birds and music like she'd never heard before, and the roar and rumble of a distant storm.

'Step into the fire, Granddaughter. And know that I love you above all others.'

The cup hummed. Rosalie stretched her foot until her toes penetrated the ring of energy around the ancient vessel. She could see the fire, but she could feel nothing except the delicious sensation of warm sun on cold skin, her husband's gentle touch, the glory and gratification of holding her newborn child in her arms. The sensuality of the simple enjoyments filled her being. She held the banksia pod with its delicate shell decorations to her heart and stepped fully into the flame.

Exultation filled her. She could see and hear everything at once. Anastasia and Florentine's determined, worried faces, the crone's soft blue gaze like a touch on her soul, the demon fading away, Drew, their menfolk, her friends at the hotel chanting in their circle. Her twin daughters travelling with Aunt Flora, her brothers mourning the loss of Mairi, Katrin bending over Ethne, Lilas standing at the abyss of life and death, even Caoimhe on a boat bound for Ireland. Further still, into the cloudy reaches of time, two ancient sisters fighting, a mother bereft. And then, Ethne, by her side.

Welcome ...

A shout, unexpected, and Rosalie staggered. The vision of Ethne M'Kynnon wavered as she was tugged viciously back to the little room beneath the fountain and the realisation that Clement Benedict had thrown the spear head at her unprotected back. It hit her like a blast of malignancy between the shoulder blades, buried itself to its hilt in her back. She had less than moments to complete her final act. Old Man Banksia could bring only one back from the fire. She'd known all along that it wouldn't be her.

Thrusting it up toward the Sheela-na-gig, she screamed, 'Come forth, Warrior Queen. Come forth! A thousand welcomes to you. Come forth!'

Red hot fire burst outward over the heads of Florentine and Anastasia, who stood horrified, struggling against the handhold of the crone. The outer vestments of the old woman dematerialised and the Cailleadch emerged, face glowing, red hair alive with potency, eyes flashing with success. Clement, caught in a fireball, had nowhere to run. He fell, hair alight, demented with fright and searing pain.

The Cailleadch lifted her face in song:

'Sister, dear sister, for too long have you cried with grief
Open the pathway and let the Warrior Queen through
She who will free our daughters from their shackles

And avenge your pain and mine.'

The fire around the cup transformed from red and orange to blue and green, the green burned away, blue became pure white. Rosalie was falling, her legs unable to hold her any longer, a gentle voice like a tumbling brook in her ears. 'Thank you, Granddaughter.'

~

The fire became incandescent as Florentine watched her mother's body sag. She could no longer look into the flame; the light was too bright and too hot. She turned her face and staggered, the crone's rough grip holding her gone. The light flickered and went out, leaving Florentine with the ghost of the fire in her vision.

At her feet, Clement Benedict had crawled through the dissipating mist and past their guard. His hand, horribly burned, held onto the lip of the cup, pulling it out of the circle. He rolled away, paying no heed to the uncontrolled flames that leapt around him, finding wood and dust, and exploding into new fires that seethed across the walls.

Florentine turned to her mother, intent on saving her, but her mother was gone. In her place, a woman sat as if she'd fallen, her face white with shock. In her hand was the strange dagger that seconds before had protruded from Rosalie's back.

'What the hell is going on?' the woman demanded.

Fire reached the ceiling, beams started to crack and fall. Anastasia grabbed the stranger's arm and dragged her away. Shocked and crying, Florentine herded her sister and the woman to the safety of the fountain pond outside. Drew, frantic, helped them stand and then started for the ladder.

'I'll get Mam!'

Anastasia stopped him with a sorrowful shake of her head. 'It's no good,' she said. 'Mam has gone.'

Drew ripped his arm from his sister and climbed the ladder as a secondary explosion blasted the underbelly of the fountain outward, knocking him back into the water. Florentine fished him out, holding him close. 'She's not there, Drew. We have to get out of here.'

Florentine looked around for the Benedicts and saw the lord huddled over his son, pulling him to his feet and half-carrying him to the staircase. They would have to follow if they were to save themselves.

By the time they reached the stairs, the lord and his son were gone and the fire was in the walls and ceiling. She didn't have time to ask questions or think beyond the immediate need to get out of the building. Anastasia led the still-stunned stranger upward, and Florentine, glancing back just in case Rosalie had made it out, dragged Drew up behind them.

At the ground floor, Florentine bumped into Anastasia. The fire had already engulfed the statue of Queen Victoria and was spreading quickly, enveloping the displays and offices, growing fiercer with every inch it gained.

The men arrived, coats over their heads to protect from popping embers.

'The whole place is going up!' John bellowed. 'What's happened?'

'Where's your mam?' Mr Michaels asked.

Florentine could not voice what had happened and had no time to try. She shook her head, fresh tears bubbling to the surface, and she could see Mr Michaels understood that Rosalie was not coming. Stricken with grief, he nodded once, and took Drew in his arms.

'Our exits are blocked.' Walls were collapsing around them, folding in like playing cards.

'First floor,' Drew said, choking back his sobs. 'We can get out on the first floor.'

Michaels turned and raced up the stairs. John held on to Anastasia like he'd never let go. The stranger stood, confused and terrified.

Alexander dodged a falling beam. 'Let's get out of here, Florrie.' He took her hand and started off.

Florentine grabbed the woman's hand as she went past. 'You're coming with us,' she said. Together they sprinted up to the first floor.

Michaels had broken through a window that led out onto a rarely used balcony and was helping Drew through the hole. John, seeing Florentine and Alexander arrive with their charge, pushed Anastasia through and waved at them to hurry. He gave Florentine a quizzical look as she pushed the stranger ahead of her.

Flagpoles attached to the outside wall gave them all footholds to climb down even as shattered glass showered them from above and sheets of iron from the roof sailed past with each new explosion. Florentine and Alexander, last to leave the balcony, climbed out over the plaster railing. As they ducked beneath its failing protection, yet another explosion rocked the building and they were forced to jump to the ground.

Sirens flailed through the night. The group hurried away from the building in awe at the height the flames reached into the early morning sky and stretching out over the harbour. A noise like thunder rolled out from the building as the scorched dome tilted to one side then collapsed inward in a cloud of flame and debris.

John and Mr Michaels gathered the women. Drew, calmer now, though from shock or grief Florentine couldn't tell, helped the stranger.

Florentine put a hand on Alexander's shoulder to forestall any questions. 'We need to get back to the hotel fast. This is not over.'

In the kitchen of the Garden Arms Hotel, Florentine sat, exhausted and grief-stricken. She didn't have the energy to look up from the table, to take the mug of coffee Bridie had placed before her, nor to answer the questions she could see on everyone's faces.

Mrs Skinner and Mrs Bell were sobbing in the corner. Honora hugged Bridie every time the girl walked past. John and Anastasia were in the backyard, his arms around hers as she cried her heart out on his chest. Alexander sat beside Florentine, maintaining a steadying presence.

The stranger was the only one in the room not stupefied with grief. Florentine noticed that the shock seemed to be wearing off. It was possible it was being replaced with anger. She didn't know who this woman was other than she must be important, but she certainly had a look of the MacKinnon about her. Her voice, though, was not accented with Scottish brogue.

The woman stared straight at Florentine. 'Would you mind telling me where the hell I am and what the hell just happened?'

CHAPTER 28

They burn witches, don't they?

Even in modern times, women suspected of doing anything remotely weird are accused of witchcraft.

Being found at the site of a mysterious fire, surrounded by strange artefacts, and air vibrating with music and voices the like I've never heard before is not going to do my reputation one jot of good.

Not that my reputation was good to start with.

Not that I'll be alive when they find me. I'm about to be burnt alive.

Witchcraft and whether I do or don't dabble will be completely immaterial.

Dead is dead.

Persephone Wells looked at the women standing in front of her. They appeared as shocked as she felt, and something more. Perhaps they'd been expecting someone else? Well, too bad for them; they were stuck, for a few minutes anyway, with ordinary old her. What did it matter when they were all about to be burnt to a crisp?

'What the hell is going on?' she asked. They were either stone deaf or too worried about pending death to answer. One of the women grabbed her hand and pulled her out of the room and into a pool. They all fell and were soaked to the skin. Persephone wasn't sure it would be enough with the fire spreading to the rest of the building so fast.

Where the hell was she? She had been outside a few minutes ago and now she was inside a burning building. The woman grabbed her again and she felt unable to do anything but follow along like a witless fool. A boy appeared. There was a struggle. She could see lips moving but couldn't quite catch the words.

She was dragged out of the water and up a staircase, pushed through a window and guided over a balcony ledge to the ground. Outside again, and not quite fresh air filled her lungs. Smoke swirled around her. Voices buzzed and they were off again, over a fence and across the road, down a lane and into another building. At least this one was safe, though she could see the reflection of the fierce fire through windows and across the sky outside.

Everyone was crying. Persephone sat and drank the strongest coffee she'd ever had. She coughed and spluttered, but the bitterness helped bring her senses out of the quagmire of confusion.

She was sitting in a kitchen around a table with people dressed in the strangest clothes. She reached into her pocket for her phone. Perhaps she could send a text off to her friend, beg a ride. Maybe order an über. Her pocket was empty. Damn!

The young woman who'd dragged her out of the fire was staring at her. She looked a lot like the one who'd spoken to her in the first dizzying moment when her world flip-flopped. A relation then. And that woman had said she couldn't return. She, Percy Wells, would have to do the best she could. She didn't like that at all. She stared back at the younger version of that woman.

'So, would you like to tell me exactly what is going on here and where on earth I am?'

The woman swallowed some of the bitter gall they called coffee. It seemed to have the same calming effect. 'I'm not sure exactly what happened, but you're sitting in the Garden Arms Hotel, Sydney. Our kitchen to be exact. Mam called for the Warrior Queen. I presume that's you.'

Persephone gulped at the hot drink. She was in a whole heap of trouble and she knew it. Except for the stupid dagger thing she still held in her hand, she'd never held a weapon in her life.

'I think you may have the wrong person,' she said, feigning a smile that she could tell was probably more of a grimace.

The woman shook her head. 'Everything else may be wrong, but I think Mam had this completely right.'

'I hope so,' another woman said, walking up from behind. A sister, Persephone deduced. 'Our mam died to bring you to us. We trust her more than anyone.'

Died? Persephone felt a rip through her gut. Not another one. She didn't think she could handle more death-wrought expectations than she was already lumbered with.

Oh, Flora. What have you done?

~ End of Book One~

ABOUT THE AUTHOR

Patricia Leslie is a Sydney author with a passion for combining history, fantasy, and action into stories that nudge at the boundaries of reality.

Urban fantasy is the ideal genre for exploring alternative history and Patricia does just this in her debut novel, *The Ouroborus Key*; a contemporary quest story set in the Rocky Mountains of Colorado. Her second novel, *A Single Light*, leaves known history behind, and joins fantasy with beach and bush south of Sydney where the mild seeming landscape becomes the setting for a potential world-altering event. Walks through the bush will never be the same again!

Patricia actively explores locations, taking photos, touching walls, and listening to her surrounds so that she can bring realistic experience to her descriptions. She is also a dedicated, some say compulsive, reader and collector of books. 'Being an author gives me the excuse I need to spend my spare time exploring, daydreaming, and reading!'

Patricia manages writing and family life with aplomb as long as there is a cup of tea or a nicely chilled glass of white wine somewhere close by.

https://www.patricialeslie.net

facebook.com/patricialeslieauthor